I0722494

On The Sixth Day

Bud Lawrence

On The Sixth Day
This is a work of fiction.
Copyrighted by Bud Lawrence ©2022
Library of Congress Control Number: 2022908827
All rights reserved. No part of this book may be reproduced, transmitted, or stored in an information retrieval system in any form or by any means, graphic, electronic, or mechanical without prior written permission from the author.

Printed in the United States of America
A 2 Z Press LLC
PO Box 582
Deleon Springs, FL 32130
bestlittleonlinebookstore.com
sizemore3630@aol.com
440-241-3126
ISBN: 978-1-954191-70-9

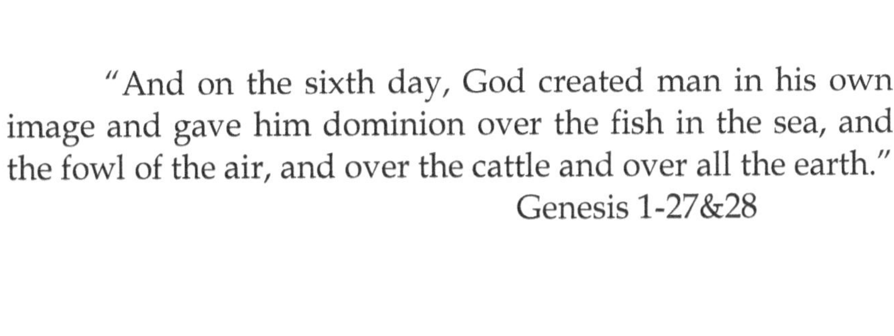
"And on the sixth day, God created man in his own image and gave him dominion over the fish in the sea, and the fowl of the air, and over the cattle and over all the earth."
Genesis 1-27&28

Contents

Foreword

1. The Battle 1
2. The Promise 9
3. Unlikely Companions 19
4. Renegades 31
5. Rosie 43
6. Bad News 51
7. Selene 61
8. In Search of a Home 71
9. Ira 77
10. Neighbors 93
11. Horses 103
12. The War Ends 115
13. Cattle 127
14. High Water 137
15. Recovery 149
16. Music Man 163
17. New Age 171
18. Anarece 179
19. Surprise Visitors 189
20. Sarah 207
21. Rustlers 219
22. Reconciliation 235
23. Ira and Sarah 251
24. Natural Perils 263
25. Changes 277
26. Jesse 291
27. Callie 307
28. Thanksgiving 327

Foreword

Caleb Melton of the Confederate army walked away from the senseless killing and maiming between Confederate and Union forces of the Civil War. He would no longer be a part of the struggle that had divided friends, families, and the nation into bitter rivals. After leaving the army, he forged a most unlikely alliance with a Negro man, William, giving both a better chance of survival from renegade soldiers of both armies and the dreaded home guard.

Their story is one of a bond formed for mutual protection that grew from a tenuous relationship between them as they traveled together, each searching for a place to call home. They faced dangers and hardships together as they built a new life. As their families grew, the bond of friendship was strained by the social structure of the south and the disparities between their races.

The two families would grow and make varied and often contradictory contributions to the settlement and growth of the area.

1

The Battle

Feb 20, 1864

Brigadier General Joseph Finegan had picked the perfect positions to repel the advancing Union Army. Union forces had control of Jacksonville and were moving west to disrupt Confederate food supply lines, capture supplies, and recruit Negro men to join their ranks.

The Confederate forces were entrenched in a small area bordered by a lake on one side and a swamp on the other. The Union forces would have to pass through on their march west. Soldiers lay behind barricades constructed for concealment and protection against the Union troops' advancement. Nerves were stretched to the breaking point as each man felt the demon of fear in his breast. There was a terrible battle coming on this clear, crisp February day.

Caleb Melton, Cal to his friends, gripped his rifle with white-knuckled hands. He could hear his heart beating as if trying to escape his body. His thoughts were that he must be brave and do his part. What surprised him the most wasn't the fear of dying but of disgracing himself with his fellow troops.

"Cal," he heard. "Cal, are you scared?"

Caleb turned to the soldier lying close to him. The man

also gripped a rifle with clenched hands. "Yeah, Jim, I'm scared. The worst thing is this waiting, knowing there are men on the way who want to kill us. The thing is, we must stop the Yankees from getting past us. Our troops north of us depend on food and supplies getting through."

"I know that Cal, but I'm not sure I can do this. I don't want to die, and I don't want to lose an arm or leg as my brother did. I surely don't want that."

Confederate soldiers were leveling their Enfield 1853 rifles on top of the barricades, waiting for the time to fire.

The rifles were newer models that had spiral grooves, called rifling, down the entire length. Rifling made the bullets come out of the rifle spinning and cut through the air with slight deflection, making accuracy possible at long distances. The old smoothbore rifles that some soldiers still carried had no accuracy. There were similar barricades set up across the field, arranged in an unbroken line facing the advancing forces.

Caleb searched the field before him for the enemy to come into view. It all looked so peaceful and quiet. In front of him was a line of trees across a broad meadow. It was hard to believe that men charging toward him will fill the space. Due to previous battles he had taken part in, he could envision men running, yelling, shooting, and dying in front of him. Some of those who died would be by his hands.

Their captain rode up with a saber in one hand, holding the reins of his nervous horse with the other.

"Okay, boys, hold your positions. The bluebellies'll be coming soon. They'll move slowly until they get within range of our rifles. At that point, they'll charge, and we'll start cutting them down. Don't waste ammunition before that and don't shoot until I give the order to fire. When I do, make your shots count. The man you miss could be the man who kills you or one of your friends."

"What about cannons, sir?" a soldier down the line

asked.

"They have cannons," the captain replied. "Scouts say the Yankees have light twelve-pound howitzers and smoothbore cannons. We know where they are and will use our artillery to put them out of business. There will be a lot of noise, so expect it. Your job is to protect your position. Forget everything except the enemy in front of you. They must be stopped one at a time. You can't stop the whole army yourself. You just stop the one in front of you and rely on your pals to do the same. You shoot the first one you see and then the one that takes his place. You keep shooting until no one is left. Load and shoot carefully. There's no time for mistakes."

Suddenly, from the trees across the meadow, a line of soldiers stepped from the trees. The line seemed to stretch forever to the left and right. Blue-clad soldiers with rifles on their shoulders began to move forward slowly.

"Here they come," someone yelled. "Here they come. Get ready, boys. We'll show these Yanks what fighting is all about. They might be high stepping to get to us, but they'll be running back to Jacksonville."

The captain rode up and down the confederate troops telling them to hold their fire until he gave the command to fire. He was interrupted by a deafening barrage of cannon fire. The soldiers instinctively ducked down behind their barricades until they realized the noise came from behind them. It was their howitzers shooting exploding rounds into the Union soldiers. A cheer went up from Caleb and his fellow soldiers as explosions from the bursting shells threw grass, dirt, and men into the air.

"Get ready, men," the mounted captain called out. The blue line of soldiers was approaching the spot where the rifles would be deadly. "Fire," he suddenly yelled. "Give it to them."

Before the men could fire their first shot, explosions bracketed their positions. The Union batteries had begun their bombardment. The shells landed and the ground erupted with the explosions. Dirt flew onto the soldiers while pieces of steel penetrated bodies, leaving men dead and injured. The men not disabled by the blasts began firing at the Union forces that had started running toward them, yelling at the top of their lungs, adding to the noise of exploding shells and firing rifles.

Caleb fought down the bile that swelled into his throat. He tried to aim at an approaching soldier. He was so nervous, and his hands shook so badly that his gun went off before he brought it down to get a good aim. The shot went into the air well above the enemy line. He recalled the captain's words about the one he missed resulting in the injury or death of one of his friends. He reloaded and controlled his shaking hands as he balanced the rifle on the log and took careful aim. He pulled the trigger and saw a blue-clad figure stumble and fall.

Many of the first shots were wasted. Fear and frayed nerves made it difficult to aim carefully before firing. The hands of some soldiers shook so severely that a good aim was impossible. One soldier, down from Caleb, fired his first shot. He then rammed another bullet into his gun. In his nervousness, he forgot to put in the firing cap. He aimed and pulled the trigger, not noticing that the gun didn't fire. He pulled down his rifle, inserted another bullet, and rammed it home; again, aimed and pulled the trigger, then reloaded again. Finally, he remembered to put in the firing cap. He aimed the rifle and pulled the trigger. The gun fired but the excess of bullets jammed the rifle barrel. The explosion of the powder couldn't go out of the end of the rifle barrel. Instead, the gun exploded, taking the top of the soldier's head off.

All around Caleb, men were settling down, sending a deadly barrage of bullets into the Union lines. Cal was deafened by the noise of the cannons and exploding shells. Time seemed to stand still. He was alone in his world of exploding shells, screams of wounded men, and horses. The hundreds of confederate troops seemed to disappear in a haze. There was only him loading and firing into the men in blue running toward him. Without feeling, he saw hundreds of Union troops running toward him. He loaded, aimed, fired, and saw red spots appear on blue coats as men fell in front of him. One man would fall and another would take the fallen man's place as the captain had said.

He didn't even notice the thud of bullets hitting the barricade, the soft plop when a shot found a man's body, or the bee-like buzz as a bullet zipped close to him, doing no harm.

The Union batteries began bombarding the barricades with solid cannonballs shot out of the smoothbore cannons. The cannonballs weren't meant to explode but to destroy the barricades. When the heavy ball hit the barriers, logs would explode and fly up in pieces, impaling the defenders with wood splinters. Men close to the impact were torn apart.

The scene was one of madness. How could a man experience the smell of blood, gunpowder, and unbearable noise of battle along with the dead and wounded men and ever again be normal? Around Cal, men lay dead and injured. Men mortally wounded moaned in pain, while others screamed for help or water. No support was coming. It was a fight for life among those that could continue the fight.

The captain rode up and down the line of soldiers. He was yelling instructions to men who couldn't hear him due to the noise of battle. As he turned his horse and faced the enemy lines, the horse reared in fright. Just as the horse reared, twelve pounds of iron cannonball struck him in the neck. The horse's head disappeared, along with most of the captain in a spray of red. The soldiers close by were spattered with blood and bone. A soldier, who was watching the captain, saw the horse's body and parts of the captain freeze in place before crumpling to the ground. The soldier, in horror, threw down his gun and fell into a fetal position, with his hands clamped to his ears to close out the sounds of battle. He would fight no more this day, if ever.

Caleb and the others fired and reloaded their rifles with deadly precision. Men in blue fell, but more took their places as the line moved closer to the confederate line. Suddenly, the Union troops stopped as one, dropped to their knees, raised their rifles, and let go a volley of deadly fire. The careful execution of volley firing was more effective than random shots as the troops moved forward. All along the defenders' positions, a hail of lead balls injured and killed men. Officers on horseback were particularly vulnerable. After the first line of Union soldiers fired their volley, they stood to reload their rifles. The second line of troops passed by those who had just fired, kneeled, fired, and was passed by the first line who had reloaded.

Suddenly, to Caleb's right, Confederate cavalry came thundering over a rise and attacked the flank of the Union lines. Before the surprised Union troops could respond, the cavalry swept through them.

Cavalrymen wielded their Dragoon Sabers and slashed at the men on foot. Even the most seasoned soldier felt fear at the sight of a horse and rider bearing down, especially when he saw the sword held high, ready to bring death or dismemberment.

Unlike the foot soldiers, cavalrymen carried pistols. Most of them had two pistols on their sides and extras carried in holsters on their saddles. A group of cavalry with swords and pistols was a formidable force. The cavalry broke through the ranks of Union soldiers and thundered on. Their objectives were cannons and artillerymen located a few hundred yards away on a slight rise.

The Union troops in front of Caleb's position were in disarray. Their leader was down and the remaining officers were giving confusing orders or orders that they couldn't hear. Some turned to fire at the cavalry while some still faced the battle line. The forward progress had slowed.

A Confederate officer rode up. He was yelling and gesturing for the confederates to mount a charge against the confused enemy. From behind the barricades, men streamed forward dressed in what had been grey uniforms a short while ago, now stained with dirt and blood. Many had minor wounds of their own, staining their uniforms. Many wore the blood of their fellow soldiers.

Caleb and the men closest to him stood and charged forward. They had bayonets fixed to the rifles, prepared for hand-to-hand combat. Fear was gone, replaced by a bitter hatred.

With little thought to personal safety, they surged forward, venting their rage, some to their death. The Union line broke and began a hasty retreat while Confederates shot at the retreating men. Caleb stopped, took careful aim, fired his rifle, and reloaded. Now that he was standing, he could load and fire three shots in less than a minute. The men around him were doing the same.

When the Union troops were out of the range, Caleb and the others headed toward the Union batteries. The cavalry had already reached the heavy artillery and the Confederates safely controlled the cannons by the time the infantry got there.

The infantry was ordered to stay and safeguard the cannons to keep them from being retaken. They couldn't be moved, for most of the horses used for pulling them had been killed. The cavalry wasn't responsible for the dead horses. Some were killed by Confederate artillery. Others were shot by sharpshooters armed with Whitworth rifles equipped with scopes. They targeted the battery as well as enemy officers. Many of the gun carriages were destroyed. The cannons, captured powder, and shot would be welcomed by the Confederates.

Caleb didn't hear or feel the explosion that knocked

him senseless.

2

The Promise

Caleb awoke hours later and was surprised to find himself sitting with his back against a tree, not remembering how he got there. The pain in his head was a living thing. He felt his head might explode at any moment. He raised his hand and felt the matted blood and swelling path a bullet had made just above his right ear.

He felt for his canteen and was pleased to find it contained water. He unscrewed the lid and took a long drink of warm water that smelled and tasted of mold, but it satisfied his thirst. He poured a little water into his cap and washed his face and neck, leaving the matted hair until he could find a source of more water.

Caleb stood up, grabbing a small tree to keep from falling. He waited for his dizziness to subside before he attempted walking.

The surviving soldiers had put up tents. Some of the men stood in small groups, engaged in conversation. Others sat alone with blank expressions on their faces. The carnage of the fight had taken away all feelings and comprehension. Many of the men had incurred injuries and wore bandages. Small campfires were scattered among the tents, over which pots simmered with a mixture of parched corn or acorns and water for a poor coffee substitute.

Caleb walked up to one of the tents. He knew the

soldier sitting in front, nursing a cup filled with a brew made from dried acorns. The man looked up at Caleb. "I see you made it. I didn't see you around, and I thought you cashed in. Join me in a cup while it is hot."

Caleb crouched down and sat on his heels. He accepted the cup offered to him. "Thanks, I need a hot drink and food. I don't know how long I was out, and I just woke up."

"Glad to have something to share. The only food I have is beef jerky." He handed Caleb a slice. "It's not bad, just a little hard and a lot salty."

Caleb chewed on the tough jerky and was glad to have food of any sort. "I don't remember much. I remember fighting, or at least shooting, and seeing men fall. I don't remember how it ended or how I woke up under a tree. Someone must have dragged me into the woods, out of the sun. I don't have a rifle or bullet pouch, and my knife is gone. I was fighting alongside my friend, Jim Sander. Have you seen him?"

"You'll find him over in the hospital tent. He got severely hit, and I don't think he'll make it; you might better hurry if you want to see him. The hospital tent is right over there. A little creek runs behind it. The stream washes away all the blood from the surgeries. It doesn't smell good, but you can clean the blood out of your hair. Just go upstream before it gets to the tent. The water is foul after it passes the tent."

"Thanks, I'll do that. Did we win the fight?"

"Oh yes, we won the fight. They lost half of their men and we only lost twenty percent of ours. We won and could have cleaned out the rest of them. Our officers never gave the order to chase after the retreating Yankees. We should have killed them all, especially the niggers who fought against us. First, the Yankees free them and then use them to fight us. It's not right to use niggers to fight us. Some of the boys made sure some would never fight us again or anyone else. We tried extra hard to kill the officers who were low down enough to lead them."

Caleb finished his coffee and walked toward the hospital tent. As he got close, he heard the moaning of men in pain. He almost lost his nerve but wanted to see Jim again. They had gotten to be good friends over the past weeks and months. Jim was a Florida man from somewhere down south. Caleb decided to wash off as much blood as possible before he looked for Jim. He waded into the creek above the hospital tent. It was clean at that point. He soaked his hat in the water and sponged away the blood from his head. It took several soakings before all the blood had been cleaned away. Caleb took off his shirt and washed it out. He put it back on wet. It felt good on his skin.

When Caleb walked into the hospital tent, the smell hit him like a physical blow. He involuntarily stepped back a step and stared into the tent's interior. Doctors were attending to the wounded as best they could in primitive conditions.

Medicine had gotten scarce as the war continued. Many operations, mostly amputations, were done without anesthesia or antiseptics. A high percentage of deaths would result from surgery, which did as much damage as the treated wounds.

Caleb walked down the aisle between injured men lying side by side on the ground. No cots were available. Many men were mercifully unconscious, and others moaned in pain or slept fitfully.

He asked everyone about Jim's whereabouts. Finally, one man pointed out where Jim was. Caleb walked over to the spot designated. Jim was there, but finding him brought no joy. Bloody bandages covered the stumps of a missing arm and leg. Caleb stood there speechless, looking down at Jim.

Jim opened his eyes and saw Caleb. He tried to raise his remaining arm, but the effort was too great. "Hello, Cal. I'm glad to see you're alive."

Kneeling, Caleb placed his hand gently on the

shoulder of his mortally wounded friend. Jim grimaced and closed his eyes tightly. He said, "Sorry, sometimes, the pain gets too much. I need to ask a favor of you. I've been thinking of my folks back home. It's bothering me that they might never know what happened to me. I know I'm not going to make it home. The fact is, I don't want to go home in the shape I'm in. I'd be no good to anyone or myself, so I'm ready to go."

As Jim paused to gather strength for other words, Caleb searched for words of comfort or encouragement, but none came. He sat in silence and Jim began speaking again, "If you get through this war, and are a mind to, I'd like you to see my folks. Tell them I was thinking of them and that I went quickly. It would ease my mom's mind by knowing that I didn't suffer. You might even make me out to be a hero. That would make my dad proud."

Caleb replied, "I'll see your folks for you if you can't. Don't give up on doing it yourself."

Jim went on. "My dad's name is Ethan Sanders. My mom is Sadie." Jim almost forced a smile to his face. "Sadie Sanders. She loved the sound of that name. Said that's the only reason she married, to get the last name. Her maiden's name was Gooch, and she hated that name. I don't blame her. They have a small ranch about a two-day ride south of Orlando, in central Florida. Anyone there can direct you to them since only a few white people live there, and they all know one another. It would be a relief to me if you went to them. You'll like it there, and it is a long way from the war, mostly unsettled."

Caleb swallowed the lump in his throat before answering. "I'll see them if I make it through this war, I promise you. Can I get you anything?"

"I'd like some laudanum to ease the hurt, but they tell me none is to be had. The surgeons are all out." With that remark, Jim closed his eyes and fell to sleep.

One of the surgeons walked over to Caleb. "This boy's about gone. He's all torn up inside as well as outside. I don't know how he lasted through the surgery." Noticing Caleb's wound, he handed him a cloth. "Here, wrap your head in this so you won't get that wound infected."

Caleb turned and walked past the rows of hurt and maimed men. He muttered as he walked, "These were good men. How did we end up with Americans hurting Americans? Life is struggle enough, without the horrors of war." He wrapped the cloth around his head and tucked the end inside the wrap.

Caleb went in search the survivors of the Sixth Florida Infantry. They were a short distance away. He found them easily enough, and they greeted him warmly. Several were missing, and the men were glad to see him. "We thought you were killed or captured, Cal. Where've you been?"

"I took a little nap in the woods, over there. I don't know how I got there. I just woke up with a sore head. Someone must have moved me into the shade, maybe left me for dead."

The soldiers were cooking the evening meal. They sat around a campfire with bacon impaled on sticks that sizzled and dropped fat into the fire. Trenching tools placed near the fire held a mixture of cornmeal, fat, and salt. The cook turned the other side as soon as it browned on one side. He handed Caleb a slab of the bread wrapped around hot bacon and, as he was ravenous, it was disposed of quickly.

The men ate their meals and, afterward, the ones who had tobacco filled their pipes and smoked contentedly.

One of the soldiers, Gavin, who was from Jacksonville, spoke, "I signed up over two years ago. I was a little tired of Jacksonville and decided I'd see a little more of the world. It sounded exciting, going off to war. I wasn't too fond of Yankees telling us what we could do or not do. It wasn't about enslaved people. We never had slaves, not exactly anyway, except for my pa. He had slaves, all right. His slaves were me, my brothers, and my ma. Maybe he wasn't mean, but he gave a good impression of being so. Anyway, this war gave me a good reason to get away from him. After what I've seen in the last two years, pa looks like the nicest, friendliest man alive."

Jack Hawkins took a deep draw of his pipe, exhaled the smoke, spit into the fire, and said, "I signed up because all my friends did. I came from Texas and that is a long way from here. I stayed with the boys from Texas until they all were killed. I joined up with other outfits. It seemed like every day I got further away from home. The Yanks drove me further and further south. I can't tell you boys about how many good men I've seen die right beside me. You see that many die, you know your time is coming. I sure would like to see Texas again before I cash in."

Gavin replied, "I know how you feel. Anyone with half a brain knows by now that the bluebellies will win out. They have all the factories to make guns. They have the gunboats to keep us from getting help from France or England. We'll run out of food and ammunition. Most of us are already walking out of our shoes and clothing. At least the weather is warmer here. The boys up in Virginia are all frost-bitten by now. My home in Jacksonville is close, but I'll never see it again. I worry about my ma. The Yankees control Jacksonville. I know they'll make all the southerners suffer."

Caleb listened to the conversations around him. All the men were sure that they'd never survive the war. Most had given up any illusion of winning the war, and they knew the Yankees would be cruel taskmasters to the southerners that did survive. He was overcome with the hopelessness of the war and suddenly weary and discouraged.

Caleb stood and said, "I'm going over to the woods where I spent the night. I need to find my belongings. I'm missing my gun, knife, and rucksack."

One of the men said, "I wouldn't worry about that.

Many men left this world today, leaving behind guns, knives, and more. Just help yourself."

"I wouldn't doubt that fact, but I'm partial to my knife. I've had it since I was a kid. I'll go look around and be back soon."

Caleb walked past the tents and soldiers towards the woods. He reached the spot where he had awoken but didn't stop or look for lost possessions.

Walking deeper into the woods, he hadn't thought of a lost gun or knife or not going back to the war. His pace quickened as he put distance between himself and the camp. He walked well into the night, finding his way by moonlight. He knew he would be branded a deserter and, if captured, he would die.

He knew he wasn't afraid to die after facing men trying to kill him and survived. He had fought with bravery and done his duty to the other men. He'd kill no more in a senseless waste of men and animals. If he stayed in camp, he would surely die. He knew that he'd be killed if captured by troops of either side, but they might not catch him. He decided to go far away from the war and find a place where they wouldn't come for him. Caleb walked for hours but, finally, fatigue caused him to stop. He sank to the ground and was quickly asleep.

Caleb awoke early. He walked steadily through the morning, keeping close to wooded areas, and avoiding open clearings. Any group of riders he'd meet would be the Union forces, outlaws, or his people seeking deserters. Any of the three would be the end of his freedom, if not his life. He kept heading south by sighting on pieces of the landscape far before him as beacons to follow, so he wouldn't walk in circles. Despite that, he knew his route wouldn't be as direct as he would like.

Water would not be a problem since there were many ponds and streams to fill his canteen. He had only to fill it once a day to have enough water to last him. He constantly refilled it at any source of water he found, never knowing for sure how far until the next one would appear.

He ate sparingly of the jerky from his backpack. Game was plentiful, but he had no way of killing anything. He could make snares, but that would mean staying in one place too long. The best idea was to keep moving and get far away from the war.

Around noon the following day, he saw buzzards circling ahead of him. Upon nearing the circling birds, he saw a large animal on the ground. Approaching, it was evident the animal was a horse. Flies buzzed around the dead animal that wore a saddle and saddlebags.

Caleb eagerly approached the dead animal and was shocked to see the body of a soldier lying a few feet from the dead horse. If the man was sleeping, he could be a danger. However, if the man was hurt, Caleb must help him. Walking very slowly, Caleb reached the man and squatted down. He took hold of the man's shoulder and slowly rolled him over.

The man was dead and quite stiff. The end of the reins was wrapped around one of the man's hands and held in a death grip. The dead cavalryman had been shot in the stomach. There was no way to know how far the man had ridden before falling from the horse or if the horse fell from its wounds throwing off the cavalryman.

A stomach wound was a terrible way to die. In the war conditions, a stomach wound was almost always fatal. If death wasn't quick by blood loss, the infection did the job. "I hate to rob the dead," he said to the dead soldier, "but you might have things I need. You no longer have any needs."

The soldier had been an officer, by the looks of his uniform. A close inspection, however, didn't turn up anything of value. There was no identification or clues to the man's identity.

Celeb walked back to the dead horse. There was a

holster on the side of the saddle with the handle of a pistol protruding. He freed the gun and, after examining it, placed it under his belt. There were two saddlebags, one on each side of the saddle. He untied the rawhide strap holding them to the saddle.

Caleb squatted and sat on his heels, opened one of them, and pulled out the contents. He found a small bag of salt, some hard beef jerky, and a bag with what looked like coffee but was ground corn, a small pot for boiling water, and a metal cup and plate.

He managed to pull the other saddlebag from beneath the horse's body by digging under it until it was free enough to dislodge. This one held little but pleased Caleb to find a handful of ammunition for the pistol and a small Bible.

He examined the pistol. It was a LeMats, made in France and smuggled into the confederacy by blockade runners. It was unusual since it had two barrels. The top barrel was for firing forty-four caliber bullets and had a nine-shot cylinder. The lower barrel was a smoothbore sixteen gauge that held one shell of buckshot. The pistol was accurate, except for the sixteen gauge, no use at a distance but deadly at close range. The fallen man must have come from a wealthy family to afford such a gun.

Tied to the saddle was a small trenching tool. Caleb took this and began digging a grave. He didn't like taking the time to bury the man, but felt compelled to complete the task. He owed the man much for the meager supplies and couldn't leave him at the mercy of animals.

It took over two hours to dig a grave deep enough with the small shovel. Caleb was drenched with sweat when he finally stood over the filled grave.

He took off his cap, looked down at the grave, and said, "I wish I knew your name so I could tell you goodbye, or something that would help me tell your folks that you were buried proper. Your folks will always wonder what happened to you, and they're not alone in that feeling. Many a good man is fallen and buried in unmarked graves."

He walked away with the saddlebags over one shoulder containing the welcome possessions. He made camp that night in a thick clump of low-growing scrub oaks.

After moving well into the oaks, Caleb built a small fire. He took the pot, filled it from a cypress pond nearby, and added ground corn plus a few tiny acorns. The water heated and began to boil. Caleb could wait no longer; he removed the pot and drank directly from it. The liquid burned his lips, but he ignored the burn as he sighed with satisfaction. He ate beef jerky from the saddlebags and washed it down.

Daylight was fading as Caleb finished his meal. He felt relaxed, and he was sure no one would find his camp. Sleep came easily.

3

Unlikely Companions

The following morning Caleb awoke to birds singing in the oak thicket. The contrast between the soothing sounds of bird songs and the horrible noises of battle only hours ago made him want to linger in this spot. The uncertainty of his future made the relaxed mood turn to unrest. He rose and drank last night's cold brew and ate a piece of jerky.

He began walking toward what he believed was south, with a small group of pine trees in the distance that served as a marker to follow. On reaching them, he saw the trees were spaced with room between them to walk through. A thick carpet of pine needles muffled his steps, and the air smelled of pine resin and was pleasing to his nose. He proceeded through the pine forest for most of the day. The pace was slow, for it was hot even in the shade of the pines. He was soon drenched in sweat and often stopped for a drink.

After finding another clearing to spend the night, Caleb opened the saddlebag and took out the pot. A small fire was soon burning with the brew wafting its earthy smell.

Caleb was accustomed to walking, but the all-day walking in the hot weather had his leg muscles complaining as he moved around. Despite the soreness, the brew and small piece of jerky were satisfying. He sat, leaned against a tree, and ate the simple meal with enjoyment.

So far, things had been going well without seeing

anyone. No farms had been passed and no smoke of campfires was seen.

After finishing his meal and extinguishing the campfire, he stretched out and went to sleep.

The sound of squawking crows brought him awake and alert. The sound surprised and alarmed him. He knew that crows were the sentinels of the forest. Anything that seemed like a danger to the crows, predators like wildcats, panthers, bears, or humans would elicit loud warning cries.

Caleb jumped up and looked carefully at his surroundings but could find no reason to worry. Still, caution kept him nervous. He held the LeMat in his hand while searching the pine forest for danger.

He relit the fire from last night and made a pot of corn-flavored water. It would suffice as breakfast. Caleb was in a hurry to get moving. He was still ill at ease from being rudely awakened by the crows, although nothing seemed to be of any immediate danger. After hurriedly drinking the hot drink, he resumed his journey south.

Between the pine forests, the land was smooth and grassy. It was in startling contrast to the war-torn land that had been so much of his life. Caleb relaxed as he walked, gaining confidence with each passing hour.

He walked steadily and covered the ground as the war fell further behind. Late in the afternoon, Caleb was walking when, suddenly, he smelled smoke. Caleb saw the smoke of a campfire. It was directly in front at the edge of a wooded area. He cursed himself for his loss of attention.

He decided to check out the campsite. Maybe it would be deserted and have something he could use. He didn't see any activity, so it wasn't either army. He decided to walk on in and see who had made the fire.

As he neared the smoldering fire, Caleb strained his eyes, searching his surroundings for danger and trying to make out who he would encounter at the fire. He could see no one but walked carefully up to the fire. It was a small campfire with a coffee pot hung from a tripod. The smell of coffee told him someone had prepared it recently.

"Hello," he called out. "I smelled your coffee. Is anyone here?"

A large black man stepped out from behind a large tree. He was dressed in ordinary cotton pants, held up by a rope belt, and a grey homespun shirt. Dark brown eyes peered out of a fully bearded face. A thick mat of black hair covered his head and thickly muscled arms showed he was used to hard work. He held a rifle in his hands, ready for use. "This is my camp and my coffee. What do you want?"

Caleb was careful not to make any sudden movements that might prompt the man to use the rifle. "I mean no harm. I was just traveling through and smelled your coffee. I'll move along and leave you be."

The Negro looked carefully at Caleb, and he made no move to lower the rifle. "You're a reb. What are you doing here? The war is north of us. Are you a deserter?"

After a pause, Caleb replied, "I was in the Confederate army. My war is over. I'm through with fighting and have no quarrels to settle. As I said, I'll move along."

The Negro stood immobile for a while and then replied. "If you are a mind to, get down, and if you are not too good to share a meal with a black man, I'll share my coffee and that pot of beans. I only have one cup and plate. I hope you have your own."

"I do," Caleb replied as he walked over to the fire and helped himself to the food and drink. He sat on the ground and leaned back on a tree trunk. He placed his coffee on the ground beside him. Holding the plate in his left hand, he spooned the hot beans into his mouth.

The coffee was delicious and the first real coffee he had in months. Even the hot beans were welcome food even though he regularly had beans in the army until lately when all supplies were short.

The Negro did the same but kept his rifle close at hand. "My name is William. I am a free man who, until recently, worked for Mr. Thornton. We drove a herd up north of here and sold them to the rebs for food. Mr. Thornton got himself shot and died. Before he died, he managed to get some supplies. He got them from a Yankee deserter, I'm thinking. I'm taking his wagon and goods back to his family. Now, tell me about you."

"My name is Caleb. As I said, I'm through with fighting." It occurred to Caleb that he had no actual plans except to get away from the war. After a moment of thought, he added, "I'm going to see the parents of a friend of mine. They live south of here. He was killed in the last battle. I promised him that I would take word back."

William took a mouthful of beans and chewed slowly as he looked at Caleb. "It seems that you have a problem. You'll run into more rebs and patrollers looking for deserters. Taking word to your friend's parents might be noble, but that won't save you from hanging as a deserter."

Caleb replied, "I'll take my chances. I made a mistake riding up to your camp. I'll be more careful in the future. I'll finish these beans and be on my way. I'll not be a worry to you."

"Hold on, don't rush off. Maybe we can help each other. You are a deserter, to be shot on sight, or hanged. I am a black man traveling alone. I'm in as much danger as you. Some reb or renegades will likely see the wagon and supplies as reason enough to kill me. If not for the wagon, they'll kill me for sport. I suggest that we travel together. You can pretend to be my boss, just coming home from delivering cattle. Together we might make it. Alone neither of us has a chance. I'm headed back to Mr. Thornton's ranch. It's just north of the town of Orlando. We can go that far together. You can go on by yourself from there."

Caleb stopped eating and looked at William. "It just might work, Will. I don't look forward to traveling with a black man, but I guess I can bear it to stay alive, so I'm willing to give it a try."

"My name is William, not Will, and don't be forgetting that. Another thing for you to remember is that I am a free man, and I mean *man*. Do not make the mistake of looking down on me. I have had enough men weaker than me, dumber than me and with less education, think they are better than me because of my skin color."

"I'll remember that; however, you'll get in a lot of trouble with that attitude. Mr. Lincoln said that you're free, but he can't change the feelings of the white men of the south, and nothing has changed in their minds except more resentment against Lincoln and Negros. You better learn to step carefully if you're in the south."

"Maybe not. We'll travel together. I'll let anyone we meet think you are the boss, but you are not. We travel together to help each other, and you are no better than me. If you can't live with that, we need to go our separate ways."

Caleb bristled at William's words and swallowed the stinging rebuke that came to his mind. He could put up with this pompous black man as long as it suited his plans, but no longer. He finally said, "We'll try to get along. Just don't sit too comfortably on your high horse attitude."

"I have an attitude, all right. My attitude was paid for many times over by the treatment of my family. I watched my folks work themselves to death with no recognition as people. Things are changing. I know it won't be overnight, and I'll have trouble. I might play the poor dumb black to get along, but I want you to know who I am. If only one man treats me like a man, it is a start."

Caleb looked at William with astonishment. His family had no slaves, but he had been in contact with many Negros. Did they all feel as William did? He was surprised to find he had never considered their feelings. He had assumed they were satisfied, if not resigned, to their roles in life. William had opened a new insight. *'Can I treat him as a man and not a Negro man?'* he thought. *'It makes no difference; I will do what is necessary for the both of us to survive. I'll be his boss if we encounter others and ignore him other times. I'll let him live as he pleases, for he won't last long with his attitude in the south. Someone will put a bullet in him in short order.'*

Caleb turned to William. "This will be hard and different for both of us. I'll do my part, and you do yours. When this journey is over, we'll both go our ways."

William replied, "Don't make a mistake and think I'm stupid just because of my color. I know southern white men think all Negros aren't human and are dumb, lazy, and unable to learn. They can cheat, beat, and even kill me with no fear of punishment. They will even be admired by other whites for doing so. I also know that the northern whites don't look at us any differently. They didn't fight the south for the sake of blacks. They fought for their reasons and used us as an excuse." He continued, "Mr. Lincoln said we were free. Someday that will help my people, but today we still must work for the whites. If the war frees us, we'll be despised more by the southern whites because of all the soldiers killed to make us free. In addition to that, many of the farms that could give us work are destroyed. My people are enslaved, but they have a roof over their heads and food to eat. If free, many will wander around with no home and no jobs. The war will help my grandchildren and their children but will be of little help today."

Caleb finished the plate of beans. He took a handful of sand and rubbed it around to clean the plate. He shook out the sand, checked the plate for cleanliness, and put it away in his pack. "If it's okay with you, William, we'll make camp here for the night and go on in the morning."

"That suits me. I'll sleep under my wagon. Just remember, I'm a light sleeper if you have ideas of doing away with me while I sleep. I'll never be done in by any cracker reb, including you."

"I have no plans of doing you any harm. I gave you my word that we would travel together. You have no reason to trust or distrust me, but I'll tell you that my word is good and I only hope yours is as well."

William cleaned his plate in the same manner, stood, and said, "My word is also good. If you can trust a Negro, I'll travel with you; even defend you, if need be, as long as you do the same."

Caleb replied, "That's fine with me. We'll be together for the journey. I don't see the wagon that you plan to sleep under. Where is it?"

"I hid it back in the trees; not sure who might come by my camp. I didn't want anyone to see the wagon and decide it was worth killing me to get it."

After saying that, William disappeared into the forest. Soon, Caleb heard the creaking sound of a wagon. The wagon came into view, pulled by two mules. William stopped the wagon near the campfire and got down from the seat. He got hobbles from the wagon and placed them on the mules before unharnessing them. After freeing the mules, he turned them loose to graze.

"They can eat grass tonight," William said, "The hobbles will keep them from wandering."

Caleb made no reply. He looked at the wagon. It carried several boxes and bags. "What are you hauling?" he asked.

"My boss traded some cattle to your army for some goods we needed back at the farm. The wagon has sugar, coffee, cornmeal, shot and powder, and other supplies. He had to do a lot of talking to get them. The army didn't have a lot to spare. Someone got a little gold out of the deal. That was before he got himself shot dead."

William handed Caleb a bundle of clothing. "These

belonged to Mr. Thornton, but he won't be needing them anymore. If you want to pass as a rancher, you better get rid of that uniform. I suggest you bury or burn it. Mr. Thornton was about your size, so the clothes should fit."

Caleb unwrapped the bundle and found a pair of trousers, a shirt, and a wide-brimmed hat. He quickly changed clothes and walked into the woods and buried his old uniform.

The two men spread blankets on the ground, making their beds for the night. They spread them a considerable distance apart. Darkness closed in as they went to their beds, William under the wagon and Caleb across the campsite.

The camp was silent, but both men found sleep coming slowly as their minds absorbed and considered their situation.

Caleb's thoughts were of the army and battles he would no longer fight. He had fought on the side of slavery, although he had never considered that was the reason he fought. He fought because the North had invaded his homeland. Now, only one day away from that conflict, he was in a partnership with a freed black man.

Caleb would have been surprised to know that the black man had many similar thoughts.

Caleb awoke to William going about stoking the fire and putting the coffee pot on the fire. He told Caleb, "There's a slab of bacon in the wagon, just under the seat. We'll fry it for breakfast if you want to slice us a few slices. There's corn pone left from yesterday, and it'll go good with bacon."

Caleb retrieved the bacon and a frying pan from the wagon. He sliced bacon into the pan. The smell of frying bacon and coffee made both men eager to set to the food. They ate hurriedly. The food was tasty, but both were anxious to get on with the trip

After cleaning the cooking utensils, they left the campsite, William driving the wagon and Caleb walking along. They had agreed to take turns riding and walking to make it easier for the mules to pull the wagon through the sandy soil.

William said, "I've been following the Bellamy Road. It cuts across Florida, southeast from Pensacola to St. Augustine on the coast. I plan to follow it for a few more days and then cut due south. That will take me to Mr. Thornton's farm. I plan to stay there and work for Mrs. Thornton for a while. You can go on from there."

Caleb agreed. "That sounds fine to me. I hope there's not too much traffic. I don't look forward to encountering many people."

"We might meet a few wagons or trail herds. If we stick to our story, we'll be all right. Our biggest worry will be renegades or bands of deserters. Most of the army is spread across a line from Jacksonville to Pensacola. The further south we get, the less likely we'll see any army men. Bands of renegades roam around, looking to steal anything they can get their hands on. They could be white deserters or runaway slaves. Either is unwelcome news, but usually are small bands who won't risk taking on two armed men. They prefer those who can't defend themselves."

Caleb wasn't happy with the slow pace of the wagon. He could have made a much better time by himself. Traveling alone would be much harder to explain if challenged. He settled into the slower trip. Traveling was hard for the wagon, for the wheels dug into the sand ruts of the road. The mules had to strain to keep the wagon moving. They were soon lathered with white foam on their coats. The hot sun bore down without mercy as they drove through Florida. Both men had to walk when the sand was at its worst.

They came to a stream with clear, cool water close to their path. They stopped to water the animals and let them rest for an hour. During this break, the men ate corn pone washed down with water from the stream. They moved into the shade of a tree and sat on the ground. They waited for the mules to rest and cool down.

The men began moving again after the rest. When he could, William would veer off the road onto grassy areas where the going was easier. Mostly they had to follow the road's ruts since trees grew close alongside the narrow road.

They made camp early that evening since the mules were exhausted. Both men knew they must not overwork the team. If they demanded too much one day, they would lose more time the next day. A slower pace would be a faster trip in the long run.

They continued the journey under a bright blue sky with no clouds the following day. "It's going to be a hot one," Caleb said, looking up at the sun rising above them. "We could use a few clouds for shade, but I don't guess the heat bothers you as much with your dark skin."

"It bothers me as much as you. The only difference is that my people were forced to work in it while yours sat on a cool porch with cold drinks. The heat is as hard on us but we had to get used to it."

The remark irritated Caleb. He replied, "You won't see any of my folks sitting in the shade. We had to work to get our food. If we didn't make it, we didn't eat. Your people had to work, but there was always someone to ensure you had food and clothing. Many of your people were better off as slaves and some of them will find it hard going on their own."

That remark brought a quick rebuttal. "I'd rather be free and hungry than a well-fed slave. You can never understand what it is not being free."

Caleb replied, "That's probably right. I can't imagine belonging to someone else. I'm just saying that being free won't put food on the table. Your people will find out that they'll have to work as hard as ever. Those that were forced to work might have trouble working on their own. I suspect we better drop this subject before it leads to trouble."

The two rode on in silence, both with their thoughts. There was no way the two would ever agree. Their paths were too different. Neither recognized the fact that neither of them were genuinely free men. They were slaves to the need for food and shelter but did have options on how to obtain either. They were tied together, at least for now, for mutual protection. Caleb could be arrested as a deserter. William, a Negro man traveling alone in the south, was in peril from several fronts.

They stopped again when the sun was directly overhead. The day was so bright the glare hurt their eyes. Sweat poured from them. The men and animals were wet with sweat. The heat was so intense they could feel it pressing into their skin as if they were covered with an invisible blanket of heat.

William let the mules drink from a pond and then drove the team under an oak tree so that they could catch their breath in the shade. The mules stood motionless, drained of energy, with little interest in foraging for grass.

4

Renegades

Caleb and William sat under the shade of a large oak tree. They heard the sounds of creaking leather and hoofbeats. Both men were startled and jumped to their feet. Caleb faced the sound while William walked over to the wagon and leaned against it. His hand was resting on his rifle. Neither man knew what to expect but prepared themselves to face friend or enemy.

Four riders came into view. Three were riding horses and one was astride a mule. The riders pulled up when they saw Caleb, William, and the wagon. Their mounts were covered with lather; their sides heaved with each breath. They had all been pushed hard.

The four men were dressed alike in coarse, gray cotton shirts and faded gray trousers. Ropes were used as belts and all had pistols tucked into the rope belts. Their clothing showed no signs of recent washing. Their faces were all covered with long, shaggy, tobacco-stained beards.

One of the riders spoke to Caleb. "Howdy. We didn't expect to see anyone out here in this wilderness. My name is Cody. Me and my men have a contract with the army to round up deserters and provide provisions. Have you seen any suspicious-looking folks?"

"No," replied Caleb. "We pushed a herd of cattle up from central Florida to the army. We're on our way home to put together another herd. We haven't seen anyone since we parted with the cattle."

The man called Cody pointed at William and asked, "Is he yours? There's also money to be made capturing and returning renegade blacks"

Caleb felt rather than saw William stiffen. Caleb looked at him, hoping he wouldn't be foolish enough to go for his rifle. "Yep," he said, looking back at Cody. "He's mine all right. He's a good man with the cattle and he's been in the family since he was born."

Cody thought for a moment and said, "We've been on the trail for a while. We could use some supplies if you have any to spare. Coffee and flour would help and a little whiskey would go mighty fine."

Caleb thought for a moment. "Sorry men, we don't have any to spare. The army is only a few days north. If you push hard, you can reach them. I'm sure they'll share with you since you have a contract with them."

Cody scowled at Caleb. He looked at the LeMat worn by Caleb and saw that William's hand was close to the rifle. "Mind if me and the boys get down and visit a spell? We've been riding hard all morning."

Caleb quickly replied, "You fellows are welcome to this spot. We're pushing on. He turned to William. Hey boy, get on that wagon, and let's get moving."

William jerked as if hit by a whip. He looked over to Caleb. Then, without a word, climbed up to the wagon seat. Caleb lifted himself into the wagon and sat beside William, careful to keep his eye on the men. The wagon started moving. He turned in his seat. Looking back at them, he said, "We'll keep our eyes out for any strangers. I wish you boys the best." He kept looking back as the distance between them grew.

Cody and his men sat on their horses, watching Caleb and the wagon move away. He saw that Caleb and William were ready for trouble. He got off his horse and directed his men to do the same. "Get down, boys. Rest your horses."

The riders sat silent as the distance between them and the wagon increased. One broke the silence and said, "You going to just let them go? It's only one man and his nigger. Niggers don't fight, so we just got one man to handle."

"Now, Shake," Cody replied to the speaker, "don't worry. We'll get those supplies. That guy was ready for trouble. We could have taken him but some of us might have a few holes in us before he went down. I'm not sure about that nigger. His hand was close to a rifle. A little rest won't hurt the horses or us. Give those two time to relax."

When the riders were lost from sight, Caleb said, "We've not seen the last of that group. They were eyeing our supplies. We had better be ready for trouble. Supplies are too scarce around here for them to just let us go."

William turned and glared at Caleb. "Boy, huh, you called me 'boy.' I am not your boy, and the fact is, I am no one's 'boy.' My name is William and remember that."

Caleb replied, "Get off your high horse. The thing we must do is survive this trip. When we're around white men, I'll treat you as they would expect. When we're alone, I'll be sure and not offend your tender pride."

William slapped the reins to keep the mules plodding along through the sand. With anger in his voice, he said, "You might be right but that doesn't make it any easier to handle. Someday, I'll find a place where there will be peace for me and those like me. There must be such a place. God did not mean for men to be treated like cattle."

They pushed on later that day, trying to put as much distance between them and the four riders. Caleb hoped the riders would go on their way but he knew that wasn't likely. They would be coming for the wagon, supplies, and William and kill Caleb without a second thought.

William pulled up the mules and said, "They're all

tuckered out. I'd like to be further away from those men, but the mules must rest. I think those four will show up tonight while we sleep."

Caleb replied, "You're right. They're renegades, pure and simple. We'll have to be ready for them. We'll build up a good fire, so they'll not think we're suspicious of them doubling back on us." He began gathering more wood than he needed for a campfire. "I'm getting extra," he explained, "We'll keep a good fire going."

While Caleb built a fire and put on the coffee, William unhitched the team.

"I'm not going to hobble them tonight," William said.

He led the two mules back into the woods and tied them to a tree. They cooked their evening meal as if nothing were amiss.

Before dark, the two men spread blankets on the ground as if ready for sleep. They placed moss on the blankets and rolled them up so it looked as if both men were asleep by the campfire's light.

Caleb said, "They'll wait until we're well asleep before they come in. I don't think they'll come in shooting because you're worth more to them alive, but they'll shoot me as soon as they can identify me. We'll spread out and find a place where we can dig in. It would help if you found a log to hide behind, facing the camp, and don't look directly into the campfire, for it will spoil your night vision. The men will be dimly lit and look like shadows. If they show up, they mean us harm, so we can't hesitate to stop them. As soon as they are in camp, shoot to kill. You shoot first, and I'll follow."

William replied, "Yes, General. I'll follow orders since you seem to think you're in charge."

Caleb said in irritation, "I don't need your attitude. If you have a better idea, let's hear it."

William gave a short laugh. "No. You seem to enjoy being the General too much for me to object. We'll do as you say. It sure is fine, having a white massa to look out for this simple Negro."

Caleb held back a retort. He stood and said, "Okay, let's take our places. If we keep some distance between us, they'll have two separate targets instead of one. We need to keep a clear line of fire between us and the camp. You take the man on your left, then the next closest. I'll take the ones on the right."

The two men moved off into the gathering darkness. Caleb found a log that would serve as protection from gunshots. He pushed it around to lay behind it where he could look directly at the campsite, being careful not to look directly at the fire.

Sounds of Williams's preparations helped Caleb locate where William would be. He didn't want to shoot William by mistake. Caleb hoped William took the same care. He lay down to wait.

Time moved slowly as the two men lay in wait. The night grew darker and the fire burned lower. Mosquitoes buzzed around and, occasionally, one would get under the clothing and deliver a stinging bite. Caleb had to endure the bites without moving. He knew he must remain still to keep his location secure.

It was well after midnight when Caleb had almost decided it was a false alarm. Maybe he was wrong and the riders had gone on their way. Suddenly, a scuffling sound came to his ears. He stared into the darkness and saw shadows of men closing in on the camp. He aimed at the shadowy figure on the right.

William's rifle boomed and a man cried out in pain. Caleb shot and his target fell as William's rifle spoke again. Caleb stared into the night but could see no further movement. The groans of a wounded man sounded in the night. Caleb collected his thoughts. *'Had only three men entered the camp or had one been out of sight when the shooting began.'* No answering fire had come from the camp.

William's voice rang out. "I got two of them. Do you see any more?"

"No. I can't see anyone. I saw the one I shot fall but don't see the fourth."

There was no longer a need to keep quiet. Their positions were no longer a secret. Caleb looked over the top of the log and scanned the darkness but no movement appeared. He heard a movement behind him. Turning, he saw a figure behind him in the scant moonlight with a pointed rifle. Even as Caleb brought his gun around, he knew he would be too late.

Caleb heard the boom of a rifle and expected to feel the blow of a bullet. Instead, the figure behind him was driven into a tree by the force of a shot from William's gun. Caleb lay in disbelief. He was sure he would die. Caleb was still lying there with his rifle pointed at the fallen figure when William walked up.

"Well, General, are you going to take a nap there or can we go clean up our camp."

Caleb arose on shaking legs. "Thanks. I thought I was a goner. I didn't hear him until too late."

William replied, "It was just lucky that I looked over this way and saw him sneaking up on you. I was afraid I couldn't get to him in time. It's a good thing I did, for he had you cold."

Caleb walked over to the fallen man. He checked for a pulse, and there was none. "Let's go check the camp and make sure the other three are done for."

The two men moved carefully toward the camp. This was a dangerous time. If the men were only wounded, walking into the camp could be a death trap. They separated and walked slowly forward.

As they neared the camp, Caleb saw the forms of three men in the dim light of the low burning campfire. There was no movement. He moved carefully to the first form on the ground. The man had been hit full in the chest and he was dead.

"This one is done for," he called out to William. William was bent over another still form. That one was dead. As William walked over to the final man lying on the ground, the figure moved and let out a long groan of pain.

William stiffened and walked over to the injured man. He had been shot in the stomach. The man rolled over and looked up at William. "I need help," he gasped.

William looked down at the man and said, "You want the kind of help planned for us?"

"This was not my idea," the man said, "It was Cody's."

"Well, I guess I'll never know for sure," William replied. "Cody can't tell us one way or the other." With that remark, William pointed his rifle and pulled the trigger, killing the man.

Caleb had been walking over to see what was going on when he saw William shoot the man. He yelled, "No!" He was too late. "Why did you do that?!" he exclaimed. "The man was down and wounded and could do us no harm."

William turned toward Caleb. Involuntarily his rifle pointed at Caleb. "The man planned on killing us; took his chance and lost. This isn't some game played by so-called honorable men. That man was my enemy and now he's not. I will kill any man who looks to kill or capture me."

Caleb looked at the rifle. "Do you plan on killing me? If not, point that rifle somewhere else."

William looked down at his rifle. "I don't plan on killing you unless you give me a good reason. He lowered the rifle. "I'll make some coffee. As soon as it's light, we'll bury these men."

His near-death and ruthless manner with which William had dispatched the wounded man still shook Caleb. He took the coffee offered to him and sat with it clutched between his two shaking hands. At William's prompting, Caleb drank the coffee before it cooled.

"General, I'm surprised. You are the trained Yankee killer. This bunch deserved killing more than the Yankees. You kill a man charging at you or one lying on the ground; they're both the same shade of dead. They were your enemy; now they are dead. You live, and that's what is important. I don't want to hear about this honor thing, for you kill or are killed. There is no honor or dishonor in killing; there is only surviving."

They sat in silence and drank the coffee. William said, "To tell you the truth, I've never killed a person before, and it wasn't something I've ever given a lot of thought to. I had fights with other men, and some of them were brutal affairs but never ended in a killing. I shot the injured man because he planned to do us harm. I didn't feel good about killing him, but I don't feel bad either. It was just something that needed to be done."

The next morning, they went about burying the fallen men. William found a shallow trench in the woods, which they took turns in deepening. They rolled the four bodies into the ditch and threw in the dirt to cover the graves. William gathered the guns and ammunition of the fallen men. "These might come in handy for use or trade," he said.

The dead men's horses were a way back up the trail from the camp. Two of the horses and the mule wore brands, quite probably stolen. Caleb said, "We can't take a chance of having stolen horses but if I had a horse to ride, we could move faster. We should take the unbranded one and leave the others."

After much discussion, they agreed to drive off the two horses and mule and take along the unbranded one for Caleb to ride. William remarked, "Shame to leave the horses and mule behind. They would have been good to trade for goods along the way, but I don't want to be hung as a horse thief.

Too many folks are eager to find a reason to hang a black man."

They removed the saddles from the horses and halters from the mule and drove the animals away. The mule stopped a short distance and began munching on grass while the two horses ran a little further before stopping.

Caleb, leading the horse, and William walked back to where they had left the wagon, picked up their blankets, and stowed them.

As soon as the team was harnessed to the wagon, the little caravan moved off, continuing their journey. Caleb rode alongside on his new mount that he decided to call Buck for its buckskin color. Buck was a medium-sized, scrawny horse due partially to a poor diet, Caleb was glad for the saddle that kept him from sitting on Buck's bony back.

No conversation was called for. Both men wanted to be away from the death site.

They made camp late in the afternoon in an oak thicket. Caleb saw tracks of wild turkeys, took a shotgun, and walked into the thick woods, moving quietly until he got close to several turkeys. With one shot, he killed two birds. After returning to the campsite, he plucked the feathers and gutted the birds, splitting them in half and roasting them over the fire. When it was done, the two men each ate half of one bird and the other was tomorrow's meal.

The men enjoyed the roast turkey after their diet of beans, so they picked the bones clean. They still had shared little conversation of last night's fight. Both had deep thoughts about the fight, but a gulf between them didn't allow for sharing personal thoughts.

William broke the silence. "That turkey was good. Before now, I didn't shoot any fresh game because the noise of a rifle shot might have attracted attention and I preferred not to be seen or noticed. We can get deer, hogs, possums, and rabbits along the way if no settlements are near. The turkey made my appetite come alive for more food. I don't expect to meet others on this trail but, together, we have a believable story for being here. We can finish the turkey tomorrow and see what we come along for the next day."

Caleb replied, "That sounds good. The only thing I've had for the last few years would be beans with hardtack if we had anything. Sometimes I was able to come across small game or bird eggs but mostly army rations."

The innocent talk of food allowed the men to begin conversing again. They stayed away from the thing that preyed heavily on both their minds. They had killed four men, men who might have families waiting. They had been evil men, but taking a life still took a toll on a man's soul.

The camp was made earlier than either man wanted that afternoon, but the mules were exhausted from pulling the wagon through the soft sand. William unharnessed them.

After unhitching them, he rubbed them down with moss he pulled from the lower branches of an oak tree. He found a good growth of green grass and hobbled the mules so they could eat their fill but not wander too far. Caleb took care of Buck. After making and attaching hobbles, he led him to another grassy spot for the night.

After tending to the horse, Caleb made a fire and heated water for coffee. He looked up, saw William getting his cup from the wagon, and walked over and poured a cupful of the hot drink.

William broke the silence by saying, "Those mules worked hard today. It's a job pulling this loaded wagon through this sand. At least it's not as hot now as it will be in the summer. We're lucky for that. It's cooler and the mosquitoes aren't so bad."

After finishing the remaining turkey, the men picked a spot to sleep for the night, well-spaced apart.

By daybreak, they were on the way again. William was driving the wagon and Caleb was riding alongside. They stopped at noon to let the mules get their breath. Again, there was little conversation as both men were still in deep thoughts about what they had been forced to do.

Camp that night was more relaxed since time had lessened the shock of killing the outlaws. They had faced death and survived, making life seem richer once the initial disgust of death was eased. They ate with relish and relaxed afterward, sitting with their backs against tree trunks. The conversation became easier.

William talked of his home. He had worked for the Thornton family for many years. His parents had been sold to Mr. Thornton when William was young. He grew up on the Thornton ranch and learned to ride and handle cattle. His parents were given their freedom, along with William, by Mr. Thornton and they stayed on as hired help. William's mom worked in the main house while William and his father worked the ranch.

Mrs. Thornton taught William to read and write alongside her son, Rory, and gave him books to read. His education was above any of the black people and many whites, but it did him little good since he had to hide his knowledge, for it was forbidden to educate blacks. It was also considered impossible to do. It was their belief that they could not learn.

Being black and educated in the south was a conflicting position. They could have knowledge but had to keep it secret among themselves. To display the ability would classify them as 'uppity' and a threat to whites who had little or no education.

It was unusual for whites to treat a black family in this manner but, on the Thornton ranch, there were no slaves. This fact brought tremendous loyalty from the blacks and, as free men, they worked harder than if they had been enslaved. They were provided a home, grew their food, and were paid a small salary by the ranch.

William had grown up with Rory Thornton, the only son of Mr. and Mrs. Thornton. William had watched Rory ride away to join the southern army. He had explained to William that he disapproved of slavery but must defend the South against the northern aggression.

Rory rode away to fight for something he didn't believe in, never to return. Now, Mr. Thornton was gone, killed in this senseless war. William relayed all this information to Caleb as they sat and smoked. William related the information while commenting on good men dying for a way of life with which they disagreed.

Caleb listened with little comment. He told William of his former life before the war. He had lived on a small farm near Pensacola. When the war broke out, all the young men enlisted and Caleb had done the same. The war was as good as any reason to get away from the farm. He felt like a hero as he and his friends marched off to join the great conflict. He had left his parents at home. He thought the war would be short and he would be home soon and be considered a man in his own right.

The war changed his thoughts in a hurry. Many of his friends were dead and others were crippled for life. He doubted he could ever go home again. He was sure he was reported as a deserter and must get deep into Florida and away from anyone who knew him. He didn't share all this with William but shared more than he had ever thought he would.

Despite their differences, a bond was forming between the two. Lives shared during times of extremes, such as war, brought the most unlikely men together. They both knew that joining forces was the reason they were still alive. Alone, the four renegades would have killed them, or at least Caleb.

5

Rosie

They traveled on for a few more days without encountering anyone. They came to a spot where William said they should turn south. "Here's where we leave this road," he said. "If you look, you can see the cattle tracks marking where there were cattle driven north. We can follow this trail straight to Mr. Thornton's ranch."

Caleb could see the path made by the cattle. "Will there be other traffic on this trail? How about the army? Do they use it?"

"I don't think so. You never know when some of them will be out on a foraging mission, but there won't be a lot for them close to here. The only town we'll see is the settlement at Starke. The railroad goes through there. Before the war, it had over a hundred people. All the able-bodied men enlisted in the army. There are mostly women, kids, and old folks there now. There shouldn't be any danger there."

William headed the wagon down the new trail. The going wasn't too bad and the ground had a good grass cover. The wagon wheels didn't dig in as they did in the sand, making the wagon move easier and faster.

They were able to supplement their food with fresh game on occasion. Caleb hesitated in using the guns, for fear of attracting company. Anyone responding to gunfire wasn't likely to be friendly. They would either be military, home guard patrollers, or renegades and none of them would be welcome.

"How long will it take to get to the ranch?" Caleb questioned.

William replied, "It's about a hundred and twenty miles. We must twist and turn some, so it'll take us about two weeks to get there, making good time. There'll be some boggy areas and deep sand that will slow us. There's no need to push the mules. We'll need them to help plant crops once we reach the ranch."

The days went by uneventfully. Caleb was surprised at the relationship between the two men. At times, he forgot to think of William's black skin. William also seemed more at ease.

Caleb laughed to himself. *'If the soldiers I fought with could see me now in the company of a Negro, I would be in for some real ribbing, if not hostility.'* This thought sobered Caleb's attitude. *'I have to remember who I am,'* he reasoned. *'Soon I'll be on my own.'* Surprisingly, he found this thought a little unsettling.

William interrupted Caleb's thoughts. "We'll be coming up to a settlement called Starke. There's a trading post outside town. It belongs to a fellow named Grainger. We might trade him a little coffee for some cloth if he has any in stock. I never mentioned it, but I have a girl for which I have plans. She would look kindly on me if I brought her a pretty piece of cloth. If the trader has any, I'll buy it for her, but if we see any troops around, we'll keep on moving."

Caleb didn't like this news but was anxious to hear any news of how the war was going. He'd keep a close eye out for danger and at any sign of any, he'd get away fast.

They came to the railroad tracks about noon. William turned the wagon to the east and followed the tracks. Soon they saw smoke rising above the tree line. A shack came into view. "There she is," William said. "That is Grainger's Store.

I don't see many folks."

Caleb saw a figure leaning over a wash pot behind the trading post. The fire under it accounted for the smoke they had seen. As they got closer, he saw that the figure was a woman. She had a wooden paddle in her hand, stirring the clothing in the wash pot. She looked up when she heard the creak of the wagon but went back to her laundry.

William pulled the wagon up to the trading post and got down and tied the mules to a hitching rail. Two skinny barefoot boys played in the sandy street, but they stopped and stared when Caleb and William appeared. When Caleb looked at them, they quickly turned and ran.

Caleb dismounted and followed William inside the store. A man that Caleb assumed was Grainger, scowled at the sight of William. "Where's Thornton," he demanded.

William took off his hat and held it in his hands, in deference to Grainger. Caleb was shocked at this act of contrition on William's part.

"Mr. Thornton got killed up north of here, Mr. Grainger. We're taking the wagon back to the ranch and we'd like to trade for some cloth if you have any."

"Who is *we*?" Grainger demanded.

Caleb walked closer, extended his hand, and said, "My name is Caleb. Thornton hired me to help William get home."

Grainger wiped his hands on his pants leg and then extended it to shake hands with Caleb. "I'm pleased to meet you and glad to see someone is looking after this uppity nigger. I don't know why Thornton put up with him for so long. Sorry, there's no cloth to be had. I haven't had a shipment of anything for a long while. The soldiers took everything I had and paid me with script. I doubt if I'll ever see any real money. I don't have powder, shot, or a gun, for that matter. They took everything not nailed down."

Caleb looked around the room at all the shelves that were empty and the barrels that were sitting around looked empty. "Why hang on," he asked, "with nothing to sell or trade?"

"Oh, I get some goods now and again. The few farmers who can still work bring in a little flour or cane sugar. Hunters trap hogs and turkeys and bring those to trade for the flour and sugar. I manage to keep a little of both, so I get by."

Caleb heard steps and looked around in alarm. The woman who had been doing the laundry came into the store. "The washing's about done," she said.

Grainger looked at her and then at William. "Hey," he yelled. "Get out of here, nigger. Can't you see a white woman is here? You know better than to hang around when a white woman is present."

Caleb was surprised by this outburst and to see William turn and walk out the door without a response. The William that he knew on the trail was a different man around other white men.

Grainger looked at Caleb and smiled. "I have a little extra business," he said. "The railroad men come in here now and then. They like to sample a little drink that I keep on hand, but I must keep it hidden. If the soldiers knew about it, they would drink it up and not pay. The railroad boys sometimes have gold to pay for a drink. They always have goods to trade that accidentally fall off the train. I keep those goods hidden. I trade flour, sugar, and game all right, but I only sell my other goods for gold. When this war is over, I plan to have enough gold to get by."

Caleb replied, "How about coffee, flour, and some cloth for a dress? If I had a gold coin, could you come up with those items?"

"I just might," Grainger said, with a smile.

"Get it," Caleb said as he turned and went outside.

William was sitting on the wagon with a sullen look on his face. "About time you came out before I kill me a man. Let's get out of this place."

Caleb walked up to the wagon. "Give me one of those gold coins you put in the wagon. You wanted a pretty cloth, and I'll get you some."

William hesitated. He reached back into the wagon, brought out a coin, and handed it to Caleb.

Caleb went back inside. "I only have one coin, but here it is. What can I get for that?"

Grainger nodded to the woman. "This coin will pay for about four yards plus a small bag of flour and coffee." He turned to the woman, "You heard the man bring us those items."

The woman turned and walked through the door.

"Where's she going?" Caleb asked.

"Why, to get your goods. I told you, I keep all the good stuff hidden. Don't worry. She'll be right back. Sure enough, she came back after a few minutes. She had a folded-up piece of floral cloth and the two sacks, one coffee, one flour. She handed them to Caleb.

Caleb took a close look at her for the first time. She was younger than he had thought. Her hands were rough and red from hard work and her face was sunburned and peeling from too much time in the sun. Her eyes were blue but had a vacant look to them. *'She had once been pretty,'* he thought. *'She maybe could be again with rest and care.'*

Grainger laughed and said, "You like the looks of her, do you? If you have more gold, we can make another deal. Her father owed me money and got himself killed in the war. I'm a reasonable man, so I let her move in with me and canceled the debt. Maybe you'd like to settle part of the debt with a little gold. If you'd like her company for a little while, I might even throw in a drink of good shine."

Caleb was shocked and embarrassed by Grainger's words. He looked at the woman, who stood staring at Grainger. Her face was red from more than the sun. She spoke, "I am not for sale. My father owed you money and I have lived up to our bargain, and the bargain did not include renting me out like an animal."

Grainger laughed. "I'll do as I please. You owe me and will do as I say. You have no place else to go. What would you do? You would starve without me."

Caleb stepped closer to Grainger. "You're wrong. I won't tolerate such treatment of a woman." He turned to the woman. "Get your things and get in the wagon. I'll take you with us. I'm sure Mrs. Thornton will give you a home on her ranch and it'll be far better than here."

Rosie said, "Anything will be better than here." She went into the back room, and Grainger started after her.

Caleb pulled a pistol from its holster and pointed it at Grainger. "Hold on mister. I have no problem shooting varmints, and you're one of the worst."

Grainger stopped. He looked at Caleb, and he could see by the look on Caleb's face that this was no idle threat. "She belongs to me. You can't just come in and take her from me. She owes me."

Caleb laughed, but it wasn't a friendly laugh. "You offered to sell her to me, and you're just not going to get the price you asked for. Your pay is that I will not shoot you unless you give me cause. She's coming with me."

The woman came out from the back room, carrying a bundle of clothing. "Go get in the wagon," Caleb told her.

As she started to move, Grainger lunged for her. Caleb was quicker. He swung the LeMat in a wide arch. The barrel hit Grainger behind his left ear, opening a large gash. Grainger stumbled and fell into the wall with a loud thud. He crumpled to the floor.

Caleb walked over to him. Blood ran freely down Grainger's face and made a puddle on the floor. Caleb looked down at the fallen man and said, "She's coming with me. If you follow us, be prepared to kill me or be killed. It'll be one or the other."

Grainger made no reply. He looked up with hate in his eyes, but he knew Caleb wasn't making an idle threat. "Take her," he mumbled. "She's nothing but trouble and I have had my fill of her. Take her and good riddance. I'll remember you, mister, until I get my chance to even the score and you can rely on that."

"Maybe so," replied Caleb. "Maybe so. But not today."

He backed slowly out the door. As he moved, he kept the pistol leveled at Grainger. He said over his back, "William, get the mules moving. The lady will be going with us."

He stood in the doorway until the woman was in the wagon. He climbed into the wagon with a quick turn and told William to get the mules started.

William looked over at him. "What's going on?

Caleb handed him the cloth. "This is for your girl. Turns out, the store had some cloth after all. The man didn't know how to treat a lady. She'll travel with us and maybe Mrs. Thornton will let her live on the ranch. In any event, we had to get her away from Grainger."

William looked at the woman. "My, my, I wanted a little cloth. Caleb has done me one better. He not only got cloth, but he also got a woman wrapped up in it. What do they call you, Miss?"

"My name is Roseanne. Most people call me Rosie. At least they used to when I had friends and a home. Grainger called me all kinds of things, but Rosie will suit me. I thank both of you for getting me out of there."

Caleb said, "Better whip up the mules a bit. We need to be far away by the time Grainger gets his senses back. He'll not like losing her, or the whipping he took. I warned him, but it won't surprise me if he follows us."

William slapped the reins against the backs of the mules. They increased their speed and made reasonable time. They reached the trail that led south, turned the wagon in that direction, and continued the journey to the Thornton Ranch.

They drove until dark set in, putting as much distance as possible between the trading post and themselves. They stopped to make camp near a small pond.

William helped Rosie down from the wagon. Caleb began gathering wood and soon had a fire going. Rosie said, "Show me where everything is stored. I'm a fair cook and will earn my keep."

William went through the wagon with her and pointed out all the provisions they carried. He filled the coffee pot from the pond.

Rosie took the pot, added coffee, and put it on to boil. She sliced bacon, and soon the smell of bacon frying filled the evening air. When the bacon was cooked and crisp, she removed it from the pan.

Next in line was preparing a mix of flour, cornmeal, and water to make bread. The mix turned a golden brown and she removed it from the fire.

Caleb had taken Buck and the mules to the pond so they could drink their fill. He led them back to the camp and William placed hobbles on the mules.

"I'll backtrack to make sure no one is following. I'll be back in a few hours." He saw a look of alarm on Rosie's face. "You're safe with William," he said, "I don't want to be surprised in our sleep tonight." She nodded her head.

Caleb walked off into the gathering night. *'She's a game one,'* he thought, *'to go off with us. Her life must have been terrible for her to take such a chance.'*

He took his mind off Rosie. He had to make sure not only she, but he and William, faced no problems with Grainger. Even though no other men had been seen, it didn't mean that Grainger didn't have more men available.

6

Bad News

Caleb backtracked for about a mile. Then, he stopped, dismounted, walked over to a tree, sat, leaned back, and began his vigil. The sounds of the night came to him. He listened to the plaintive call of the whippoorwills and the swoosh of the bull bats as they dove for insects. Tree frogs added their songs to those of their pond living relatives. He heard the soft flap of the flight of an owl and the following squeak of an unfortunate mouse. All these noises were comforting to Caleb, but he strained his ears to pick up a sound that didn't fit into nature.

As the hours slowly passed, no noise came to him that didn't belong to the night. He mounted the horse and rode back to rejoin his fellow travelers. Before seeing it, he walked right up to the camp, for William had doused the fire. *'A wise move,'* thought Caleb. *'A fire, even a small one, would be an easy beacon for anyone following them.'*

He was startled when William spoke out, "See anything, General?"

"No," replied Caleb. "We're alone. Don't sneak up on me like that. I might have shot you and stop calling me 'General.'"

"Oh, I don't know about that. You have been in two battles so far and won both. That's a good record. I think 'General' will fit, that is, until you lose a battle. When that happens, I might demote you. Get some sleep. I took a nap while you were gone. I'll go back down the trail and keep a lookout until daybreak. I don't want to wake up to the sight of Mr. Grainger. You noticed that he doesn't particularly like me."

Caleb welcomed the chance to get some sleep and placed a blanket on the ground. Laying down, sleep came quickly. He awoke to the smell of coffee boiling and bacon frying. He sat up, surprised that daylight had come without his wakening.

Rosie and William sat by the fire, drinking coffee. William turned to Caleb, "Finally woke up, I see. We thought you would sleep the night and day away."

Rosie filled a cup with coffee and brought it to him. He took the cup and took a healthy drink. "Hey," he said, "that's good coffee. Thanks. I'm not used to being waited on."

Rosie placed bacon on a tin plate and brought it to him. "I'll spoil you for a while. I must repay you for getting me away from Grainger. A little spoiling never hurt a man."

"No," he replied, "a little spoiling doesn't hurt. When you get used to being spoiled and it stops, that when it hurts."

Rosie laughed. It sounded good. She had a lovely laugh. "Thanks," she said, "for the laugh. I haven't laughed in a long time. I must thank you both. At times, I wanted to die. Grainger made a lot of promises when my dad was killed. None of the promises came through. I was just his slave." As she said that, she looked at William and blushed.

"No need to be ashamed," said William. "Nobody likes being a slave or being treated like one."

Caleb finished his breakfast. "We better get going. The further from Grainger's we get, the better I'll feel."

Rosie began cleaning up the plates and William retrieved the animals and hitched two mules to the wagon. He jumped up into the seat and reached a hand to Rosie to help her up. She hesitated a moment but then reached out her hand for his assistance into the wagon. She took her seat and the wagon began moving south. Caleb mounted Buck and rode off in the opposite direction, still unsure if they were followed.

"How did the two of you get together?" she asked. "The two of you seem like an odd pairing."

William hesitated a moment and spoke, "We've only been together a short while. We thought two men traveling together would make more sense than traveling alone. I'll be stopping at the Thornton Ranch since I work there and Caleb will be moving on. He's a good man, but he has some settling to do."

Rosie said thoughtfully, "I suppose Caleb and I have something in common. I also have some settling to do. I'm ashamed of the time I spent with Grainger and I'm sure Caleb looks down on me for that."

"Don't be doing his thinking for him, Rosie. You never know what a person will think or do. He risked a lot to take you away, so he must have not thought badly of you. Keep your head up. Don't let anyone put you down, for trying to get by. This war has eaten up a lot of pride. Pride won't feed you or keep you warm. A body must do what it called for at the time."

They rode on in silence.

They stopped at noon and the mules were unharnessed and allowed to eat grass and roll in the sand. Little was said during the stop. Caleb rejoined them and reported no one was visibly following. William reharnessed the team and the journey continued.

Caleb stayed behind to watch for pursuit whenever they came to higher ground that offered a view of their back trail. When they camped for the night, he caught up with them and reported that they still had no followers.   After dinner, Caleb walked down to a small creek to wash away some dust and shake it from his clothing. After rinsing off, he decided to be alone with his thoughts for a while.

Rosie finished cleaning up from the meal. She walked down to the creek and sat by Caleb. "I want to tell you how much I appreciate the risk you took by freeing me. It wasn't my plan to end up there. My mom died some time ago, so I lived with my pop on our farm. A boy from a neighboring farm was to be my husband but he was killed early in the war. My father took a wagonload of corn to sell to the army. He was shot from ambush. We never knew who fired the shot. I only knew Pop was dead. Soldiers came to the farm and took all the livestock and grain. I had no food or a way to get any. Grainger pretended to be concerned for me. He offered to marry me and take proper care of me. All those I loved were dead. I thought Grainger's offer would be as generous as any I was likely to get. He seemed sympathetic. As soon as I agreed and went back to his place, he changed. He said marrying was foolish, just words on a paper. When I tried to get away, he beat me. I had endured all I could take when you came along. If you hadn't, I don't know what would have become of me. I just know I couldn't live that life anymore. I want you to know that I'm not an evil person. I'm deeply ashamed. I know I'll never get respect from others or myself."

Caleb put his hand on hers and said, "Don't be thinking your're the only one who has acted against their beliefs. This war has not only maimed and crippled our country, it has made us do things we would have never thought possible. What has happened is over. Respect and pride will come back to you, and I hope to me. We must go forward with our lives."

Caleb stood and offered his hand to her. Rosie placed her hand in his, and he gently lifted her until she stood by his side. Together they walked back to the camp.

William had watched the exchange of words. '*Well now,*' he thought, '*Maybe the General has found more than he expected. They have been badly bruised and need healing, and they can heal together.'*

This thought made him think of the girl who waited for him at home. She was seventeen now, a grown woman. He had plans for her and had for a long while. He had also seen her looking at him. *'A man doesn't need a lot of words to know what's going on,'* he thought. *'It's high time I got home and settled down with her.'*

Caleb and Rosie got back to camp. She took three blankets out of the wagon and spread them on the ground, one for each of them. "Hold on there," William said. "Don't spread your blanket on the ground. Look, missy, I've made room for you in the wagon. No more sleeping on the ground for you, with the snakes and bugs. You can sleep in peace while we men get eaten up."

Rosie walked over to the wagon. Sure enough, William had cleared a place for her to sleep in the wagon. Tears came to her eyes. It had been a long time since anyone cared for her. "Thank you, William. Thanks more than you know."

William pretended not to notice the tears. "You're welcome, missy. A lady like you shouldn't have to sleep on the ground. You go on now and get some sleep. Me and Caleb will set up a spell and talk."

William walked over to where Caleb stood. They looked toward the wagon, where Rosie was settled in her bed. "That was a good thing, William. She'll be comfortable in the wagon."

They sat on the ground and talked as the night darkened. "Do you think we should keep watch?" William asked.

"I don't think so. If Grainger was going to follow, he would have done it right away, while we were close. It makes no sense for him to wait for us to get this far. I could have killed him, but the law might be after us if I had, and that would be worse. Although there has been so much killing for the last few years. I doubt anyone would notice one more."

William rose and went to his blanket. Soon, he was asleep. Sleep would not come easy for Caleb. He sat long after darkness came and looked into the night. About two in the morning, William walked over to Caleb and said, "Okay, you get some rest now. I'll stand watch until morning."

Neither man realized it, but a working partnership was forming between them. Without talking about it, they had worked out a guard routine.

Caleb went to his blanket and slept soundly until the stirrings of Rosie around the campfire awakened him.

They journeyed on day after day. The going was good most of the time. Swamps had to be avoided as much as possible. Sometimes the wet areas spread too far. The mules labored hard to pull the wagon through shallow water and muddy ground in those cases. Cottonmouth moccasins slithered out of their way. A few of the larger snakes refused to be intimidated by the travelers. The snakes would coil with open mouths displaying the cotton-white mouths that gave them their name. These snakes were more dangerous and aggressive than rattlesnakes. If possible, they'd veer around the snakes. Caleb would dismount and kill them with a long stick if it were impossible to avoid them. He didn't want to shoot his guns to avoid attracting attention.

All three of them had to walk to lighten the wagon. The scrub was also home to rattlesnakes, so care was taken to avoid them.

The territory was getting more familiar to William. One day they crossed a well-worn roadway that ran from east to west. "That's the road to Ocala," he said. "We're getting close. A few more days will get us to the ranch."

This information brought mixed reactions from Caleb and Rosie. Rosie had grown comfortable with her travel companions. She felt secure in their presence. The new challenge of meeting new people was unsettling. She surprised herself by wondering what Caleb would be doing.

'Would he stay or keep traveling on his own?'

A big smile covered William's face as he pulled back on the reins, stopping the wagon. "This is it," he said. "We turn off here and follow that road." He pointed to a well-worn trail leading off to the left. "The ranch is just down this road, about a mile.

William turned and looked at Caleb, "Well, General, I guess this is where we part company. My destination is down this road to the Thornton ranch and my girl. My journey is almost over. You can go on south on the road we've been following. It'll take you where you need to go."

Caleb looked at Rosie's troubled face and, after thinking it over, replied, "No. I'll go with you to the Thornton's for I feel responsible for Rosie and need to see her safe in a new home. I'd have no peace of mind until I know she's safe."

William said, "Okay. We'll travel a little further together. I'm sure Mrs. Thornton will welcome Rosie, but come along and make sure if it'll make you feel better."

William turned the wagon and headed down the new route. He was anxious to get home but knew it would be awkward facing Mrs. Thornton. She probably had gotten the news of her husband's death but seeing her would not be easy. Mixed with dread of seeing Mrs. Thornton was the anticipation of seeing his girlfriend's face when he gave her the pretty cloth, which made him eager to see her.

Finally, he saw the ranch house, a typical Florida country home with a steep pitched, rust-covered tin roof placed lengthwise facing the road. The house was divided into two parts by a covered breezeway connecting the kitchen on one end to the bedrooms on the other.

William drove the wagon up to the house and was surprised by the lack of activity. There should have been workers going about running the ranch and no smoke came from the kitchen stove's chimney.

The ranch house's front door opened and a man stepped out on the front porch. He wore black trousers, a grey shirt, and black boots. A toothpick dangled from his lips which he removed, saying, "What can I do for you folks? Are you lost? We don't have anything if you're looking for a handout."

William said, "I live here and aren't looking for any handout. Where are Mrs. Thornton and all the help, and who are you?"

The man gave William a long brooding look. "My name is Wilson. I own this farm. This 'Mrs. Thornton' you speak of might have been the previous owner. I don't know about that, but this place is now mine. All the worthless niggers ran off when they saw I wouldn't put up with their shiftless ways."

"This is the Thornton Ranch!" exclaimed William. "I don't care what you say, this is not your land!"

The man, who called himself Wilson, scowled menacingly at William. "You better watch your mouth, boy. As I said, this is my place now. He reached back inside the open door and his hand came out holding a rifle. "Now, you folks better move on down the road. If there's a problem, take it up with the sheriff at Ocala. He will explain it, and he might want to talk to you anyway. There're a lot of deserters around here and runaway slaves. He just might like to talk to you, for sure."

Caleb spoke up. "We're not looking for trouble, Mister. William here used to work for the Thornton's. Do you know where Mrs. Thornton might be or the people who lived here?"

Wilson replied, "It's mighty suspicious that you let this nigger do all the talking. That makes me wonder. However, I want no trouble either. I heard that some of the niggers I ran off moved down the road to the Hagins' farm. If your boy did work here, he knows where that is. Now, I want you folks to move along and, if I see any of you again, I'll figure you're not friendly and handle the situation accordingly."

William looked as if he'd protest more. Caleb said to him, "Come on, William. Let's go before there's trouble. We'll find out what happened and we can come back if we need to." He turned to Wilson. "We'll leave for now. That rifle doesn't scare me. I've faced much worse than one man with a rifle. You need to understand that if we come back, you can be sure it won't be as friends."

Wilson replied, "I don't think you'll be back, and I don't think you want to talk to the sheriff. You rebs and niggers just don't know when you're licked."

William turned the wagon and drove away from the ranch house. They drove down the road until they came to the end of it. William stopped the wagon. "I don't know what's going on, and I'm not just going to ride away until I do."

Caleb said, "I'm with you on this. We need to find out what happened. Do you know where this Hagins' farm is?"

"Yes. It's about ten miles from here. This road will take us right by it. We'll go there. I hope my pretty little girl is there."

7

Selene

William turned the wagon south again. They traveled the ten miles and then turned off onto the new path. They proceeded until they came to another house like the Thornton place, except this one had activity.

Besides the main house, several smaller houses were uniformly bleached grey by the Florida sun. Men worked in the nearby fields and Negro children ran and played beyond the home.

William drove right up to the ranch house and a man with a long, grey beard stepped outside. William assumed that the man was Hagins. The man raised a corncob pipe to his mouth with his left hand. The right arm of his shirt was folded up and pinned at the shoulder. He saw the visitors glance at the empty sleeve. "Lost that arm right off," he said. "I was in my first battle when a six-pound cannonball took it clean off, making my army career short. You folks get down and rest a spell. You look as though you've been traveling awhile." He looked at William. "I know you," he said. "You worked for Thornton. I heard he got killed, and it was a shame about Mrs. Thornton."

"What happened?" William asked.

"Well," Hagins replied, "she heard about her husband being killed. A couple of days later, the sheriff came out with papers. He said Thornton owed money on the place and, since he was dead, he couldn't pay. The sheriff had a man named Wilson with him; he said he was the new owner. That was all too much. The poor woman killed herself, then and there. I don't know if Thornton owed money or not. He wasn't there to say yea or nay. Anyway, Wilson took over and ran off all the help. Most of them took up here. I've been doing my best to feed them."

A thin woman came out of the house and stood beside Hagins. She spoke in a weak, reedy voice. "My man here has lost his manners. My name is Emmy and he is Sy Hagins.

Rosie answered her, "My name is Rosie and he is Caleb," she said as he pointed to him. "The other man is William."

"Well, Rosie, climb down from that wagon seat and come in the house. I'll give you a good drink of water and put on the coffee pot if you're of a mind for that."

Rosie climbed down from the wagon and followed Emmy into the house. She took the offered glass of water. It was cooler inside and it felt good to sit at the table, a welcome change from the wagon seat. She sat quietly as Emmy stoked up the fire. She filled a coffee pot with water, then added a brownish mixture to the pot and put it on the stove to boil.

"It's not coffee," Emmy confessed. "It's parched corn with a little chicory, but it tastes okay if you pretend just a bit." She came over to the table and sat across from Rosie, awaiting the coffee to boil. "What are you folks doing, traveling down this way? Is that your husband?"

Rosie hesitated, "Well, no. Not really. Caleb and William helped me out of a bad spot up near Starke. I'd hoped to stay with the Thornton's until I got things sorted out. I'm not sure now what I'll do."

"You can always stay a spell," Emmy chuckled. "We take in all kinds of folks. We offer nothing fancy, but we somehow manage to keep body and soul together. You can make a pallet on the floor and the men can sleep in the barn. You're welcome if you'd like to stay. It'd be nice to have a white woman to share gossip. Old Sy is not much for womanly conversation. If he didn't talk about farming, hunting, or fishing, he wouldn't have a word to say."

As the women talked, Caleb and William got down from the wagon. They stepped up to the porch under the shade of the roof. Both sat and leaned back against posts supporting the roof. Hagins looked surprised when William sat alongside Caleb but didn't comment.

Caleb asked, "How do you manage to feed everyone? The armies of north and south must have taken all the corn and livestock."

Hagins laughed. "You're right about that. The rebs took our food and left us worthless script. The Yanks outright steal it. Either way, we're left with nothing. I keep two fields, the one that you see the men working in, so that the armies can steal the corn. We have another field hidden in a clearing back in the woods. We harvest that and keep it stored out of sight. So far, that has worked. The armies took all the cows, pigs, and chickens, so we make do with fish. Some of the boys keep traps in the woods. They catch possums, coons, and turkeys and we gather anything edible. Growing enough to eat was hard enough before the armies started helping themselves."

William had been quiet. Suddenly, he asked, "What happened to the girl, Selene, that used to live at the Thorntons'?"

Hagins thought a minute and replied, "She's here. She lives in the house down at the end with her ma and pa. You can find her there now."

William jumped up and strode off toward the house indicated by Hagins. By the time he reached the house, he was breathing hard from exertion and excitement. He called, "Selene, are you in there?"

The front door opened and a black girl came out. She was tall and ebony black. "William," she said. "I was afraid you'd been killed, and I got no word from you."

He stared at her as if he'd never seen her before. She wore an ordinary cloth dress that covered her from her neck to well below her knees, and it hung straight with no belt. Despite the formless dress, there was evident pride and confidence in her stance.

When William found his voice and was able to speak, he said, "I'm back now. I just rode up on that wagon. I went to the ranch, but everyone was gone."

She replied, "Yes. We all had to leave. That Wilson man is mean through and through, and he doesn't grow any crops. He and the sheriff share some crooked business between them."

"I'm back now. I came here for you and I brought you a present."

He turned and ran back to the wagon and got the cloth. He walked proudly up to Selene and gave it to her.

Selene unfolded it carefully and looked at it. She held it to her chest. Her eyes were bright with pleasure and devilment. "It's so pretty," she said. "Do you think you can ride in here with a little cloth and win me over? It'll take more than that, Mister. How did you get it? No one has seen anything like this for a long time. I might keep it just to humor you. It's too pretty to make into a dress. I'd be afraid to wear it. I'll just wrap it up and keep it."

William laughed with pleasure. "I bought that for a special reason, Selene. You'll make a dress and wear it, and that dress will be your wedding dress. Me and you are going to get married. I want you for my wife."

The devilment didn't leave her eyes. She wouldn't make this easy for him. "I don't know. I'll have to think about that. I didn't know if you were alive. You show up with this cloth, and now tell me we're getting married. There might be someone else making a better offer."

"You take your time, girl. Get used to me being back. You'll marry me and I pity any man who looks at you while I'm alive. In your new dress, you'll be the prettiest girl ever married in these parts. Get started on making it. I don't plan on waiting too long before we're married." Then, William told her, "I'll be back later to talk to your folks. I don't care if they approve or not, but I'll give them a chance to speak their mind." With that, he left and walked back to the ranch house.

Selene watched him walk away. She clutched the cloth close to her breast and smiled as he walked away. She would go with William but not without giving him a rough time. He wasn't the only one with pride.

Caleb and Hagins still sat on the porch. When William walked up, Caleb said, "Hagins here was telling me that there's land south of here just waiting to be settled. It belongs to the government and anyone can claim a section. You must build a house, live on the land for five years, and it's yours to keep. It's good grazing land according to Hagins, with plenty of water. I'm going there. Would like you to go with me?"

William was taken back by this turn of events. He had only thought of marrying Selene, with no idea where they would live. "You need to know that I'm getting married," he stammered. "I'll have a wife to go with me."

Caleb replied, "That's fine. You can start your new family in a new land and we'll be safer further south. Just maybe you'll not be shot by someone over your attitude. Let me do your talking and you might live to old age."

William bristled. "Are you trying to claim land for yourself and show up with your own slave to do your work? No, thanks. I told you that I was a free man, and I plan on staying that way."

"I didn't say anything about a slave, or you're doing my work." Caleb's face reddened. "You can see that there is little for you around here. I don't have any money to hire you, but if you help me, I'll share what we make and help you start your own home."

Hagins interrupted, "Are you going into partnership with a nigger? I never heard of such a thing. Folks will run you off if you try such a foolish notion. You better go way up north for those kinds of thought."

William retorted, "You hear that? Your kind will run you off if you dare treat me like a person."

Caleb held his position. "I don't care what others think. If I can claim and tame a section of land, that'll be one hundred and sixty acres. We'll have plenty of room to get along. Besides that, two men will stand a better chance of getting by in these troubled times."

William considered Caleb's words. He knew if he stayed around here, he'd get in trouble with Wilson. A clean start further south might make sense. If he tried it and it didn't work out, he could always leave. He surprised himself with a sudden decision. "Okay," he said. "We'll go with you, Selene and me. Don't think, suddenly, that you own Selene or me. We're free, and the first time you forget that we're gone."

Hagins shook his head. "I don't know what this world is coming to. This war confused me enough, and now a white man and nigger are going to share. That's unbelievable."

Emmy came out the front door. "Rosie will be staying inside tonight. You men can sleep in the barn. There's straw there to make your beds. You can let your mules loose in the corral. You had better be ready to hide them if you hear any army boys coming. They'll, what they call, commandeer them. That is legal stealing, but they'll be gone just the same. Caleb, you can eat with us tonight. Food will be simple, but filling. I'll ring the bell when dinner is ready."

Hagins stood up. "Well," he said, "the boss has spoken. You boys take your wagon down to the barn and let your animals loose in the corral. You might find a little hay to give them. I'm afraid there's no grain for them, but there's tall grass beyond the barn and a scythe to cut it with if you're a mind to give them fresh forage."

William drove the wagon to the barn and Caleb followed, riding Buck. Once the wagon was inside, William unharnessed the mules and turned them into the corral. Caleb did the same with Buck. There was a small mound of hay and William used a pitchfork and threw some into the corral. The animals drank from the water trough and then began munching on the hay.

William and Caleb stood in awkward silence. Neither knew how to proceed. A turning point in their lives had been reached.

Caleb thought, '*Can this work?*' He had asked William to go along with him, without giving it a lot of thought. He had been brought up thinking Negros were inferior in all ways to a white man, yet William had proved to be trustworthy by saving Caleb's life. His conversation proved him to be intelligent. He was proud and, while he didn't look for trouble, he avoided it if it arose. He was surprised to realize he trusted William and even more by the fact that he liked him.

Caleb would have had more doubts if he knew that William also had concerns. Any black man knew that white men looked on a black man as a beast of burden. Many whites were not cruel to blacks, but even the kindest overseer felt blacks were beneath them. For a black man to trust a white man was almost impossible.

The two men faced each other. Finally, William broke the silence. "I'll take the scythe and cut some fresh grass for the animals. As soon as I'm done, I'll see my girl. Maybe she'll offer me something to eat." He picked up the long-handled scythe and went out the barn's back door.

The scythe was sharp. William grasped the short handles and swung the scythe back and forth in long swings. As it cut wide swathes of grass, the swish of the blade was satisfying. He pulled hard to get the blade to cut through the grass and then pushed it back to raise it high overhead before the next downward sweep.

As satisfying as it was, William realized it had been a long time since he had done this kind of work. Soon, he was covered in sweat. He could feel his hands begin to blister, along with cramps in his upper shoulders. He finished cutting enough grass, gathered it into large armfuls, and gave it to the animals. They began eagerly eating the fresh-cut grass.

After watching William cutting food for the mules and Buck, Caleb washed his arms and hands in the horse trough and walked to the ranch house. He stepped up on the porch and through the open doorway. Rosie and Hagins were sitting at the table. Emmy stood over the stove, stirring a pot of stew. Caleb took one of the empty chairs and sat down.

"You're in luck," Hagins said. "Some of the boys caught rabbits in their trap. We even found a few potatoes in the field. We'll have rabbit stew. That's hard to beat. The rabbits are getting scarce around here. We have too many people living on game. There was a time that we only hunted rabbits when nothing else was available. Now, even the rabbits are getting scarce. I hear folks are even eating rats now. I don't think I could handle that. Of course, if I got hungry enough, I suppose I would."

Emmy retorted, "There won't be any rats in my stew, Mister. We'll boil and eat roots if that's all we have. No rats, no way."

Hagins laughed. "That always gets a rise out of Emmy. I couldn't stand that myself, but I was serious. I hear people living in towns have done just that. Living in town doesn't provide the chance to hunt for food in the woods or fish, for that matter. We can always scare up something to eat. The woods, lakes, and rivers will provide. We might be down to crawfish and marsh reeds, but we'll eat."

Emmy brought the cookpot over and ladled a sizeable

portion of stew for each of them. She added a plate of corn pone. The stew smelled terrific and Caleb realized he was famished. Conversation lagged as each of them ate heartily of the stew and corn pone. They washed it down with water.

"We used to have milk every night," commented Hagins. "The army saw fit to eat the milk cow. We haven't been able to find a replacement, so water will have to do. At least we don't have any kids that need milk to drink."

They finished the meal and the women cleared the table. The men got up and walked outside. Hagins lit up his pipe. "I'm down to smoking corn shucks instead of tobacco. One thing I look forward to one day is to have real tobacco for my pipe. Not likely, but a good thought."

Caleb was concerned about William. Hagins saw his discomfort and said, "Don't worry about your nigger. He'll be spending time on his own. They don't like being around us any more than we want to be around them. He's doing well, probably down with Selene. She's a real beauty for a black wench."

Hagins puffed on his pipe. Caleb questioned him further about the land to the south. "The land there is scarcely settled. There's lots of free land with plentiful grass and plenty of water. I've been there and thought of moving there, but I've been here too long to pick up stakes and move. It's terrific land for a young man, and that nigger looks strong enough to be of help. If he takes Selene, they'll breed you some healthy workers."

Caleb said, "I meant what I said to William. If he goes along and carries his part of the deal, I'll share with him, whatever the gain. It's hard for me to explain, but William is the only one I know and can trust. He is a Negro, but I've found no fault with him, except too much pride. That will get him in trouble one day."

Hagins chuckled, "If you think he's proud, wait until you meet Selene. You would think she was the queen bee.

With their attitudes, you'll have a job keeping the two of them from being lynched. You just might be hung with them if you're not careful."

The door opened. The women stepped out onto the porch. "This breeze feels good," Emmy said. "After standing over that cookstove and cleaning up, I need a breath of fresh air." She looked at Hagins. "Not that I can get a breath of fresh air with all that smoke. I don't know why men have to stink up the air with those awful pipes."

"It's easy to tell that Emmy is healthy," said Hagins. "If she can complain, it means everything's okay."

8

In Search of a Home

Caleb stood. "Rosie," he said, "how about you and me taking a little walk; maybe work off the good stew we ate."

Rosie looked surprised but stepped down from the porch and looked up at Caleb. "Alright, a walk in the cool evening would be great. Where should we go?"

He stepped down from the porch and joined her. Together they walked from the house. "Hagins says there's a lovely little stream just a little way from here and we can go there, maybe put our feet in the cool water."

They began walking in the direction that Hagins had indicated the brook. They quietly walked until they came to the clear running stream. Rosie leaned down and put her hand in the water. "It's cold," she said. "It must be the runoff from a spring." She sat on the ground and dipped her hand in the water. She raised her chin and rubbed her damp hand on her throat. She had loosened her hair and it fell freely down her back. "The water feels good," she said. "You should try it."

Caleb, still standing, looked down at her upturned face. She looked so lovely in the moonlight that was replacing the day. Her brown hair was streaked with gold, and her face had lost many of the stress lines she had worn only a few days ago. "Rosie," he began, "William and I are going further south. Hagins says there's land to be claimed and I'll start a new life there, either a farm or ranch, depending on the land. It'll be a lot of work and take years to make a life. I'll give William a share of whatever we make if he stays with me."

Rosie sat silently, looking down at the water and her dim reflection in the half-light. "I understand," she said. "I hope you and William do well. I thank you both for what you've done for me. Emmy says I can stay here with them. I'll be fine."

Caleb looked down at the top of Rosie's head and heard the sadness in her voice. "Rosie," he said, "I know you've been mistreated, and I wouldn't blame you if you never trusted another man. I also know that I have no right to ask and it's too soon, but I'd like you to go with me. We can start as friends. If that's all you ever want, I'll respect your wishes. I know that I feel at peace with you, and I'm not too fond of the thought of leaving you behind. Will you come with me?"

After a still moment, Rosie looked up at him and asked, "Are you sure? You know about Grainger. Can you forget about me being with him?"

Caleb gently placed his hand on top of her head. "Rosie," he said, "What either of us did before we met is unimportant. I've done things that shame me. I imagine we all have. We'll begin life with a clean slate if you go with me. Yesterday is only important if it ruins our tomorrow, and we'll not let that happen."

Rosie got to her feet. She moved close to Caleb and leaned her head into his chest. He closed his arms around her and gently held her. "I'll be a good wife for you," she said, "and make sure you never regret taking me along."

They stood together for a long while. Finally, he backed up, took her hand in his, and turned back toward the ranch house. When they got there, Hagins was outside holding a lit lantern. "Come on," he told Caleb. "I'll walk you to the barn. There's plenty of straw for your bed and you can stay long as you want. Rosie will sleep in the house."

Rosie started to protest his leaving. Caleb squeezed her hand and spoke. "I'll see you in the morning, Rosie. We have much to talk about."

The two men went inside the barn and she went inside the house. Emmy had a lantern going so Rosie could see the pallet made up for her. She lay down and heard Hagins come inside. The lanterns were extinguished and darkness claimed the night.

Rosie awakened to the sound of Emmy fixing breakfast. She sat up, embarrassed that she overslept. She hurriedly got up from her pallet. "Here, Emmy," she said, "let me help. I'm sorry for sleeping so late."

Emmy replied, "Don't you fret yourself. You looked so peaceful there sleeping, and it made me feel rested. You can do all the work when you get to your new home. Am I mistaken, or will you be making a home with Caleb?"

Rosie was embarrassed all over. "Yes," she said. "Caleb has asked me to go with him. How did you know?"

"I'm not blind, girl. I saw how he was looking at you. He would be a fool not to ask you. Where else can you find someone like you? I'm surprised you didn't figure that out for yourself. I saw you looking at him, and don't tell me you didn't want him to ask."

"I don't know. There are things you don't know. I was afraid he wouldn't want me, and I didn't dare think he would."

"That's all behind you now. You and he will get along. You're both young, with lots of time to get to know each other. I imagine you'll have a whole brood of kids before you know it."

The door opened. Caleb and Hagins came in. Hagins had his hat off and was carrying something in it. "Look at this," he said. "I found a whole clutch of quail eggs. We'll eat well this morning. Caleb has bacon left from his pack. We'll eat bacon and eggs. It's been a long time since we had that pleasure."

Emmy gently took the hat full of eggs. She placed them on a table near the stove. She sliced bacon into a large iron skillet. The bacon began to sizzle and give off an irresistible smell. When she considered the bacon done, she cracked the quail eggs and put them on to cook. The eggs cooked quickly. She ladled eggs onto four plates, added the bacon, poured coffee, and everyone sat down to eat. It was a merry foursome who enjoyed the meal.

Hagins had been told of Caleb and Rosie's plans. It amused and pleased him. "Makes me jealous," he said, "you two young folks going off to start a life together. It makes me feel how old I am. But I'm proud as if you were my kids. I imagine you'll have company. After Selene gives William a rough time, she'll go off with him. We'll have a double broom ceremony."

"Hush up, Sy, you'll embarrass them. You're too anxious to send them off down the road. I had hoped to hold on to Rosie for a spell, to tell the truth. Her company would have been a good chance. I guess I can't be selfish. They need to get on with their life. Don't you two forget to come back and visit sometime, after you get settled."

The men went outside while the women cleaned up the dishes. Hagins had just lit his pipe and settled down when William walked up. He stopped in front of the porch and stated, "I've just got myself married. My new wife, Selene, will be going south with us. Do you have any problem with that?"

Caleb replied, "I don't suppose that'll be a problem. Rosie will be going on with us. It seems we both have new partners."

William smiled broadly. "That beats all. We haven't even started our new home, and we've already doubled our numbers. We better hurry or the crowd will be too big to travel."

Hagins joined in the conversation. "You might be right. The more I think of you going makes me want to pack up and go along. It all sounds exciting. There's nothing much going on around here."

Emmy came out the door and heard that comment. "Don't go talking that way, Sy. We're going nowhere. My old bones are too brittle to bounce around in a wagon for days. We'll stay right here. You just get busy and provide food for our table."

Hagins breathed a deep sigh. "You boys sure you want to get yourself tied to apron strings? You'll never know a day's peace again or run your own life."

William spoke to Caleb, "We're ready, General, to get on the move as soon as you're ready. Selene has her clothing packed and mine's still in the wagon."

Caleb looked at Rosie. "What do you think? Are you ready to go, or do you need a few days' rest?"

Her reply came quickly, "I'm ready to go. I had just as soon be further away."

William and Caleb knew she was referring to Grainger. Caleb had told Hagins about the trouble with Grainger and the threat he had felt from Wilson at the Thornton Ranch.

Hagins said, "You folks don't worry. If anyone comes here looking for you, I think we can manage it."

Caleb thought for a moment. "William, let's get the wagon hitched. As soon as the women folks are ready, we'll get on our way. It's early yet. We can cover a lot of ground today."

William replied, "I'll go tell Selene. She'll be ready by the time I get the wagon hitched." He walked away toward Selene's house.

In short order, all were ready for departure. 'Good-byes' were exchanged with Emmy and Sy Hagins as the wagon, driven by William, moved away with the women riding, sitting alongside William. Riding Buck, Caleb rode alongside.

Emmy wiped a tear from her eye. "It was like we had a daughter. They were only here a brief time, but I'll miss them."

"You women," retorted Hagins. "Always getting soft. Fix me a cup of coffee. It'll get your mind off them."

Emmy went inside to get the coffee. Hagins stood and watched as the small procession left. *'Getting a little soft myself,'* he thought. *'It was nice, having them young folks visit, and I might just miss them myself.'*

He turned and went inside to Emmy and his coffee.

9

Ira

The four travelers moved steadily all day, except for a stop to let the mules and women rest. The women chose to walk after riding for hours. The wagon seat was hard and sitting in the wagon was rough riding. Sore muscles needed the kinks worked out. It also gave the mules a break as they had a lighter load to pull.

Caleb dismounted Buck and walked with Rosie. Selene walked alongside the wagon with her hand on its side for support. William climbed down from the wagon seat to walk with her. He kept the reins in his hand to control the mules and urged them on if they began to slow the pace.

They stopped for the night and Caleb was anxious to see how the two women would get along. He had accepted William but was unsure how Rosie would manage the situation. Rosie was from the south and had grown up with prejudice toward black people. His fears turned out to be groundless as Rosie and Selene shared the camp duties.

'It's odd,' mused Caleb. '*The four of us alone seems natural enough.*'

The problems would come when they were around others and people would expect Caleb and Rosie to be in charge, William and Selene subservient.

On the third day of the trip, they came to a small homestead. There was a house made of faded cypress. Two barefoot boys played in the white sand of the yard, wearing well-worn overalls and no shirts. Both had the sun-bleached, blond hair that was common in Florida. When the boys spied the wagon, they ran beyond the house yelling, "Pa, there are folks here!"

Beyond the house, Caleb saw two figures working in the field. A man with leather straps over his shoulders was pulling a plow. A woman was bent over, holding the plow handles as she guided it on a crooked path.

The man stopped and looked toward the two boys. He also wore faded overalls but had a shirt. The overalls and shirt were drenched in sweat. He wiped a hand across his brow. The woman let go of the plow handle, put a hand to her lower back, and stood upright with evident effort.

Caleb told William to wait with the women and wagon and walked over to where the man and woman still stood. "Hello," offered Caleb.

"Howdy," the man replied. "We don't have any food to spare, nor anything of value. The army has taken our mule. They killed and ate it. I hope they don't see me pulling this plow. They might decide that I'm a mule and kill and eat me!"

Caleb looked around. He knew that the plight of these people was a common one in Florida. People struggled to live and finding food for each day was a big challenge. "We don't want anything," he said. "We're traveling south, looking for a family called Sanders. They live south of here. Can you give us directions?"

The man looked at Caleb, deciding if he presented a danger. Finally, he answered, "There are a few ranches down that way, but I've never heard of any Sanders. The fact is, I don't know anyone around there. There's a trail made by cattle moving north. If you follow the trail, you'll find cattle and ranchers. You can ask about the Sanders along the way. The ranchers will know of Sanders if he has a ranch."

Caleb thanked the man and rode back to the wagon.

He looked back and saw that the man had resumed pulling the plow. His wife stumbled behind, trying to keep the plow turning over the sandy soil. He passed the information along to the others. The journey resumed.

Later that day, Caleb saw a building off to his left. They drove over to the building to inquire about Sanders. The building had a sign crudely printed on the wall with the name 'Bascomb's' in faded paint. Two men sat on the front porch and could have been twins. Both were thin and had long, grey beards stained by tobacco. They greeted Caleb in unison with a, "Howdy."

Caleb asked, "Is this a trading post?"

One of the men laughed. "I'm Bascomb and this used to be a trading post back when there was anything to trade. All we trade now are lies. Sit down if you'd like. We're tired of our lies and would enjoy some new ones."

Caleb laughed and said, "We're looking for the Sanders ranch. Do either of you know of it?"

One of the men replied, "Yep. I know one family with that name. They live south of here. You head straight south until you see a sizeable lake. Turn right and follow the lake. Don't get too close to the lake or the mosquitoes will eat you alive. If they're the ones you want, the Sanders place is about twenty miles from here. You'll have to cross a wide creek. You'll have to look for a shallow place to get your wagon across. Once you pass the creek, the land is wide open. Just keep headed south and you'll see the Sanders place. You might come across some of the cowboys chasing cows. They can direct you if you get lost."

Caleb thanked the men. William turned the wagon around and the little group headed in the direction given by Bascomb.

Caleb said, "We'll see the Sanders and tell them about their son. They can likely tell us where we can homestead some suitable land."

They headed south again and made camp that night. Everyone was excited that the trip was almost over and soon they would make a home and settle down.

They reached the creek the next day. It was wide and looked too deep for the wagon to cross. They turned west, following the stream's path until they came to a sandbar. Caleb walked ahead of the wagon to test the firmness of the bottom. It was hard-packed sand and would hold the weight of the wagon. William drove the mules into the river. They balked at first, but the crossing was achieved with little trouble. When they were safely across, they rested the mules.

Caleb looked back at the creek. "It seems like that creek separates our old lives and our new ones. Let's hope the water will wash away our past problems and give us a clean start."

"It most likely won't be that easy," countered William.

After resting the mules, William slapped the reins. The wagon began moving again over level ground. They started to see cattle tracks quite often.

"This looks like cattle country alright," Caleb said. "Maybe we can get in the cattle business. There'll be lots of calls for meat."

Late that afternoon, they stopped and made camp. Caleb gathered wood and started a fire. As the four of them prepared to eat, they heard hoofbeats. Two riders rode up on small horses. The two wore cotton pants, boots, long-sleeved cotton shirts, and well-worn, creased black hats with wide brims.

"Howdy," one of them said. "My name is Oliver. My ugly friend here is Hiram. What are you folks doing out here?"

Caleb answered, "We're looking for the Sanders place. Can you tell us where it is?"

"You're close," Oliver answered. "Keep on south for a couple of days traveling with that wagon. You'll come to a pond of cypress trees. Turn west and you'll see the Sanders house a few miles ahead. Are they expecting you?"

"No, they're not. But, we bring them news from the war. Will you and Hiram get down and have a cup of coffee?"

"I guess we will. We haven't had real coffee for a long time. The Yankee blockades have kept any supplies from getting to us. We used acorns and baked corn for coffee, a poor substitute. Better ration your coffee, for you're not likely to get anymore around here."

The two cowboys squatted on their heels. They showed pleasure at the taste of the coffee. "That's mighty tasty," Oliver commented. He didn't show it if he seemed surprised by the two white people sitting and eating with the two Negroes. "Are you folks looking for work? My boss could use more cowmen. Help is hard to find with the war on."

"No," Caleb replied. "I understand there is land to be homesteaded. We plan on finding unclaimed land and filing a homestead."

Oliver looked over at Caleb. "Well," he said, "there's a lot of government land here and a lot of water. Most of the land is used by a few ranchers, and they think the land is theirs since they have been here so long. We don't see a lot of government around here. My boss and the other ranchers think they are the government."

Caleb didn't like hearing this information and he decided to drop the conversation. "We haven't seen a lot of cattle, although we have seen tracks."

Oliver replied, "We round them up and sell them to the army. Taking cattle to the army is why we're not in the army. The army decided ranchers and cowboys were more valuable in providing beef than serving in the army. We and the other cattle owners are part of what the army calls the cattle guard. The other day I heard the boss say that he might slow down the shipping. There is some question about the value of the script the army pays with and the confederate dollars. That's none of my concern. I do my job and let the boss worry about that."

Oliver stood. "Thanks for the coffee. We have a long ride to get back to our beds. You folks take care. Hope to see you again."

With that remark, the two mounted and rode away. The next morning, they were all anxious to get going. After a hurried breakfast, they were moving once again. When they reached the cypress pond that Oliver had described to them, they turned to the west and saw smoke rising. The smoke came from a house that Caleb assumed was the Sanders' place.

Like others they had seen, it was made of sawn cypress wood. Boards were placed upright with smaller boards covering the cracks where the boards met. The wood was unpainted and bleached to a dull white by the Florida sun. Hand-hewn cypress shingles covered the roof.

A small covered front porch was joined to the house. The house showed neglect and disrepair. A boy holding a rifle in his hands stepped out of the house onto the front porch. "What do you want?" he demanded.

The boy was clad in worn cotton pants and shirt but was barefoot with an uncombed mop of hair.

Caleb said, "We don't want anything, son. Is this the Sanders' place?

The boy didn't lower the rifle.

"Is your Ma and Pa home?"

"My Pa's inside, but he's sick. We buried my Ma last week."

Rosie spoke, "If you let us come in, maybe we can help your pa. Don't shoot us, for we're friends."

The boy, who said his name was Ira, lowered the rifle. "I'm not going to shoot you, for I don't have any powder or shot to shoot you with." He leaned the gun against the wall. "You might as well come in. I can't stop you."

Rosie got down from the wagon and went inside,

followed by Caleb. The inside of the room was dark and smelled of sickness. Against one wall, a thin figure of a man lay on a mattress, soaked with sweat. He slowly raised his head and looked at the visitors. "I don't know you," he said. "You'd better not get too close. I have a fever. Ira's mom died from it, and I won't last much longer."

Rosie walked over to the bed. "My name is Rosie, and my man's name is Caleb. We'll try to help. Caleb was a friend of your son, Jim."

Rosie told Ira to bring some water. He went outside and returned with a large gourd filled to overflowing. She soaked a piece of cloth in the water and bathed Ethan Sanders' sweating face.

"That feels good," he said. "I thank you." He looked over at Caleb, who stood nearby. "You know my boy, Jim? You're here, so I guess he's killed."

Caleb lowered his head. Bringing unwelcome news to a sick man made the job more complicated. He looked up. "Yes," he said. "Jim was a good man and he died bravely. His last words were of his family. You can be proud of him."

The old man dropped his head back on the bed. After a few minutes, he raised it again. "What are your plans?"

"We plan on homesteading some land. I hear there's government land that we can settle to farm or raise cattle."

Sanders nodded his head. "There are two ways to go. The cattle business is okay but might not stay that way. This land is also good for growing oranges. Plant some now and, if the cattle business gets bad, you can fall back on the oranges. You might have trouble homesteading around here. There are big cattle ranchers and they have run cattle on all the land for years. They think it's theirs and they'll give you trouble if you try to claim any land."

"How about you, Mr. Sanders? They let you stay."

"My pap settled this place a long time ago. We own a full section of land. Much of it is a swamp, but there is lots of dry land when the floods don't come and it's good for cattle to graze. This ranch is as old as any others, but they have just gotten bigger."

Caleb was upset with this information. First, the cowboys had warned him, and now Sanders was reinforcing their words.

Sanders said, "I got me a good boy there in Ira, but there's no one to look after him. I don't want him growing up to be wild. I'm dying, and nothing will stop that. I have no family except for Ira, with Jim gone. Ira is too young to take over and the ranchers around here would take over my land. One of my neighbors would take Ira in, but I don't know how he'd be treated. Most of them have more mouths than they can feed already. I'd like Ira to grow up here, in his home. We can work something out to help each other. If you give me your word to look out for Ira and raise him into a good God-fearing man, I'll sign over my land to you. I only ask that you give him a good home and when he's grown, give him a start in life."

Caleb was speechless. Rosie spoke up. "Don't worry about Ira. We'll look after him, and you don't have to give us this land; we wouldn't desert a young boy."

"No," said Sanders. "I want you to have this place. I have a whole section that you can live on and improve. It makes my going easier, knowing someone will carry on for me and take care of Ira. This will relieve my mind a whole lot. Ira, get the pencil and paper that ma was using to teach you numbers and give them to this lady."

Ira went to a rough cupboard and retrieved a pad of yellow paper and a worn-down pencil. He handed them to Rosie.

Sanders said, "Can you write?"

Rosie nodded that she could.

Sanders directed her to write out words that would give the place to Caleb and Rosie. Caleb interrupted. "It's not fair to Ira giving this place to us, and it should go to him."

Sanders thought a while, then finally said, "My deal is, I'll give you this place. Your deal with me is that you'll improve it and raise my boy. There are cattle on this land, branded with the double S, after my wife. When my boy is grown, give him the value of the cattle. That'll give him a start in life. If I left this place to him, someone would take it, along with the cattle. I'm happy with our deal. Finish the paper, Rosie, and I'll sign it."

Rosie finished writing the paper and gave it to Sanders. He signed it, saying. "I'm much relieved, knowing that Ira will be looked after. He's a good boy and will make a good man with proper guidance, and I believe you folks will provide that."

Rosie took back the signed paper then, folded it and put it in the cupboard.

Caleb walked back outside to the wagon. William stood beside it. Selene still sat on the wagon seat. "We'll be staying here. The old man is dying and his wife is already dead. This is our new home. There's a barn out back to park the wagon and a corral for the mules."

William had a questioning look on his face. Caleb said, "Sanders turned this place over to us in exchange for raising his son. We can all make a good home here without upsetting the local ranchers."

Caleb began walking toward the barn. William followed with the wagon. The barn was old, weather-beaten, and needed repair but still serviceable. Caleb looked around saying, "I reckon we can make do. There's straw for beds so that we can sleep here for now. We can repair the house and barn."

Selene got down from the wagon seat. She looked around the barn and said, "Looks like I made a good choice in my man. He took me from a nice house and, now, he's putting me in a dilapidated barn. I thought you wanted a wife, but it seems as if you thought you bought another mule. The next thing you know, you'll be feeding me hay."

"Hush woman," William replied. "We'll make do with what we have for now. You'll get your house. At least we have a roof over our heads. That's more than we had last night. Help me unpack the wagon, then can go up and help Rosie."

Caleb left the two of them to their friendly bickering. He walked back to the house and went inside. Rosie still sat by the bed. Ira stood to one side, looking down at his bare feet. Sanders was still alive, but his breathing was irregular and shallow.

Rosie looked up. "I don't know how long he'll last. It looks like he's ready to go now that Ira will be taken care of."

Caleb walked over to Ira. "Come on, Ira. Show me where the chopping block is and we'll chop some wood to cook supper."

Ira looked up at Caleb. He didn't speak, just slowly walked out the front door. Caleb followed. Ira walked over to a woodpile next to the house. An ax was sticking up from a chopping block. Caleb pulled it free and began chopping wood. "You heard your pa," Caleb said. "We'll be caring for you from now on and we want to be your family. We can't replace your ma and pa, but we'll care for you. You don't have to be afraid."

Ira retorted, "I'm not afraid. I was ready to fight to defend this place if you forgot. I'm almost grown-up, and I can do a man's work. I'm not afraid."

"Of course, you're not. And I remember you were ready to defend this place. I'm right glad you're here. You can help me look after Rosie. A woman needs men to look out for her."

"Okay, I can do that. Just remember, I'm not afraid.

Caleb said, "I can see that. If you'd like, you can carry some of this cut wood to Rosie so that she can start a fire."

Ira took a hefty armload of wood and walked toward the house. Caleb watched him walk away and thought, *'I have to be careful with him. He lost his Ma and soon his Pa. His whole world is turned upside down. It will take all I can do to get him to accept us. I'm glad I have Rosie, for she'll be much better than me.'*

Caleb chopped another armload. He swung the ax and buried its blade in the chopping block. After picking up the cut wood, he carried it to the house.

Rosie had started a fire in the cookstove. She had brought bacon and cornmeal from the wagon to cook for their supper. "There's a garden out back," she said to Caleb. "It's in poor condition, mainly weeds, but maybe I can find some things to eat. You or William can bring in some game to go with the vegetables."

The kitchen had a table with two chairs and two benches. When supper was ready, Selene called William to come to supper. She and William sat together on a bench and Caleb and Rosie took chairs. Ira sat on the other bench.

"I've never eaten with niggers before," he spoke. "Folks around here would not put up with that."

Caleb said, "You're probably right, but we'll be taking meals together. The work around here won't know if a Negro man or white man is doing it, and the food is the same way."

"I was just saying I've never done it before," Ira replied. "I didn't say that I wouldn't do it, just that I never have."

"Did your pa have Negro help?" William asked.

"No. He never did. Some of the ranchers have nigger help and some of the cowboys are niggers."

Rosie said, "Ira, I think it would be better if you referred to William and Selene as Negros, not niggers."

Ira looked confused. "That's all I've ever heard them called," he replied. "I don't mean anything. That's just what everyone calls them. I thought that's what they were."

William laughed. "You're right, boy. There are Negro men and there are niggers. Sometimes it's hard to tell them apart. Selene here comes from a line of Africans and her grandmother was an African Queen. She can tell you stories about Africa that will keep you up nights."

Ira looked at Selene with wide eyes. "Are you really a queen?" he asked.

Selene laughed with her rich, deep voice. "No. I'm not a queen, even though a certain gentleman promised to treat me like one. But, my ancestors were royalty back in Africa. Someday I'll tell you stories about them."

Ira looked at Selene in a whole new light. "How about you, Mrs. Rosie? Were you a queen?"

"No, son, I'm afraid not. I'm just your run-of-the-mill girl, so Selene will be our only royalty."

Everyone fell to the eating of supper. Once they had all finished, Rosie took a plate over to Sanders. She tried to get him to eat. All he wanted was a drink of water. He was getting noticeably weaker. Caleb told Rosie they would sleep in the barn that night and Ira could sleep inside. Rosie told Ira to get them if his father worsened. The four walked together to the barn. They piled straw into mounds and placed blankets on top, forming comfortable beds.

Caleb and William stepped outside the barn. Caleb said, "We have a place to stay now but still have a job to do. We're almost out of food, so we might have to live off the land until we get in a garden."

William replied, "I saw some old hoe-heads in the barn that need new handles and an old plow. We got the mules to pull the plow, so we can get in a crop if we can find seeds."

When Rosie and Selene reached the house the following day to prepare breakfast, Ira was standing on the front porch, staring off into space. Rosie touched him on his arm.

Ira turned to her and said, "Pa's gone. I tried to give him a drink this morning and he was gone."

"I'm so sorry," Rosie told him. We'll get him ready for

burial."

"Thank you. I'll dig him a grave next to Ma." He stepped off the porch and walked toward the barn.

Rosie and Selene went inside. Rosie washed Sanders' face and straightened up his clothing. The fever had made him lose weight, making him easy to move. He was still wearing his rough cotton pants and shirt. She found a pair of shoes next to the bed and put them on his feet. "I reckon that's all we can do for him."

Ira went inside the barn. He picked up a shovel and softly said to Caleb, "Pa is gone. I'm going to dig him a grave."

Caleb replied, "I'll help. Sanders seemed like a good man and I know you'll miss him."

"No. I'll dig the grave myself. He was my Pa, and it's my job to dig the grave. It's the last thing I can do for him."

Ira walked out of the barn with the shovel in his hand. Caleb stood and watched him go. He nodded his head in understanding.

Ira went to the place where his mother was buried. He looked down at her grave. Tears ran down his face. "I'm bringing Pa to join you. Don't worry about me. I'll get by. It'll be hard, for I've missed you. Now, I'll miss you both. The two of you always took care of me. I'll not forget that or the things you told me. You know I didn't like learning to read and figure, but I promise to keep at it. You don't know Rosie but she'll help me. She's not you but seems nice. You'll sleep better with Pa beside you. I promise never to do anything to shame your name."

Ira selected a spot next to her grave and began digging. Soon, he was drenched in sweat. It was early in the day but already hot. The sun bore down on his back as he dug. Sweat mixed with tears ran down his face as he toiled.

William walked up to the gravesite. "Can I help you dig?" he offered.

"No, thank you. This is my job."

William squatted down and sat on his heels. "I had to bury my pa a long time ago. I know how you feel. It's hard to lose your Pa. It'll take a long time for the hurt to go away, but it will. You'll always remember him. His words will come back to you when you need them. He'll never completely go away. He and your ma will live on in you."

Ira kept on digging. It was strange that William, a Negro man, had mourned his father's death. He had never considered that a Negro might feel the same things that Ira did. He didn't say anything, just kept digging under the watchful eyes of William.

Rosie walked out to the barn. She carried a cup of coffee for Caleb. She handed him the coffee and cold corn pone and he took them gratefully. He sat on a crate, drank the coffee, and ate the corn pone. Caleb said, "I'd like to build a coffin, but we don't have the planks or nails to make one."

Rosie said, "Sanders is ready. We can wrap him in the blanket he slept on."

Caleb walked to the gravesite where Ira was still digging. "I believe the grave is deep enough," he said.

Ira stopped digging but didn't look up at the men. He didn't want them to see the tears in his eyes. Caleb motioned for William to follow. They went to the house and went inside. Rosie and Selene had wrapped the body in the thin blanket that Sanders had lain on. Caleb and William picked up the covered body and carried it to the grave. They gently lowered Sanders in the open grave. Ira stood there looking down into the grave. Rosie put her hand on his shoulder. "Is there someone we should notify about your Pa?"

"No, Ma'am, I don't think so. No one came for Ma's burial and Pa will have more at his with you all here."

Caleb stood at the head of the open grave. He took off his hat, as did William. "Lord," he said. "we're sending Ethan Sanders to You. We didn't know him well, but he seemed a good, caring man. With so many folks dying, You might have left Ethan to raise his boy. We'll not question Your plans, but sometimes they're hard to understand. This leaves a good boy without a pa or ma, but we'll look out for him. When the Sanders join You, Lord, tell them their boy will be cared for and not worry. Amen"

Rosie said, "Ira, it's right for you to throw in the first shovel of dirt."

He pushed the shovel into the mound of dirt. He lifted and threw a shovel full into the grave. He stood staring at the earth he had just thrown onto his father's covered body.

William reached for the shovel. "Let me help you."

Ira hesitated. He looked down at his hands holding the shovel and both were blistered from the rough shovel handle. He mutely handed the shovel to William.

When the grave was filled and mounded over, Rosie took Ira's hand and led him to the house. Once there, she offered him food, which he declined.

She went outside. The two men stood about aimlessly. An awkward time follows a funeral, making men think of their own mortality.

Rosie had a cure for that. "Hey," she called, "you men build a fire under the wash pot and fill it with water. I'll need a lot of hot water. The house and everything in it must be scrubbed."

While the men carried on that job, Rosie and Selene went into the house. They removed all the sheets, blankets, and window curtains. Selene took them outside and placed them in the pot. The water wasn't too hot yet, so she took a bar of lye soap and scrubbed each piece of cloth before putting them back in the pot. In the meantime, Rosie instructed the men to bring buckets of water into the house. She opened all the cupboards and scoured the insides. Nothing was spared her attention. No one mentioned lunch, as the women went about getting everything clean and hopefully free of the fever that had taken Sanders.

William said, "Caleb, you and Rosie sleep in the house since it'll be easier for Ira. Selene and I will make do in the barn."

Caleb told William, "We'll build another house for you and Selene as soon as possible. You can take your meals with us."

William replied, "We'll be fine, for now. This barn will keep the rain off."

10

Neighbors

They spent the next few days cleaning and repairing. The women scrubbed the house clean. "I thought they'd scrub the floor away and we'd be standing on dirt for a floor," Caleb complained.

They had just finished their evening meal and were sitting on the front porch when three riders rode up. Two of them were the cowboys, Oliver and Hiram. The other was an older man. He had a broad face topped with gray hair. His blue shirt was sweat stained but in good shape. He wore dark blue trousers that disappeared into high top black boots. "My name is James Roberts. I understand that Sanders is dead. His boy's not old enough to run this spread. Does he have any family? I'll give him some money to take with him. I'm taking over this ranch. Sanders shouldn't have settled here. My cows have been on this range for years."

Caleb stepped into the yard. "I'm glad to meet you, Mr. Roberts. My name is Caleb Melton. Sanders signed this place over to me, just before he died. We'll be living here now and taking care of Ira. I hope we can be good neighbors. Would you and your men like to get down for a spell?"

Roberts was startled by this news. Scowling, he said, "You have no right to this place. It should be mine since I have run cows here for years. I knew someday Sanders would be gone. It's a hard land and not many can take it. I'll pay you a reasonable price to move on and leave to me what is rightfully mine. I have nothing against you, folks, but you need to move on. I'll even give you a job. You'd be better off. I know this land and how to manage it. You might grow enough food and hunt to get by, but all you'd do is just get by. The first bad year, you'll be gone. Working for me, your family would have food and lodging. I'd pay you wages, both you and your nigger. Things will go tough for you if you stay."

Anger filled Caleb at Roberts's words. "We're here to stay and raise our families and Ira. We had hoped that any neighbors would become friends, for we want no hard feelings. I'm sorry you feel as you do, and I understand, but the land is ours now. You're still welcome to visit with us but as a neighbor only. I hope you didn't intend your words to be a threat. If they were, I suggest you reconsider."

"Roberts looked down at Caleb and noticed William had taken a couple of steps closer. "No. I don't need to threaten you. Your problem will be this land. You need horses if you plan on ranching, and you'll find the army took all the horses except for the ones we ranchers needed to raise and drive cattle. You'll not find any for sale around here. Some of my stock runs free along with my cattle. It goes hard on anyone who helps themselves to my stock or those of other ranchers. My stock has double notches on the right ear. Some of the others brand their stock, and some use notches. I'm giving you a fair warning not to help yourself to either. There's no law around here, so each man does what is needed to protect his property."

Caleb was ready for a reply when William stepped up beside him. William looked up at Roberts and said, "Since we're going to be neighbors, I think we should get to know each other. My name is William, and that is my wife Selene over there. I'm no one's nigger. I'm a free man and I expect to be treated as free and a man."

Roberts looked at Caleb and William standing side by side with the two women behind them. He wasn't accustomed to anyone not bending to his will. Now, Caleb defied him, and a black man sassed him. He thought, *'It must be the war that has driven everyone crazy.'*

Caleb interrupted his thoughts by saying, "We welcomed you as a neighbor and you greet us with threats, like thieves. We're honest, hard-working, and offer to be good neighbors. If pushed, we'll push back. I've seen more trouble and bloodshed than any man should see in a lifetime and hope to avoid more. That doesn't mean we'll be bullied or threatened. I'm told there is unbranded stock running loose. We plan to add stock and use Sanders' brand as our own. We won't touch any animal with another man's brand."

The little group watched as Roberts wheeled his horse around and rode away. Oliver and Hiram sat there for a moment, not believing the exchange they had just witnessed. Oliver spoke, "Mr. Roberts isn't an evil man, he just doesn't take to not getting his way and he had counted on this land. Give him time and he'll be okay." With that, the two cowboys turned their mounts and rode away.

Caleb said, "I doubt if Roberts will ever be our friend. I don't like the idea that he thought he could just come in and take over."

William replied, "That's just a small sample of what black men have known as a way of life. Not only threats, but those threats are carried out."

Roberts was soon forgotten as they faced what must be done for food and supplies. Their first concern was the garden. It was time to plant the summer crops. There were still greens from the winter garden but they had been left untended by the ailing Sanders, allowing weeds to crowd the collard and cabbages plants. The women used hoes to chop and clear away the weeds. Some wouldn't be gathered for food but left to form seed heads for the following year's planting.

William was at work plowing a larger area for corn planting. He had one of the mules harnessed to the plow with the harness draped over his shoulder and plow handles in hand as he watched the grass turn under and the rich soil exposed. The corncrib alongside the barn held a few ears of corn from last year's crop.

The two men took what was left of it to the shade of the barn and sat on crates where they shelled the corn kernels from the cobs. Caleb picked up a cloth bag filled with shelled corn. He placed the bag's strap over his shoulder and walked up and down the rows, dropping corn seeds a few inches apart. William came behind with a hoe and covered the seeds.

Caleb said, "We need additional seeds to plant the rest of the garden and Roberts will be no help. We must find another source for seeds."

After the corn was planted, the two men went back to the barn. Caleb said, "If you'll stay here with the women, I'd like to saddle Buck and look around the land. Maybe I can bag some game for our next meal."

William readily agreed since he wanted to make the barn as livable as possible.

Caleb saddled Buck and rode away toward some distant pine trees. The land was mostly flat and grassy except for wet areas dotted with bay trees called bayheads. He didn't get too close to them, for the mosquitoes were so thick he could hardly breathe. He saw a few cattle but couldn't get close enough to see if they carried brands. They shied off anytime he tried to approach them. He saw a lot of deer and torn-up grass where wild hogs had rooted.

Caleb came to a wide stream that wound lazily and was bordered by trees. It appeared deep enough to provide them with fish. He decided he would take Ira fishing here. He rode on and came to higher land. Here, the grass gave way to a pine forest. He rode into the woods. Pine needles covered the ground, and the wind whispered through the treetops. It was a peaceful place. He dismounted and lay on the carpet of pine needles.

He awoke, surprised that he had fallen asleep. It was time to remount and go home. Before he exited the forest, he spied a deer stepping timidly out of the woods to feed on the grass. Carefully, he pulled his rifle, aimed, and fired. The deer dropped to the ground. Caleb rode over and dismounted. He used his knife to field dress the deer and hung it over Buck's back. Once it was tied into place, he mounted and headed for home. The deer meat would be a welcome treat.

When Caleb arrived back at the cabin, Rosie stood in the doorway looking at the deer. She said, "That'll be welcome. I'll fry some for supper. I also have a pot of poke salad greens that I picked earlier. I've already boiled them twice and threw away the water, so the poison will be all gone and the greens will be good to eat."

After skinning the deer and stretching out the hide to cure, Caleb sliced several slabs of venison and took them to Rosie to cook.

The five enjoyed a meal of fried venison steaks for supper along with the pot of greens and corn pone. After the evening meal, the men and Ira sat on the porch.

Caleb said, "We'll need seeds for the garden and we'll need horses to round up cattle. They are wilder than the deer and will roam free with no fences; they'll be almost impossible to catch."

Ira spoke up. "Pa built a holding pen a little west of here. Every year, after calving time, he would get help in rounding up all the calves so that they could be branded. The rest of the time, they run free. Mr. Roberts usually makes a drive once or twice a year to sell the cattle. He takes cattle from other ranchers along with his and sells them. Everyone knows how many are theirs because they all help in the roundup. He pays four dollars per head for any that he sells for someone else. Pa said that Mr. Roberts gets ten dollars, or better for them when he sells them."

"Why don't other ranchers do their own drives?" Caleb asked.

"He's the only one around here with enough men to make the drive. He has a pack of dogs to help drive the cows. It's hard to drive these wild cows without dogs to keep them in line. There are no men to hire to drive cattle since many are in the war. The small ranchers just have to take what they can get."

William added, "If we had horses, we could round up the cows and brand them. The mules will help but not good as cattle handling. Ira is old enough to ride and Selene can ride. That would give us four riders and we could do the job with four. We still have a few gold coins to buy them with."

Caleb said, "I'll ride to the Bascomb's tomorrow and see if knows where there any are for sale."

The following day, he saddled Buck and rode away. He followed the same path they had used earlier. He reached Bascomb's around noon. The same two men as before sat on the porch. One of the men Caleb recognized as Bascomb from the last visit. He dismounted as Bascomb said, "Hello, didn't expect to see you again so soon."

Caleb replied, "We're settled at the old Sanders' place. He passed away and left us the ranch and his son, Ira, to raise."

Bascomb replied, "I heard he was ailing. I'm sorry to hear that he died. What brings you here today?"

"I want to buy some horses and we need seeds for a garden. Do you know of anyone who has either for sale?"

"Nope. I can't say I do. Every horse around here that could still move was sold to or stolen by the army. Be sure and bring your wife next time. She can visit with mine, for we don't get much company. Everyone who lives here has heard all our lies and we need new folks that don't know better," he laughed.

Caleb was disappointed. He regretfully thought of the horses of the four renegades that he had released.

Bascomb spoke, "Folks here use parched acorns for coffee, wild honey for sugar, and ground corn for bread. I've not seen powder or shot for ages. I used to go to Fort Mellon on the St. Johns River, east of here, once a month and buy anything available. A few boats brought goods down the river, but these days, none gets through the army blockades. I can tell you where you might find a horse or two and maybe seeds."

Caleb eagerly asked where he could find either.

Bascomb replied, "There's an Indian who has a camp on the creek you passed to get here. His name is Pony. Sometimes he traps a horse or two and breaks them to ride. When you get to the creek, head off to the right and follow it until you come to the camp where he lives. Further along the same creek lives a man named Taylor. He might have seeds for sale. None of the ranchers are likely to help you, for they don't welcome newcomers. Taylor is a farmer and might help."

Caleb thanked the man and, after mounting Buck, rode away, retracing his path home. He reached the creek and veered left. After riding about an hour, a thatch-covered, open-sided structure came into view. A small, dark-skinned man with black hair stood alongside the shack. He wore homemade clothing and moccasins on his feet.

Caleb dismounted and said, "Are you known as Pony?"

The man replied, "White men call me Pony. That is not my real name, but it is how I am known."

Caleb nodded and said, "My name is Caleb Melton. I live at the old Sanders' place and need some horses. Bascomb said you might be of help. Do you have horses for sale?"

"No. Evil men stole my last horse, so now I must walk

until I can catch more horses. I know of wild horses near to here. My people catch and train them. They know how to live off the land and are excellent for chasing cattle. We can catch them if you help. I trap and sell horses, so white men named me Pony. Evil men stole my last horse, so now I must walk until I can catch more horses."

"I need horses," Caleb replied. "What must we do?"

"We must go to where they live and build a pen to catch them. It will take us three or four days to get there and catch them, and it will take me another two weeks to train them."

Caleb had his doubts, but he did need horses. "Okay, what will you charge?"

"I will not charge anything but will keep half of the ones we catch. I will train yours and mine for riding."

Caleb mounted and looked down at Pony. "Okay, we'll catch some horses. How will you travel without a horse?"

"I will go on foot. I am used to that."

Caleb told him, "I must go see a man named Taylor before I go home."

Pony said. "I will be ready when you come back this way. I know the man called Taylor. He is a two-hour ride from here."

Caleb rode away. Before long, he came to a house just off the creek and surrounded by large trees bearing yellow fruit. He rode up to the house and a man and woman emerged. The man greeted Caleb. "Howdy, stranger. Get down and rest a bit. I'm Enos and this is Edna. We're the Taylor's."

Caleb dismounted and shook Enos' hand and introduced himself. "I'm told you might have seeds for a garden. We're at the old Sanders' Ranch. Sanders died and left the place for my wife and me to run and raise their son."

Enos said, "I'm really sorry to hear that. Always hate

to lose a good man. It's good the boy has someone to look after him. Come in and sit a spell. Have you eaten anything?"

Caleb replied that he wasn't hungry, but Edna quickly said, "I've never seen a man who couldn't eat a bit. Come in. You two men can talk while I fix up a plate for you. Won't be fancy, but it'll be filling." With that, she turned and walked into the house.

"Come on in, Caleb. She's made up her mind to feed you. No sense arguing with her."

Caleb followed Enos into the house and took a chair offered to him at a plain, but clean, table. Edna bought him a plate of greens and a serving of something the color of potatoes but smaller pieces, along with a pone of bread. At his questioning look, Edna said, "As I told you, nothing fancy. Just some poke salad greens, boiled swamp cabbage, and bread made from coontie flour. The war took all the real flour."

Caleb began eating. All the items on his plate were new to him but that didn't keep him from enjoying the food. Edna also placed a cup, made from a gourd, full of an orange-colored drink in front of him. "Orange juice," she said. "First of the season."

Caleb took a drink and savored the taste. It was cool and sweet-tasting. The first sweet tasting thing in months.

After the meal, the men talked. Enos took Caleb to the barn and provided seeds for a garden. He had seeds for cowpeas and beans. Caleb explained he already had corn and would harvest collard plant seeds from the old garden. After thanking them for the food and seeds, he mounted Buck and rode away after promising to be back to learn about raising oranges.

11

Horses

Caleb rode back to meet with Pony and found him waiting for him.

They waded across the creek and soon were moving briskly along. Pony never seemed to tire, but Buck was breathing heavier than Pony. They reached the ranch house at dusk. William was sitting on the front porch.

He took one look at Pony and said, "Well, General, he looks like a poor specimen of a horse. I hope you didn't pay too much."

Caleb said, "I'm sorry, but there are no horses for sale. This is Pony. He's a Seminole Indian and knows where there are some wild horses. He'll catch and train them for us."

Rosie came out of the house and looked questioningly at Caleb and Pony. She went back inside and came out with fried venison between two slices of corn pone. She handed one to Caleb and the other to Pony. "My name is Rosie. That's William and his wife is Selene. We have a boy named Ira. You'll meet him shortly."

Rosie turned to Caleb. He repeated the story to her about the plan to catch horses.

The next morning Caleb saddled Buck for the hunting trip. He packed a few supplies into the saddlebags and took along ropes and halters in case they caught some horses. Rosie also packed a small pot, frying pan, and cornmeal. The men would get fish and game for meat. Pony rode one of the mules bareback. The mule wasn't accustomed to being ridden and it took Pony some time and effort to settle it down.

Finally, the items were packed and the two rode out to the southwest, as Pony directed. They made camp the first night. Pony had jumped off the mule and chased down a possum, dispatching it with a tree branch.

Caleb sat with a cup of parched corn coffee and watched the fat possum sizzle and drip fat into the fire. Soon, it was a golden brown. The two men pulled off pieces and enjoyed it and had enough left for their noon meal the next day. They traveled for another day and stopped again for the night.

Supper that night was a gopher tortoise that Pony picked up during the day. It was roasted in its shell on top of the fire. When it was done, the shell popped open, and steam escaped. Caleb was a little unsure. He poked gingerly at the gopher with his knife and cut off a small piece. The taste was different but okay. Soon, he ate the meat as eagerly as Pony.

They ate in silence until the meal was finished. Caleb said, "How soon will we find the horses?"

"We are close to them. We will come to a swamp in the morning and we must cross it to reach the island where they live. White men do not know this place, so the horses are still there. I have caught horses there before and I always leave the young ones to grow up. We will catch some nice horses."

Daybreak found them on the move. Later in the morning, they came to the swamp, a dark and foreboding place. "We can cross now," Pony said. "In a few weeks, the mosquitoes will be so thick it will be almost impossible to cross. The winter froze many of them but their eggs will hatch soon and there will be many of them. To cross here then, with the mosquitoes, you would have to cover yourself and your horse. If you do not, you will not be able to breathe."

Pony led off into the swamp, weaving around to find

the firmest bottom to keep the animals from sinking into the muck. Water moccasins were everywhere. The horse and mule snorted with alarm when one got too close. Mosquitoes were still plentiful. Caleb covered his arms and face as best he could. Still, many mosquitoes got through and delivered their painful stings.

They traveled through the swamp for over an hour. *'It's no wonder no one else comes here,'* Caleb thought. *'I would have never done so.'*

Pony led Caleb out of the swamp onto higher ground. The land was covered with lush green grass. "There is always good grass here," Pony said. "With all this water, there is never a drought. The horses are healthy and fat."

Pony led Caleb along the swamp's edge until they came to a slightly wooded area. When they got close, Caleb saw a makeshift pen. Pony had threaded grapevines and tree limbs in the trees around a small clearing. There were long cypress poles that would close the opening once the horses were inside.

"How do we get them to go inside the pen?" Caleb asked.

Pony replied. "This is an island. The ponies will not go into the swamp. I will ride in one direction and you in the other. When the horses see us, they will try to keep their distance. If we do it right, we can direct them into this opening. Once we do, we put the poles in place."

Caleb was anxious to begin. They rode off in opposite directions. After about an hour, Caleb spied a group of horses. They were all looking his way. The stallion pawed the ground, then whinnied and trotted off. The mares and colts followed.

Caleb rode slowly, keeping the horses moving in front of him. Soon, he saw the leader stop and sniff the air. In the distance, Caleb could see Pony on the mule coming his way. Pony rode toward the group of horses at an angle to start them going in the direction he wanted them to go.

The two men drove the horses slowly toward the waiting pen. Caleb was sure the horses would break away and run in the wrong direction. Today, the men were in luck. The horses weren't overly alarmed due to the slow pace of the men and went into the pen. By the time they realized that there was no way through the trees, Pony had dismounted and slid the poles in place. The horses were securely inside the pen. There were seven horses and two foals.

Caleb and Pony watched as the horses circled and whinnied, tossing their heads while looking for an opening to escape through.   Pony said, "We will let the mares and their colts go free. We will also turn loose the stallion, for he's needed to breed other horses. That will leave us four to take home, two for each of us. I come here every year and get horses. Two more herds live here. I take a few and leave others to breed."

Pony added, "There are other horses running free closer to your ranch, but most of them have escaped and have brands. If I catch one of those, I turn it loose. If I did not, they would hang me as a horse thief so I make sure any horse I catch, carries no brand. We will make our camp close to the horses. They will get used to us being here. Tomorrow, we will begin to tame them."

The men went about setting up camp. Their meal was corn pone. The horses snorted and milled about in the pen. They weren't accustomed to the smell of men.

The two ate leftover corn pone for breakfast. They were anxious to get to the horses. "First, we must release the stallion," Pony said. "He will fight to protect his mares. They will be much calmer with him gone. You stand by the gate. I will drive him to you. If he comes alone, remove the poles, and set him free. You must block the entrance quickly or the rest of them will escape. Wait until only the stallion comes your way. Do not let him see you, or he will turn back."

The two men walked over to the entrance. Pony removed all but one pole. It was about four feet from the ground. Pony stooped over, went under the pole, and slipped inside the pen. He moved slowly toward the horses.

The stallion turned and faced Pony, pawing the ground. Pony moved off to one side, trying to get between the stallion and the mares. The mares were all bunched against the back of the pen. They were wide-eyed and nervous.

Pony managed to get between the stallion and the mares. He moved toward the stallion, slowly waving his arms. The horse turned and ran away from Pony, straight toward the pen entrance. Caleb stood to one side, behind a large bush. He saw the horse coming and slid out the one remaining pole. The horse raced out the entrance. Caleb quickly replaced the pole and two others, securing the mares inside. The stallion was still running, kicking his rear hooves high in the air as he ran.

Pony walked up to Caleb. "That went well. Usually, it takes longer to get them separated. Now we will go to work."

He turned and walked toward the group of horses. He moved slowly, talking to the horses as he walked. He was speaking the Seminole language, so Caleb understood none of it.

The horses moved away from Pony. He followed slowly, all the time talking to them. This went on for three hours. The horses still shied away from him, but the distance between man and horses had lessened.

Pony joined Caleb outside the pen and said, "They will get used to me being close. They do not like it, but they will learn to trust me. We will put the mule in with the mares. That will settle them down more."

Caleb removed the poles to allow the mule to enter the pen. Pony led the mule over and released him to join the mares. The mule took a few steps and began to graze. One at the time, the mares moved closer. Soon, the horses were all around the mule and his presence calmed them down, just as Pony had predicted.

Twice more that afternoon, Pony went back into the pen and repeated the routine from the morning. He walked toward the horses, speaking softly to them. They weren't as restless as they had been that morning, partially because of the presence of the mule and partially from getting accustomed to Pony's presence. After a few hours, he left the pen.

The next morning, Pony walked into the pen. The horses ran as far away from him as possible. Only the mule stayed where he was. Pony walked up to the mule, speaking softly. He grabbed a handful of mane and jumped on its back. Using his knees, he directed the mule toward the mares. They were confused since they'd gotten accustomed to the mule without a man on his back. Pony sat without moving. The mule went back to grazing on the sparse grass that the horses' hooves hadn't destroyed. After a few minutes, the mares moved closer to the mule and Pony. They didn't get as close as the day before, but did come close.

The mule would take a step, looking for more grass. The mares would be startled. Pony didn't move. He sat motionlessly and let the mule do all the moving. After a few hours, they accepted Pony as part of the mule and they ignored him.

Pony knew that any movement on his part would startle them, so he sat still. When he thought he'd spent enough time in the pen, using only his heels, he directed the mule over to the opening. The horses didn't follow, for they saw Caleb. Pony dismounted and went outside the gate.

Caleb had watched Pony's action with interest. "That's a peculiar way to break horses."

"It is the Indian way. I will not break their spirit. When I am finished with them, they will see me as a friend. My horses will never try to escape. You can go back home and I will stay with the horses. When they are ready, I will bring them to you."

Caleb agreed to this. "When will you ride them?"

"I will ride among them on the mule and begin touching the mares tomorrow. Soon, I will be able to put halters on them and teach them to follow the pull of the halter. After that, I will begin putting pressure on their back. Once they are used to that, I will slide off the mule and onto their back. They might buck a little but not much since they will know me by then. I will teach them to eat fresh grass from my hand. It will take me two or three weeks to train them."

Caleb decided to leave after breakfast the next day. Pony retrieved the mule from the pen. He rode the mule, led Caleb back through the swamp, and headed him toward home.

Caleb offered to leave the cooking utensils, but Pony said he didn't need them. "I will cook over the open fire. There are many small animals that are easily caught with snares. There are plenty of fish and turtles in the swamp. I will not be hungry."

Once they were through the swamp, they stopped. Caleb looked back. He didn't relish ever going back without Pony to lead him.

Pony said, "I will bring the horses to you as soon as they are ready."

Caleb nodded his agreement. He turned Buck toward home and urged him to a jarring, but ground covering trot.

When Caleb arrived at the house, it was late afternoon. He was pleased to see smoke curling up from the cookstove. He hadn't realized how much he missed Rosie and the others. It hit him that he had a home and family. It made him feel warm inside. *'I'm getting soft,'* he thought to himself. The thought made him smile.

Rosie came outside to greet him and was followed closely by everyone else. William looked at him and said,

"Well, General, where are our horses and that skinny little Indian?"

"He'll be along in a few weeks. He's training the horses in his style. They're good-looking horses and we'll be lucky to have them. There'll be a horse for each of you, and you'll all be chasing cows before long."

The group sat around the porch, talking excitedly about their plans. Caleb looked around. He knew how lucky he'd been so far. Now, he had a decent home, his own woman, and a son. He had loyal friends and helpers in William and Selene. Caleb made a solemn vow to take care of all of them.

Three weeks later, Ira came running into the barn where Caleb worked on a broken harness. "They're coming," he yelled. "The horses are coming."

Caleb put down the harness and walked outside. He saw the group of horses coming toward him. Pony, astride the mule, was following. Caleb opened the corral gate to let them enter. He stood to one side as Pony herded the horses inside. Caleb was surprised to see one of the mares had a young filly in the group.

Everyone came to the corral to see the new horses. William said, "They're small. Are they full grown?"

Pony replied, "That is the size of their type. Many years ago, my people told me that men wearing metal clothing brought the little horses with them. The ones we have come from them. They can go all day without stopping and live off the wild grasses."

Ira looked with wide eyes at the filly. "Look at her," he exclaimed. "Just look at that little lady." The filly he was looking at stood with its front legs slightly spread and stared back. She was a deep brown with a white spot on the front shoulder. "She likes me," Ira said.

Pony said, "She will be yours if you promise to look after her. You will have to train and teach her to be your friend."

Ira looked at Pony and then over to Caleb. His eyes were wide with excitement. When Caleb nodded his approval, Ira went back to looking at the little mare

"You belong to me, little horse. I'll teach you to be my friend."

The grownups walked back to the house. The women went inside to prepare the noon meal. The men sat on the porch.

Pony said, "You trusted me when many would not. When I told you to go home and I would follow, you did not doubt me. For this reason, I brought the mare and foal for you. I will my two but the rest are yours, except for the one I gave to your son. I will stay and work with the horses a little longer if you would like. I must teach them to carry a saddle and wear a bridle. I have only ridden them bareback, with a halter. If your women plan on riding, I should train the horses more."

Caleb said, "We must remember that others don't want us to last, so we must brand the horses. Otherwise, anyone can claim them at any time."

Pony replied, "This, I do not like, but I understand. I have had horses taken from me by men who said they were not mine. Please make a paper selling the two I take with me to show white man's paper that the horses are mine."

Caleb said he would have Rosie prepare such a paper.

William said, "This little group just keeps getting bigger. A few weeks ago, I was all alone. The next thing you know, I have a white man to look out for, two women, a boy, and now an Indian. We can start our own army."

Caleb added, "We might need an army to protect you from our neighbors when they hear your uppity talk."

Pony looked from Caleb to William. This was a strange white man who treated blacks and now an Indian with respect. He knew that most whites looked down on Indians and blacks alike.

The women called them in to eat. Pony was startled when he was invited to eat with them. He hesitated, afraid he had misunderstood until William urged him to come inside. Caleb had called Ira to eat. He knew that wasn't likely and the filly would get all of Ira's attention.

Pony ate his meal nervously. He was unaccustomed to sitting at a table or eating in the presence of white people. He excused himself to go outside. He walked over to the corral and stood by Ira. "The horse has a free spirit," he said. "They are meant to run free, but they must learn to work for men. It would help if you made the horse your friend, for you ask her to give up much. Treat her with respect. Never mistreat her and she will serve you well. I will teach you how to train your horse."

Ira replied, "I'll be good to her and do all you say. Does she have a name? Can I call her Blaze for the white on her head?"

"She is your horse, so she will be Blaze if that is what you want."

"Yes," Ira said. "Hi, Blaze. You're my horse."

The summer months brought a good rainfall and the garden flourished. They ate fresh vegetables straight from the field. Rosie and Selene cooked them for a welcome treat. The beans and peas that weren't eaten were dried. Some of the dried ones would be used for seeds next year and some for cooking.

As soon as they had gathered the peas and beans, the fields were replanted. There would be plenty of Florida sun to make two warm-weather crops before they planted collard, cabbage, and turnips for the winter crop.

The corn they didn't eat was left on the stalk to dry. When it was dry, they gathered it. Ira drove the wagon down the cornrows. William and Caleb tore the ears from the stalk, removed the husk and threw the cobs, full of yellow kernels, into the wagon. They filled the corncrib until it was ready to overflow.

As needed, they had a small hand-cranked grist mill to grind the corn into grits or cornmeal. They didn't grind more than they could use at the time. The cobs would keep in the crib. Once ground, care had to be taken to keep out weevils.

Pony spent a month working with the horses. He had them all broken to bridle and saddle. He spent hours with Ira and the filly named Blaze. The filly grew fast. Pony instructed Ira to put a strap around Blaze's abdomen so that she would be accustomed to its strange feel. He told Ira to add a little weight for her to carry, increasing it gradually. This way, she would be ready for Ira's weight when she was old enough to ride.

Ira followed Pony's instructions and spent many hours leading Blaze around, first with a halter and later with a bridle in her mouth. He fed her fresh-cut grass and even handfuls of wild berries that he gathered for her, and she followed him eagerly.

The women gathered huckleberries, blueberries, and blackberries, to make into jelly. They had to use honey for sweetening since no sugar was available.

Pony had located a wild beehive in an old oak tree. He took Ira to go with him to gather honey. Ira followed along carrying a large pail made from a gourd and a hand-carved spoon. Pony told Ira to stay back as the bees flew in and out of a hole in the tree.

Pony built a fire from pinewood that was rich with resin to create as much smoke as possible. After smoke covered the entrance used by the bees, Pony cut an opening in the tree, exposing the honeycomb. He dipped honey into the pail using the spoon, almost to the top, then stood slowly and backed away from the tree and handed the bucket to Ira.

Pony went back to the tree and sealed the opening with mud. "This will dry and seal the hole and you can come here again and gather honey. Never destroy a hive or take all the honey. Leave enough for the bees to eat. They will make more and you can gather it again."

The women were glad to get the honey. They stored it away in containers to be used as a sweetener until the men could raise sugar cane for sugar or trade for some. They placed some honey in a bowl and covered it with a cloth.

The honey was a real treat for everyone. After their evening meal, they sat and chewed the honeycomb, letting the sweet honey run down their throats.

Pony came to Caleb one morning. "The horses are ready," he said. "They do not need further training, just need to be ridden regularly to keep them used to the weight on their backs. I will take my horses and go."

"Where will you go?"

"I will visit my people who are far south of here, past the big lake. I will take my horses with me, but I might sell one or take one to the father of an Indian girl that I would like for my wife. Her name is Oconee. She is very pretty, and many men show an interest in her, but she waits for me."

Caleb had come to count on Pony. He taught him and Ira much about the land and Indian customs and horse care. "You have a place with us if you'd like. Bring your girl back with you. She'll be welcome."

"I thank you, Caleb. Your family has made me most welcome. I will think about your words. I must go. It is up to Ishtohollo, the Seminole god, to determine. I have lived well here and will not forget."

He went to the corral, put halters on his horses, and rode away to the south without looking back. Caleb watched him until he was lost to view. He would miss the Indian.

12

The War Ends

The evenings were starting to get cool and a second warm-weather crop had been gathered. They planted a winter garden of collards, cabbage, and turnips.

Caleb rode one of the new horses to see Bascomb to see if any goods were available.

Bascomb talked of the war. "I hear things are going rough for our boys. The Union blockade has totally shut us down and our army is running out of everything. When our boys go into battle, many don't have powder or shot. They walk along with their empty rifles. If a man with powder goes down, someone else picks it up and continues the fight. Much of our supplies must be taken off the Yanks and our men sneak in and out of battle zones, looking for powder or food. Soldiers are hungry, sick, and have little powder and shot. They have men handy with knives carving bullets from oak wood since they don't have lead for melting down. I don't think they can go on much longer, for almost half of our Florida troops are killed or crippled."

Caleb left the store as soon as possible. He didn't like to hear of the war and felt guilty about running away. "I'd do it again," he thought. "I have a family now, and it was the right thing to do."

One morning, Caleb walked out of the house. A chill was in the air. He thought of the smokehouse that was empty of food and needed repair. Close inspection showed a few missing boards but it could easily be repaired. He went to the barn and found William inside.

Caleb said, "Winter's coming and the weather is cool enough to cure some meat. We can repair the smokehouse and smoke some for later."

William replied, "I agree with you, General. Some pork would be good but the last time I looked, we didn't have any hogs."

"We don't. But, I saw some tracks made by them not far from here. They're wild hogs, known as piney woods rooters, mostly muscle and bone but better than nothing. We can trap some and save our bullets for deer. We don't have many shots left and no telling when more will be available. Tomorrow, we can use the wagon to take what we'll need to make the trap."

The next morning, they harnessed a mule to the wagon and loaded the tools and materials they needed. After a few hours, they came to the place that showed the activity of hogs that came out of the woods at night to forage for food. The hogs pushed up the dirt with their noses looking for edible grubs, roots, or anything else.

"We'll make our trap close to the woods," Caleb said.

They followed the tracks made by the hogs to the edge of a wooded area. They looked it over and decided it would do for a place to put a trap. A cypress pond was nearby, so they were able to cut cypress poles. They loaded the wagon with fresh-cut poles and went back to the trap site.

William took a shovel and dug four holes to place the corners for the trap. He dug them deeply, for the hogs were strong and would knock the poles down if they weren't anchored securely. Caleb took a drawing knife and removed long strips of cypress bark, leaving bare poles wet with sap.

They used smaller cypress poles that were flexible to make the sides of the trap. The strips of bark made good ties to hold the trap together.

After working hard for four hours, the work was complete. Caleb had fashioned a trap door before they left the house. It fit in an open space at the front of the trap. It was raised above the opening and would drop to catch the hogs once they were inside.

The trap door was designed to drop when a hog tried to eat an ear of corn tied in the back of the box. Caleb suspended ears of corn from a line that led over the top of the pen to a trip lever that controlled the trap door drop. He put the corn at the back of the trap in hopes that several hogs would enter the trap before it sprung.

The men took a bag of shelled corn and spread it around the trap. They made a path of corn into the trap and liberally sprinkled corn around the inside and examined their work.

"I hope it'll hold them," Caleb commented. "We did a lot of work for nothing if it doesn't."

"By the time you get through wrestling with one of those wild boars, you might wish they had gotten away. Those things are mean," William warned.

For now, there was nothing else to do, so they drove home.

Early the next morning, the two drove the wagon towards their trap. Before reaching it, they heard the squeal and grunts of pigs.

There were three sows and several small pigs inside the trap. The sows backed against the back wall when they saw the two men. They were thin and covered with long, wiry hair. Their snouts were long, well suited to tearing up the ground looking for food. They stood against the back wall with back bristles raised in a row along their backbone.

William said, "We have them in the trap. Now what do we do."

"We have to get them out of the trap."

The two had rehearsed the next move. Caleb went to the back of the trap while William squatted down behind the trap door. As soon as Caleb neared them, the hogs ran away from him to the other end of the trap. The hogs turned to face Caleb.

While Caleb distracted the hogs, William was able to reach over and grab one by the rear legs. The hog squealed in fright and fury. William held tight to both back legs of a squealing, trashing muscle bundle. With a mighty heave, he lifted the hog over the side of the trap.

The hog was squealing, kicking her rear legs, and digging in with her front. She tried with all her might to turn around and bite William.

With a quick move, William flipped her over onto her side. Before she could recover, Caleb jumped astride her and pushed her neck to the ground. This allowed William enough freedom to take the small rope from his pocket and tie the rear legs together. He then did the same to the front legs while Caleb held her down.

The trussed-up hog squirmed and popped her teeth together. The two men stood and looked down at the hog. Both were wet with sweat and breathed in short, nervous breaths.

They loaded the hog into the wagon bed. The sow continued to squirm, squeal, and tried to bite. They double-checked the rope for a loose hog in the wagon wasn't a thing they wanted to happen.

They caught the other two and loaded them alongside the first using the same method. William went into the pen, grabbed the piglets on at a time, and handed them to Caleb, who tied their legs together and placed them in the wagon. They re-baited the trap and drove home with their catch.

They put the hogs in a secure pen next to the barn. The hogs ran around the pen, looking for an escape. They stood side by side in one corner of the pen when none was found, staring at the men. William placed wooden troughs filled with water and shelled corn in the pen with the hogs, but they ignored the food and water.

The women and Ira came out to look at the captives. "They don't look like they have much meat on them," Rosie ventured. "They're nothing but skin and bones."

"They'll fatten up some," Caleb said. "They'll never be as fat as domestic hogs, but they'll give us some meat. We'll feed them corn and Ira can gather acorns for them. A mix of corn, acorns, and table scraps will put weight on them. We'll feed them good for two months and, by then, they'll be as fat as they'll ever get."

The following two days, the men captured two more hogs. They were young boars and had lower tusks curled up on either side of their snouts. These had to be handled with care since the tusks were deadly weapons and could slice open a man with ease.

Before the boars were released into the pen, the men cut off the tusks and neutered them. They did this so the flesh wouldn't have a musky taste when they were butchered. They used pine tar sap to seal the neuter incisions and prevent infection.

William and Caleb planned one more trip to get all the hogs they had room to keep and enough pork to last the winter. As they neared the trap, they heard squeals of rage. By the time they got to the trap, it wasn't only empty, but partially demolished. Large gashes were cut into the poles.

William got down from the wagon to inspect the damage. He quickly looked towards the woods when he heard a peculiar grunting-huffing sound.

The sound came from a huge boar hog at the edge of the woods. He was an old one with long, wicked-looking tusks, yellow with age. The hog had scars along both sides of his lean body, showing proof of fights with other boars. William saw that the boar's open mouth was dripping with saliva.

With a loud roar of rage, the boar charged, running with surprising speed, his head swinging from side to side as he ran.

Caleb, still in the wagon, saw the hog begin his charge. He grabbed the rifle and aimed at the animal. The shot hit the boar in the body and the bullet's impact knocked the boar to the ground but it quickly got up, squealed loudly, and resumed his charge toward William.

A second shot hit the beast in the chest. Again, the boar was knocked to the ground and managed to get to its feet again. The saliva in his mouth was now a bloody froth as he continued staggering, heading for William.

Both men were amazed as they watched this deadly animal, still intent on killing. The boar closed the distance between himself and William, the object of his rage. Caleb jumped from the wagon and ran over to the hog, pointed the LeMat pistol, and shot the boar in the ear. It fell for the last time and, with a few short gasps of breath, it was finally dead. Both men stared at the fallen hog.

William said, "He sure is an ugly thing. His meat will probably be tough, but we might as well butcher him."

He took his knife and cut a wide gash in the hog's throat. Bright red blood gushed out of the opening. They stood and waited for the blood to stop flowing. William sliced open the hog's belly and removed the insides. Once that was done, the two men lifted the carcass onto the wagon and took their seats with William driving. He turned the wagon and headed home. Neither mentioned re-baiting the trap. Both knew they were through hog hunting for now.

When they got back to the barn, they filled the big iron kettle used for laundry with water and heated it until it was boiling. The men lifted the hog by its front legs and lowered the back half into the boiling water. They took it out after a few minutes and put it in the front half. It was too bulky to fit all of it in the kettle at once.

Now, they'd be able to scrape off the bristly hair. When all the hair was scraped off, they cut the hog up. Caleb cut slices from the rear haunch and took them to Rosie to cook for their supper while Williams continued cutting up the meat. Once the rest of the hog was cut into portions, he took the hams and cuts for bacon to the smokehouse to let them cure. The rest would be cooked down in the kettle to provide lard for frying.

Rosie fried the pork slices and served them along with cowpeas. No one finished their portion of the meat. Not only was the meat tough, it also had a foul taste.

"That old boar was mighty riled up when he died," William said, "making the meat sour. All his male meanness got soaked up in the meat."

Caleb was quiet during the meal. If he'd been alone today, the outcome would have been different. It was a lesson well learned, and he'd never underestimate a wild boar.

As the days came and went, Caleb knew they must use the rifle sparingly and take advantage of the dwindling shots he had left; hunting carefully and never wasting a shot. He used the rifle to hunt deer only.

The fattened hogs were butchered. Pork and venison that Caleb brought home soon filled the smokehouse. The smell of the hickory wood smoke gave off a pleasant aroma. They were fortunate that no troops, Northern or Southern, came to this part of the state on foraging expeditions.

One morning, William walked up to Caleb and said, "General, it's time for me to build a cabin for Selene. The barn was okay for a while, but now with hogs in the back yard for our neighbors, it's time to move. I've found a nice spot to build on right under the big live oak tree. It'll keep the cabin cool in summer."

Caleb couldn't object to William and Selene wanting a cabin of their own. "I know the spot," he said. "It's a good place for a house."

The following day William rode to the nearest pine forest. He took his ax to cut logs, corn pone for his lunch, and a jug of water.

Looking at the trees, he searched for the right ones to fall. They must be small enough to drag back to the building spot and as straight as possible. Fewer limbs would make trimming easier. He found what he was looking for in a place where the trees grew close together. They were smaller in diameter in their reach for sunlight and grew straight up with few branches.

He dismounted and tied the mule to a tree. Taking his ax, he began chopping away at the base of a tree. Soon, it fell with a crash onto the ground. Stepping off the length he wanted, he cut off the remainder of the tree, then trimmed off the branches leaving him with a log of the correct diameter and length he wanted for building.

He worked all day, taking time off for lunch and drinks of water. He removed his shirt and his body glistened with sweat caused by his labors.

Chips flew from the tree as the ax rose and fell with precision. His powerful arm and back muscles' flexing made him feel strong and in control. By late afternoon, many logs lay ready to drag away.

William put on his shirt, picked up the ax, and rode home to the barn and a waiting Selene. She gave him a piece of corn pone and a slice of venison. After his long day cutting logs, he was tired and they were both soon asleep.

The next morning, they walked over to where Caleb sat outside drinking his coffee. Selene went inside to see Rosie.

William said, "I can cut logs for the walls but need some boards for a door and framing out the windows. I can't cut them with only the ax. The floor is another problem. I can put down a pine needle or sand floor but would like something better. The roof will have to be thatched until I have time to cut some shingles."

Caleb replied, "I can ride over and see Bascomb and see if he knows where we can get some cut boards. If not, we might have to go over to Fort Mellon to find any."

William finished his coffee and returned to the barn to prepare for another day's work cutting pine for the walls.

Caleb rode off to see Bascomb in case some precut lumber was available. Upon arriving at Bascomb's, he inquired about lumber.

Bascomb thoughtfully scratched his beard and finally said, "There would be some at Fort Mellon, but maybe there's some closer. About five miles from here, a family settled and built a home. The man was killed in the war and his wife went back to live with her folks. I don't know if anything remains of the house but it would be worth looking over. No one else has settled around here, so maybe something useable would be there."

After getting directions from Bascomb, Caleb headed Buck to where the old homestead was supposed to be. A few hours later, he found what remained of the house. It was in poor condition. Vines grew on and in it. The door was lying on the ground, and the roof looked like it might fall in at any second.

Caleb dismounted and walked up to the front door. He stepped inside and could tell from the odor that animals had made this their home. Rats scurried away at his presence and a snake's tail slithered out of sight. Not much was left to mark the family who tried to make this a home. A few broken bottles and rusty cans lay scattered around. Despite this, he saw that there were some materials that William could use. He walked back outside to Buck, mounted, and headed home with thoughts of returning with the wagon to salvage what he could.

The next day, Caleb and William took the wagon back to the abandoned house and began salvaging what they could. At the end of the day, the wagon held enough materials to aid William in the construction of his home.

Once William had enough logs cut and dragged them home by the mules, he began construction. Each log must be notched on each side of both ends.

Once the notching was complete, William and Caleb began the task of constructing the house. William stepped off the length of the walls and drove stakes into the ground to mark the four corners. Next, he marked where the doorway would be located and the location of a window on each side of the house.

The largest of the logs were picked for the foundation logs. They placed the base logs into position and were now ready to begin building the walls, leaving openings for the door and windows.

Working together, William and Caleb lifted the logs into position, making sure the notches cut into the logs were uniform in depth so they would fit close together, making a tight fit. If the notches were cut too deeply, the logs wouldn't fit together securely. Where the doorway would be, they cut a log into small sections and these were placed at right angles to the logs forming the wall. The wall logs were nestled into these shorter sections to secure them in place. The same procedure would be used to secure the openings for windows once the walls were the height of the intended windows.

The work was strenuous and both men were soon drenched in sweat. They stopped often to drink water, but refused to stop for lunch as they wanted to get as much work done as possible. If they stopped, sore muscles would make restarting difficult.

It took two long days to complete the construction of the walls. The topmost logs were too much for the two of them, so mules and ropes were used to get the final logs in place.

They drove the wagon to a bayhead and cut long

cypress poles for the rafters and smaller poles for cross joining the rafters together.

After the rafters and cross poles were tied together with strips of cypress tree bark, they spent a week gathering swamp cabbage palm fronds to thatch the roof. It took several layers to make it rainproof but, finally, it was done. The door and windows, which swung out to allow ventilation, were made from the abandoned homestead wood.

William and Selene stood looking at their new home. "It's not much," he said, "but it'll do. I promise you a better home someday. One with real glass windows and cookstove so you won't have to cook outdoors."

She laughed, "Well, it'll have to do for now. But, I'll hold you to that promise."

They moved in the next day with what possessions they owned. Furniture would have to be made by hand.

13

Cattle

The two men were sitting on the porch, with Ira staying close. "I've been thinking about the cattle," Caleb told William. "We need to figure out a way to catch and brand them before someone else does. We have horses now, so we can round them up and put our brand on them."

With Ira's help, the men cut cypress poles and built a large pen to hold cattle. Caleb, William, Selene, and Ira rode out in search of cattle. All of them carried long whips like the local cowboys used. The sharp crack of the whip makes it easier to get the cattle moving. Selene and Ira had been riding since acquiring horses and both had become capable riders.

Selene wore a pair of Sanders' pants. She looked elegant sitting straight in the saddle and William looked at her with pride, knowing she would do her share.

They spread out and began their search. After a short time, two sharp cracks of Ira's whip rang out; the signal used to notify each other if cattle were seen. The other three rode over to where Ira awaited them. He was excited. "I found some," Ira said, "right over there."

He pointed to where eight cows grazed on the long grass; three had calves. Selene and Ira rode slowly, directly at the cattle. The cows saw the riders and began moving away from them. The slow movement kept them from running in alarm. William and Caleb rode on either side of the herd, well away from them.

The small herd kept moving slowly in the right direction. When they tried to veer to one side, either William or Caleb barred their way. It took a couple of hours of slow moving before they reached the pen. They had beginners' luck and the cows went into the enclosure. Caleb slid poles in place to close off the opening.

They built a fire inside the pen and, as soon as it was burning bright, the branding iron was heated. Caleb rode his horse close to the milling cattle. They ran to stay away from him but, eventually, he was able to throw a rope over the head of a cow. She let out a loud bawl and tried to get away. Caleb was almost pulled off his horse before he could wrap the rope around the saddle horn.

The cow jumped around wildly, trying to escape, but the relentless pull of the rope dragged her bawling and protesting away from the rest of the cattle.

When the cow was isolated from the rest, William dismounted and put his hand on the taut rope and followed it to the head of the wide-eyed cow. He grabbed her by the horns, twisted hard, and threw her to the ground.

Caleb dismounted and removed the rope, then sat on her rear legs. The two men held her securely while Ira picked up the branding iron, his hands wrapped with cloth to keep the iron from burning him. He walked over to the cow and touched the cow's flank with the iron. The smell of burned hair filled the air as the cow thrashed and bawled.

"Push it harder," Caleb said. "It would be best to push down harder on the iron so the brand will burn into the skin. That time you only burned a few hairs."

The boy was embarrassed. He reapplied the iron and, this time, he pushed it hard into the cow's flank until Caleb nodded to him that it was enough. Caleb told Ira to get away from the cow before she was released. Once released, the cow ran back to the other cattle.

They repeated the process with the unbranded ones. Two had brands of other ranches, one of which had a calf. The calf was left unbranded.

After all the cows were branded, they opened the gate. The cows rushed through the gate and ran into the distance. It was a decent start, for they had put their brand on four cows and two calves. Two cows belonged to another ranch, and two already wore the SS brand.

SS was the brand of the Sanders ranch. Ira said that the brand was derived from his mother's name, 'Sadie Sanders.' William and Caleb had agreed to keep the same brand for any cattle they acquired.

They spent two months rounding up and branding all they could find. At the end of that time, they decided to stop. Some of their cows had wandered farther away, but they had branded some unbranded stock that strayed from other ranches. Florida was an open range state, so cattle roamed freely. At least now, no one could claim any of their branded cattle.

On the last day of branding, the riders headed home. William and Caleb rode side by side ahead of Selene and Ira. Caleb said, "That was hard work but we got the start of a herd. We can keep the garden going and, with the wild game for meat, we don't have to butcher any cattle, so our herd will grow. We can sell a few if we need some money."

They rode in silence until William stopped his horse. Puzzled, Caleb looked back at him.

William said, "We caught some cattle all right but we need to talk about whose cattle they are. It seems to me Sanders gave the land to you and Rosie. That leaves Selene and me as hired help."

Caleb replied, "When we started this journey, I told you we'd share whatever we made together. That still stands with me."

William quickly asked, "That means half the cows are

mine?"

Caleb, beginning to get aggravated at the conversation, said, "No," he said. "That means they all belong to you, me, Selene, Rosie, and Ira. There is no yours or mine. We share ownership of all we have and also any further gains. If you want that in writing, say so, and it'll be done. I keep my word and Rosie feels the same. As far as the land, it has the same owners. I add Ira since he deserves a place in everything since his family owned it."

Looking a little embarrassed, William nodded his head and, urging his horse on, rode along in silence.

On reaching the ranch, Selene helped Rosie with the evening meal. The men unsaddled the horses, fed them, and turned them loose in the corral.

Caleb learned that the war had ended when he visited Bascomb. Lee had surrendered on April 9, 1865 and Florida's governor, John Milton, had committed suicide only eight days earlier. Milton had said he'd rather be dead than live under Yankee rule.

State Senate President, Abraham Allison, inherited the governor's job but resigned a little over a month later. Allison went into hiding but was captured by Yankee troops and imprisoned. President Andrew Johnson appointed William Marvin, a New Yorker, as provisional governor. Bascomb had said that a few battles were still fought after that date before all the men heard the news. Men still died after the war was over. Some Southerners refused to accept the surrender, and bands roamed the South making isolated raids on union encampments. Many of them, whose lives and homes were destroyed, turned to outlaws, preying on anyone.

Caleb felt a relief that he hadn't felt since walking away from the war. If the war was over, no one should come looking for him. He went about his work with a lightened heart.

One day, Caleb saw Roberts riding up to the house.

Surprised, he watched in silence. Roberts looked around, noticing the garden and full corn crib. "Looks like you're here to stay. My boys tell me they see fresh branded cattle with your mark."

Still cautious, Caleb replied, "We only branded cattle or steers with no brands or notches. Any of your cattle or any other branded we released along with their calves."

"My men told me as much," Roberts replied. "We're planning a roundup to drive some cattle to sell at the port in Tampa for shipment to Cuba. If you and your nigger want to help in the roundup, your cows can be part of the drive."

Caleb, looking dubious, said, "You sure about that. Last time here, you were ready to drive us off."

Roberts replied tersely, "I don't apologize for anything I said. I wasn't happy to see you here and not getting this land. Plus, any cows you branded might have been branded for me. Despite that, you're here and you seem to be going to stay, so I might as well get used to the idea. If you want to join with a few other ranchers and me, it's okay with me and the others."

Caleb pondered a moment and then said, "That's fine with me. As I told you before, we prefer to be good neighbors. Fighting with you helps no one, and we'll join with your men. Another thing is that William isn't mine and is a free and proud man. He's part owner of this ranch and part of any decisions."

Roberts made no reply, turned his horse, and rode away.

Caleb and William joined Robert's riders. Ira stayed home with Rosie. He wanted to go on the roundup, but Caleb wanted him to stay. "You need to protect the ranch while we're gone," he told him.

The roundup took three weeks, covering a much more extensive territory than Caleb was prepared for. Unbranded cows and calves were roped and branded. Per the agreement with Roberts, the SS brand was put on some of the unbranded stock rounded up. It was three weeks of hot, dirty work. Roberts was surprised by the number of cows wearing the SS brand.

"You've been busy," he told Caleb. "Maybe I should've run you off before you get too big to run off."

Caleb didn't answer that remark. "I want to sell twenty head," he told Roberts. "The rest we'll leave to grow our herd."

Roberts agreed to take the cattle to market with his. "I'll pay you three dollars per head right now or four dollars when I return, for every one of yours that makes it to market. We'll likely lose some to varmints, rustlers, or river crossings, and it makes no difference to me."

Caleb talked with William and, with his agreement, said, "We'll take the three dollars now. That way, we won't have to worry about how many make the trip."

Roberts counted out sixty dollars in gold coins. Caleb took the money and gave Roberts twenty dollars back, saying, "We need some forty-four shells and powder and shot for the shotgun. Plus, we need seed potatoes. I don't know if either is available, but maybe some things are available since the war's over."

The remaining forty dollars was the first money they had made. As the men rode home, it occurred to them that while the money felt good in their pockets, it was only worth what it would buy. If no supplies were available, money had little value.

Weeks later, Roberts rode up to the barn where Caleb was working, leading a pack mule loaded with bundles. He dismounted and said, "I got the seed potatoes you wanted plus some other items."

After saying that, he untied a bundle from the mule and dropped it on the ground. He took another bundle from the mule and handed it to Caleb. It contained two Henry repeating rifles and a bag of forty-four shells.

Caleb took the rifles and examined them. "How," he asked, "did you manage to get these rifles?"

Roberts laughed and said, "A boat landed from Cuba just as we got to the port. The Captain was short on gold but had some Henrys and shells. Probably stolen, but they work. I'm sure they'll come in handy for you. I'm just trying to make up a little for our rough start. I think we'll need all the guns we can get if the rustling gets any worse. There's a lot of drifters now that the war's over, plus there might be trouble with all the freed slaves who are going to be starving since they don't have the plantations to feed and clothe them. Be ready if you get a call from me or the other ranchers. We have troublesome times ahead even though the war's over."

Caleb was pleased and shocked at the good fortune that the rifles promised. They could hunt freely and fill the smokehouse with food. He thanked Roberts.

After Roberts rode away, Caleb turned and walked over to the barn where William was working. Caleb handed one of the Henrys to him. William took the rifle in his hands and looked at Caleb with a puzzling look.

"Roberts brought back two of these from Tampa," Caleb said. "He also brought seed potatoes."

William handled the gun carefully and said with a laugh, "Well, General, we can start our own army."

Caleb returned to the house and went inside to see Rosie and handed Ira a rifle. Ira took the gun from Caleb and sat at the kitchen table making sure the Henry Rifle wasn't loaded. He looked up a Caleb in awe. Then, he put the rifle up to his shoulder and pointed it at imaginary targets all around the ranch. After this, he asked, "Can I shoot it sometime?"

Caleb took it from him. "It's time you learn to shoot. We'll go hunting tomorrow. You can get your first deer."

He took time to show Ira the right way to aim the rifle and operate the lever.

The next morning at breakfast, Ira ate nervously. He wasn't sure that Caleb would remember the promise to take him hunting. Caleb finished breakfast and Ira watched as Caleb got up from the table, walked over to the stove, and poured a cup of the hot brew from the pot. He went out on the porch and sat down to drink it. The delay made it impossible for the boy to sit still.

Finally, Caleb said, "Ira, why don't you go saddle up a couple of horses for us. It's time we went hunting."

Ira jumped up, ran to the barn, and was back in short order, leading two saddled horses. Caleb went inside and retrieved the rifle. They mounted the horses and rode off.

Caleb talked to Ira as they rode. "Make sure that you never shoot towards the house. This rifle can kill a man at over a mile. You make sure of what you're aiming at and if you're not sure, don't shoot."

They rode to the edge of a wooded area, tied the horses to tree limbs, and walked into the forest. Ira proudly carried the rifle. Birds sang in the trees above and they could hear wild turkeys in the distance. They took up a position close to an open glade in the forest. Caleb had shot deer here before and was sure some would come into the glade to feed. The two hunters were concealed by trees but had a clear line of vision.

Caleb whispered to Ira, "The first deer you see, I want you to aim at it." He explained to Ira the spot to aim at for a clean kill. "Don't shoot, but keep the gun aimed at it as it moves; but don't fire the gun."

Ira looked at Caleb. He didn't understand why he couldn't shoot. Despite his thoughts, he nodded his head in agreement. After a few minutes, a deer came out of the forest. It was a doe that looked around cautiously and, seeing no danger, began to feed.

Ira pointed the gun at the deer. His hands were shaking so badly he couldn't keep it aimed at his target. The deer walked forward, looking for tender grass. Ira followed her with the rifle as best he could. The deer walked out of their line of sight.

"You did well, Ira. Another one will be along in a minute and I want you to do the same thing. Aim, but don't fire."

As Caleb had said, another doe walked into the clearing. Ira pointed the rifle but his hands weren't shaking as much. He was able to keep the gun pointed toward the doe until she passed out of sight.

Ira looked at Caleb in confusion since he had hoped to shoot a deer. All he was allowed to do was point the gun.

Caleb saw a buck step out of the woods. He knew the smaller does would come first and that the buck would wait to be sure it was safe. He whispered to Ira, "Aim at the spot where I told you and, this time, when you're sure of your shot, you can shoot."

Ira aimed the rifle. His hands still shook a little but he was able to take careful aim and squeeze the trigger. The deer jumped high into the air and fell back to the ground without moving. "Good job Ira!" exclaimed Caleb. "You got him!"

The boy grinned with pride. Caleb had made him aim at the first two without shooting for two reasons. First, he was sure that a buck would follow the does, but the main reason was to get the boy's nerves under control. Each time he aimed, his nerves calmed down a little more. If he'd shot at the first deer, it would've taken a miracle for the shot to be successful. Talking about it wouldn't help, only experience would do the job.

They walked out into the clearing to where the deer lay. Caleb told Ira to stand back. He walked up to the deer and nudged it with his foot. The deer didn't move. It was dead. He called Ira over. "Always make sure an animal is dead for sometimes they're only stunned. You can get hurt badly by a *supposedly* dead animal."

He gave Ira a long-handled knife and explained how to field dress the deer. As Ira went to work with the knife, Caleb walked back to retrieve the horses. He came back with them and watched as Ira finished with the deer.

Caleb lifted the deer carcass and tied it behind Ira's horse's saddle. An extremely proud boy mounted the horse and headed for home, anxious to show off his trophy to Rosie.

Rosie came out to greet them. Ira sat straight up in the saddle, trying to keep a big grin from his face, but was unable to do so. William and Selene also came outside to greet the returning hunters. They all bragged on Ira's hunting ability.

Caleb took the deer from the back of the horse. He directed Ira on how to skin the deer and cut up the meat. They hung in the meat in the smokehouse after cutting slices for Rosie to cook for their dinner. They scrapped the skin of the deer, stretched it out, and attached it to the outside wall of the barn with pegs to cure.

Rosie looked at Caleb with a smile. "Our boy is growing up. The next thing you know he'll be bringing home some little girl."

Ira's face turned red, "No, Ma'am. You don't have to worry about that. I'm going to stay here and take care of my horse and hunt. I don't want any girl."

14

High Water

Caleb and William were riding across the range to check on the cattle. They took along the branding iron in case they found unbranded calves since the young calves could be roped from horseback and were easy to throw and brand. They built a fire wherever they roped one. The calf would strain against the rope and bawl piteously while the fire heated the iron.

They had to be careful of protective mothers who would charge at them and impale them with sharp horns. Even worse, were the bulls who defended their flock with deadly focus. On two occasions, bulls had to be shot to protect the horses and men from harm.

Caleb said as they rode, "You know, William, I've been thinking about orange trees. If you remember, Sanders mentioned that this land is good for growing oranges. If the cattle business plays out, we'll have something else to fall back on."

William replied, "We've been getting by really well. We have game to eat, a good garden, and the cattle herd is increasing. We have plenty."

"You're right, but we have to look to the future. Our families will grow. Ira will be grown in a few years and have a family of his own. We need to think ahead and plan for our children and their children."

William replied, "How do we get an orange grove started?"

"I've talked to Enos Taylor. He's the man who has a big grove close to us. His house is right on the creek, and the orange grove is there as well. I think he'll sell us some young trees to get started."

The two decided to see Taylor and the grove the next day. When they were ready to leave, Ira wanted to go with them when they prepared to leave and Caleb agreed to let him come along. If their future held orange trees, Ira might as well learn about them.

They rode to the creek and followed the directions to Taylor's farm. They found the house easily since it sat right on the creek. A dock was built out into the creek and two boys were fishing off the end of it.

Caleb knocked on the front door, but no one answered. One of the boys called out, "They're in the orange grove. If you want to see them, look up the opening between the rows and you'll find them. They won't be far."

The three riders walked their horses along the edge of the orange grove until they saw a wagon coming toward them down one of the rows. They rode toward the wagon and Enos, the man driving the wagon, pulled back on the reins and brought the wagon to a stop when he neared the riders. Edna sat next to him.

"Howdy," he called out. "Good to see you again, Caleb."

Caleb replied, "It's good to see you again. This is William," nodding toward him, "and Ira Sanders."

Enos replied, "Hello, William and Ira. My name is Enos Taylor and this is my wife, Edna. Enos and Edna go together, don't you think?"

Both were dressed in grey cotton shirts, faded blue trousers, and flat-soled boots. They hadn't recognized Edna as a woman from a distance, for she was dressed just like Enos and wore a wide brim hat.

Caleb explained that they were interested in oranges. Taylor seemed glad to talk about oranges and invited them back to the house where they could talk while Edna fixed them lunch. Enos slapped the reins and the wagon began to move. The riders moved out of the way and followed the wagon when it passed.

Enos parked the wagon and he and Edna got down. She went to the house and went inside.

"We've been picking," Enos explained. "Edna helps me since it's hard to get help due to the war. We need more help to finish the picking, so I'll make you a deal. You leave the boy and your man to help us pick, and I'll teach them all about oranges."

"That'll be up to them," Caleb replied. "William here is a free man and he'll have to decide. If he wants to stay, Ira will remain with him. How long would you need them?"

"I'd say, about a week. I'll take a little time every day and teach them about the oranges. Edna will feed them well. What do you say?"

William had never seen an orange grove and looked at wonder at the orderly progression of dark green trees with bright yellow oranges contrasting with the green leaves.

He said, "I'll stay, for I like the look of those orange trees. They're right pretty, and I just might eat all the ones I pick."

"I'll take that chance," Enos replied.

Edna came out with a plate of fried chicken. The men hadn't had such a treat in a long time. She gave them glasses of orange juice and they all had more than one glass.

Caleb left after lunch and made his way back home. He'd been impressed by the oranges. Sanders might have been right about them.

Rosie met him at the door. She saw that Ira wasn't with him and was alarmed at his absence. "What happened to Ira?"

"Nothing. He and William are staying with an orange grower named Taylor, learning the orange business."

He gave her an orange that he brought back and was pleased with her expression when she tasted the juice. "Well, we'll have oranges one day and people will buy them. There's a good future in oranges."

Nine days later, William and Ira rode up. William had a bag full of something strapped to his saddle. "Taylor gave us some trees to get us started. They're in this bag. He wrapped them in wet moss to keep them alive until I can plant them. We need to decide just where this orange grove will be."

They picked some land that was free of native trees to plant their grove. William volunteered to plant the young trees. The following day, he took a hoe and began planting, sighting on a tree in the distance to keep the trees in a straight line.

Taylor had told him to step off six big steps between plantings. Ira drove the wagon loaded with kegs of water. William would dig a hole and pour a dipperful of water into the open ground. He would then put in the tree and press dirt around the roots. He followed that with another dipperful.

William planted a hundred trees by late that afternoon and was tired. He looked with satisfaction at the rows of trees. Something was pleasing about the uniform plantings. Taylor had told them to water the trees every two days until they took root and began to grow. After that, if no rain came, they must be watered once a week until they were a year old.

William took on the job of looking after the orange trees. He drove the wagon and watered them on the schedule Taylor gave him. Some days it rained and he was relieved of the watering.

William walked down the rows and checked for growth every afternoon when the other work was done. He rejoiced every time a new leaf unfolded. The trees were taking root and doing well.

William also dug up a plot to plant orange seeds in his garden. Taylor had given him a big sack of them. He planted the seeds two inches apart and figured he had planted about four hundred. When the planting was completed, he thought, *'Someday, these tiny seeds will make a big grove.'* He smiled when he envisioned a large grove of trees covered with green leaves and golden oranges.

Three weeks later, William saw the ground popping up in little mounds. The seeds were sprouted and were pushing their way into the sunlight. Soon little rows of orange seedlings grew. It was hard to imagine these tiny plants growing into large trees full of golden oranges. Taylor said they'd be mature enough in seven years to start yielding a crop big enough to market.

William had to run a bunch of cattle away from the first rows of plants. Some of them had been damaged by hooves. With Ira's help, he and Caleb cut cypress poles and built a fence around the whole field where the orange grove would be. The hundred already planted plus the four hundred seedlings would cover a large area. With cattle roaming free, everything had to be fenced in, including the houses to keep out the wandering cows.

Caleb was working in the barn and was startled by two figures that appeared at the barn door. They were two Indians. He recognized Pony and walked over to greet him. Pony was even thinner than before and the other one was even more delicate.

The other Indian was a girl with a slight figure, and would have been pretty except for the thinness of her face. Her long black hair framed large black eyes that looked at Caleb. Both of their clothing showed a lot of wear.

"Welcome," Caleb called out. "It's good to see you again, Pony."

Pony spoke up, "It is good to see you. This is Oconee,

the one I told you about. We have come a long way from Pahokee and would like to stay for a while. Things are not good with our people and many bad whites live in the everglades. They shoot our people without reason. It is dangerous for us to hunt."

"You're welcome here. Come to the house and Rosie will give you something to eat."

Rosie gave them a warm welcome. Oconee was hesitant to go into the house but did so after urging from Pony. Once inside, Rosie gave them fried pork, greens, and corn pone on plates. There was no talking as the two ate with gusto. Both ate as if they hadn't eaten for some time.

When the meal was finished, Caleb told them they could stay as long as they liked.

"It is not our way to live inside," Pony told him. "If you allow it, we will build a chikee for our home. We will sleep outside unless rain comes before we get it completed."

Caleb told them that they were welcome to do so. He also told them to help themselves to the garden and meat from the smokehouse. He told Pony that he could help locate and brand cattle once they were settled.

Late in September, dark, ominous clouds covered the sky to the east. Caleb stood in the yard and looked at the sky. Pony walked up to join him. "The big wind comes," Pony said. "There will be much wind and rain."

That afternoon, the rain came. Water poured from the sky; unlike anything Caleb had ever seen. It went on well into the night and the wind blew steadily. It increased until it was howling around the house.

The house trembled with the blowing wind. The wind lasted the rest of the night and throughout the next day. The rain continued to fall and was blowing sideways with the force of the wind. The animals would have to go untended until the weather improved. Caleb was afraid at times that the house couldn't stand against the high winds.

The wind lessened during the night, but the rain kept falling. When Caleb ran to the barn to check on the animals, he had to wade through water to reach the barn. Water covered the ground as far as he could see. The barn had water covering the floor and the animals all stood in the water. The rain continued to fall. After three days, it finally stopped.

Caleb walked out onto the porch. All he could see was water. The garden was completely covered and water came up to the top step of the house. A little more and it would have come inside.

William rode up on his horse. The horse waded in water almost knee-deep. "What do we do?" he asked Caleb.

"Not much we can do. The water is covering everything. We'll have to wait until it goes down."

By the next day, the water hadn't receded. Caleb and William pulled bean plants up by the roots and hung them in the barn to dry. After three days, the remaining garden was ruined, and the vegetables had all turned yellow as they began to rot.

Pony walked up to Caleb. "The cattle must be moved for the grass is destroyed. We must move them to higher land. I know of such a place."

Caleb had been so absorbed with the garden that he'd forgotten about the cattle. He, William, and Pony saddled their horses and rode out to inspect the cattle. They slogged through the standing water.

"Why does the water not soak in?" lamented William.

Pony replied, "The big lake overflowed and we are now part of the lake. We must wait for the lake to go down, and it will take a long time."

The pastureland was all underwater. The cattle had moved to the higher spots trying to escape the water, but water covered the whole land. The cattle tried to feed on the bushes and trees standing above the water, but that wouldn't suffice for long.

The men went back to the house and packed all the food and cooking utensils on one of the mules. The wagon couldn't be used. Caleb told Rosie that they must leave and find higher land. The horses and cattle would get hoof rot from standing in water and must be moved to dry land. They would have to camp out until the water receded enough to return home.

Soon, all was ready to go. William rode the remaining mule. Selene, Rosie, and Caleb rode horses. Pony and Oconee shared a horse and Ira rode his pony, Blaze.

The procession sloshed slowly through the water. The ground underneath was soggy and the going was rough for the animals. They'd be gone for several days. They rode through water all day and snakes were swimming everywhere. The horses shied when one swan to close.

Pony said, "Do not fear the snakes, for they struggle to live and offer no threat as long as we leave them alone."

Rosie replied for them all, "Don't worry about that. We sure won't bother them. I just hope they remember to leave us alone."

The snakes mostly swam clear of the riders. Sometimes, one would swim too close, making the animals nervous.

Pony explained that most of the snakes were not poisonous. The rattlesnakes and cottonmouth moccasins swam with their heads held high above the water, and rattlesnakes raised their rattles out of the water. The water snakes, blacksnakes, garter snakes, puff adders, and others swam with their heads and tails level with the water.

Everyone was shocked by the number of snakes swimming in every direction. Some had taken refuge on low-growing branches. The water snakes and moccasins would survive, but many other snakes wouldn't if they couldn't climb into the low-growing trees.

The bodies of many small animals floated on the

water's surface. Alligators left the swamp ponds and swam where dry land had been. They gorged themselves on drowned animals. Thankfully, they swam away from the herd and riders. One giant alligator grabbed a young calf and it disappeared in a swirl of water. The riders were helpless to go to its aid. Buzzards circled overhead. They couldn't land to join the feast of drowned animals.

The group rode for a full day before they came to a high enough hammock above the water level. They all dismounted and stretched stiff muscles. They decided to make camp and dry out as much as possible.

Dry wood was gathered and soon a campfire burned brightly. A pot was filled with water and boiled to make drinking water. The water surrounding them wasn't safe to drink without boiling.

After they dried off some and the horses' legs wiped down with moss from the trees, Pony said, "We must find the cattle and drive them to higher land. There are higher lands west of here another day's ride. This hammock is big enough for a camp but too small for the cattle."

The men, Ira, and Selene saddled up and rode back into the water. When the riders returned from gathering cattle, Rosie and Oconee had gathered wood and prepared a hot meal.

The cattle, when located, stood in small groups on the highest land they could find, though still in the water. The first small group they came to held about ten cows plus five calves. They stood in a tight group, wide-eyed and bawling. They weren't as skittish as usual and offered little resistance to being herded toward the hammock.

William and Selene took this group and headed back to dry land. Caleb, Ira, and Pony continued the search. The next group held about the same number. Caleb and Ira headed them towards the hammock while Pony continued the search.

William and Selene reached the hammock with the first group. The cattle spread out and began grazing on the grass covering the hammock. William unsaddled and wiped their mounts down with Spanish moss. Caleb and Ira drove the second group onto dry land two hours later. This group joined the earlier arrivals and began munching on grass.

Pony arrived soon with more cattle. He drove them ashore and dismounted. After looking after his horse, he walked over to the campfire and Oconee handed him a plate of food.

Pony explained that the cattle must be driven further west to find higher land with enough grazing for the animals. "I know a place," he said. "It's another day's travel from here with much land that does not flood."

The weary travelers spent a night sleeping on the ground, waking stiff from the previous day's ride and sleeping on the ground. The morning was bright and clear and no clouds dotted the blue sky. They gathered the small herd of cattle and tried to drive them to the west.

It took a lot of effort to get the reluctant cattle to enter the water. After much shouting and cracking of whips, they got them moving. Rosie and Oconee stayed in the temporary camp as the others herded the cattle away westward from the hammock.

The sun came up and the reflection on the water was blinding. The water mirrored the sun's heat, making the day unbearably hot. Later that day, they drove the herd into shallower water.

They rode all day, occasionally crossing small hammocks of green more often as they went west. They drove the cattle out of the water and onto dry land that stretched out before them late in the afternoon. They were pleased to see many cows had made their way to safety, both theirs and other ranchers.

Deer and wild hogs that had been driven west by the

rising water dotted the fields. Food wouldn't be a problem for cabbage palms were plentiful and the hearts of the palms would provide food to go with the plentiful game.

Pony said, "This is the place. It will remain dry and the cattle can be moved about for grass."

The cattle began to graze eagerly on the green grass. The exhausted riders spread blankets on the dry land and slept soundly. Everyone was too tired to think of food.

The next morning, they awoke, brewed parched corn coffee, and fried bacon. Pony told them, "The cows will not wander, so we can go back and round up more. Many that are left behind will starve or be killed. The cattle here must be kept close together and allowed to graze and one of us must stay with them. The high water will drive bears and panthers to any dry land and they will be hungry. The calves will be easy prey unless someone protects them."

The men agreed to leave Ira to watch the herd. He was given one of the Henry rifles. Ira watched the riders ride away, leaving him alone for the first time. Ira spent a lonely night by himself, except for the cattle. He heard something moving in the bushes and built up the campfire during the night. Whatever made the noise didn't appear but, still, Ira spent a restless night.

Two days later, late in the afternoon, Ira heard splashing sounds. William and Selene rode up driving a small bunch of cattle. The horses and cattle were breathing heavily from wading through the water. Ira had put on a pot of beans earlier in the day. The three of them enjoyed a hot meal.

Later that afternoon, Caleb and Rosie also arrived back with a group of cattle. Pony and Oconee arrived just before noon the next day. They drove in a sizeable group of cattle. Ira fixed them plates of food since they had only eaten jerky carried with them for the last two days. They were accustomed to going hungry, so it was no hardship to them, but they did enjoy the hot food.

Caleb waited until Pony had finished eating. "Have you seen high water like this before?"

"Yes, but not this bad. Every few years, we get high winds and it rains for days. The big lake fills up and spreads over the land, for the land is only a few feet above the lake. The swamps fill up and add their overflow to the lake's water."

"How long will it last?" Caleb asked.

"It will take two or three weeks for the water to go down. After that, it will take a couple of months for the grass to come back. It is all dead now, but the roots will survive. The land will be green again in two or three months if we do not get another big wind."

This was distressing news for Caleb. The water had caught him off guard and he mused, *'I wonder what other surprises Florida has in store for me.'*

Pony added, "There is grass here for the cattle to eat. Someone must stay and keep them together. If we allow them to wander this far from home, we will never find them again."

Later that day, William, Selene, and Rosie rode through the water and joined the others.

Caleb said, "We must camp here until the water goes down. Pony says it'll take a few weeks for that to happen."

They moved a good way away from the water to avoid the worst of the mosquitoes and went about setting up a more permanent camp. They cut young sprouts from the cypress trees growing at the water's edge to make a softer bed and keep them off the ground. They fashioned a tripod to hang the cooking pot over the fire.

Twice more, Pony and Oconee, along with William and Selene, rode back into the water and came back with more cattle. After three days, they had quite a few gathered up.

15

Recovery

Caleb had taken some dried jerky and ridden west. Pony had told him to ride one day to the west and he'd find a trail headed north and south. If he turned north, he should come to a trading post and supplies could be obtained there.

They'd need seed to start over when the flood went away and there'd be no seed available back to the east where they lived. Caleb found the trail made by cattle drives and turned north. A few hours later, he rode up to a small building with sun-bleached cypress.

A man came out the door and greeted Caleb. "Howdy. Get down and rest yourself. There's a water trough out back to water your horse and a corral you can let him loose if you'd like."

Caleb led the horse around the building and found the water trough. He allowed the horse to drink, tied him to a hitching post, and walked back to the front where the man still stood.

"My name is Gillins," he said. "Welcome. Come on in and sit. I can offer you water or something a little stronger if you'd like."

"Water's fine. I'm a little dry from riding," replied Caleb.

They went inside. Caleb saw a rough table and chairs in the dim interior. He took a seat and took the offered gourd full of water.

"My name is Caleb Melton," he volunteered.

"I live over east of here and got run out by the flood. We're camped out south of here until the water goes down. I need a few things if you have any to sell."

Gillins replied, "Don't have much. Things didn't come at all during the war. Now that it's over, I hope to get some goods. I can offer you a couple of tents traded to me by some soldiers who passed through. No powder or shot and no flour, coffee, or tobacco. Folks around here have been using corn or acorns for coffee. Some pick pinecone seeds for coffee, but it's too much work to gather them."

Caleb wasn't pleased to hear that news. He said, "I'll need seeds to replant my garden. Do you have any?"

"No," Gillins replied. "No seeds at all. Soldiers took all the planting seeds I had and ate them when no other food was to be had."

Caleb said, "Okay. I was afraid of that but I'll take the tents."

He rode back to the camp. He reached the herd and was relieved to see that everyone was safely there. The herd was spread out over the fields.

William told him that they'd kept the herd moving to find plenty of grass. He told Caleb that some other herds were nearby. At least some of the ranchers could reach dry ground with their herds. All the ranchers had lost cattle and, some, whose ranches were far from dry land, had lost most of theirs.

Rosie and Selene were disappointed at the news of no seeds but were glad to get the tents. Pony had been busy and made a palmetto covered, open-walled chikee for himself and Oconee

Roberts rode up to the camp. "Hello," he called out. "Should've known you'd make it, glad you did. My herd is just south of here. We saved a lot of cattle but lost a lot. We've had floods before, so they're not new to us. This was the worse but the news isn't all bad. It's extra work for us, but the ones we save will be worth more money. Folks will be hungry for beef. We plan to stay around here for two or three months. We'll let our herd wander and not push them so they'll put on weight. I plan on driving some of them to market in a month or so after they gain some weight. I'll buy some of yours if you want to sell them or you can help me on the drive. Yours will bring you the same price I get for mine. I expect to get fifteen dollars a head but I need more men to drive the herd, including yours. We'll be gone about two months."

Caleb considered the offer. He had fifty head of cattle. That would give him seven hundred and fifty dollars. That was more than he had ever seen and would help buy supplies to last them until the garden was producing and the game came back. Caleb looked at William and he agreed to go on the drive. Caleb told Roberts that the two of them plus Ira would go with him.

William said, "My woman can go with us also. She can drive a wagon as good as any man and she's a good cook."

Roberts hesitated a moment and then said, "That's okay with me. I'm sure the men will be happy not having to cook. Not many of them can cook anything edible. We'll pass at least two trading posts on the way. I'll pay for the supplies and take your share from the sale proceeds. We brought two wagons so you can share one of them. You can mix your herd with mine. We'll make a count when we sell the herd and we'll be paid with gold coins."

A few days later, the drive began as Roberts led the herd westward. The pace was leisurely as they allowed the cattle to graze along the way.

Roberts hoped to put some weight on the stock before they reached their destination. The men took turns riding alongside the herd or trailing it. Roberts had dogs trained to keep the stragglers moving and retrieve any cattle that tried to veer away from the path.

When Caleb saw how effective the dogs were, he decided he must get some. He asked Roberts about the dogs.

Roberts replied, "The breed of dogs, Black Mouth Curs, are bred for cattle drives. One dog can do the work of three men. They can drive cows out of places a man and horse can't go. I wouldn't want to try a cattle drive without the dogs. You need dogs if you want to raise any livestock. They also protect the calves."

The drive went smoothly. Twice, the cowboys killed panthers that decided the cattle were fair game. They spotted riders that might be rustlers in the distance since they didn't ride in to greet them or share a meal. The number of cowboys plus Caleb and William were too many to tackle. Despite that, Roberts posted sentries at every night's camp.

Six weeks later, they reached the port at Tampa. Roberts reported a Cuban boat was there to buy beef. He brought buyers out to see the herd and a deal was made. The cattle were driven to the stock pens and gold coins were exchanged for the cattle.

Roberts counted out seven hundred dollars in twenty-five-dollar gold coins for Caleb and William's forty-six cattle at the count. They had lost four along the trail, either to wild animals or just lost.

The Cuban boat had brought in supplies desperately needed by the townspeople and the cattle drivers. Caleb, William, and Ira went shopping.

The first general store they came to, they turned and walked inside. The shopkeeper came over and said, "This store is for whites only. If you want something," he said, nodding at William, "come around back of the store and I'll pass you your goods through the door."

Before William could react, Caleb said, "He's with me. We have gold to spend. If you don't want it, we'll go somewhere else."

The shopkeeper replied, "What do you want?"

Caleb asked for twenty pounds of coffee and one hundred pounds of flour. "We all want new outfits. We need shirts, pants, boots and a hat. I need a dress for my wife, new shoes, and maybe a do-dad for her hair."

"Does that new outfit go for him too," he said, looking at William.

"Yes," William replied. "It does."

The storekeeper valued the size of the order, so he begrudgingly judged the measure of all three and threw pants, shirts, boots, and hats on the counter.

"I can only give you five pounds of coffee and fifty of flour. That's all I have."

"We'll take that," Caleb said.

William also bought men's pants, a shirt, and boots for Selene. She'd requested this since, as she told him, she couldn't do ranch work in a dress. She liked to ride and work alongside William.

Caleb asked about seeds to replant their garden and was directed to another business that sold farming and ranching supplies. The store had a good supply of seeds, so Caleb bought seeds for cowpeas, beans, corn, collards, cabbage, and, to his surprise, tobacco seed.

They all left the Port of Tampa with the supplies loaded in the wagon. Selene drove it and followed the horse riders as they headed home.

When they arrived back at the campsite, Rosie was glad to see them and was surprised and pleased with her new dress. They spent the night at the camp.

The following day, they viewed their surroundings. The water had receded but, beyond the high land that they had camped on, the land eastward was bleak.

The ground was still spongy and water-soaked. Most of the vegetation was dead and lay decaying in the sun. The cypress trees came through fine and their greenery was a welcome sight in the greyness of rotting vegetation.

Caleb and Rosie, along with William and Selene, were anxious to get home and see how things had come through the flood.

Before leaving, Caleb went to the wagon and picked out an object. He handed it to Ira and told him to unwrap it. Ira took the package, looking questioningly at Caleb. As he did so, he realized it was a small-caliber rifle. Suddenly it hit him and he asked, "Is this gun for me?"

"Sure is," Caleb said. "If you're going to supply us with game, you need a gun. It's a brand-new Winchester 22 caliber and it's light weight and very accurate. I bought several boxes of bullets, so you should be able to bag a lot of animals. This rifle is perfect for shooting rabbits, squirrels, or other small game."

They headed home with the wagon loaded with their camping supplies and purchases. Pony and Oconee agreed to stay with the cattle. Caleb told them someone would be back to help them as soon as possible, for two Indians with all these cattle were a tempting target for unscrupulous ranchers and renegades.

The ride home was through a landscape changed since they last came this way. The bay heads were still green with cypress and bay trees. The higher ground showed shoots of green pushing through. Lower land was still water-soaked and it would be a while before anything would grow back.

Few animals were seen. The bay heads held many snakes and alligators. Possums and raccoons climbed among the bay trees. Bones dotted the land from animals, including cattle, who had perished in the flood. The bones were picked clean by vultures.

The bodies of bloated fish lay in the dried-up ponds that the receding water had trapped them in. They passed by the mummified remains of a cow that had reared up to eat moss out of a tree out of desperation for food. As the cow lowered itself, its neck was caught in the vee of two tree trunks. Trapped there, it died of hunger and thirst. The body hung there as a silent reminder of the tragedy that had struck the land.

After a long ride with little conversation, they reached the house and barn. There was much to be done.

The smell of mud and decayed plants filled the air. The water had risen higher after they left and mud filled the floor of the house and barn. The corncrib held a mess of rotted corncobs. The smokehouse door was hanging off its hinges. Nothing was left inside.

The house hadn't been high enough to remain out of the water. At least the garden area was okay. The influx of mud would help replenish lost nutrients lost by continual plantings. They planned on replanting the garden as soon as possible with the seeds bought in Tampa.

There would be cowpeas and beans in two months and corn in three. Food would be hard to come by for a while. The supplies they brought wouldn't feed them until the garden produced a crop. They'd have to depend on what they could gather and get by hunting and fishing.

Rosie, Caleb, and Ira slept on the front porch the first few nights. Selene and William slept in the wagon.

Rosie and Selene spent the first day cleaning the mud out of the house. It had dried and stuck to the wooden planks of the floor and the lower part of the walls. They broke it loose and swept it out the door. After removing the mud, they washed and cleaned the house's interior. Next, they went to Selene's cabin and repeated the process.

Caleb and William turned their attention to the garden. It was still too wet to plant. Ira kept them supplied with the small game that he shot and quail that he trapped following Pony's instruction for making traps. He'd bring home any gopher tortoises that he found outside their burrows.

Rosie said gophers weren't her favorite food and wouldn't cook them once regular food was available. She was okay with turtles that were caught in the fish traps. They seemed somehow more palatable than the tortoises.

No big game had returned to the land, but smaller animals had escaped the flood by finding refuge in trees. Squirrels, 'coons, and 'possums were easy prey for Ira's new rifle. They still had some cornmeal left, but it was going fast. The next few months would be rough and they must live off the land.

William drove the wagon to the pine forest, which was on higher ground. He dug and gathered roots from the abundance of coontie ferns that grew wild. The seeds were pounded into a pulp and washed to remove the poison.

The pulp was left to ferment for two weeks. Then, the fibrous parts were drawn off and the resulting material spread out to dry in the sun. When dry, it was pounded into a coarse material like cornmeal and could be made into bread.

Caleb gathered the young leaves of poke salad, which Rosie cooked to go with the game Ira gathered. In addition, Caleb gathered leaves from the wild thistle plant, which was edible and nutritious.

They also learned to eat the young sprouts of cattails that grew around the wetlands. Caleb used the cattail stalks to weave fish baskets the way that Pony had taught him to do. Swamp cabbage provided a hearty meal when the hearts were chopped out and diced before boiling. This Florida life was demanding, but also offered a way to survive.

The orange trees were all dead, the planted ones and the seedlings. William was devastated at the loss. '*I'll replant*,' he thought. He was eager to see Enos Taylor and see if any of his oranges survived.

Caleb saddled his horse and rode out the next morning to try to find more supplies. A packhorse trailed behind. He arrived late in the day. Gillins was waiting on his front porch when Caleb rode up. "Howdy," he greeted Caleb. "Good to see you again. I hear you went with Roberts to ship cattle.

Hope everything worked out."

Caleb assured him it did. "I need supplies. Our garden is dead and we need supplies to last until the garden comes back."

Gillins shook his head. "I'm afraid not. What few things I get are used up by my closest neighbors. Items weren't available for so long folks naturally grab up anything they can. If you need supplies, you'll need to go to Orlando. Some soldiers passed through here and said Orlando was getting supplies regularly. They have wagons that go to the Port of Tampa and get goods arriving from Cuba and England now that the blockades have eased. You could go to Tampa yourself, but Orlando is closer."

Caleb asked about the availability of land nearby. Gillins replied, "There's lots of land and most of it belongs to the State, but ranchers have grazed cattle on the land for years and they feel they're the owners. Florida is a free-range state, which means cattle can roam anywhere they please. Plus, the new laws passed by our Yankee government made it illegal for anyone who fought against the north to homestead property."

Caleb was thankful that Sanders had signed over the land; otherwise getting land would be hard.

Gillins broke into his thoughts, "If you're going to Orlando, you're welcome to stay the night in my barn. Stable your horse there too. I might even rustle up a little pone and bacon for your dinner."

Caleb thanked Gillins and took his horse out back and turned it loose in the corral. As soon as the horse was freed from the saddle and bridle, it lay down and rolled in the dirt of the corral. The mule, likewise released, just walked slowly to the far side of the corral and munched on some straw.

Caleb walked back up to the trading post and went inside. Gillins had a cup of coffee poured for the two of them along with a plate of corn pone and fried bacon. Caleb hadn't eaten all day so he was glad to eat the food.

Gillins offered a drink of whiskey he made but Caleb declined. Gillins didn't refuse a drink himself. He filled a cup with the yellowish liquid and took a deep drink. He grimaced, coughed, and said, "Great stuff," as he took another drink.

After the dinner, Caleb paid Gillins for the night's stay and food. He went back to the barn and fell asleep in the hay after throwing some hay into the corral for the horse and mule.

Bright and early, he rode off with the mule in tow, following a trail north and then east that would take him to the settlement in Orlando. He carried pone and bacon wrapped in a greasy cloth Gillins had provided him.

As he turned and started eastward, he passed an occasional farmhouse. All were the same sun-bleached cypress or log houses. Some had smokestacks indicating a fireplace, while others had cooking pots outside held by an iron tripod.

It took him two days to reach the settlement. He spent a dry night under a large oak tree. After a night's sleep, he mounted and continued his journey. Late that afternoon, he reached the small community.

The trading post was at the end of a dusty street. He tied his horse and mule to a hitching rail in front and went inside. The room was long and narrow, with shelves running down both sidewalls. The shelves were stacked with clothing, lanterns, leather goods, and jars and cans full of various things.

The center of the room was full of barrels. The back of the store had a glass front counter across the room's width with shelves behind. The operator of the post was talking to another man. He nodded to Caleb and said he would be right with him.

Caleb wandered about the room. He saw the barrels that contained flour, meal, salt, sugar, dried peas, and beans.

There seemed to be no shortage here.

The store manager walked up after the other customer left with his packages. "Hi," he said. "My name is Josh."

Caleb introduced himself and explained what he needed.

Josh told him, "I just got in three wagon loads from Tampa. I should be able to furnish what you need. Looking around, Caleb wished he'd brought the wagon. He settled for all the flour and dried beans he thought the mule could carry. He added bags of coffee and salt that he would tie behind his saddle.

Caleb returned by the same route, stopping overnight at Gillins' trading post. Gillins told him, "If you go again for supplies, take a wagon. You can haul more, and I'll pay you to haul some for me."

Caleb replied, "I might have to make another trip. If I do, I'll come by here and get your order."

In Caleb's absence, William decided to see Enos Taylor. Early one morning, he hitched up the wagon and drove to the Taylor farm to see how Taylor's oranges had come through the flood. He neared the Taylor house and saw the green of orange trees.

Taylor greeted him as he drove up. Taylor said, "First, you must find hammock land to plant your trees," when he was told the news. "You must plant them high enough to handle the floods. We get them often enough. Then, you still have to mound them up and create drainage between the rows."

William looked at Taylor's grove. The trees started on a gentle rise well above the creek water level. Taylor continued, "The trees should be planted on raised mounds so water could stand between the rows without drowning the plants. Even my trees suffered from the high water. All the young fruit fell off before ripening. I lost a whole year's crop. All my seedlings were drowned. Only the mature trees made it through. We lost our garden the same as everyone else. We had enough seeds saved back to replant the garden, but food and supplies have been scarce. Plenty of raccoons and possums took refuge in our trees, but we're tired of eating them. We get fish from the creek and a turtle now and then. The flood drove out all the big game. No pork or venison for a long while."

William told Taylor of the trouble he and Caleb went through. "We did save some cattle, so maybe I can trade you some beef for more orange trees."

Taylor replied, "It'll be a while before I can trade you any trees. I'll have to replant. It'll be a couple of years before the trees will be big enough to transplant. You'll have to go further west to find any trees. Everything from here to the east coast is flooded out. This flood was the worst one we've had."

William took his leave from Taylor's. He was disappointed at the absence of orange trees for a new grove but pleased with the latest information on how to prevent further flood damage.

William was an angry man who didn't realize that fact since anger was a thing that lived in him and was a part of him. Every day was greeted by him with distrust and a feeling he had to keep his guard up.

For the first time in his life, William found something that gave him the sense that he was in control and provided peace for him. The planting of seeds that sprouted into tiny trees and grew into large trees decorated with golden globes of color gave him order and reason. The trees' planting, caring, and nurturing were in his control, subject to nature, of course.

When he returned from Taylor's, Selene ran to him and they embraced. They went inside with his arm around her and he told her of his plans for a new grove.

"I know a place with high ground I need to plant my oranges," he told her. "Higher land and mounding the rows will keep the trees free from any floods. This time, I know how to make it work." His excitement brought a smile to Selene's face as she listened to his plans.

William worked at various jobs around the barn and garden as he eagerly waited for Caleb to come home. A few mornings later Caleb rode up, followed by the laden mule. He helped Caleb unpack. After the new supplies were safely packed away, the two men sat on the front porch, anxious to share information.

Caleb replied, "I talked to Roberts. His house is built on a high hammock, so his house doesn't flood. The land around him does, but he has men that herd most of his cattle west of here on free-range. He still has cows ranging close to here, but he's ready to move them at the first hint of flooding."

William thought for a while and then said, 'We can do the same thing with our cattle. Selene and I, along with you and Rosie and Ira, can use the wagon to carry supplies and travel along with our herd until we can afford to hire more help."

Caleb replied, "We need to get through the next few months. We should put in a large corn patch and raise up and increase the size of the corncrib. If we grow enough corn to fill it, we'll have enough to last us all year for cornmeal and have some for feeding the stock. It would be good to have enough to fatten some hogs. I want to be ready for the next flood with plenty of corn, dried beans, and cowpeas to eat and replant a new crop After that's done, we can move our cattle to higher ground for grazing."

Caleb and William looked proudly at the overflowing corncrib three months later. There was corn enough to see them through tough times. The grass grew high in the fields and the trees that survived were green with new growth. Animals had returned to the land and were available to hunt without traveling great distances. It was hard to keep Ira doing his chores. He was constantly out in the woods trapping for animals. The barn sides were covered by the curing hides of coons and deerskins. Caleb told him to stay clear of panthers and bears.

16

The Music Man

Caleb told William that a trip to the settlement at Orlando for more supplies was necessary. If they took the wagon, they could bring more back. William readily agreed to go, so they left around noon, accompanied by Ira, riding Blaze.

They planned to stay overnight in Gillens' barn and continue the trip the following day. William drove the wagon pulled by two mules and Caleb rode Buck. They arrived at Gillins' late that afternoon, and he again greeted Caleb from his front porch. He said, "I didn't expect to see you again so soon."

Caleb told him of their plans and asked if they could stay in his barn.

Gillins replied, "Sure. And, as soon as you take care of your animals, you and the boy can have supper with me. You can take some pone and greens out to the barn for your nigger."

Caleb felt William tense at the remark, so he quickly said, "Thanks, but we brought food."

William couldn't constrain himself. "I am no one's nigger. I'm a free man," he said, glowing at Gillins.

Gillins looked at Caleb and said, "Better get that boy some manners. Folks around here won't take kindly to his sass. He can be what he wants around his people, but needs to learn his place if he wants to avoid trouble."

Caleb said, "We'll stay in your barn tonight and be on our way in the morning. I'll put away our animals and be back to talk to you soon."

With that, he led William and Ira to the barn. He and Ira unsaddled the horses and turned them into the corral. William unhitched the mules and let them join the horses.

Caleb walked back to talk to Gillins, who didn't appear as friendly as before. He said to Caleb, "I meant what I said to that nigger. I need to add that folks might not go for your riding with him."

Caleb replied, "I understand, but he saved my life before and is a good, hard-working man. He has a little trouble with his attitude, but can be trusted. He has a good woman and the two will be an asset to this land. We all want to be good neighbors and not invite trouble. Lord knows we've seen enough."

Gillins said, "We need good neighbors to rebuild our land. He might be okay if he lives long enough. We lost a lot of good men to Yanks because of his likes. Don't expect him to be welcome around here, and he better learn to stay in his place. We don't need uppity niggers."

Caleb explained that they were going on to Orlando for supplies and might have room for a few supplies for Gillins.

Gillins' mood shifted to a friendlier tone at this news and he quickly told Caleb, "I need anything you can bring back, especially coffee, flour, sugar, dried beans, and any powder and shot. I saw your rifles, but many folks here still own muzzleloaders and not rifles using shells. I'll give you some gold coins to buy all you can for me. I'll also send along a pack mule to carry my goods."

Caleb agreed to Gillins' request. Caleb went back to the barn and joined William for the night. They awoke early, saddled the horses, and hitched up the mules.

Gillins came out of the house. He caught one of his mules and put on a halter and lead rope and gave Caleb several rough fabric bags for the goods he needed. He went back inside and came back with a coffee pot and three cups. "Here," he said, "a hot drink will get you started."

He also gave Caleb a tin plate filled with corn pone. Caleb took the pot of coffee, cups, and corn pone to the barn and shared with Ira and William. As soon as they finished eating, they were on their way to the settlement in Orlando.

They made camp that night just outside Orlando and rode in early the next day. Arriving at the trading post, they were greeted by Josh. Caleb, Ira, and William walked up the steps and started inside.

Josh, pointing at William, said, "Not you. You wait outside. If you want anything, wait until I'm finished waiting on the white folks, then come around to the back door and I'll take your order as long as you have money to pay for them."

Caleb said, "We travel together, and both have money to spend. We have a big order to place and will go to someone else if you don't want our money."

Josh looked at Caleb, then at William. "Okay," he said. "Come on in. If one of my regular customers comes in he'll have to wait outside, especially if it's a white lady."

Caleb angrily replied, "If one of us must leave, we'll all leave along with our money. If your customers are offended by being around us, tell *them* to stay outside."

This remark made Josh's face turn red as he was startled at Caleb's anger. He stammered out, "I didn't intend to offend you. It's just that folks around here have a certain way of living and you're certainly not in tune with them, but I'll fill your order and if I get other customers, I'll ask them to wait."

Slightly satisfied by Josh's words, they wandered around the room looking into the barrels and examining other goods available. Caleb gave his order to Josh along with all the things Gillins requested.

After tallying up the bill, Josh said, "If that's all, you

can pay me. I'll help with the loading."

William spoke up, "That's not all. I need some things too."

Josh looked surprised and said, "I thought you were all together."

William replied, "I have my own place, so I need some things. Don't worry, I can pay you for what I need."

He told Josh what he wanted. As the clerk put the supplies in bags, William walked around the room. Picking up an ax, he leaned it against the counter, added two hoes, and asked Josh for the total. When told the amount due, he reached into his pocket and pulled out gold coins to pay the bill. "I pay for what I need," he said. "I'll need other things as we go along. In the future, should I come here for things or would you rather I go somewhere else?"

Josh looked hungrily at the gold coins in William's black hand. "Long as you got gold to spend, I'll take it. It would help if you remembered your place. Most folks aren't as friendly as me."

William laughed, "You're real friendly, alright."

They carried the supplies outside to load them on the wagon. Before they began loading, Caleb reached in and grabbed a bundle of raccoon skins. "We want to trade these furs that Ira here trapped and cured."

Josh fingered the furs, looked at Ira, and said, "Yes. I can use these. You did a good job. Come on in and let's see if we can make a trade."

Caleb and William began loading the wagon and packing the mule while Ira followed Josh back into the store. "Look around," Josh said. "See what you want, and maybe the skins will pay for it."

Ira went straight over to a display counter, picked up a knife, and carried it back to Josh. He handed the knife to him and looked at Josh to see if the skins would be worth enough to buy it.

Josh said, "Well, boy, that's a real fine knife. It costs a pretty penny."

Ira stood there looking up at Josh. Finally, Josh said, "Okay. I see you're a good trader. I'll take the skins and you keep the knife. Let's see now, you might have a little more credit." He reached into a glass jar, picked out a piece of hard candy, and handed it to Ira.

Ira took the candy and the knife and walked proudly out of the store.

He showed Caleb and William his new knife. They both told him it was a fine knife. They completed loading the supplies and Josh came back outside to see them off.

They started the ride home, William driving the wagon, Caleb and Ira riding their horses. A black man dressed in shabby homespun clothing stepped into the street and walked toward the wagon at the edge of town. Curious, William pulled back on the team, stopping the forward progress of the wagon. He looked down at the man.

"My name is Freman," the man addressed William. "I'm looking for work and will work hard for a place to stay and a little food. I had a good job a while back, but renegades killed the farmer that gave me work. I escaped, but times are hard and work is scarce."

William, from the wagon seat, looked the man over. He noticed a guitar hanging from a well-worn strap. "You play that thing?" he asked.

Freman smiled and replied, "I sure do. And sometimes my music is all that keeps me going. Although the music doesn't fill me up when there's nothing to eat, sometimes people give me a little money or food when I play my music for them."

William moved over in the wagon seat and said, "Get on up here and play a bit while I drive. If your music is passable, maybe we can give you a job, in addition to entertainment."

Freman jumped into the offered seat with a smile and said, "I sure am thankful for the ride and promise you won't regret taking me on."

William looked at his passenger. "Freman is a funny name for your mom to give you."

Freman, looking pensive, replied, "I didn't get that name from my mom. When my last boss told me I was a free man, I decided I would be called Freman to remind myself that my family was enslaved."

They made camp that night and, as soon as a fire was made and dinner cooked, the four men sat on the ground and ate. Freman ate like he hadn't eaten for a long while. After the meal, William told Freman it'd be good to hear some music before going to sleep.

Freman picked up his guitar and, after adjusting the strings, began playing a melody none of them recognized. He started singing and the men were pleasantly surprised at the sound of his voice. It was a rich baritone that rose and fell with the song's words.

The men looked at Freman's worn clothing, shaggy hair, and beard and were amazed that so pretty a sound could come from such a sight.

Ira asked, "Where did you learn to sing like that?"

With a slight smile, Freman replied. "I sure hope you liked it. I learned to sing from my mother. She said a person could put up with a lot of hardship if you keep music in your heart. She is passed on now, but she was right. My music has given me a lot of pleasure and made some bad times bearable."

The next day, they arrived at Gillins' place. Gillins was glad to see them and eagerly examined the goods his money bought. They brought him flour, dry beans, sugar, and the powder and shot requested. He said to Caleb, "I might want to hire you to haul supplies for me, maybe a trip to the Port of Tampa. I hear they're getting good supplies there. I'd pay you for your time and the use of that wagon and mules."

William spoke up. "These are my mules and wagon."

Gillins looked surprised. "Well now," he said, "I might pay you to do the hauling. I can have my wife write down a list of things for you to take along. I doubt if you could remember a long list. I never learned to write myself, but I can make change."

William laughed, saying, "I'll let you know. We have lots to do, but we'll talk it over. If you see me show up with my wagon, you'll realize we agreed. As far as a list, your wife can tell me what you need and I'll write the list myself."

William laughed loudly at the shocked look on Gillins' face as he drove off with Freman sitting beside him on the wagon seat.

Caleb and Ira mounted their horses to follow. Gillins said, "That nigger will get himself shot or worse with his attitude. Can he really read and write?"

"Yes," replied Caleb. "He can. As for getting shot, I wouldn't be surprised. It's just that if someone tries, he better be careful it's not the other way around."

Gillins turned back to go inside, shaking his head as he walked.

William drove the wagon with the new addition to their group. Caleb rode his horse up to the wagon's side and asked, "What are you going to do with your guitar player when we get home?"

William laughed and said, "That's a good question. I was just wondering how to present him to Selene. We don't have any room for him in the house, so I guess he'll have to sleep outdoors until we can make other arrangements."

Caleb replied, "I suppose he could stay in the barn and we can give him a job working in the garden."

Freman spoke up, "No place can be any worse than some places I've stayed. I can farm or work stock as far as work, and I've done plenty of both."

They arrived home and Caleb introduced the new man to Rosie, who didn't seem surprised, saying. "I guess one more mouth to feed will be all right. We can use help around here looking after the garden. Ira here spends all his time in the woods hunting or trapping."

17

New Age

The years following the end of the war were tumultuous. The Yankee reconstruction program started with good intentions of improving life in the South, and the plan was to rebuild the South while upgrading the lives of black people. The project didn't take into consideration the greed of northern carpetbaggers and ambitious Southerners.

The two groups, through questionable dealing, kept the black people in poverty and did little to rebuild the South unless doing so was highly profitable to themselves.

Part of the reconstruction plan was disqualifying any leading Confederates from running for office or voting, but black people were given the right to vote.

Harrison Reed, formerly of Massachusetts, was now governor and further alienated the white Southerners by appointing a black person, Jonathan Gibbs, as Secretary of State and as the Lieutenant Colonel in the Florida Militia.

Gibbs was an educated and qualified candidate for the jobs, but was a known abolitionist before the war. He was also known for working to improve the life of impoverished blacks. Southerners were upset that a black man was appointed to such a high-ranking job and was sure he'd put the needs of blacks above that of the whites.

During these times, the Southern whites developed attitudes that would last for many years. The limitations placed on the South by the ruling North and the sting of losing the war instilled more hatred of the North.

The most convenient thing to vent their anger on was the black people, resulting in the Negroes of the South living in conditions, in many cases, worse than before slavery ended. Where whites, before the war, looked at black people as a source of cheap labor, they now blamed them for the war and its aftermath of poverty.

The white population of Florida banded together to oppose the northern invaders and the rules imposed by the new government.

New immigrants from northern states looked down on the southern whites and black people alike. They were also more favored by the government imposed by the North.

Black people who had been oppressed and believed that freedom would solve their problems found that little had changed. Home ownership for southern black people was scarce because of economic restrictions and limited opportunities to purchase land.

Employment was almost nonexistent since farmers had no money to hire and little food to spare. Scattered landowners struggled to feed their families, let alone take on other mouths to feed.

Some black people stayed on as free men on the same farms they were formerly slaves, but little change in their life occurred. There was no money to pay them a wage, even if the owner was of a mind to pay. They still labored long days for meager food and clothing. Those who did leave in search of better conditions often wandered about with few chances to better themselves. A few lucky ones with learned trades could find employment but the monies earned didn't provide much of an existence.

Black people like William and Selene dared to challenge the situation and make their way. However, the many limitations and frustrations made it challenging to maintain a positive outlook. Despite dreams of freedom, many found those dreams replaced by confusion and then anger at the environment that kept them away from true freedom and opportunities.

Newly freed black men, as well as returning southern soldiers and drifters, turned to theft to provide food for themselves. All were held in low esteem, but it was easier for the honest victims of thievery to believe it was just the nature of the black people to be lazy and steal and, to a small degree, they forgave the whites as being victims of circumstances; namely the northern aggression and freed slaves.

Never had our country been subject to the conflicting emotions of various classes of people, black and white, trying to survive but still having the capacity to hate those different from themselves.

Politics had little effect on Caleb, William, and their families. While politicians planned and legally robbed, northern investors clamored for favorable land purchases through paid political influence. The ranch prospered and provided a good living for both families.

Annual drives to the West and northern markets brought in money to buy the supplies not provided by the ranch. Excess gold coins were carefully put away for future use.

The orange grove flourished under William's care, and they were selling barrels of oranges for shipments up north.

Former Confederate Major J.H. Allen opened a trading post north of Lake Tohopekaliga and formed a small settlement known as Allendale. Supplies were now regularly available from trading posts in the area.

William adopted the last name of Thornton, the name of his former owner that had given him his freedom. He and Selene had two boys named Jesse and Jairus plus two girls, Adaza and Hiba. Selene spent time instructing the children and William spent time going over what they had learned every night.

"You must learn," he told them. "Education is what will move our people forward in the world."

Being isolated kept the children away from prejudiced whites. Still, as best he could, William explained the differences between Negros and whites, dreading the day that his children would be subjected to discrimination.

"How do I explain to them," he thought, *"that they're as good as any other race, with the same wants and needs, while telling them they must adopt a lifestyle of subservience to have a good relationship with whites."*

So far, his children had never experienced the hatred and mistreatment that Negros had at the hands of southern and northern whites.

William spent his time working on the orange grove that he replanted. He and Caleb agreed that William would oversee the oranges and Caleb would manage the herd of cattle.

The orange grove was William's calendar. He marked the coming and going of the seasons by the changes in the orange trees.

Spring brought the intoxicating smell of orange blossoms that filled him with wonder. The trees seemed to wake from a long winter's sleep and burst forth with brilliantly white blossoms and bright green new leaves that painted the trees in contrasting white and green.

From inside his house, he could hear the buzzing of bees as they went about collecting nectar and spreading pollen as they moved from one blossom to another.

Spring was an exciting time for William for he knew the white blossoms would fall away, and small green oranges would form and, in a few months, the oranges would increase in size and turn a golden yellow. William swore that nothing on earth could be as pretty when the trees were loaded with ripe oranges.

Summer heat meant the oranges were maturing and ripening. Every day, William walked among the trees and checked the size of the fruit. This was also a time to be concerned about the trees getting enough water. If not enough rain fell, William had to haul water for irrigation, especially the young trees.

Fall announced the harvest time for his fruit. This was the time of picking the oranges. Picking and packing them into barrels for shipment was hard work, but it was also a festive time as William's and Caleb's families gathered for the harvest.

When winter came, the trees seemed more somber as the bright green leaves of spring turned a deep green in preparation for colder weather.

William had conflicting emotions at this time of year. He felt sadness and a sense of loss when the final orange was shipped, but also felt gratitude that the year had been success.

William and Selene's daughter, Adaza, was his constant companion. She was tall for her age and promised to grow into a tall woman. William looked down at her small round face as she clung to his hand and asked constant questions about the trees and their care. William felt a softness that was new to him and vowed to look after her and the rest of his family.

Selene told him he might as well sleep in the grove so he could watch the oranges grow, but Adaza had to spend more time at home so she could learn the ways of housekeeping and cooking. Still, Adaza joined William as he tended his trees.

In contrast, Hiba was smaller, with a narrow face and a serious look on her face most of the time. She learned the tasks of housekeeping readily but had a curiosity about everything.

Jesse chose to be alone whenever he could. He'd be a big man, like William, but was quieter. He was most content when he was outside and wandered off into the woods, giving Selene many anxious moments.

Jairus was smaller than Jesse and was content to spend a lot of time in the house with Selene. He did chores assigned to him but daydreamed a lot.

William was proud of the new home he and Selene built with lumber and other materials that were now available. The pride of ownership swelled in his chest as he thought of the home they now lived in and the oranges.

They had moved out of the log home, leaving it intact. He had built a house of rough-sawn lumber with a shingle shake roof.   William had made several trips for Gillins and the money that he earned was enough to buy the lumber to build his new home without using any of the money from the oranges or cattle sold.

Building the new home was easier now that nails were available since the war was over. The windows were glass paned and the floor was made from planking newly cut at a local sawmill.

William sometimes thought of his parents, who lived and died in slavery, and then of his life as a free man. He had a family and owned his home, which was unthinkable a few years ago.

One morning, Jairus, the younger of the Thornton boys, couldn't get out of bed for breakfast. Selene had called the children to breakfast and was surprised that Jairus, who usually was eager to eat, didn't take his place at the kitchen table. She left the other children eagerly eating their breakfast of cornbread and fried pork fat.

Going to Jairus's bedside, Selene called his name and asked why he was still in bed. When he didn't reply, she put her hand on his shoulder and felt it covered with sweat.

Jairus slowly opened his eyes and said, "I don't feel good. Just let me sleep for a while."

Selene wiped his face with a fold of her dress. "Okay,"

she said. "You sleep for a while and I'll check on you later."

Selene returned to the other children who were finishing their breakfast. "Jesse," she said, "go to the barn and tell your Pa to come to eat breakfast. You can take over the milking. Adaza, you go with him and bring me any eggs you can find if the creatures haven't seen them first. Hiba, you pick up all the dirty clothes and take them out to the wash pot."

They left to go about their duties as William walked through the door.

"Come in," Selene said as she poured him a cup of steaming brew from the coffee pot on the woodstove.

He took a drink and said, "Next time I go to Allendale, I'll buy some real coffee. A drink made from parched, ground corn gets as hot as real coffee, but that's all it does that resembles real coffee. If they have any coffee and sell us some, we can mix a little coffee with the ground corn to stretch it out."

Selene laughed as she poured herself a cup and sat down across from William. "I remember a time we would've been proud to have this drink. When the war was going on, we drank hot water many mornings, and that was all we had for breakfast."

The two finished breakfast. William left to tend his orange trees while Selene cleared up from breakfast and straightened up the room. She went back to check on Jairus. He was still hot to her touch and listless.

He looked up at her and said, "I'm so sleepy but I can't sleep because of pain in my arms and legs. What's wrong with me?"

"Hush now," she said. "You just rest in bed today. Tomorrow you'll feel better. Would you like something to eat?"

"No, Ma'am," he said. "I just don't feel like eating right now."

The next morning, Jairus was still running a fever. Selene couldn't get him to eat the milk and cornbread mix that she offered. She was getting concerned that he wasn't getting any better.

When William came home that night, she expressed her concern. "I'm really worried," she told William. "None of the kids have been this sick before and I don't know what's wrong with him. If he's not better tomorrow, then you get Anarece to come to see Jairus. She's a Root Worker and some say she can cure just about anything as well as being in touch with spirits who help her cure sickness or personal problems of people."

"I never heard of her," William replied. "How do you know of her? You know I don't believe in that conjure stuff."

"That may be, but your son is mighty sick and you know that no white doctor would come to our house, even if there was one around. The closest one is in Orlando, but even then, if he came to our house, none of the whites would have him in theirs. He won't risk that, even if he wanted to, which he doesn't."

The next morning Jairus was even more listless. It took Selene a while to get him to take any food. His arms and legs seemed limp and he made no effort to move them.

More alarmed than ever, Selene left his bedside and went out to the barn where William was mending a harness. He looked up, surprised at her presence.

"Stop what you're doing," she commanded. "Our boy needs help right away. I'm afraid he's going to die. I don't know what's wrong with him and have never seen this illness. Go now and get Anarece!"

Surprised at her statement's firmness, William replied, "Okay. I'll get her if I can. Just tell me where to find her."

"She stays at the Roberts' farm. Her boys work for Mr. Roberts and he gives her a cabin to live in."

18

Anarece

William took the newly mended harness and, going outside, caught and harnessed one of his mules. It only took a few minutes to back the mule up to the wagon, and soon he drove up to the front of the house.

Selene came out and handed him a sack. "There's cornbread and fried squirrel for your lunch. You'll be asked to spend the night with her family, but don't do that. Tell her Jairus is badly sick and needs help right away. You can make it back by tonight if you don't waste time."

William was irritated by the tone of her words. He looked sharply at her but didn't reply. He could tell of her concern for their son. He replied, "I'll go as fast as I can."

With those words, he slapped the reins against the mule's rump and began his journey to get help. He knew the way to Roberts' farm as he and Caleb had made the trip several times, driving cattle.

His thoughts wandered as the mule slowly covered the distance. *'I should have been a little more patient with Selene. She's mighty worried about Jairus.'* He began to be more concerned as he drove. *'Selene isn't one to worry over nothing,'* he thought.

The concern made him slap the reins and urge the mule to a faster pace. The mule refused to be hurried and the wagon slowly covered the distance.

Under a sky of blue, the wagon moved through broad

meadows covered with golden sagebrush, the pale green dog fennel, and the dark green poke salad plants.

William had to drive around cypress ponds where the wagon wheels would sink into the dark-colored moist ground and made the going tough for the mule.

William stopped by one of the ponds and picked some blackberries growing in the rich soil. He ate them with the bread and meat Selene packed.

William finally arrived at the Roberts' ranch. It was an odd collection consisting of Roberts' home, barn, and various other buildings, all constructed of unpainted cypress bleached a dull grey by the Florida sun.

William heard a noise coming from the barn and drove the wagon up to the open door. He entered and found a black man working at a forge. The heat from the forge heated the entire barn and the man was drenched in sweat. He looked up with a questioning look on his face when William approached.

William said, "I'm looking for Anarece. I got a sick boy at home and I understand she can help him. Tell me where to find her. I need her quick!"

"Okay, okay," the man replied as he led William out of the barn. Pointing down a rutted road, he said, "Just follow that road about half a mile and you'll come to her cabin. It's the first one you come to."

William thanked the man, jumped into the wagon, and drove down the road that led to Anarece's cabin. Soon, he arrived at a small wooden house nestled among trees and shrubs of various sizes and shapes. The door to the house opened and a small black woman stepped outside.

William couldn't judge her age. He saw that she was old for sure, but how old was impossible to tell. She wore a simple cotton dress, but it was dyed many colors. Her hair was piled high on her head. It was all grey but decorated with bits of colored cloth. She walked up to the wagon and climbed in next to William. He noticed she carried two bags, one small and one larger.

"My name is Anarece," she said. "Let's go and not waste time."

William looked confused and said, "I came to see you about my sick boy."

"I know," she said. "I've been expecting you."

"How could you be expecting me?" he asked.

Her reply was, "That isn't important. Just take me to your boy. I have roots and herbs in this sack." She pointed to the smaller bag. "And my clothing in the other in case I have to stay awhile."

William questioned the woman as they drove toward his home. Anarece only said, "You don't have the feeling to understand, so explaining to you would do no good. Just take me to your boy."

When they reached home, Selene was standing in the open doorway. She ran quickly to the wagon and welcomed Anarece. Anarece walked quickly passed Selene and into the cabin. Walking directly to the bed where Jairus lay, she put her bag down and knelt by the bedside.

Anarece put her hand on his forehead, felt its heat, and frowned. She then pulled his eyelids open wide and looked into his eyes. Next, one by one, she lifted his arms and legs.

Selene and William stood by as the woman did her examination. They watched helplessly as Anarece finished and reached into her bag and retrieved a box, opened it, and took out small bags containing finely ground herbs of varied colors. She placed a shallow bowl next to the bed and mixed them.

Anarece looked at Selene and said, "Bring me some hog tallow that hasn't been used for cooking."

Selene went to the stove and returned with a container of the yellowish-tinted mixture. She handed it to Anarece, who took a handful and mixed it into the bowl containing the herbs. After mixing thoroughly, she began rubbing the mixture into Jairus' arms and legs.

"You do this every day for two weeks," she told them. Handing them another bag, she continued, "Mix a spoonful of this with water and have him drink it every day. It'll make the fever go away."

William could wait no more and exclaimed as he asked, "What's wrong with him!?"

Anarece looked at him and said, "I don't know the name for what's wrong, but I've seen it before. He'll live, but might lose feeling in his arm or leg. Only time will tell. What I did is all I can do with what I have. I must go back to Mr. Roberts' and pick up more things."

As Anarece prepared to go with William, she saw Hiba looking at her with wide eyes. "Who are you?" Anarece asked.

With no shyness, Hiba replied, "My name is Hiba. Who are you?"

Anarece looked at the girl for a long time and said, "I'll be back later. You and I will talk, for I want to get to know you."

William hitched up the wagon and drove Anarece back to the Roberts' ranch. During the ride, she asked William questions about the little girl she had just met.

William replied, "Her name is Hiba. Selene picked that name from her ancestors in Africa. It means *'gift.'*"

Anarece nodded her head at the information. At her cabin, she dismounted and told William to wait. She made several trips from the cabin to the wagon. She loaded a sleeping mat and cover and several gourds that were painted different colors.

When William questioned her, she replied that she was moving in with him and Selene to care for Jairus. "He's a special boy," she said. "He'll need me to look after him. He'll never be whole, but I'll do all I can for him."

William didn't know what to do or say. This thing wasn't something he could fight. He feared for his boy and what Anarece had foretold for him. This country was hard enough for a healthy person to survive. Jairus' sickness made William feel helpless, a feeling he didn't like.

The two arrived back and Selene greeted them with a concerned look. "He's no better," she said. "He doesn't have the strength or energy to move or even eat."

Anarece got down from the wagon and told William to bring her belongings.

"What's happening?" Selene asked.

William replied, "This woman said she's moving in. She didn't give me a choice. She said she's moving in with her sleeping mat to take care of Jairus."

Selene was glad to see Anarece back. As strong as Selene and William were, this was more than they knew how to handle.

Anarece went directly to where Jairus lay, barely moving. His breathing was slow and laborious.

Anarece pulled the plug out of one of the gourds and poured a foul-smelling liquid into her hand. She reached for Jairus' right arm and, starting at his shoulder, she applied the liquid and, applying pressure, she pulled her hands down from his shoulder to his fingertips. She repeated the move ten times and then the same process with the other arm and legs.

She looked up at Selene's troubled face, saying, "I must try to release the thing in his muscles. I'll do this every day. I'll make a broth for him to eat. We must hope that will be enough to make him live and the oil I rub will make him recover."

"What are you putting on him?" Selene asked.

Anarece looked at Selene for a long time and finally said, "No one knows my secrets, but I'll tell you how to use the mixture in each of my gourds. Some of them can kill a person if used wrongly as well as not exactly as I say."

She continued, "The mix I use on Jairus is made from ground-up poke salad berries and they're deadly if you don't know how to use them. It has its uses and they can help Jairus if I rub him with them daily."

William and Selene looked on hopelessly as, twice a day, Anarece massaged ointment into the limbs of a listless Jairus.

When she wasn't busy taking care of Jairus, Anarece spent time with Hiba, asking her questions and answering her questions. Hiba began to help care for Jairus and soon both Anarece and Hiba could be seen tending the sick boy, with Anarece explaining the care.

When questioned by the two concerned parents, Anarece replied she was doing all that could be done.

After what seemed like an eternity, Jairus showed some improvement. He was able to eat sitting up but was very weak. His left arm had no sensation and the muscle had shrunk in the upper and lower arm.

Anarece continued her twice-daily massages. After another week, he was stronger and, with help, he could walk around the room.

Anarece still did the massages twice daily and added twice daily walking him around the room steadied by holding him around the waist.

His walking improved but there was no help for his left arm, and it hung motionless at his side. He'd sit for hours looking out the window and the world outside. He particularly liked watching the small animals and birds teeming in the bushes behind the house.

He never tired of watching and was fascinated by the colors of the various birds; the scarlet red of the redbirds, the greys that blended on the mockingbirds, the ebony black of the grackles, and the copper of the thrushes.

Later, when Anarece took him for walks outside, he marveled at the red and black of the Red-Headed, Ivory-

Billed, and Pileated woodpeckers.

One day, Anarece brought him several gourds. When he removed the tops, he saw various colors of liquid in each of them. He looked at Anarece for an explanation. She smiled and showed him a paintbrush she had made.

Jairus watched as she dipped the brush into one of the gourds. She removed the brush and it held some of the liquid on its tip. She then picked up a piece of a board and moved the brush across it. It left a trail of color. Jairus was spellbound.

Anarece handed Jairus the brush and watched as he took it carefully in his hand, dipped it into a gourd, and followed her example by making a streak of color on the board.

"Now," she told him, "you can paint pictures of the birds you see and many other things you admire. I'll teach you to make the paint out of things that grow wild in the woods and ponds." Anarece walked out the door without looking back at the boy who was just introduced to a miracle of colors and brush.

The next day, after tending to Jairus, Anarece told Selene that she needed to talk with her. Once the two were alone, Anarece began. "I was afraid I wouldn't find the right one to continue my work, but I knew that my search was over when I met Hiba. I should have trusted the powers more and not doubted. Hiba is the chosen one and I'll teach her the gathering in preparation of various herbs that are used to fight injury and disease."

Serena replied, "While I'm intrigued by the variety of powers and liquids you possess, the thought of Hiba, young as she, following in your footsteps, is too early. Maybe when she's older."

Anarece simply stated, "She must start young, for there's much to learn. Now, you have concerns, but it's her destiny. Would you take that from her? If my parents had stopped my learning, I wouldn't be here to help your son. Would you deprive another mother's son of the same by denying Hiba her destiny? I promise that if any time she decides it's not her life or I think she can't continue, I'll stop the teachings of my art."

Selene thought about Anarece's words. If it was meant to be that Hiba be a root woman, she couldn't stand in her way. She nodded her approval.

William was chopping wood for the fireplace when Anarece walked up to him. She said, "William, I want you to take me back to Roberts' farm so I can get the rest of my belongings. It's my place to live with you and teach Hiba in the ways of my medicine. I know that she's the one to continue my work. Jairus will also need my care to regain his strength."

William was shocked at this news. He laid down the ax and turned to her. "What do you mean? You want my daughter to learn all you know about caring for folks? Why she's just a little girl. Wait for her to grow up, and then maybe."

Anarece looked at William with a fixed stare. "You and I have no control over some things in life. I was brought here to help your son and never expected to do more but, meeting the girl, I knew she was born to be a root woman, just like me. She's a chosen one and I believe she knows."

His final remark was, "You better talk to Selene about that."

Anarece smiled.

William went to hitch up the wagon and, once the team was ready, he drove it up to the house. Anarece came out and climbed into the wagon seat. William had questions but decided to wait and let Anarece tell him in her own words. The two rode along in silence for a while.

Anarece began to speak, "My mother before me had the healing powers and the ability to see things that other people couldn't. Some people think this is a blessing. Those who have the power sometimes think it's a curse, for you can't escape it and you can't misuse the power. I hesitate to pass this power on to Hiba, but I feel in her a special power that makes me know she can handle the responsibility."

William replied, "She's so young and should be enjoying the short time she has left as a child, not learning about sickness and death. Why not wait until she's older and see if that's the life she wants?"

The reply was quick. "I didn't plan to become what I am, and neither did those before me who had the gift. We do not choose. We are chosen, the same as Hiba."

When they arrived at the Roberts' ranch, he drove directly to the home where he first met Anarece. He dismounted from the wagon and helped Anarece down. They went into the unpainted little house and she began gathering up her belongings, including the rest of her gourds filled with medicine and potions.

They completed loading her possessions and were ready to begin the trip back home when Roberts rode up, stopped his horse, and looked at Anarece.

"Where're you going with all your belongings? The folks that work on my ranch depend on you to help them when they're sick or hurt. I don't like the idea that you're moving away,"

Anarece replied, "It's commanded by a power stronger than me that I should move in with William and Selene, for their daughter is to take over my work when I no longer can. I'll still treat those that need me, but they'll need to come to William's house to find me, where they'll be welcomed as well as any of your family looking for my help." She turned to William and said, "Let's go."

William clucked to the horses and the wagon began moving slowly away. When they arrived home, all the family came out to help unload and carry Anarece's possessions into their own home.

As soon as William and Selene were alone, he said, "Did you know that Anarece plans to teach all her black magic or whatever she has to our daughter?"

Selene answered, "Yes, I do. We talked about it and, the more we talked, the more I realized that Hiba is different. I'm not surprised that Anarece understood. I'm not sure I like it, but I'm not sure it's not the right thing to happen."

Life resumed to a sort of normalcy. William went to work with the oranges every day, often accompanied by Adaza.

Jesse completed or avoided being assigned chores and spent his days wandering in the woods. William had bought Jesse a small twenty-two caliber rifle, so Jesse often came home with small game for their dinner table.

Selene went about her housework and, occasionally, when she could corral Adaza or get Hiba separated from Anarece, she had the girls help with the household chores and taught them the duties of taking care of a house.

Teacher and student spent hours together. Some of the time was spent taking care of Jairus and, the rest of the time, they walked together close to the swampy areas or among the tall pine trees, gathering samples of roots, tree bark, and berries.

Anarece explained the preparation and the usage of natural remedies for sickness and wounds. Hiba was an eager student and learned rapidly.

19

Surprise Visitors

Caleb's family increased by one. His daughter Callie was a prim, blond-haired beauty. She was now seven, going on twenty. She didn't care for the outdoors, and she would rather stay in her mother's footsteps.

Callie insisted on helping Rosie with household chores and told her mom in confidence that she'd marry Ira as soon as she was old enough. Caleb longed for a son but no other children came along. He felt of Ira was his son and treated him as such. He taught Ira all he could about farming and ranching. Ira had grown into a strong young man and carried his share of the work.

One day, Caleb stepped out the front door. He was startled to see two horsemen approaching. He knew Roberts' riders, but these were not Roberts' men.

As the riders grew near, he saw one of the riders seemed familiar. One man was average size, around six feet tall. His shoulders were broad, and he might have been a little beefy at one time but, now, he was thin as was common after the war. Years of poor food and sometimes none at all had reduced his stature. Caleb recognized him. It was Jack Hawkins, the Texan that everyone called Tex.

Tex recognized Caleb and a smile came to his face. "Cal," he said, "word was that you were killed. I'm glad to see you made it through." He continued, "I don't think you ever met Joe Standish here. He's a good fellow; just talks funny like they do in Virginia, but otherwise a good man."

Joe was a thin, sallow-faced man with one arm. The sleeve of his left arm was pinned to his chest.

Caleb relaxed as he realized the riders didn't know of his walking away from the war. He told the men to get down and then asked, "Where're you headed. This place isn't on the road to anywhere so, while I'm glad to see you, I'm surprised you showed up here."

The men dismounted and Caleb shook hands with them.

Tex answered, "We met a fellow named Bascomb who said there were ranches in this area that might need help. He mentioned your name and I wondered if it was you. It looks like you're doing well and you have a home and family. Maybe you could use some help. We'll work for food and a place to sleep."

Caleb replied, "If you'd like to stay on here, you can sleep in the barn until we can build you a place to stay. I can use some help with the cattle."

Tex was quick to speak up, "We'll be glad to stay. Since the war, we've roamed around, working a week in a place and then moving on. We're tired of being on the trail and would welcome a regular place to stay."

Caleb knew that some ranchers no longer let the cattle scatter into the woods and swamps. The cowboys kept them formed into a large herd. They'd follow the herd as it moved from place to place, looking for good grass.

This was necessary to combat the cattle rustling that had become common. Many men with no roots settled in Florida and rustling cattle was a lucrative trade. Some cattlemen would buy cattle with little concern about where they came from. With cattle bringing fifteen dollars each, protecting them was important.

Caleb told them he'd welcome their help. "But, before

you agree, you need to know that I have a partner in this ranch. His name is William and he's a black man. He and his wife live nearby and are frequent visitors and they have meals with us. Also, another black, Freman, is sleeping in the barn and works here. Sleep in the barn tonight and think things over. You can tell me in the morning if you still want to stay. I understand if you don't but, after meeting William, I understand that though a man may be a different color, they're people too."

Tex and Joe looked at each other and then back at Caleb.

Caleb continued "There won't be any money for a while. All I can offer you is a barn to sleep in and food when we have it. Sometimes it gets a little scarce."

He looked questioningly at Joe.

Seeing the look, Joe said, "Don't you worry about me. I may not be the whole man I once was, but I'll earn my keep. Anytime I don't, just say the word and I'll be gone."

Caleb, embarrassed, replied, "I'm sure you'll do. I need all the help I can get. I'm glad you men came along, Both of you.

The door opened and Rosie and Callie stepped outside. Caleb said, "This is my wife, Rosie, and our daughter, Callie."

Both the men took off their hats and nodded. Tex said, "We're glad to meet you both." Looking at Caleb, Tex continued, "You've done really well, Cal. I'm glad for you."

Caleb replied, "Thank you Tex. You and Joe take your horses to the barn. There are corn shucks you can throw down for them to eat and maybe a little corn also. After you see to them, come back and Rosie and Callie can rustle up some food."

Tex replied, "That'll be fine. Food has been scarce on the trail. We've eaten so many rabbits that our ears are getting long."

The men led their horses to the barn, unsaddled them,

and turned them loose in the corral attached to the barn. Tex found the corn shucks for them to eat. With that, the men walked back to the house. Joe led, followed by a bowlegged Tex.

Rosie opened the door and invited the men inside. She had tin plates filled with beans and cups of hot coffee.

Another plate held a mound of corn pone. Each plate had a spoon carved from oak wood. The men sat and began eating with no conversation. After a while, they finished the food and pushed back from the table.

"That was fine," said Tex.

Joe nodded his agreement. "It's been a while since we've sat at a table. I wasn't sure we still know how to sit at one and have a meal."

With a smile, Rosie said, "Well, you boys might not remember a table, but you sure recalled how to eat."

They laughed, "Yes, Ma'am. We know how to eat just fine, just haven't had much practice lately."

Caleb and the two men sat at the table with cups of coffee and discussed the war and conditions since it was over. Soon, the men, tired from their journey, went to the barn to sleep. Caleb walked with them and introduced Freman.

Tex looked at Freman and said, "Well, Freman, I guess the world is changing and we all have some changing to do. We'll be staying for a spell and I have to warn you, I snore a lot but, if you can put up with that, we'll be okay."

Freman looked dubious, but nodded his assent. Tex and Joe each retrieved a rough cotton blanket from their saddlebags and spread them over corn shucks, pleased to be sleeping with a roof over their heads.

After breakfast the next morning, Caleb went to see William. Selene invited him in and poured him a cup of coffee. Caleb said, "Two men from my old regiment showed up at my door yesterday afternoon looking for work. I told them we could use their help. They'll work for their keep for now and later we could pay them."

William thought for a few moments, "What about the army? What do they think about your desertion?"

Caleb replied, "They thought that I'd been killed, but now think I served out my time. There doesn't seem to be a problem on that account. With their help, we can gather more cattle. Once we get enough for a herd, we'll have enough help to follow the herd as it grazes and also enough to make our own drives to market."

William agreed with the idea and promised to meet Caleb the next morning and begin gathering more cattle.

When William arrived the next morning, Caleb had a wagon hitched up and loaded. It contained tents, cooking utensils, and food. In addition, it held irons for branding. He introduced William to Tex and Joe.

Joe drove the wagon and followed the riders. They rode for a few hours until they came to the corrals Caleb and William had used on other occasions. Caleb stopped the group and asked Joe to set up a camp.

While he did this, the others spread out and searched for any unbranded cattle or those who carried the SS brand. Freman was left behind to tend the garden and water the orange trees.

William, Caleb, and Tex rounded up a few cattle, but they were still scarce from the flood. Those around were extremely wild and hard to catch. Cattle were experts at hiding in the brush and palmetto thickets. They had corralled eight cows and no calves at the end of the day.

The camp was moved every couple of days and new areas were searched. The men combed the woods, collecting cows when they found them. The wagon was stocked with coffee and cornmeal.

Ira was given the task of hunting for game to supply meat. He returned to the camp every afternoon with small animals he had shot with his rifle. Joe occasionally cut swamp cabbage and collected berries.

Every afternoon, after an exhausting day of chasing cattle, roping and branding them, the men gathered around a campfire Joe made.

After eating whatever Joe had prepared, the men would sit around and talk. These were memorable times for Ira. While he enjoyed Caleb and Rosie's company, listening to the new men speak about the outside world was exciting. Ira listened with wonder as they talked.

Tex did most of the talking. In his slow drawl, he told stories of Texas. Ira listened with wonder at the tales. Tex told him these Florida cattle were toy animals compared to the wild steers of Texas. Ira couldn't imagine cows so large and, according to Tex, horns that were longer across than Ira was tall.

Ira listened to the stories of grasslands that swept for miles with no swamps. He couldn't imagine so much dry land and couldn't believe there was land with no alligators or cottonmouth moccasins. Tex did tell him that rattlesnakes were everywhere and bigger and meaner than Florida snakes.

"In fact," Tex said, "rattlesnakes are so long in Texas when ropes are scarce, we just tie two rattlesnakes together to make a lasso."

Tex told him of cattle drives that took months to complete and all the country he'd seen. When he told the stories of men who wore six guns on their side and of gunfights, Ira imagined himself walking down a dusty street with his own pistols strapped to his side.

Ira asked Tex if he thought he could take his horse, Blaze, out west with him if he went to Texas. Tex laughed and said, "Why boy, that little horse would be laughed out of Texas. We grow them *big* in Texas. Everything is bigger in Texas. It's a big land with big men and bigger animals. I'm six feet tall and considered a midget in Texas."

Ira took this all in. He decided to go to Texas one day

to see all that Tex had described. He was more than a little disappointed that Blaze would be looked down on in Texas and didn't like the thought of leaving her behind. He could just visit Texas and come back to his horse. He wasn't sure about living where all the men were as big as Tex described.

One night, as Tex extolled the bigness of all of Texas, Joe made a rare comment. He said in all seriousness, "I suppose there might be big things in Texas, but I know they raise the biggest storytellers."

Tex replied with a hurt look on his face, "Why, Joe, I'm hurt that you think I don't tell the truth."

Joe said, "Now, Tex, I never said you would tell a lie on purpose, but I do think that you might stretch the truth a mighty long way."

At the end of three months, the men had collected over one hundred head of cattle and branded all of them. The steers were neutered and the older bulls would be among the ones driven to market on the next drive.

William and Caleb alternated going home during that period of time to catch up with work around the ranch. They each spent two weeks helping with the cattle and two weeks at home.

The men kept the cattle bunched and, as a section of grass was depleted, they moved them along to another grazing spot.

Caleb looked over the herd. The number of livestock was encouraging, and they gathered more as they moved along so that in a few months there would be enough to drive some to market and leave enough to grow the herd.

Caleb told Tex and Joe that he and Ira would look after the herd to give them a break to go back to the ranch for a few days and visit the settlement. He gave them money to replace their clothing and boots since all of theirs were worn and threadbare from riding through the rough brush.

Caleb enjoyed these days with the cattle. He felt

disconnected from the ranch when he was no longer the sole protector of the cattle. He needed the men, but having them made him think he was avoiding his duty.

Occasionally, they saw wolves, bears, and panthers that were a threat to the calves. The grown cattle were in no danger. The bulls, with their sharp horns, protected the herd from predators. The cattle had grown up in the wild and could take care of themselves. The calves were vulnerable if they could be separated from the herd.

Caleb told the men to shoot any alligator that was large enough to do damage to cattle drinking from the swamp waters. A large alligator could drag a full-grown cow into the water.

After the men returned wearing new clothing, Caleb and a reluctant Ira rode back to the ranch house. There was work to be done and the garden had to be enlarged to help feed their increased number.

Ira missed the campfire talks with Tex and his stories of Texas. He told Caleb and Rosie that he was going to Texas to at least look around. "I just might move out there. It sounds like a great place to live with lots to do."

Caleb was sitting on the front porch after breakfast one morning, when he was surprised to see Roberts riding up.

After exchanging greetings, Roberts dismounted and sat by Caleb. He said, "Some of the men are getting together at the Yates' Ranch about a five or six-hours ride from here. I'd like for you to come along with me. There'll be a discussion about some common problems we ranchers face."

Caleb replied, "I'll ride along. What kind of problems are we discussing? My problems are with natural things like weather and wild animals killing my calves and not much can be done about those things."

"No, Caleb. You're right about that. But, there are other problems that, while they don't bother us now, could in the future. It's a good idea for us to get together because it's better to have all of us face any problem rather than facing it alone."

"Okay. Give me a few minutes to tell Rosie. I suppose we'll be gone overnight. I can also get William to come along since he's involved with the ranch as much as I am."

Roberts hesitated a moment and then said, "I think it'll be better for just the two of us to go to the meeting. Some ranchers might be a little uncomfortable with William. He's a little outspoken."

Caleb didn't like leaving William out but agreed to go with Roberts. He said, "Okay, but I'll bring Ira also. He's a man now and needs to be a part of anything concerning the ranch."

After telling Rosie, the three rode off towards the Yates Ranch. They reached the ranch and saw that several wagons and saddle horses were already there. They rode up to the barn where the men had gathered. Roberts knew many men, including Yates and introduced them to Caleb and Ira. Yates introduced those Roberts didn't know.

Yates stepped up on a raised platform so the men could see him and announced, "Okay, men, everyone is here that's coming. I want to thank all of you for showing up and I believe we'll all benefit from getting together. Some of us have been talking about two problems that some of us already have and all of you will be affected to some length. The first one is cattle rustlers. I think all of us are missing cattle, and we won't know how many until roundup. Even then, it's hard to tell due to the size of the range they cover. I'm told that a ranch due west of us is buying a lot of cows and isn't too particular about brands. There are a lot of men home from the war who either can't find work or choose not to. Many of them have taken the easy way to make a living by selling our cows. Then, too, there are the freed slaves roaming the country with no way of making a living. They steal anything they can get their hands on. So far, the men appointed by the Yankees to positions of authority aren't interested in doing anything about the problem."

Yates paused as the men made comments among themselves. He held up his hands for quiet and said, "The second problem is the 15th Amendment that the Yankees just passed. It gives the freed slaves the right to vote and elect our officials. This law means the sorriest nigger out there counts the same as the best of you, and the Yankee government will back them up."

This time the comments from the assembled men were angry outbursts and spoken threats.

"Hold on, men," Yates called out. "We have to get together on these problems. Singly, we can't solve either problem, but together, there are some things we can do. We have a sheriff now, but this is a big area for him to cover. He must get along with the Yankees, so he might be of little use to us. I don't think he'll interfere if we handle some of our own problems. I suggest that we form a group like the Cattle Guard during the war. We can track the rustlers, thieves, and crooked ranchers and deal with them. When anyone discovers cattle are missing, the call will go out and our riders will assemble to track down the rustlers or anyone who has our cattle."

"How about the nigger vote?" someone called out.

"Why, we'll handle it the same way. We'll volunteer some men to help the sheriff safeguard the voting places during election time. If some of our boys discourage the niggers from voting, that's how it'll be."

The comments from the crowd were clearly in favor of this. Roberts called out, "Wait a minute. Yates, are you talking about forming a band of Klansmen?"

"No," Yates replied. "The Yankees would be all over us if we tried that. I'm talking about a cattlemen's group to safeguard our property and chase down outlaws. Everything we do will be legal and above board."

"In that case," Roberts said, "I'm in favor. Me and my

boys will ride with you."

Many other men joined in their approval and willingness to ride with Yates. They all knew that some of the activities wouldn't be considered precisely legal to the Yankees, but the ranchers had to stick together.

Caleb was uneasy about the whole affair. While he could see the threats from rustlers and would readily ride against them, the voting thing would take some thinking.

Yates ended the meeting, but invited all who had ridden a distance to stay the night in his barn. "Lots of hay here," he said, "for you to sleep on and feed your animals. The women folk will be bringing out food for everyone and I just happen to have a couple of jugs to fight off the cold, cure snakebite, or help your rheumatism."

Everyone laughed at this declaration and had spirited discussions about which ailment they needed tending. All in all, everyone there found a reason to sample the contents of the jugs. Soon, laughter and good-natured kidding filled the barn. Caleb joined the group and took a glass of the brew. He sat and sipped it slowly and considered the results of this meeting.

The barn door opened and a woman came in carrying dishes of food. Yates introduced her as his wife. Everyone nodded their 'hellos.' She was followed by two girls who were also carrying food. The food was placed on a board suspended on two barrels at either end.

Yates said, "These are my two oldest girls. The taller one is Sarah, and the shorter one is Janie."

Caleb joined the other men as they moved to fill tin plates with food. He looked around for Ira and saw him motionless, staring at Sarah Yates. Caleb had to speak to him twice to get his attention.

Finally, Ira followed Caleb to the makeshift table with another glance toward Sarah. Sarah stood at the end of the table and offered him a tin plate for his food.

"Hello," she said. "My name is Sarah. I haven't seen you before."

Ira tried to reply, but no words would come out. He just stood there and stared at her. She pushed the plate into his hands and he managed to grasp it in one hand before it fell to the ground. He looked down at the plate as if surprised by its presence.   Looking back at her, he managed to say, "Ira. My name is Ira."

After saying that, he moved along, placing food on the plate given to him. He followed Caleb and took a seat against the barn wall.

Caleb said, "I see you might have a new friend. She's very pretty."

Ira's face turned bright red. "No such thing," he said. "I just told her my name. That's all."

Caleb laughed at Ira's discomfort. He realized how remote they'd been on the ranch with only the men for Ira to meet. Caleb finished his meal and moved away to talk to a group of men. Ira had barely touched his food.

Sarah walked over to him and sat next to him. "What's the matter," she asked. "Aren't you hungry? Don't you like the food I cooked?"

Startled, he replied, "No, uh, yes."

"Which is it, no or yes?"

Her nearness had his mind reeling and words almost impossible to form.

He stammered, "The food is fine. I'm just not hungry."

"Since you're not going to eat my good food, would you like to go for a walk?"

"What?" he again stammered.

"Walk," she replied. "You don't eat, but you're here, so I suppose you can walk."

He looked around the room for some relief. Stalling for time to get his thoughts settled down, he managed to say. "I'm not sure. Caleb might need me for something."

"Come on, silly," she said. "A little walk won't hurt you. I'm sure Caleb will find you if he needs you."

She took the plate from his hand and stood. "I'm going to put your plate away and be right back. I can help you get up if you have a problem."

After saying that, she walked away with the plate. Ira's eyes followed her every move. She placed the plate on the table, turned around, and walked toward him. He quickly rose to his feet and stood nervously waiting for her. She walked over, took his hand, and led him through the barn door to the outside. He followed along in a trance.

After a while, Sarah said, "You don't eat much and you don't talk much, do you?"

Ira replied, "I eat lots and I talk a lot to the men I work with. I don't know how to talk to a girl."

"Well," she said, "you talk to girls the same way you talk to men."

He reddened when he recalled some of the talk around the campfire. That talk surely wouldn't be proper for a girl. Searching for a safe subject, he said, "I have my very own horse. Her name is Blaze. I named her myself. I can show her to you if you'd like."

She smiled, "You can talk. I'm glad you have a horse, but horses are all I see around here. Maybe you could come over again with Blaze and take me for a ride."

Ira was speechless again. As he tried to unscramble his brain, Mrs. Yates came outside and called for Sarah to come back inside and help clean up the food and plates.

Before leaving, Sarah touched Ira's arm, squeezed it lightly, and said, "Don't forget you owe me a ride one day very soon."

Before he could answer, she walked away to join her mom. The spot on his arm where she had squeezed seemed to burn with the memory of her hand. He recovered enough of his senses and walked back inside the barn. He was disappointed that he couldn't get another look at Sarah. He sat on an overturned barrel and thought of all the things he should have said.

The men broke up their groups. Most of them found a spot on the barn floor to spread their blankets for a bed after gathering hay to soften the hard floor.

Ira found a place for his bed. Soon, snores filled the barn as men fell asleep; some sleepiness was aided by Yates' jugs. Ira lay awake long after most of the men slept. His mind was a jumble of thoughts. One thought brought him fully awake, and that thought was of Sarah.

The next morning, Caleb told Ira to saddle the horses for the ride home. Ira searched around for a final look at Sarah. She didn't appear. After saddling the horses, Caleb, Roberts, and Ira left the barn, mounted, and started the journey home. As they rode past the ranch house, Sarah walked out onto the porch, waving to Ira as he rode by. "Don't forget," she called. "You owe me a ride."

Ira's face turned red and he nodded as he rode past.

Caleb looked at Ira. "What's this?" he asked. "You've found a girlfriend? I didn't know you were looking for one."

Ira nudged Blaze in the ribs and moved ahead of Caleb and Roberts. He couldn't ignore the chuckles of the two men and he didn't share their mirth. He needed to talk to someone. He just wasn't sure who.

As Ira rode ahead of the two men, Roberts commented, "I guess this could give you a rough time with William."

Caleb rode for a while and then answered, "William is a good man. He saved my life and I want him by my side if we chase rustlers. He'll take voting seriously and trying to stop him will be trouble enough for anyone, and I fear what that'll bring."

Roberts, after a delay, said, "I'm not a man to tell another how to live his life, but you seem like the kind of man we need. You might have to come to a decision about your dealings with your own kind and what's good for your family."

Caleb didn't reply to that comment. They continued riding.

Rosie greeted the men when they reached home. She invited Roberts to come inside and eat. "Thank you for the offer," he said, "but I better get home. My wife will be concerned." With that, he turned his horse and rode away.

Caleb dismounted and took Buck to the barn, unsaddled him, and wiped him down with corn shucks. He then turned him loose in the corral and returned to the house. Rosie had a meal on the table and they sat down and ate. Ira seemed distracted and had little to eat.

When Rosie questioned him about this, he said he was just not hungry. Caleb didn't comment. He was quite sure he knew what was on Ira's mind.

He told Rosie about the meeting and his misgivings about how it would affect William. He explained that the ranchers and farmers getting together to protect their livestock and facing the Yankee invaders as a group was a wise move. What he feared was that many of the group would think it their duty to punish any Negro who tried to improve his life. Many men who once were indifferent to the Negro now hated them, for they were everyday reminders of the stinging loss by the hands of the North. Caleb would fight for the ranch and stock but wouldn't be a part of harassing the Negros.

"You should ride and tell William and Selene," Rosie told Caleb. "They must be on guard."

"I know," he replied. "I feel trapped between two sides. I know and respect William and Selene and will do all I can to help protect them. On the other hand, I don't want to be at odds with the other ranchers."

"I understand that," Rosie said. "But William and Selene are our friends. It's only right to put them first, and we must do what is right."

The two finished the meal in silence, Caleb in deep thought. After eating, he told Rosie he'd ride over to see William. He went to the barn and saddled another horse for the ride, leaving Buck to rest after the morning ride. Buck raised his head and watched Caleb ride off as if wondering why he wasn't being ridden.

Caleb rode up to William and Selene's home. They greeted him from the front porch. William was leaning against the wall, smoking his pipe.

Caleb dismounted and stepped onto the porch.

"Hello," William said. "Welcome. Come and sit and have a smoke."

Selene asked, "Can I get you a drink of water?"

"No, thank you, Selene. I just came over to talk to William. In fact, you should probably sit in on the conversation since it concerns you and your family."

Caleb looked at William, who had a puzzled look on his face but didn't ask any questions. He pulled up a chair for himself and offered one to Caleb. The two men sat and puffed on their pipes, looking across the field in front of the house rather than at each other. Selene went inside and came back out and took a seat.

Caleb told the two about the meeting and formation of men to fight cattle rustling.

William took a mouthful of smoke and gently blew it out, watching the smoke curl into the air. He then said, "I take it from the fact I wasn't invited to this meeting that there's more than rustling involved. I'm sure your white friends wouldn't object to me being shot at by rustlers. There must be a reason I wasn't invited. What about you. Are you to be a party to this?"

Caleb replied, "You're my friend and as far as I'm concerned if there's trouble for either of us, we'll face it together. I'll ride with these men to stop rustlers or other lawbreakers and would like for you to ride with me. But, I won't be a part of denying any man's legal rights, be they black or white. I'm concerned that some men might not think the same way."

William sat and watched more smoke curl up from his pipe. Selene put her hand out and placed it on his arm. He finally spoke, "I appreciate you for bringing me the news, Caleb, and your friendship. I know what's coming. The men will try to stamp out rustling. Once that's done, they'll go about keeping us in our place. You might tell your friends not to come around here, bothering my family. They won't be welcome."

Caleb rode home with his mind in turmoil. He had thought that after the war was finally over, the land could find peace again. It seemed that men would always find differences in their concepts of right and wrong. Once the concepts were accepted as facts, men would go to any extreme to reinforce their opinion.

Men of similar concepts would band together and soon find enough differences from other groups to accelerate hard ideas. Differences would begin as minor things, but misunderstandings and misconceptions would escalate from irritation to anger and, in some cases, violence. The differences could grow within groups making the separation more remote.

20

Sarah

Rosie commented to Caleb her concern that Ira seemed distracted and went about his daily chores with little interest. He laughed and told her about the girl that Ira had met. Rosie told him it wasn't funny. Ira had no contact with girls and needed some input on how to handle himself around them.

Callie overheard the conversation. After Caleb returned to his work, she said to Rosie, "I don't want Ira to have a girlfriend. I plan to marry him as soon as I'm old enough."

Rosie put her arm around Callie and said, "Don't you worry about that. It'll be long before I'm ready for you to consider marriage. Besides that, Ira's like your brother."

Callie replied that it didn't matter and she'd wait until she was older, but Ira was the one she wanted.

Rosie decided to talk with Ira. That evening, after dinner, she directed Callie to clean up the dishes. She walked outside and saw Ira at the corral feeding his horse.

Rosie walked up to him and said, "Ira, we've lived apart from other people and I know it's difficult to learn to talk to strangers, especially girls."

Ira responded, "I'm going back to join Tex and the others with the herd. I'm at home with them and have no problem talking. When I get around others, I get confused and don't know what to say."

Rosie chuckled, "You mean around girls?"

Ira's face turned red as he replied, "I've only talked to one girl and don't plan to do so again. As I said, I want to help with the cattle. Tex has told me all about Texas and I plan on going there, maybe with him."

"Maybe so, but come talk to me if you change your mind. Remember, I used to be a girl and know what a young girl wants to hear."

Ira looked startled, looking at Rosie. He'd never thought of comparing her with the likes of Sarah. The two were different in his mind. Rosie was Rosie, but Sarah... he was unsure exactly what she was. He only knew that he was anxious to see her again but afraid to do so. It was much simpler to go back to the campfire with the riders.

Rosie remembered her days as a girl and thought a girl would be lucky to have a man like Ira. She told him, "Okay, Ira. Go back to the cattle. Think about Sarah. Remember, a pretty girl doesn't like to wait. Some other man will come along and she might be gone."

Ira felt a tight feeling in his chest. He had no idea of going back to see her, but the thought of someone else seeing her was unsettling. He thought for a few minutes and said, "Maybe I'll ride over to the Yates' ranch after all. I want to look at their ranch and get ideas for our cattle."

Rosie smiled. "That would be a good idea. And, you might learn something new."

'And,' she mused, 'it has nothing to do with cattle or ranching.'

Ira saddled Blaze and headed to the Yates' ranch. He rode with confidence but, when he saw the ranch house, he began to get nervous about how to proceed.

On reaching the house, the door opened and Sarah stepped out onto the porch. "Took you long enough to come to see me," she said. "I thought you'd forgotten about me."

Ira sat on his horse and looked down at her, unsure

what he should do or say.

"Well," she said, "I see you're still as talkative as ever. Good thing I can talk enough for us both. Get off that silly horse and come inside. You're just in time for supper."

Ira dismounted and was shocked when Sarah took his hand in hers and led him inside.

Yates was sitting in his favorite chair, smoking a pipe. He looked up and didn't seem surprised to see Ira standing with Sarah.

He stood and walked over to Ira, shook hands, and said, "Welcome Ira, it's good to see you again. Have a seat"

Sarah led Ira to a sofa. She sat down and motioned for Ira to sit by her. He sat just as Mrs. Yates and Janie walked into the room.

Janie giggled and said, "Sarah has a boyfriend"

Mrs. Yates told Janie to be quiet and added her welcome to Ira.

Ira realized he hadn't yet spoken a word since arriving. He stammered, "I didn't mean to put you out. I mean feeding me and all. I just came over to look over your ranch."

Mrs. Yates smiled and Mr. Yates replied, "I'll be glad for you to look over our place. Maybe Sarah can show you around before supper."

Sarah looked at Ira. "Silly me. I thought you had come to see me. Now, I find out you'd rather look at cows than me."

Ira stammered, "No, No. I don't want to look at cows. I like looking at you just fine."

Then, realizing what he had just said, his face turned a crimson red.

Janie laughed and said, "He likes to look at Sarah. Sarah has a boyfriend."

Yates tried to come to Ira's aid. "You girls stop picking on Ira. He's our guest and we need to treat him as one."

He turned to Ira and asked about Caleb and his cattle. Ira was relieved at this rescue and was able to carry on a conversation with Yates while not looking in Sarah's direction.

Ira was relieved when Yates pushed back his chair and said, "Ira, let's me and you sit on the front porch."

Ira eagerly followed him out the door and both sat.

Yates explained his operation and answered Ira's questions. The door opened and Sarah came out. Yates got up, excused himself, and went inside.

Sarah appeared and held out her hand to Ira. "Since you came to see the ranch, you can take me for a walk while you look at it."

Ira stood and Sarah led him outside. She was different from the teasing girl she had been earlier. Without her customary smile, she looked at him and said, "I'm glad you came to see me, Ira. I've been looking forward to seeing you again and was afraid you might not come."

Ira walked along in a daze. He not only was walking with this beautiful creature and holding her hand, but she had been afraid he might not come to see her. The day took on a whole new light for him. He was ten feet tall and nothing could hurt him. He wanted to yell out something but couldn't think what or who. Instead, he said. "I'd like for you to meet Rosie."

"Who's Rosie? Is that your mom?"

"No. Rosie is Caleb's wife, but she treats me like a mom. My real mom died from the same fever that killed my Pa."

Sarah quickly said, "I'm so sorry about your folks. I don't know what I'd do if I lost mine. But I'd love to meet Rosie. When can I?"

Ira was not prepared for the question. "Well," he said after a long pause, "I guess any time you want to meet her, you can."

The reply came quickly. "Right away. It's too late today, but how about tomorrow?"

Thoughts raced thru his mind, for things were moving too fast for him to absorb it all. *'I want her to meet Rosie,'* he thought, but how to explain to Rosie when he had denied the existence of a girlfriend last week.

Ira thought, *'Is she a girlfriend?'* Rosie asked this in a round-about way. She hadn't said so in words, but her actions seemed that she had taken it for granted they were more than just friends.

He chose his words carefully, "I'll go home and come back later with the wagon to take you to meet Rosie. In fact, I'll also introduce you to our friends, William and Selene."

"Nonsense!" was the quick reply. "I don't need a wagon. I have a horse and know how to ride. Did you take me for someone who could only cook and clean up the dinner table? You need to understand right now if we're to be together, we'll be together. Anything you do, I'll help you do. Come now. We must tell my folks we're going to meet your family tomorrow and that you'll be calling on me in the future."

This statement brought another scene to Ira's mind that he hadn't envisioned. The thought of facing Mr. Yates with this information brought waves of dread to his mind. He had little time to dwell on this new challenge, for Sarah turned and, pulling on his hand, said, "Let's go right now and tell my folks the news."

They soon reached the Yates' yard. The door opened and Mrs. Yates stepped outside. With a wave of her hand, she said, "Come on, you two. You're back just in time for supper. Following her inside, they were met by Sarah's younger sister, Janie, who, with a smirk, said, "Sarah has herself a boyfriend, or she used him to get out of helping fix supper. I suppose she'll have an excuse not to help me clean up."

Ira's face burned with embarrassment and was at first relieved and then panicked by Sarah's reply to her sister. "It's none of your business, busy body. Just run along and tend to your own business. I'll help clean up and wash the dishes since Ira will want to talk to dad after supper."

Yates took a seat at the head of the table and motioned for Ira to take the seat on his right. Sarah sat next to Ira and Janie sat across the table with Mrs. Yates.

Ira had never eaten with anyone other than at home and was nervous and afraid to make a move. Yates carved the beef roast that Mrs. Yates had cooked. Everyone passed their plates to him and he placed generous portions on them and passed them back. Once everyone had slices of roast, Mrs. Yates passed around bowls of vegetables, potatoes, and bread.

Ira spooned portions from the bowls onto his plate, trying to keep his hands from shaking due to his nervousness. It all looked good and he was hungry since he hadn't eaten since breakfast. He waited until Sarah picked up her fork to begin eating before picking up his. He saw that she had placed a napkin on her lap so he did the same.

Ira was startled when Yates said, "Well Ira, how was your little tour of our ranch?

Ira had just taken a bite of the beef and almost choked trying to answer. "It was fine sir, you have a nice ranch."

Ira barely tasted the food as the family carried on a conversation around him. They asked questions to get him involved in the talk. He answered them but offered no other input.

After what seemed forever, the meal was finished. Mr. Yates stood and said, "That was a fine meal, and now Ira and I will go outside so I can smoke my pipe while you girls clean up."

With that, he motioned Ira to follow him outside. They both took seats. Ira sat in silence as Yates took out his pipe and rapped it on the chair leg to clear any debris left to form the last smoke.

Next, came the placing tobacco in the bowl and

tamping it down with his thumb, then lighting it. Placing it in his mouth, he took in a long draw breath and blew out a cloud of smoke.

Turning to Ira, he said, "Nothing like a good smoke after a meal. It makes a man feel really at peace with the world. A bit of liquor would go well, but Mrs. Yates frowns on that. Are you a drinking or smoking man, Ira? Not that I'm against it, mind you. I just want to know before I offer you either."

"No, sir. I don't do either. Never got around to doing either."

They sat quietly for a few moments, which seemed like hours to Ira. Yates broke the silence. "I overheard Sarah tell her mom she's going with you to meet your folks. I'm taking from that you're serious about my girl."

"Yes, sir. I like her fine. She confuses me a lot and I don't know how to act around her, but I like her and like being around her."

Yates laughed. "Son, you might as well get used to that. No man ever understood a woman, and they change about the time you figure them out. Believe me. You're not the first or last to face that problem. Sarah is old enough to make up her own mind and too stubborn not to change it once she makes it up. I do ask you to go slow and be sure before you take her away. She's dear to me and her mom, and I'd take it poorly if you or anyone else does her harm."

Ira could only reply, "Yes, sir."

Ira had planned to spend the night in the barn. When he mentioned fixing himself a bed in one of the stalls, Yates said, "There's plenty of room in the house."

They stepped inside and were met by Mrs. Yates. She told Ira to follow and led him to a small room at the back of the house. It was furnished with a small bed and a nightstand with a lighted lantern on its top.

"You should be comfortable enough here. It's nothing

fancy, but the bedding is clean." She turned and walked out the door, closing it behind her.

Ira sat down on the bed, more of a cot than a full-size bed. The bed was of no concern to him. His mind swirled at today's activities. He took off his shoes and lay back on the bed, leaving the lantern glowing on the nightstand.

He lay there going over a myriad of thoughts. The sounds of the house came to him with the stirrings of the Yates household. Soon, everything was quiet. Still, Ira lay there. Sleep was a long way off since he couldn't stop his mind from thoughts of Sarah.

He heard a soft, shuffling noise and the door to his room opened. Sarah stepped through. Leaving the door open, she walked over and sat on the edge of the bed.

Ira was petrified, afraid to move or say anything. Sarah laughed her little teasing laugh and said, "You didn't tell me 'goodnight,' so I brought you another blanket in case it gets cool tonight." She placed the blanket on the bed, and with a soft, "Good night," she leaned over and kissed him quickly on his cheek. "You go to sleep now and I'll wake you for breakfast. Then, we can go meet the rest of your family."

She rose, lifted the globe of the lantern, and blew out the flame. Then, turning, she left the room, leaving Ira in the dark and confused.

Hours later, he finally slept but was awake early. He heard noises of the household beginning to stir and, after a soft knock, heard Sarah's voice directing him to come for breakfast. He had slept in his clothes so, putting on his shoes, he went to join the Yates family for breakfast.

Breakfast was a little better for him to handle and he ate heartily. After breakfast, he and Mr. Yates walked to the barn and Ira helped with the morning chores. He gave Blaze fresh hay to eat and saddled and bridled her for the ride home.

Yates saddled a horse for Sarah. The two men led the

saddled horses to the house and arrived as Sarah stepped outside.

Seeing her horse ready to ride, she said, "Thanks for saddling my horse for me, but I just want you to know I could've done so myself."

Yates laughed, "Quit giving this boy a rough time. I saddled your horse. Wouldn't blame him if he rode off without you."

Sarah looked at Ira. "Is that right? Are you thinking of riding off without me?"

"I told you to stop it, Sarah," her dad replied. "He had no such thoughts, but might be better off if he did."

Ira stood mute. Then, putting his foot in the stirrup, he swung into the saddle. "I guess we should be going. It's a good ride to my house."

Sarah swung into the saddle of the other horse, saying to no one that, since no help was offered, she must reach the saddle by herself. Yates again told her to behave and, with Ira leading the way, began the ride to see Rosie.

They rode side by side, warmed by the bright Florida sun. Neither was aware of their surroundings. Ira rode as if in a dream, occasionally sneaking a look at Sarah. The ride over seemed to go on forever and he was shocked at how quickly they arrived at their destination.

They rode up to the cabin and Rosie came out at the sound of the horses. She looked at Ira with a quizzical look and waited for him to speak.

"Rosie, this is Sarah. She's a friend of mine and I'd like you to meet her. Sarah, this is Rosie."

Rosie, with a broad smile, stepped forward and said, "Welcome, Sarah. Get down and come inside. You must be thirsty from your long ride. Ira, you can look after the horses while we get to know each other."

Sarah got down and followed Rosie inside. Once inside, she saw Selene sitting at the kitchen table drinking a cup of coffee. Rosie said, "Sarah, this is my friend, Selene. Selene, this is Sarah, a friend of Ira."

Selene rose to greet Sarah. "I'm glad to meet you, Sarah. Rosie told me Ira had found a new friend and looks like he found a pretty one," she said with a smile.

Rosie saw the hesitancy on Sarah's face and said, "Sarah, let me get you a glass of water as I promised."

Sarah looked at Rosie and said, "I really should go and help Ira with the horses. Mine gets a little skittish at times."

Sarah turned and hurriedly went outside, walking fast to the barn.

Ira was inside, taking off the saddles and preparing to wipe down the horses. He looked up in surprise as Sarah came into the barn and was more surprised and alarmed at the tears in her eyes.   "What's wrong?" he demanded.

Sarah walked up to him and said in a trembling voice, "A black woman is sitting at your table and Rosie says she's a friend. No black woman dares to sit at a white person's table and especially not introduced as a friend."

Ira, wiping her tears away, thought, *'I should have told her before coming over about Selene and William.'* It hadn't occurred to him that it would be a problem.

Ira gently took Sarah's hand, walked over to an upturned wooden crate, and asked her to sit. He began, "Selene is the wife of a man named William. Remember I told you that I'd introduce you to them?"

The reply came quickly, "You never told me they were Negroes. A white man doesn't introduce a white girl to black people. It's not proper."

Ira thought, *'How did my life get so complicated? Too many things are coming at me at once.'*

Collecting his thoughts, he began trying to explain about William and Selene. "Sarah, I know how folks feel about blacks and, until I met William, I felt much the same. William and Selene are different. They are smart and educated and work harder than anyone I know. You must understand, for they're part of my life and are partners with Caleb. William saved Caleb's life at some point in the past. Please try to understand."

Sarah looked at Ira with a look he couldn't decipher. "Saddle my horse for me, please, Ira. I'm going home."

Ira, feeling hopeless and with a sense of loss, complied. Once the horses were both saddled, Sarah said, "You need not ride with me. I know the way."

Ira quickly replied, "I'll ride along to see you safely home."

"Very well, but don't talk to me."

Rosie and Selene sat looking at each other after Sarah left the room. Selene broke the silence. "I'm sorry, Rosie. My being here was a shock for the girl and too much for her to accept."

Rosie replied, "It's not your fault, Selene. She would have to know about you and William at some point. Ira should have told her, but I'm sure he never thought of it. Men are short on common sense sometimes."

They heard hoofbeats and went outside and saw the two riders going away.

Ira tried to ride by Sarah's side, but she urged her horse to pull ahead every time he did. Finally, he reined Blaze to a position behind Sarah's horse and mutely followed.

Sarah dismounted and turned to go inside when they arrived at the Yates' ranch. The door opened and Yates, with a puzzled look on his face, said, "Well, I didn't expect you back this quick. Ira, do you want to get down and come inside?"

Sarah quickly retorted, "No. Ira has to get back home to his friends."

Having said that, she walked inside through the open door. Without further word, Ira turned his horse and rode away back down the trail towards home. His mind a whirlwind of confusion and a heart-rending feeling of loss.

218

21

Rustlers

William sat on the porch late in the afternoon, smoking his pipe and thinking about the progress achieved. He was proud of the orderly rows of trees and was content with the oranges and his family. The limitations placed on Jairus gave him mixed feelings of pity for Jairus and anger that illness had afflicted his son. He and Selene and the other children were healthy and robust.

As he sat with his thoughts, William was surprised to see a horse approaching. There were two figures on its back. He stood and the horse stopped at the edge of the porch.

The two people on the horse were Pony and Oconee. Pony was in front and sagged forward. Oconee sat behind him with her arms wrapped around him to hold him in the saddle.

William quickly went to the horse, catching Pony as he slipped from the saddle. Blood soaked the front of his shirt. William, holding Pony, looked up at Oconee. Her arms and dress front were also bloody.

William asked, "What happened?"

She replied, "We were driving some cattle that Pony had captured. We were taking them to add to the herd. Bad men shot him and stole the cattle. Pony tried to tell them that the cattle belonged to you and Caleb. They said they did not care. They shot him and took the cattle. I brought him to your home for I hear a root woman stays here."

Selene had come out of the house when she heard the conversation. She told William to bring Pony inside. Oconee dismounted and Selene went to her. "Are you hurt?"

"No, I am okay. Pony is hurt bad and needs help."

Selene followed William as he carried Pony into the house. He laid him on a bed and stood. Anarece appeared at his shoulder. She quickly knelt by Pony and began removing his shirt.

"Bring me hot water and a cloth," she ordered.

William, glad to have something to do, went to heat a pan of water and returned it to the bed where Pony lay. He watched as Anarece washed away the blood.

The bullet hole in Pony's chest was still bleeding. Anarece stood and went to her bed. Reaching under it, she brought out a gourd that had a corncob stopper. She walked back to Pony's side. "Bring me a lot of spider web," she ordered William. "It will stop the bleeding."

The spider web was easy to gather, as spiders were plentiful around the cabin. He brought it to Anarece, who was rubbing an ointment onto Pony's chest. She took the spider web and pressed it into the bullet hole.

She had William help turn him over and treated the area where the bullet had exited his back, which she plugged with more spider web. Pony groaned as they turned him over.

Anarece looked up into Oconee's anxious face. "He's lost a lot of blood, but the bullet went cleanly through. He should be okay, but he'll need to be quiet and rest up for a while."

William got down his rifle from pegs on the wall. He went to a shelf high along one wall and took down a pistol. He told Selene, "I must get the cattle back."

He walked to the barn and, after saddling a horse, he rode off to alert Caleb. He found Caleb working in the barn with Freman. He told them of Pony's being shot and the stolen cattle. Caleb quickly saddled his horse and told Freman to saddle one for himself. He went to the house and got rifles for both Freman and himself. He told Rosie what was going on. She made him wait while she packed a sack with corn pone, dried meat, and a coffee pot.

They didn't push the horses too hard, for they knew the herd couldn't move fast and a steady gait would catch up, keeping the horses fresh enough to follow.

They found the spot where Oconee had told them the cattle were when the rustlers had struck. The trail was evident, as the cattle were no longer slowly grazing as they moved but were compacted into a tighter bunch for driving at a faster pace. The rustlers weren't interested in the cattle gaining weight and they wanted to move as fast as possible to sell the herd before the pursuit, if any, could catch them.

William, Caleb, and Freman stopped around dusk and made camp for the night. They thought they could catch sight of the cattle the next day. They unsaddled and hobbled the horses. Soon, they had a fire going and boiled coffee. Dinner was corn pone that Rosie had packed.

As they sat around the small campfire, they were surprised to hear a rider approaching. William quickly got his rifle from the saddle scabbard. Caleb and Freman moved away from the campfire and took cover behind trees.

When the rider got close, he stopped the horse and called out to the camp. They were surprised to hear Ira's voice. William said, "Come on in. What are you doing out here?"

Ira rode into the camp and dismounted. He tied his horse to a low-hanging limb. William saw that Ira was leading a pack mule carrying burlap bags.

Ira replied, "I'm taking supplies to Tex and Joe. I followed the cattle tracks, thinking it would lead me to them."

Caleb told him about the cattle being stolen and Pony being shot.

Ira said, "What are you waiting on. They're getting away."

Caleb cautioned him to sit and have a cup of coffee. "We should catch sight of them tomorrow."

Ira was impatient to chase after the rustlers, but was finally convinced that caution was the best plan for now. The rustlers had proved by shooting Pony that they'd result to violence to keep the herd.

The trail was easy to follow, but it was evident that more cattle made the tracks than Pony had said he was driving. Around noon they came to where the rustlers had camped for the night. It looked like there were four men from boot tracks with more probably watching the herd. That would make at least five or six rustlers.

Ira was ready to pick up the pace to find the herd. Again, he was cautioned to keep calm. William said, "We'll catch up tonight. We'll hang back and then decide what to do."

Late that afternoon, they heard the noise of the cattle as they were being driven. William motioned for his group to stop. "We'll stop here and make a camp. The night is close and I don't want to stumble into their camp accidentally. I'll ride ahead and see when they stop for the night."

The others were unhappy to be left behind while William rode ahead, but finally agreed when William explained that it would be easier for one man to stay concealed. If he was spotted, one man alone wouldn't concern the thieves.

William rode ahead slowly, often stopping to listen. He stayed clear of open spaces and kept to the cover of trees or tall bushes. He circled to the left when he thought he was close to the herd. He estimated he was about a quarter of a mile to the west of the herd.

After riding at a fast walk for an hour, he rode slowly toward where he thought the herd would be. He rode to the edge of a group of thick scrub oak trees. He could see the herd through the openings between branches.

He dismounted, tied his horse to a tree, and proceeded on foot to the very edge of the scrub. Crouching low, he peeked through the leafy branches. He didn't think he could be seen from there.

The cattle were grazing and two riders circled them, keeping them closely bunched, but allowing them to feed on grass. William could see the smoke from a campfire set among pine trees just off the clearing.

He watched for a while but couldn't make out how many were around the camp from his vantage. He went back to his horse and led him away on foot to keep the noise down. As soon as he was far enough from the rustler's camp, he mounted and rode back to join his little party.

As they were having breakfast the next morning, they heard more riders coming. As the riders rode up, Caleb was surprised to see Yates riding with two other men.

Caleb said, "We're tracking rustlers who stole some of our cattle and shot our man who was driving them. They're not far ahead of us, so we can catch up."

Yates replied, "They stole cattle from me too, so we're all chasing the same outlaws."

Caleb said, "William, this is Mr. Yates. He owns a ranch near here. Mr. Yates, this is my business partner, William."

Yates replied, "Yeah, I've heard about him. We'll get the rustlers and then talk more."

Yates glanced sideways at Ira but didn't comment. Ira followed suit.

Yates asked. "How many rustlers are there?"

William replied, "There are at least five, maybe six or more, but I think six."

Yates looked around at the group of men. He brought two riders with him; one called Tyler and the other, Sam. The three added to Ira and Caleb meant five whites. William and Freman, made a total of seven.

Yates turned to Caleb and asked, "How much can we count on these?" He nodded at the black men.

Before Caleb could reply, William stepped up, "I have the same doubts about you and your men. Don't be concerned about us; just do your job."

Yates jerked as if struck. Being addressed like this by a black man was unheard of.

Caleb spoke up, "I'll vouch for these men. I've seen William in action. I feel sorry for any enemy of his."

Yates composed himself and said, "I know this trail. I've driven cattle south to Fort Bassinger more than once and that's probably where they're taking the cattle. They must make a big swing to the west to go around a big swamp. They can't drive the cattle through it, for it has deep water. We can cut across there and, traveling as fast as possible, come out in front of them. They'll be looking back for anyone chasing them. We can surprise them if we get in front."

No one disagreed with Yates, so the party followed his leadership. He led off, followed by the rest of them. They caught up to the tracks of the cattle, and the tracks turned to the west.

Yates led them to the east. Soon, they came to the swamp, and single file entered a world of cypress trees and coffee-colored water.

Yates knew his way and avoided deep water. As the group traveled, water snakes were bountiful, swimming slowly away from the riders. Some were harmless, according to Yates, but some were the deadly cottonmouth moccasin, whose bite would cause the flesh around the bite mark to die and a person or animal could lose an arm or leg or even their life. The horses sensed this and shied away from any snake that got too close. He warned the riders not to shoot the snakes. The gunfire would alert the rustlers.

Four hours later, the party left the swamp and everyone was glad to be on dry land again. They stopped for an hour to let the horses rest and eat. There was little conversation as the odd collection of riders sat on the ground.

The journey continued until Yates stopped the procession and said, "We should be ahead of them, and there's a good place for them to stop for the night a mile back."

They made camp in a group of trees and awaited the rustlers to catch up and stop for the night. Surprise would save lives when they confronted the gang.

Just before dusk, they heard the noise of cows bawling and the crack of the riders' whips as they drove the cattle.

William volunteered to head toward the sound of the cattle and report back as to the position of the herd and riders. After an hour, he returned and reported the rustlers had made camp as anticipated and only one man was minding the herd. "That rider will be a problem, for there's no way we can surprise them with him able to sound an alarm."

Freman spoke up, "Just point me in his direction and I'll take care of him."

Everyone looked at him in surprise, for he rarely spoke.

Feeling their stares, he said, "Trust me, I move quietly. It's getting dark now and I'm even darker. He'll never see me until it's too late."

They all mounted their horses and rode slowly until they could hear the movement of the cattle. Stopping, they all looked at Freman, who nodded and dismounted, handed his horse's reins to William, and said, "I'll be right back."

William looked at Freman. "You know you can't let that rider make any noise. A gunshot will alert the others."

Freman handed his rifle to William and said, "Here, take this. I have no need of it for this job and, you're right, no noise."

Freman went to the side of his horse, reached into the saddlebag, and took out a sheath with a knife handle protruding. As he pulled the knife free, the blade glistened in the moonlight.   Caleb shuddered at the sight of the knife and for what it would soon be used. He couldn't believe this mild-mannered man with a great singing voice could be taking on this job.

Freman turned and walked into the surrounding brush and trees and soon was out of sight.

The remaining men dismounted and tied the horses to limbs of nearby brushes. They'd go on foot from here once Freman returned. If he failed and an alarm was sounded, they'd remount and charge the camp. All dreaded this thought, for that meant some of them would suffer gunshot wounds, maybe fatal.

An hour passed and the men began to glance nervously around, for the waiting was the hardest of all activities. Each minute seemed to be hours.

And then, out of nowhere, Freman returned, leading a saddled horse. The dark stain visible on the saddle in the moonlight made no questions necessary. Someone was no longer a threat, thanks to Freman's deadly knife.

The men went according to their plan. Spreading out, they walked in a line toward where the rustlers had settled for the night. As they got closer, a fire was burning, and what looked like a coffee pot was hung from a tripod over the flame.

They crouched as low as possible and approached the fire. In the light of the fire, they could see the sleeping figures of four men. No one appeared to be awake. Silently, the men approached the sleeping rustlers. In short order, the four outlaws were rudely awakened, disarmed, and trussed with ropes.

Thanks to Freman taking care of the look-out rider, they'd all been captured without a shot. Freman was sent back to the waiting horses and led them to where the captives were being held.

William was concerned that he was sure there were at least six men, but only five were accounted for so far. When he brought this up to the other men, Yates assured them there must be only five, and he was wrong about a sixth man.

The rest of the night passed slowly. Caleb and Ira agreed to watch the trussed-up outlaws so the others could sleep. They'd decide the fate of the cattle thieves in the morning.

Hours later, Yates arose and woke his man, Tyler. He told Caleb to rest. It was daylight when the sound of an approaching rider was heard.

The horse carrying a rider rode up to the camp. The rider assessed what had happened and, turning his horse, dug his heels into the sides of his mount in an attempt to escape. William was awake and realized that this was the sixth man.

Yates untied his horse and quickly lifted himself into the saddle. He turned to Tyler, "Come on, he's getting away."

Tyler hesitated and said, "Mr. Yates, why don't we let him go. We got all the rest, and there's no sense chasing after him in the dark and getting shot ourselves. He won't be a threat anymore since his friends are all caught."

Yates didn't answer, wheeled his horse around, and raced after the sixth rustler. Tyler stood for a moment, shook his head, mounted his horse, and chased after Yates.

Yates could hear the hoofbeats of the escaping rustler as he rode through the small trees and brush. He came to the end of the wooded area and saw the outlaw riding across a level meadow.

Yates stopped his horse, pulled his rifle from its scabbard and raised it to his shoulder, aimed carefully, and pulled the trigger. The fleeing horse stumbled and then fell forward and flipped over, throwing the rider forward.

Yates spurred his horse to where the rustler's horse convulsed in death. His shot was a mortal blow to the animal. He found the rider on the ground, groaning and holding his shoulder. No gun was visible, so Yates dismounted and walked over to the fallen man.

Hearing an approaching horse, Yates turned to see Tyler riding up. "Get down, Tyler, and help me tie this one up. We'll take him back to the others."

When Tyler made no move to discount, Yates again told him to dismount and help. Yates was shocked to see Tyler pointing a rifle at him. "Afraid not, Mr. Yates. I asked you to let him go, but you wouldn't listen to me. Now I'll have to tell the others that the rustler shot you and got away. I recognized the horse and knew the rider was my brother. I tried to warn you off. It's a shame, but I can't let you live, Mr. Yates. If I do, you'll never stop chasing my brother and now me."

Yates looked into the barrel of the rifle. He knew he couldn't bring his gun to bear in time. He started to try and talk his way out of the situation when he heard running hoofbeats. Tyler heard them too and looked surprised to see William charging toward him on a horse.

Tyler got off one hurried shot before William's horse slammed into his horse, knocking it off its feet. Tyler rolled away from the horse and reached for his holstered pistol, having lost his rifle in the collision.

Before he could bring up his pistol for a shot, William leaped off his horse and landed on top of Tyler. He knocked the pistol out of Tyler's hand and flipped him over, placing his knee in the middle of Tyler's back to keep him from moving.

William turned toward Yates and saw that Tyler's brother had regained his senses and was searching for his pistol. William pointed at the man and yelled for Yates to look out. Yates still had a pistol in his hand. He pointed it at the rustler and said, "Stop looking for your gun and walk over here."

The man did as he was told. Yates tied his hands behind his back and walked him over to where William still held Tyler on the ground.

Yates saw that William was pressing a hand to his right side. He saw blood seeping out from a bullet wound on Williams's side.

"Guess Tyler got me a little bit before I got him," William said.

Yates replied, "I was a goner for sure if you hadn't shown up when you did. What made you come, and why didn't you shoot Tyler instead of ramming into his horse?"

"I saw Tyler acting a little strange at the camp. Then, when he tried to keep you from chasing after the other man, I thought something wasn't right with him. I'm embarrassed to say I jumped on my horse and forgot I'd removed the rifle from my saddle holster." Then, William added, "If you'll cover Tyler with your pistol, I'll get off his back."

Yates nodded. William slid to his left, getting off Tyler and sat on the ground, holding his side. Tyler slowly got to his feet and turned to face Yates. He looked over at his brother and said, "You understand that I had to help my brother. I didn't approve of his life, but he's my brother."

Yates replied, "I understand and you understand that I can't let you go after planning on killing me and shooting William.

Tyler nodded and put his hands behind his back for Yates to tie them together.

With Tyler now secure, Yates looked at William and asked how bad the gunshot wound was.

William looked down at his side and said, "It hurts a lot, but the bleeding has slowed. I don't suppose you want to carry me, so I'll ride."

He started to stand and was surprised when Yates

walked over and, grasping William's hand, helped him rise.

"Thank you for saving my life. In doing so, you could have lost yours, and as it is, you're wounded."

William grimaced with pain from his wound and said, "Well, I'm sure you would have done the same for me."

With Yates's help, William got into the saddle, and they rode back to camp. Yates led Tyler's horse with Tyler and his brother riding double with their hands tied. They soon reached the camp where the others waited. Everyone was surprised to see two men riding Tyler's horse.

Caleb saw that William was wounded, and said, "William, we need to get you back home so you're wound can be tended."

The reply came quickly. "I'm not going anywhere until I see these men pay for stealing our cows and shooting Pony."

The four rustlers were still tied securely, and all had a look of dread about their fate.

The oldest of the tied-up men spoke up, "Okay, you got us in a tough place here, but you need to understand we were hard up for food and clothing. No one had money to pay us for work, so we went wrong. We once were honest working men. So, let us go and we'll leave and you'll never see us again."

Yates walked over to the man, who had long hair and a beard that was beginning to show gray. He looked at the other three; one was a young man with terror in his eyes and one was a stern-looking man with black hair and a long beard. He returned Yates' look with a hard stare. The fourth was a black man. All wore worn clothing that hadn't been washed for a long time.

Yates said after a short pause, "You might have been honest men once, but now you're cattle thieves, and cattle thieves get hung. You knew that before you decided to steal from us."

Freman said, "Why don't we just shoot them. I don't

go for hanging anyone. I lost a brother and uncle to hangmen's nooses. They didn't do anything, except be born black. I know these men must pay, but I sure don't like hangings."

All the others remained silent, surprised at the statement, and realizing that sometimes people are hung for no reason.

Freman continued, "I understand that they're evil men and deserve to die. I just don't want to see men hung. Shoot 'em or use my knife on 'em; just don't hang 'em."

Yates replied, "You can't shoot men or use a knife on them while they're tied up. The legal way is to hang them like a sheriff would do."

"So, shouldn't we take them and turn them over to the sheriff?" Caleb asked.

"Why," replied Yates, "They'd only end up the same way and be a lot of trouble to us. Let's find a suitable oak tree and get this job finished. Sam, put a rope of these guys and get them on their feet."

Sam did as he was told. He looped his rope around the neck of the first outlaw and ran the same rope to the necks of the other three. After getting them on their feet, he mounted, holding the end of the rope and, joined by the other men, made a small procession as they rode and walked to a live oak tree a short distance away.

William, understanding Freman's plea, said to him, "Freman, you start driving the herd back. We'll catch up later."

A relieved Freman mounted his horse and rode off to gather up the herd. He didn't want to see men, especially another black man, hung. He said, "I have no problem killing a man who's intent on killing me but hanging a man is against my nature."

Four ropes were placed over a large limb of the tree, and the ends tied into a noose and secured around the necks of the four, who were then lifted onto horses' backs with the reins of each held by Yates.

Yates Looked up at the three men and said, "Anything you want to say before we drive these horses out from under you?"

The older of the men spoke again and said, "We knew what we were getting into and the price we would have to pay. The boy is only fourteen years old. Can you give him a break?"

The kid was young. His lips trembled and tears seeped from his eyes.

Yates said, "He's old enough to steal cattle and maybe shoot men, so he deserves the same as the rest of you."

Suddenly, the hoofbeats of several horses were heard. Everyone looked toward the sound and saw a group of riders coming toward them. One man rode in front of the group with a badge pinned to his shirt that glistened in the sunlight.

The man, who was quite large and had bright red hair, said, "My name is Sheriff Copeland. What's going on here?"

Yates stepped forward and said, "My name is Yates. I own a ranch close by. These men stole cattle from me and from these other men, so we're fixing to hang them."

Sheriff Copeland replied, "I reckon not. They probably deserve hanging all right, but that's to be decided by the law. I appreciate you men catching them for they stole from others also. I'll take them and see that justice is done."

Yates was clearly upset by the Sheriff's interference, but saw no way out of complying. One of the sheriff's men removed the nooses from the rustlers.

The sheriff saw Tyler and his brother still sitting on Tyler's horse with their hands tied. Looking at Yates, he said, "What about these men. Are they rustlers?"

Yates pointed at Tyler and said, "No. He's not a rustler. He worked for me but just tried to kill me to save his rustling brother who's sitting behind him on the horse. You might as well take Tyler along with the rustlers. I'll testify to whatever charge you can make against him. I don't want him hung but he deserves punishment, even though he was trying to help his brother."

The sheriff rode over and took the reins of Tyler's horse and said, "I'll take him and he'll pay for his mistake. But, I must tell all of you, we have laws now to handle things. It'll go hard on anyone who takes the law into their own hands. In the future look to those who are hired to catch and punish lawbreakers."

With those words, the sheriff and his men rode away, taking the rustlers and Tyler with them. Everyone at the camp watched them ride away. Some were disappointed, but some were relieved that the sheriff arrived when he did.

Yates said, "Okay, it's over, so we might as well catch up with the cattle and go home."

They all mounted and moved out. Caleb rode beside William and they talked of the future.

William said, "The herd is getting bigger, and there'll be other rustlers. More and more desperate men are arriving that were in the army, with no means of making a living. Some are good, but others aren't. I think Freman should join the other men in looking after the cows."

Caleb agreed, "That's a good idea and, with another man, we can catch and brand more cattle."

The two of them turned their horses and headed home to get William tended to while the others continued driving the recovered cattle. The ones carrying the SS brand would be turned over to Tex, and Joe. Yates and Sam would take the others. As they rode, Yates talked to Ira.

22

Reconciliations

The last few days had been hard on Selene. When William rode away, she tried not to worry, but a chance that he could be hurt or killed was a real possibility.

Anarece tended to Pony, who was in her care. Every day, she cleaned his wounds with a solution of powders made from blackberry roots and pieces of the bark off the east side of bay trees and fresh ginseng, all mixed in rainwater. She burned bay tree leaves and fanned the smoke so that Pony would breathe it in.

Anarece explained that these steps would keep the wound from getting infected. A similar mixture was made from dried saw palmetto berries, which she had him drink to keep his lungs clear.

Jesse spent as much time as he could with Pony and Oconee. He was fascinated by the Indians and asked question after question about how they lived. He wanted to know their customs and habits.

Selene often chased Jesse out of the house to do chores outside the house or orange grove. He completed his chores quickly and was soon back talking to Pony or, if Pony was too tired, talking to Oconee.

One day, late in the evening, Selene heard riders approaching. She rushed to the door and went outside and immediately saw the horse riders were Caleb and William.

With a fright, she saw William's blood-stained shirt and the way he sagged in the saddle.

Selene ran to help William dismount and she and Caleb helped him inside. Calling for Anarece, Selene lay William down on the closest bed. He gave little resistance to her care, for he was weak from blood loss and the long ride home.

Once William was settled, Caleb told Selene that he must go home to let Rosie know he was okay, "I'll put William's horse away before I go."

"No," Selene said. "You go on home to Rosie. She's as worried as I was. Jesse can take care of the horse."

Caleb was relieved that he'd have to delay no longer, went back outside, mounted his horse, and rode away.

Anarece removed William's shirt and began cleaning the area damaged by the bullet wound. "William will be fine. The wound isn't infected and he'll heal quickly. We'll treat him just like we treated Pony."

Selene was relieved at these words but still concerned. She had two wounded men to look after.

The next morning, William was listless and, when Anarece saw moisture on his brow, she placed her hand on his head and felt what she feared; he had started running a fever.

Calling Selene, Anarece told her they must soak William several times a day in the mixture she had prepared.

Anarece poured hot water into a cup and then mixed a powder from one of her gourds along with honey. She went to William and told him to drink the mixture. Selene worriedly looked on.

Anarece said, "We must make him drink this several times a day to fight the fever."

Selene nodded her assent.

After a week, William had regained some of his strength back but still not enough to do any work, even on the orange trees. He was well enough to complain about not being able to go about his normal life. Selene was content to listen to him, glad that he was alive and getting better.

Another week passed and Pony was well enough to leave, so he and Oconee thanked Anarece and Selene for their care and went to live in their chikee. Jesse stood and watched them leave. He would miss them.

A month passed. Selene and William sat on their front porch to escape the house's heat one afternoon. They heard riders approaching, and they were surprised when they recognized their visitors.

William knew Yates and Selene recognized his daughter, Sarah, riding with him. William told Selene that Yates was with him when they chased down the rustlers.

Selene added, "The girl is Sarah, who was Ira's girlfriend"

William slowly stood to welcome the visitors. Selene quickly rose, took his arm, and walked with him to greet them.

Yates and Sarah stopped their horses and Yates asked if it was okay if they stepped down.

William, totally surprised by this visit, told them they could, although he was still puzzled by this visit.

Yates got down from his horse, turned, and helped Sarah dismount. He took Sarah by her hand and said to William, "Sarah and I would like to talk to the both of you."

William and Selene exchanged quizzical looks before William said, "Of course, Mr. Yates. Would you like to sit, or is this just a short visit?"

Yates replied, "No. This might not be a short visit so, yes, a seat under your shady oak tree would be nice and a glass of water would be good, as we just finished a hot horseback trip."

Selene hurried inside and returned with two tin cups filled with water.

Yates took a drink of water and motioned Sarah to do the same. Yates stared at his cup and then, looking up at William and Selene, said, "The two of you need to understand that we had a long ride over here and an even longer journey to drink out of these cups."

This remark brought anger to Williams's face, but Selene squeezed his arm before he could say anything in return. She recognized what Yates was saying.

Yates continued, "I had heard of you two and the word was you were trouble, so I was surprised and shocked to understand that Caleb considered you a partner and his wife entertained you in their home. The way you handled yourself when we were after the rustlers caught me off-guard. Men have respect for you and your leadership. On top of that, you saved my life. You not only saved it, but you also risked your own to help me. I don't forget when I owe someone a debt, and I owe you a big one."

Yates took another drink from the gourd and began talking again. "I rode over here to get some things out in the open. I'm not saying that my family or I have changed our way of thinking, although, we'll try. I'm not saying we'll be close friends because we won't. What I am saying is that you and your family will have nothing to fear from me or mine. We had rustlers, and we'll have more plus other enemies. I'd like you to come to any meetings I hold in the future even though explaining you to my neighbors isn't going to be an easy task."

William struggled to restrain his anger at Yates. He tried to understand what Yates had gone through to bring himself to this visit while, at the same time, angry that Yates felt he was making a sacrifice in recognizing William as a person, second class, but a person. His first response was to run Yates off and reject his gestures of whatever it was.

Before he could answer, Selene tugged on his arm. "Excuse us," she said, "there's something inside we must check on right away. We'll be right back."

William gave her a funny look but didn't say anything as he let her lead him away.

Once inside the house, she said, "William, I know you're upset with Mr. Yates, but please stop and consider his situation and yours. The man made a considerable sacrifice to the beliefs that he was taught and has been a part of his life forever. He's trying to get along and it would be in our best interest not to reject him. You have more than yourself to think about. We have four children and they don't need to lose a father just because of his pride. Of course, he's prejudiced. He never considered a black man more than a work animal, but he has come here and brought his daughter, something he would never have dreamed of doing before you chased after those rustlers. I don't expect you to act like he's your master and you, his slave. Instead, give him credit for recognizing you. If we can get white men, even one at a time, to speak to us as people and not animals, it'll make things better for you and your family."

William didn't reply but turned and walked back out the door. Selene followed. Once outside, he walked over to where Yates and his daughter still sat.

William said, "Thank you, Mr. Yates, for coming this way. I know it was an awkward thing to do, especially bringing your daughter along. Without offending you, I must tell you that I'm a man with the same wants and needs that you have. I was born black and you were born white. Consider for a moment you were born with black skin and I was born with white. Do you think that because you wore black skin, you'd be a different man inside? I think not. Again, I do thank you for coming over."

Yates stood and said, "I understand your situation and know your people have been mistreated."

William couldn't ignore this remark and said, "Mr. Yates, unless you understand what it would be like if you were a six-year-old to have the white overseer come to your house and run you outside, close the door and, when he comes out, to go back inside and see your mother crying. Then, seeing your father hold your mother in his arms and tell her it wasn't her fault. Then, when the overseer came back again, except this time when you go inside, your mother has tried to hang herself rather than face the indignity. When you cry and hold on to her, she doesn't complete the hanging, just holds you and cries. Then, your father comes in and, seeing her, knows what has happened again. He takes her in his arms and says, 'Never again.' That night, your father wakes you up and the three of you run into the night to escape the overseer. You run as far as you can and then your father picks you up and continues running, carrying you. You hear the dogs early the next morning and, by noon, they catch up to you and the riders are close behind. They take your family back and tie your father to the front wheel of a wagon and your mom to the back wheel after stripping off both their clothing. You watch the overseer take a cow whip and beat both of them brutally until both pass out. He continues the beatings until both of their backs are crisscrossed with deep cuts from the whip. You, a six-year-old, sit by your mother's side for a night and the next day, for they are left tied to the wheels as a lesson to other blacks. Mr. Yates, I say to you. When you understand all that, tell me again you understand my life or the things that led me to be the man I am today."

Yates looked down at the ground and then up to William. "No, William. I can't say I understand what that must have been like for you, but I've come here to offer my thanks for what you did for me. I was wrong to say that I understood. I can't change the past but I promise you or your family will never be abused or looked down on by me, my family, or those who work for me. Again, thank you for what you did. We have another reason for our visit. We must go to see Ira. I think he has been misjudged and deserves an apology."

Turning to Selene, Yates said, "In case William forgot to tell you, he risked his life to save mine. As I said, I will not forget that. Come, Sarah, it's getting late, and we have another stop to make."

Sarah stood and looked at Selene. "I too, have an apology to make to you, Selene. I promise I'll never respond the same way again."

Turning to William, Sarah said, "I'm so sorry William. No child should ever face what you did. What happened to your folks?"

William replied, "After they recovered from the beatings, we were classified as 'problem niggers' and consigned to a slave auction. The only good luck we ever had was being bought by Mr. Thornton, who freed us."

Yates and Sarah mounted their horses. William and Selene watched them ride away.

Selene said, "I'm proud of you. I know you wanted to run them off, but I feel that would have been a mistake."

William replied, "Maybe so, but not running him off doesn't make me feel any better."

The two went back into the house, walking arm-in-arm.

Yates and Sarah rode until they arrived at Caleb's home. Rosie was in the front yard as the two stopped their horses. "Welcome," she said, puzzled at the unexpected visit.

Sarah spoke up. "I need to apologize to you, Rosie, for the abrupt way I left on my last visit. I wasn't prepared to see you with a black woman in your home. It wasn't fair to Ira and I'd like to tell him. Is he at home?"

Rosie replied, "He's out behind the barn working on the fence. I can call for him if you'd like."

Sarah replied, "No. I'll go to him."

Sarah dismounted and headed to the barn. Walking around the barn, she saw Ira hard at work.

Sarah walked right up to Ira before he noticed her. "Hello, Ira. I suppose you're mad at me and I wouldn't be surprised if you were. I'll go if you want."

"What do you want, Sarah. If I recall, you didn't want to talk to me or even be near me."

Ira looked closely at her and was startled to see tears in her eyes. He said, "Are you okay? What's wrong?"

She turned her face away from him and he could see her shoulders were trembling. He felt compassion for her for a moment then, collecting his thoughts, he remembered the long miserable ride to her house and back and a tinge of anger replaced his other feelings.

Sarah turned back to face Ira and, with tears still welling from her eyes, she said, "My dad just went to see William to thank him for saving his life and he took me with him. I met William and, as you know, I already met Selene. They're not what I expected and I can see where you might consider them friends. I was just shocked at the encounter. Maybe if you had warned me, it might have been different."

The anger left Ira as he thought the situation over. He thought, *'What she said made sense, and maybe explaining about William and Selene to her might have softened the blow. He had to accept blame for not telling her, but she hadn't given him a chance to explain, and she didn't share her thoughts.'*

He walked over to Sarah and, placing his hands on her shoulders, looked intently into her eyes, and said, "I should have told you about William and Selene, but it never occurred to me that it would be a problem. They've been a part of my life for so long I don't consider them black or white, only as friends that I respect. William is honest, works hard, and Selene comes from a royal family in Africa. I care for you, Sarah, and would like us to be friends again, but William and Selene would remain my friends. They'd be your friends too if you'd give them a chance. Try to forget that they're black and look at them as people. I feel lucky that they're my friends and I can look to them for any help I might need."

Sarah replied, "I do want us to be friends again, Ira, and I'll try to accept the two of them as part of our life. You must be patient with me, for this goes against all that I've been raised to believe. I'm riding home with my father tonight and I'd like you to come over for dinner on Sunday."

Ira took her hand and the two walked to the house where Rosie was talking to Yates. As Ira and Sarah approached, Rosie saw them and a smile came to her face.

Yates laughed and said, "I guess the two of you had a good talk. I'm glad, Ira, for we missed your visits and I thought no one would take Sarah off my hands. She eats a lot and hardly does any work."

Sarah hit him gently on the shoulder. "Don't listen to him, Ira. He's just trying to scare you off again."

Everyone laughed at the friendly banter that relieved any tension they might have felt.

Yates said, "We better get going. It's going to be late by the time we get home. Mrs. Yates will be worried. Rosie, the next time Caleb comes over, you must come with him and meet Mrs. Yates. Looks like our family might be close from here on out."

Sarah was embarrassed and Ira felt the world had been lifted from his shoulders. Yates and Sarah mounted their horses and rode off, heading home. Ira went back to his work. Rosie, feeling pleased, went inside to make the evening meal.

Bright and early Sunday morning, Ira saddled up Blaze and rode to the Yates' ranch and was met by Mr. Yates, who said, "Welcome, Ira. It's good to see you again. The girls are fixing dinner so we can sit outside and talk until it's ready."

Yates took a chair and motioned Ira to do the same, as he lit his pipe and leaned back contently.

The door opened and Sarah came out to get the two for the meal. Ira followed Yates inside. He saw Mrs. Yates, Janie, and a man he didn't recognize. The man walked over to Ira and put out his hand to shake Ira's.

Yates said, "Ira, this is Reverend Sommers. He'll be sharing our meal, and I'm sure blessing it before he lets us eat."

Reverend Sommer laughed and said, "Glad to meet you, Ira. Sarah here, just won't stop talking about you. I feel I already know you."

Ira looked at Sarah, whose face was blushing red.

The meal progressed after a lengthy blessing by the Reverend. After the blessing, Yates said, "Ira, you have to admit this food has been liberally blessed. Why I heard one family actually starved to death waiting for one of Reverend's prayers to end."

Sommers laughed and replied, "I better include a blessing in my next prayer for the Lord to forgive some of his children who bend the truth a bit."

Everyone laughed and began eating. The mood was good and much small talk accompanied the food.

The meal was finally over. Yates pushed his chair back. "We'll get out of the way so the women folk can clean up."

He motioned for Ira and Sommers to follow him outside. He led them to the barn, where he wanted to show off a new bull he just bought. The three leaned on the fence and looked at the latest addition to the farm. He was larger than any bull Ira had seen.

As they looked at the animal, Sommers turned to Ira and said, "I travel around a bit and don't have a regular church. Good folks like the Yates give me a bed to sleep in and right good food to eat. I spread the word of the gospel and preside over baptizing babies, weddings, and, sadly, burials. I don't recall seeing you before. Do I know your family?"

"No, sir. We live a good way from here and no preachers have come along our way."

Sommers replied, "And you, Ira, what are your beliefs on religion?"

"I never gave it much thought. Ma used to tell me

about the Bible and I believe in God okay, just never been to no church or heard of one nearby."

Ira was relieved to see Sarah approaching. She called out, "Ira, you promised to take me for a walk. It's a lovely day and a shame to waste it." Taking his hand, she led him away. She looked at him and spoke, "I'm sorry about Reverend Sommers. I didn't know he'd be here when I invited you over. I don't know if he just happened along or my mom sent for him. We're not engaged, are we?"

Ira thought, *'I've trapped many animals and, as good as I am at setting traps, it looks like I just walked into one. The problem is, I don't mind.'*

They walked along and Sarah held his hand in silence. Ira laughed at his next thought. *'She asked the question about engagement and now is waiting for me to say something, one way or another. She sure knows how to bait a trap and wait for me to get caught in it.'* Again, he didn't mind.

Ira said, "I wouldn't mind getting married if you're of the mind to do so. I want you to know that I want to go to Texas someday. My friend, Tex, told me all about it and I'd like to go."

Sarah spoke now, having sort of a commitment from him, and said, "Did you just propose marriage to me?"

Ira looked across the meadow they were walking by and then turned to her. "Yes, I suppose so. What will your parents say?"

A small giggle left her mouth. "Silly, they've been planning that since they first met you. We did have a little setback after I met your family, but it's okay now. If we were married and you wanted to go to Texas, I guess we'd go. I certainly wouldn't stay home while you went." She wheeled around, pulling Ira with her, and started walking back home. "Come on. We have to go tell my folks. I know they're waiting for us."

The telling of the engagement, though expected, brought merriment to the Yates household and seemed to be shared by Reverend Sommers.

After handshakes and back-slapping, Reverend Sommers announced, "I'm sure your mom wants you to be married by a preacher, so you two need to set a date and I'll be there."

Ira's mind was reeling and it was too much to take in all at once. He thought, *'Where will we live? What are Caleb and Rosie going to say? Before I made plans, I should have talked to Rosie, but it came along too fast. I must talk to Rosie and Caleb before I go any further.'*

Ira told everyone that he must go home and tell Rosie and Caleb the news. Mrs. Yates agreed with Ira and said much was to be done and Rosie could come over to help with arrangements or Mrs. Yates could go to her.

Ira and Sarah sat on the front porch and talked by themselves. Ira was grave and thoughtful and Sarah was animated and talked on and on, while all the time wearing a smile on her face.

Mrs. Yates came outside and said, "Okay, you two. Time to come inside. Ira, I made up the same room you stayed in last time for you."

Mrs. Yates led the two inside and, after leading Ira to his room and telling him goodnight, led Sarah back to the kitchen and poured them both a cup of coffee.

"Lots to talk about," she said.

The two sat up much of the night talking plans and Mrs. Yates answering Sarah's questions about married life.

After another sleepless night and a large breakfast, Ira bade the family goodbye and rode away to talk to Caleb and Rosie. He rode deep in thought but found himself smiling and chuckling. *'Trapped sure enough,'* he thought. *'And there is no escaping.'*

The idea of telling his adopted parents would be no problem but, when he thought of telling Tex and the others, he knew he was in for teasing. Well, he could face that too.

When he arrived home, he saw that Caleb and Rosie

were there, along with William. The smiles on their faces told him that they expected the very news he was bringing.

Caleb asked, "Where will you be living? Here or with her family?"

This question came as a surprise. Ira always assumed he'd live here and hadn't considered any place else, which he told Caleb. The problem was the house was a little small for all of them.

"We'll build you a house," William said. "You just pick out a place you like. My mules and wagon will haul lumber for its construction and it'll be up in no time."

The wedding took place two months later at the Yates' home. Reverend Sommers was there to perform the ceremony. Caleb, Rosie, and a reluctant Callie, arrived early.

When Rosie told Callie about the marriage, Callie responded, "I don't want to be there, and I'll hate Ira forever for not waiting for me. I wanted him to marry me."

Rosie tried to soften the blow for Callie, saying, "Sarah will be a big sister for you, Callie, and you'll learn to love her."

Callie replied, "I don't want a big sister and I hate her too."

Rosie told a distraught Ira to give Callie time and everything would work out.

The wedding was the first social event for a while, so Yates had food for everyone and a little snort of corn whiskey for the men and a couple of the women. Yates closest neighbors were in attendance and more came a long distance.

The visitors slept in their wagons and the barn. Roberts and his wife, along with his cowboys, Oliver and Hiram. Tex, Joe, and Freman left the herd to wander for a day so that they could attend. Tex insisted that Freman attend.

Yates' neighbors looked in shock as William and Selene rode up and were welcomed by Caleb, Rosie, and even Yates. Anarece had stayed home with the children.

The ceremony was completed with voluminous

prayers by the good Reverend. Most of the men and a few women sneaked drinks from the corn liquor jug that was circulated.

Afterward, dinner was served on long planks set on top of barrels. As soon as everyone had filled themselves with food, musical instruments appeared and lively music filled the air. All the men wanted to dance with Sarah, some of whom were single and jealous of Ira's good fortune.

She danced with several but, finally, with a face blushed from the activity and short of breath, she went to Ira's side and said, "How about you? You want to dance with me?"

Embarrassed, Ira said, "I don't know how."

Sarah laughed, fanning her fan in front of her face for cooling air, and said, "That's okay. I'm tired anyway. But, by the time a dance comes around again, I'll see that you know how."

As soon as they could, Ira and Sarah went to the wagon Sarah's parents gave them. It was hitched to two horses and ready to go. Helping Sarah up to her seat, Ira stepped up, took a seat next to her, and urged the horses into movement, driving away amidst laughter and good-natured insults hurled at the couple.

Gifts given to them as wedding presents were in the wagon, mostly items they'd need for setting up housekeeping. One gift Sarah kept in her lap. It was the family Bible given to her by her parents. In it were the records of generations of births and marriages of the Yates family. It was a cherished gift that told of her history. The wedding was recorded and pages were left for Sarah and Ira's children and grandchildren. William and Selene rode along with them.

Everyone watched the two newlyweds drive off. Then, someone yelled, "Hey, those two love birds are gone, but the party's still here, so kick up the music and let's have fun."

Everyone moved to the barn, where lanterns shed their light. A makeshift stage had been erected along one wall for the music makers. The players took the stage and, immediately, the music and dancing began.   Young and old filled the dance floor as the caller stood and began calling instructions to the whirling dancers.

It wasn't long before the older dancers left the floor, took seats, and watched the younger ones dance. Even the hardiest dancers were too tired to dance as the night wore on. The musicians began packing up the guitar, banjo, and fiddle.

Tex strode to the abandoned stage and called out, "Wait a minute, folks. I have a special treat for you. Just hold your places for a while."

He went out the door and returned, carrying a guitar, and leading a hesitant Freman with him. Mutterings of discontent and outrage were heard from the onlookers.

Tex held up his hands and spoke. "Hold on, folks. I promised you a treat, so give me a chance to keep my word."

He handed the guitar to Freman and said, "I know you're nervous and I forced you to come here; just pretend we're back with the cattle."

Freman took the guitar and gently began to play. Everyone except Caleb's riders was shocked into silence as Freman began singing in his deep melodious voice. He sang words to a song that no one had heard before.

When the singing stopped, the crowd was silent. Finally, one of the young men called out, "Well, we all know them niggers can sing. And, I guess this one is better than most, but still a nigger and shouldn't be around our women."

Tex walked over to the speaker and, with a roundhouse blow, knocked the man to the floor. Tex looked down at the man and said, "You shouldn't have said that. That man is the best singer you've ever heard and he writes his own songs. If you refer to him again, call him Freman, which is his name, or you can call him the song man. Anything else, I'll not look kindly on."

One onlooker called out, "Sing us more songs like that

last one."

Tex motioned for Freman to sing more. The crowd sat silent as they listened to songs that he'd written. There were songs about lonely times alone herding cows, happy songs about things that pleased him, and his favorite, religious songs praising God and thanking Him for blessings.

Tex walked up to the stage and said, "That's enough for now, Freman. Save some for later."

Many of the onlookers began to clap their hands in appreciation of the songs. Others had walked out during the performance. Some stayed but didn't join in the clapping.

Freman nodded his head in recognition of the applause. Tex motioned for him to follow and the two walked out into the night.   Caleb and Rosie, who planned to spend the night with the Yates, and the other two riders followed them. Tex, Joe, and Freman mounted their horses and headed back to the herd.

23

Ira and Sarah

William and Selene rode along with Ira and his new wife until they reached the new home that was just completed.

William said, "Look over your front door and you'll find a present from Jairus. Anarece taught him to paint and we taught him his letters. Now, he's making signs as well as pictures. He has a talent for painting."

William and Selene said their 'good nights' and rode away to their own home.

Ira sat on the wagon seat beside Sarah. He had felt confident when people were around and even when there were accompanied on the ride home. Now, his courage failed him, and he was hesitant to make another move.

Sarah looked at him. "Ira, are we going to sleep in the wagon tonight? It might be a little uncomfortable."

Her voice startled him. He quickly said, "No. We'll go inside our new home."

Ira helped Sarah down and reached back inside the wagon for a glowing lantern. They walked to the house and saw the sign over the front door. It was white with black letters and said, 'Ira and Sarah Sanders.'

Both were pleased to see their names marking this as their home and were amazed at Jairus' talent.

Ira and Sarah went inside and Ira watched as Sarah, by lantern light, inspected the room and the simple, but serviceable, homemade furnishings. Ira, Caleb, and William had built the house and furniture, but Sarah hadn't seen it.

Sarah turned to Ira and said, "Ira, I just love it. We'll be happy here, and I promise to make you a good wife."

Ira, who had been waiting tensely for her response, was relieved and suddenly very happy with her approval.

For the next two weeks, the two spent every minute together. Ira made new furnishings for the house that Sarah asked for while she sewed and hung curtains in the windows. Neither could believe their good fortune in finding each other and it scared them both to think they could have lost each other over Ira's friendship with William and Selene.

At the end of the two weeks, Ira told Sarah he must get back to his work, mostly helping gather and tending the cows.

Sarah said, "I understand. Just don't expect me to stay home by myself. I can ride and chase a cow as good as any man and want to share life with you, and I mean your work, your friends, and all you do."

Ira was pleased by her remarks, but a little apprehensive about facing everyone as a married man for the first time. He thought, *'They'll give me a rough time but maybe go easy on me with Sarah with me.'*

On the first day Ira decided to get back to work, he saddled up their horses. He and Sarah rode to Caleb and Rosie's house. Caleb greeted them with, "Get down and come in for a cup of coffee."

Ira and Sarah dismounted and followed him inside. Rosie rushed up to Sarah and hugged her. "Come on in," she said. "Let the men talk about work and we'll get to know each other better."

The two men went into the kitchen to have their coffee and talk about the work to be done. Ira was assigned to take supplies to the men who followed the herd as it grazed slowly across the grasslands.

Caleb walked with Ira to the barn where two mules

stood with packs strapped to both sides of each of them. Caleb said, "There are enough supplies to last the men a few weeks. I bought flour, real coffee, tobacco, and even sugar. They'll be glad to get the supplies. You'll find them south of here. They shouldn't be hard to find. Just follow the tracks."

Riding side-by-side, Ira and Sarah headed off to deliver the supplies. Ira held onto a rope that controlled the mules.

It was a gloriously lovely Florida day with few clouds in a blue sky as they rode together. Sarah marveled at the green expanse of grass and the animal life that abounded.

Songbirds sang from the thickets, and Sarah laughed at the procession of the mother quail who scurried to get out of the path with her hatchlings furiously moving tiny legs to keep up. She heard the male quail calling out to locate his family as the horses moved away.

Ira set up camp early in the afternoon. He erected the small tent Caleb had packed for them and built a fire to make coffee and dinner.

After eating, they sat with a last cup of coffee and listened to late evening sounds. The lonesome call of the whippoorwill floated on the air as nighthawks made a swooping sound as they dove after insects in the air.

Sarah looked up in time to see an owl fly overhead on silent wings on his way to find prey.

"Everything's so beautiful and peaceful here," Sarah commented to Ira. "I'm so glad I came along with you. I wouldn't miss this for anything."

Ira smiled at her happiness and he, too, felt at peace. He saw the land and all that inhabited it through Sarah's eyes.

Morning came and they packed up and continued their journey to deliver the supplies. Late that afternoon, they heard the noise of the cattle. Urging the horses to a faster gait, they soon caught up with Tex, who rode at the back of the slow-moving herd.

They rode up to Tex, who turned in his saddle and said to Ira, "Well, I lost another bet, for I bet the others that you wouldn't be back to minding cattle since you became an old family man."

Tex laughed loudly with his remark and was joined by Sarah who then said, "Tex, I guess you didn't hear that since you were getting a little old for this kind of life, I'll take your place while you go back and ride a rocking chair."

His face flushed red at this unexpected kidding from Sarah.

Ira laughed loudly at Tex's discomfort, loving Sarah more for her defense.

Tex recovered his composure and laughed too. "Ira," he said, "looks like you got you a good woman here and, once you have a brood of little Ira's and Sarah's running wild on this land, I'd hate to be anyone or anything that comes between her and hers. Why she'd be worse than a mama bear with babies."

They circled the cattle into a close bunch for the night. A campfire was soon burning bright and the new supply of food was turned into a good meal. Sarah didn't recognize the meat browning in the Dutch oven.

Joe, who was cooking, answered her question, "That's steaks sliced from the hindquarters of a panther. Tex shot him earlier today and it'll taste good. That panther thought he could eat one of our young calves and Tex shot him just in time." Motioning with his hand, he added. "That's his hide rolled up right over there. We'll get a few dollars for it next time we go to town."

Sarah wasn't sure she could eat panther meat, which showed on her face.

Tex saw the look and said, "Sarah, that panther steak will be good eating. Now last night's meal was one you did well to miss. I killed a rattlesnake and Joe here, skinned him, and fried him for dinner. It must've been a Texas rattlesnake that got lost and ended up in Florida. It was small for a Texas snake but big around enough that you could only cook one slice at a time in the frying pan, and one slice barely fit."

Tex's statement started the other men telling tall tales that grew more far-fetched as the meal was consumed. Night softly covered the land, cattle, and men.

Before everyone went to sleep, Freman, who had joined the others in tending the cattle, sang two of his favorite songs. His voice filled the night and all were slow in making their way to bedrolls for the night.

The following day, Tex secured several animal hides to one of the pack mules for Ira to take back and sell the next time he went to a settlement. There were hides from panthers, wild cats, wolves, and bears. The men gave Ira a list of things they'd like to buy with the sale of the hides.

Before Ira and Sarah left, Freman walked up to Sarah and handed her a folded piece of paper. He said, "I was working on a song last night and wrote a little something but couldn't set it to music, but I like the words and thought you might also. You can read it tonight when you make camp."

Ira and Sarah rode away and were sad to leave the company of the riders. Ira especially had wanted Sarah to hear about Texas. He still had plans to go to Texas one day.

The trip home took two days. They rode together, enjoying the sights and sounds of the county. They stopped that night at the same spot that they had stayed before. Ira built a fire and Sarah prepared the evening meal.

As they ate, Sarah said, "This spot is so lovely, I could spend a lot of time here."

Sarah and Ira never dreamt of being this happy, but they were and cherished these moments.

Sarah remembered the paper Freman had given her and pulled it from her pocket. She was anxious to see the words. She unfolded it carefully and a tear came to her eye. And by firelight, read it to Ira.

It was titled, 'The Moon Spoke.'

The Moon Spoke

I heard the moon speak today
With my ears or in my heart
I am not sure.

The moon said I see: your moves, your thought,
Your plans, your triumphs, and misdeeds.

I spread my light to guide your way,
Unfeeling, uncaring you spend your day,
You chase the things you do not know
Instead of basking in my glow.

Trust your heart, forget your mind
For the heart lends true, it knows no wrong,
The heart will lead and life define

I shine in your heart to gladden your days,
Shun the shadows bask in my rays,
My wish is that my light will lead you true.
And that you see yourself as I see you.

Sarah said, "That's so pretty. A black man wrote it. I never considered blacks as anything but a source of labor. Now that I've met William and Selene, and now Freman, I'm ashamed of how I thought of blacks. It'll take time but I'll be better. I promise you."

The next two years went by and the two spent as much time together as possible.

At first, Ira was concerned about Sarah joining him because of the demands of the ranch. But, after a while, he came to depend on her help in rounding up cattle for she became an excellent horse rider. Even the men who tended the cattle looked forward to her visits with Ira, even though it meant cleaning up some of their stories.

One day, Sarah told Ira that she wanted to visit Rosie for the day and didn't ride with him. When she knocked on the door, Rosie invited her to come in and, after a quick hug, the two sat down for a cup of coffee and conversation.

They talked of the ranch and other items of interest, until Sarah put down her cup and said, "Rosie, I think something's wrong with me. We've been married long enough to have children and I'm getting concerned. Ira hasn't said anything but I know he'd like at least a son."

Rosie took Sarah's hand and replied, "I wouldn't worry. There's plenty of time. You're both young, so be patient. You could try talking to Anarece. I understand she might have some advice for you and maybe some medicine."

Sarah thanked her for the information and, after spending most of the day with Rosie, went home to cook dinner for Ira.

Several days later, Selene was surprised to see Sarah ride up on her horse. After welcoming her warmly, Selene invited Sarah to get down and have a drink.

Sarah dismounted and nervously said, "I'd like to talk to Anarece."

If Selene was surprised at this, she didn't show it. She simply said, "Of course. Wait just a moment."

She turned and walked back into the house. A few minutes later, Anarece walked through the door and stepped out to the front porch. "You want to see me?" she asked.

Sarah said, "Yes. Can we take a walk? I'd like to ask your advice."

They began walking and, after a long silence, Sarah said, "As you know, I've been married for a few years and we have no children. Ira hasn't complained or said anything, but I'm sure he'd like children. Can you help me with that?"

Anarece said, "Sometimes it's God's will whether

children come into your life or not, but I have the power to help in some cases. Come back in two days and I'll have a medicine for you and give you instructions on its use. You understand there's no guarantee. But, the medicine and advice I'll provide has helped others in the past."

The two turned and walked back to the house. A very relieved Sarah said, "Thank you, Anarece. I'll be back in two days and I'll do what you tell me to do."

With that, Sarah mounted up and rode away.

The following day, Anarece and her young student, Hiba, walked to a pond nearby where bay trees grew. Anarece showed Hiba how to cut the bark from a young tree. "You must find a vee in the trunk. Cut bark from the inside of the tree, never the outside."

After that, they found blackberry bushes growing wild near the water's edge and, together, they dug up some roots and added them to the bag. Anarece searched the edge of the water until she found empty shells of snails bleached by the sun. She added them to the bag.

Anarece and Hiba moved away from the pond, entered a wooded area, and searched until they found a wild ginseng plant, which they dug up and added its roots to their collection. Anarece was satisfied with what was in the bag, so they went home.

Anarece instructed Hiba on grinding the snail shells into a fine powder. Next, she ground ginseng, bay tree bark, and blackberry roots together. The remaining ginseng was added to the snail powder.

The next day, Sarah appeared. Anarece met her at the door with two gourds. One held the powder, which she instructed Sarah to mix a small amount with water and drink the mix every morning. The other mixture she would add to her bathwater.

Anarece told her, "Don't go on any long horseback rides, get plenty of sleep, and don't watch animals killed or skinned for food for three months. You must drink milk every day, cow's milk is okay, but goat's milk is better. Get plenty of sleep. It's okay to cook fresh meat, but have Ira bring it into the kitchen ready for the stove."

The instructions sounded strange to Sarah, but she agreed to do as told.

The following day, Ira and Sarah sat enjoying a cup of coffee. After their breakfast, Sarah said to him, "Ira, it would be nice if we had a milk cow. I want to start having milk with our meals and I'm sure Caleb and Rosie would like that also."

Ira replied, "We own lots of cows, but none of those who would give enough milk to provide much to drink. Not only that, they're so wild that it'd take four men to milk one."

Ira promised to talk to Caleb and see if he had any ideas. He went to Caleb and Rosie's the following day and they agreed it was a good idea to have a milk cow, but didn't know where to get one.

Ira said he would ride into Allandale to see what was available. He saddled Blaze and rode off in the search of a milk cow. When he arrived at the town, he obtained the name of a rancher who had a different kind of cow that was said to give lots of milk.

But, the opinion was that this new breed wasn't suited for the harsh conditions that Florida offered. After getting directions, Ira rode off to see the rancher who had this unique breed.

Following the directions, he arrived at what must have been the right ranch. There was a house with a picket fence around it and, off to one side, a large barn. The house was a surprise since it was painted white. All the other homes he'd seen were unpainted and uniformly bleached a dull grey by time and the sun.

Noticing activity at the barn, he rode over. Remaining mounted, he called out a loud, "Hello."

It was rude to dismount without an invitation, which

was considered improper.

A man in blue overalls walked out of the barn and said, "Hello."

Ira was invited to dismount and did so. He walked over and introduced himself.

The man, who introduced himself as Sam Joyner, said, "Welcome, friend. We don't get many visitors and it's always a pleasure to meet new friends."

Ira liked Sam immediately and found he was sincere in his greeting. He told Sam the reason for the visit.

Sam laughed and said, "I'm glad someone told you to see to me. I do have a new breed of cattle for this area. Most folks in town think I'm a little, if not a lot, crazy. They believe my cattle aren't rugged enough for Florida. I'm always glad to talk about my new cows. Come with me."

Sam turned and walked back to the barn. As they entered, Ira saw cows in separate stalls. They were larger than any cattle he had seen. They were all white with black spots. Ira looked to Sam for information, who was more than eager to talk about the cows.

"These are Holsteins," he said. "Cattlemen from up north imported them from the Netherlands, so I'm told. They're finding their way south since the war ended. One of these will provide all the milk that two families can drink, with some left over."

Ira saw that the cows had large udders that promised a lot of milk. He told Sam that he wanted a milk cow so his wife could have milk to drink and that he'd like to buy one if possible.

Sam scratched his chin as he thought about Ira's request. Finally, he said, "I have a cow with a calf almost old enough to wean off nursing. I hadn't planned on selling one, but since it's for your wife and I bet a house full of kids very soon, I'll sell you the cow and throw in her calf for fifty dollars."

Ira was shocked at the price for cattle were usually bringing less, but he agreed and handed Sam the amount asked for in gold coins. Sam looked at the coins and said, "I'm glad to see some gold. Most folks around here must trade goods or services since they don't have money to spend."

It was late in the day, so Sam insisted that Ira have dinner with the Joyner family and spend the night in the barn. Ira agreed and, after washing their face and hands, the two men walked to the ranch house for dinner.

Sam introduced his wife Edith and five boisterous children, all whose names Ira promptly forgot. Dinner was a noisy, but cordial, event and Ira enjoyed the company. He was impressed by Sam's family and looked forward to having children of his own, not knowing of Sarah's attempts to accomplish just that.

The following day, after another family meal, he rode off on Blaze leading his new cow followed by a miniature duplicate. The calf kept trying to nurse as they walked but couldn't as long as the cow moved. Ira stopped a couple of times during the day to let the calf nurse and then continued his way home.

24

Natural Perils

Ira and Sarah were having dinner by lantern light when he told her it was time to take more supplies to the riders watching the herd. "We can go tomorrow," he said, "and camp along the way just like we did last time. It'll be fun."

Sarah hesitated and said, "No. I don't think I'll go this time, Ira. I promised Rosie I'd help her preserve some berries. So, you go along and I'll stay with her until you get back."

Sarah saw the hurt look in Ira's eyes and felt guilty, for she would have liked to go with him. Anarece's words rang in her head, *'Don't take any long horseback rides.'*

Ira reluctantly said, "Okay. If that's what you want. But I'll miss you."

They both went over to Caleb and Rosie's house the following day. Sarah went in to tell Rosie she'd be staying with her for a while.

Ira went to the barn with Caleb, where the packhorses were loaded with supplies for delivery. Sarah came out to the barn to tell him 'goodbye' and that she was sorry for not going with him. He looked questioningly at her but mounted his horse and rode slowly away with the lead rope from the pack animals in his hand.

As he rode, the world didn't seem quite as bright as the last trip with Sarah. The bird's singing wasn't as good and the air seemed oppressively hot. He made camp that night but didn't even start a fire, just ate cold corn pone and drank from his canteen.

The following day, he searched for the herd, which had ranged farther south. It took him two days to catch up, but he felt better when he reached them.

It was good to see the men and he always enjoyed talking to Tex. They sat around the campfire that night and told tall tales and he heard more of Tex's stories.

Ira had told Sarah that he'd spend time with the men, who were glad to have his company, as they followed the slow-moving cattle as they grazed.

Ira stayed with them for three days. Evenings became more festive with songs by Freman and the off-key singing of Tex when he tried to join in.

The herd had increased over the years with new births and strays caught and branded. Ira decided to talk to Caleb and William about driving some to the market. He'd heard that there was a shortage of beef north of Florida since the war had decimated all the herds.

On the fourth day, he prepared to head back to the ranch. He rode off after more than a few good-natured remarks about him being an old married man who had to get back to the apron strings.

Ira camped alone on the first night. It felt strange after spending time with the riders. Since he and Sarah had been together, he was rarely alone. He looked forward to getting home and seeing her. But, on the second day, the sky turned dark and the wind began blowing.

At first, he thought nothing of this. For being caught in rainstorms and getting wet wasn't a new happening. There was a rain slicker tucked in the saddlebags. He camped that night and was surprised that the wind had picked up more.

Awakening the next morning, the wind had increased and the sky seemed angry. Black scurrying clouds raced across the land. He rode a couple of hours leaning into a fierce wind with driving rain. Despite the rain slicker, his clothing was soaked. Soon, it was evident there was no way he could pitch his tent in the now howling wind. He pushed on, hoping to come to a place to get out of the wind.

The wind increased to an even greater howling wail and thunder, the loudest he had ever heard, crashed all around him. Next, came the lightning strikes. Bolt after bolt streaked across the sky.

Suddenly, the lead packhorse reared and tore the lead rope from Ira's hand. Before he could recover, the packhorses raced away from him. He had trouble controlling his frightened horse as the lightning and thunder crashed.

Ira saw animals running across the fields, running in front of the wind. Flocks of birds half flew, were half-blown across the sky. The wind grew worse.

Ira saw trees were being stripped of their leaves and the wind blew limbs and debris through the air. He knew he must find a place to get out of the wind. At any moment, a wind-carried branch could crash into him.

He saw a high mound off to his right in the dim light. He directed his horse toward a large patch of palmetto bushes growing on a higher spot. He reached it and the wind lashing the palmetto fronds was a crescendo of noise.

Ira dismounted and removed Blaze's saddle and bridle. Freed from the restraints of the reins, Blaze took off running.

Ira struggled against the wind towards the palmettos. It was hard to stand or walk. Reaching the palmetto clump, away from the wind, down on his hands and knees, he parted the palmetto fronds and squirmed into the cluster. He made his way to the middle of the palmettos and lay down between the big trunks that lay flat on the ground.

The palmetto fronds above him were being blown sidewise by the wind. They formed a layer of protection as the wind shrieked through them. *'If I wasn't down between these trunks,'* the thought occurred to him, *'those fronds would cut me to pieces."*

Ira snuggled down further. These were old palmettos, so the trunks were as thick as he was. They crisscrossed and formed protection from the thrashing fronds. Rain was coming down in sheets, but he couldn't get any wetter, so he pulled the rain slicker over his head as best he could and prepared to ride out what had to be a hurricane.

The next morning, the rain continued and the wind still blew. Ira realized it might be necessary for him to spend the entire day waiting for the wind to stop. Ira lay face down with his head cradled on his arm. As he was lying there, he tried to sleep, but it seemed impossible. He detected the musty smell from all the rain and, suddenly, saw a flicker of motion out of the corner of his eye.

Before Ira could react, the large head of a rattlesnake appeared inches from his face. Ira froze. If he tried to move in this cramped space, the snake would bite him before he could get out of its reach. The snake slowly crawled forward and Ira saw the large triangular head pass by within inches of his face.

The snake moved more and the thick body slowly passed as Ira stared. He felt the heavy body of the snake as it crawled up his shoulder and across his back.

Ira tried to stop the tremor that moved through his body. He felt the snake make a coil in the middle of his back. It seemed to have stopped there, probably because of the warmth of Ira's body.   Ira lay petrified. To move meant a certain snakebite. Snakebite out here far from home would mean death; a slow, painful death.

The rain finally slowed and stopped. The palmetto fronds stopped their frenzied wind dance. Ira felt the body of the snake move and crawl off his back and into the palmettos.

Carefully, Ira turned and sat. No trace of the snake remained. He sat for a while, trying to slow the racing of his heart and the tremors in his arms.

Finally, he stood and exited the palmettos, taking a path away from where he thought the snake went.

The landscape had changed. Bay and oak trees stood stripped of their leaves. Only a skeleton of the trees remained. The palms and palmettos bent with the wind and thus survived with their fronds, though shredded, intact. Around him was a sea of water.

There was no sign of his horse, so he began walking toward home. Late that afternoon, he saw a wagon approaching. It was Caleb and Sarah. Never had he seen a more welcome sight. Trailing behind the wagon were the two packhorses that Ira thought he might never see again.

Sarah jumped from the wagon and ran to his arms. They stood in an embrace as Sarah cried and as Ira tried not to shed any tears.

Caleb sat in the wagon and waited on them until Ira and Sarah came over to the wagon and climbed aboard. Caleb turned the wagon around and they headed home.

Sarah said, "We were so worried when Blaze came home without you, afraid you were hurt or worse."

Ira replied, "No. I'm not hurt. But the wind was so bad and things were blowing around. I found refuge until the storm was over and am glad that Blaze came home okay, and you were able to see me. I thought I might have to walk a long way home. But where did you get the packhorses? I lost them in the wind."

Caleb replied, "We found them contentedly grazing on some tall grass a few miles back. They don't look any worse for wear."

Caleb dropped Ira and Sarah off at their house and drove away, relieved that Ira was home and okay.

Late that night, Caleb and Rosie were awakened by the sound of the animals in the barn and something making noise near the fence behind the barn.   Caleb arose, got dressed, and lit a lantern. Picking up his rifle, he headed for the door.

Rosie called out, "Be careful, Caleb. You don't know what's out there."

Caleb said, "It's probably nothing but a fox trying to get into our chicken coop or maybe a bobcat."

Caleb went out the door and walked towards the barn, hearing the restless stamping of horses' hooves moving around in the barn and snorts of fear. He thought, *'If the horses are afraid, it's probably more than a fox. It could be a bear wandering around.'*

He took a close grip on his rifle and, holding the lantern high, closed the distance between him and the barn. Once inside, by the lantern's light, he could see the whites of the horses' eyes as they moved restlessly in their stalls.

Caleb thought it was unusual for the horses to be so afraid. The lantern allowed him the assurance there were no animals inside the barn other than the horses. He moved on through the barn and opened the back door, walking toward the corral where more animals were held.

A small noise made Caleb turn around, holding the lantern high with his left hand. He only saw a blur of motion before a panther, in a mighty leap, struck him and knocked him to the ground.

Caleb felt the teeth of the panther bite into his left shoulder, biting all the way to the bone. The panther made a howling scream as he bit harder into Caleb's shoulder.

The blow from the panther's leap had knocked the rifle from Caleb's hand. The panther wrapped both front arms around Caleb, digging claws into his back, holding him close with his shoulder still in his mouth.

The panther's two rear legs with their knife-sharp claws were moving up and down Caleb's left side and thigh, tearing clothing and flesh with each swipe.

Thoughts raced through Caleb's head. *'Am I to die like this?'*

He knew no help would be forthcoming in time to help him escape from the panther. Caleb pounded on the panther with his right fist, but it made no difference. The panther still emitted the horrible noise and continued biting and scratching. Caleb looked desperately for any weapon that he might use to fight this formidable enemy.

The only thing in sight was the lantern. It had landed upright and was still lit. Caleb was able to reach the bail of the lantern and, with all his might, he swung it into the head of the panther.

The lantern's glass shattered on contact and fuel ignited from the lantern wick splashed onto his attacker. The panther screamed again, this time in pain as the flame enveloped his head and neck.

The panther released Caleb and began rubbing his head with his front paws, rolling on the ground and screaming. The panther managed to extinguish the flames but, by then, it had forgotten all about Caleb and ran off into the darkness.

Caleb lay on the ground. He knew that he'd suffered terrible wounds and was unsure if he could make it back to the house. His left arm was useless, hanging limply by his side and his left side was covered with blood.

Suddenly, he was aware that Rosie was there. She had heard the noise and ran out to check on Caleb and held a pistol in her hand. The minute she saw Caleb lying on the ground, covered in blood, she knelt on her knees, forgetting danger to herself.

Rosie saw that Caleb was unable to walk. So, putting him partially in a sitting position, she got behind him and put her hands under his arms. Rosie walked backwards and slowly dragged him to the house. Once inside, she managed to get him onto the bed.

Rosie knew Caleb was severely injured, and she began trying to treat his wounds. Tearing cloth from a sheet, she wrapped the lacerations made by the panther's claws and bound up his shoulder, trying to cover the huge puncture wounds that were deep into his shoulder and seeping blood.

Rosie heard a knock on the door. She hurried over, opened the door, and saw Ira standing there.

"I saw the light on and was curious what you were doing up at this time of night."

Rosie didn't answer, just took his hand and led him to Caleb's bed. Ira looked at Rosie with a questioning look and all she said was, "Panther. I've done all I know how to do. He's hurt badly."

Ira walked over to Caleb's bedside and looked helplessly down at the injured man.

Caleb saw Ira standing there and rasped out the words, "Go get William."

Ira went outside, quickly saddled a horse, and thundered off into the night. As he neared William's house, Ira began calling William's name. William came out of the house, followed closely by Selene. Ira told him what had happened and that Caleb wanted to see him.

William said, "I'll saddle my horse and be right with you."

Selene said, "I'll go also."

William replied, "No. You stay with the children. I'll take Anarece with me. She can help tend to Caleb."

William quickly saddled two horses. He, Anarece, and Ira rode off as fast as the horses could carry them.

William thundered through the front door and went to Caleb's bedside. Rosie rose from her chair and moved aside.

William, pushing the chair away, kneeled and looked at Caleb, who lay swathed in bandages that were soaked thru with blood.

Caleb looked up at William and said, "I'm glad you're here. I don't know if I'll recover from this. In case I don't, I'd like you to consider Ira your new partner and give him the help and respect that you've given me."

William reached over and took Caleb's hand and

pressed it to his chest. He looked at his wounded friend and the thought of losing Caleb made him realize the depth of his respect and feeling for this white man. He felt tears form in his eyes. Still holding Caleb's hand, he looked up as Anarece came into the room.

In a troubled voice, William said, "Help him. Use all your power and medicines to help my friend. Tell me what to do."

Anarece walked over to the bed and said, "Rosie, build up a fire and put pots of water on to heat. Tear bandages from a clean sheet and put them in a pot and let them boil."

Rosie rushed off to do as she was told. After she had pots of water heating up, she came back to the bedside and asked, "What else can I do?"

Anarece replied, "Do you have any whisky?"

Ira spoke up, "I do. Someone gave us a jug at the wedding and it's at my house. Should I go get it?"

Anarece said, "Yes, and hurry." Then she added, "The wounds, while bad, won't kill Caleb. The bigger problem is what is in the wounds. The panther's claws have bits of anything it has walked through plus dirt on them. The scratches on Caleb's body must be cleaned of all that to keep down a fever. As soon as the water's hot, I'll clean them as best I can. Then, after the water, I'll rinse them out with the whisky. If I can get the wounds clean and then wrap them in clothes that have been boiled, Caleb has a chance."

They waited for the water to get hot. In the meantime, Ira returned with a jug. Anarece took it from him and sat it by the bed.

Caleb began talking in a weak voice, "Ira, William has agreed for you to be his partner in my place if I don't recover. It'll be William, Selene, you, and Rosie working together."

Rosie heard a soft sob behind her. Turning, she saw Callie standing there, holding her doll. Tears streaked down Callie's face as she said to Rosie, "I don't want my daddy to die. Please don't let him die."

Rosie walked over and took Callie in her arms. "Go back to sleep, Callie. Anarece is here to help. I pray that your dad will be okay, but sometimes God's will must be obeyed, no matter how hard."

Callie replied, "I don't like God if He would take my daddy. He let Ira marry someone else and now wants my daddy."

Rosie led her to bed and tucked her in, saying, "We'll take care of your daddy. So, go to sleep."

Rosie sat with Callie until she heard the soft breathing of sleep. Once she was assured Callie was okay, she went back to assist Anarece.

William still knelt by the bed. He squeezed Caleb's hand and said, "Don't think about us. We'll get along and continue our work. Just concentrate on yourself and don't give up. With Anarece's help, you'll be just fine. Think of that and save your strength."

Rosie came into the room with a basin full of hot water and said, "The water's hot. Now what do we do?"

Anarece removed the bandages covering the scratches on Caleb's body. They were deep slashes. She took the fingers of one hand and spread the wounds open as far as she could. Taking a ladle full of hot water and, one at a time, she rinsed them.

As soon as she completed cleaning a scratch, she squeezed the flesh around it, making it bleed. She said, "Washing the wound will help end even though Caleb has lost lot of blood. I want fresh blood to help wash the wounds out more."

After all the scratches were treated in the same way, she reached for the jug of whisky and poured it into the open wounds, further cleaning them. Once she completed the cleansing process, she had Rosie bring in the other container of hot water holding the strips of cloth. She bandaged all the scratches and wrapped them up tightly.

When she completed bandaging Caleb's thigh wounds, she uncovered the shoulder with the puncture wounds from the panther's teeth.

She looked at William and said, "I can't clean out the bite marks, but they must be treated. Heat a knife blade in the fire and bring it to me."

Rosie gave William a knife and he held it over an open fire until it was heated and then took it to Anarece.

She inserted the point of the knife into the punctures. The pain was so intense, that Caleb passed out. A hissing noise and smell of burning flesh made everyone look away, except Anarece who moved the blade from side to side.

After treating each bite puncture, she reheated the blade. She treated all the punctures, poured whiskey over them, and re-bandaged the shoulder.

When Anarece finished, she stood up and looked down at Caleb who was mercifully still unconscious and said, "That's all we can do for now. He has a chance of making it but we must clean his wounds and re-bandage them every two days, always using bandages that have been boiled in water. I'll stay here with Rosie and keep an eye on Caleb."

William said, "I'll stay too."

Rosie interrupted him and said, "No, William. There's nothing you can do. I appreciate your concern but you need to go home and be with your family. We'll let you know if anything changes with Caleb."

Before William left, Anarece told him to bring back the medicine she would need to treat Caleb. William rode home with a terrible dread in his heart. He realized he cared very much if Caleb lived or died.

At times he'd been aggravated, but now realized that Caleb was the best friend that he ever had and most likely ever would have again.

William rode home and explained what had happened

to Selene. She fixed him a cup of coffee and sat at the table with him, knowing he wouldn't go to sleep.

Ira lingered a while, but went home to Sarah after telling Rosie that he'd be back in the morning to check on Caleb.

Anarece told Rosie to get some sleep and that she'd watch out for Caleb.

Rosie replied, "I can't sleep. I appreciate what you've done for Caleb and I'll sit up with him tonight. You get some sleep so you can look after him tomorrow. As you said, there's nothing more you can do for him tonight."

Anarece replied, "Okay. But I'll stay and help you tend to Caleb until he's better."

Rosie nodded.

In the following days, Anarece cleansed the wounds, applied her medicines, and replaced the bandages. She was pleased to notice there was little redness around the wounds, just a lot of bruising, particularly around the shoulders where the teeth had bitten deeply. The bites had been her biggest concern, but seemed to be healing; although the scars would always be black from the cauterizing of the hot knife.

William and Ira were frequent visitors and sat with Caleb. After a short visit, Anarece would send them away, saying, "You have work to do and you're only tiring Caleb. I'll look after him and if any change for the worse occurs, I'll send for you. For now, we just have to wait and hope."

The first couple of days, Caleb would awaken in a lot of pain and Anarece would give him a drink from the jug of whiskey. It did him little relief. She said to Caleb, "I know you're hurting, but that's good for it means you're still alive and recovering."

Anarece or Rosie fed Caleb hot broth with a spoon three times a day for two days. On the third day, he said he needed solid food and was able to eat corn pone softened with water. After a week he was able to eat a little meat and vegetables.

Caleb was in bed for two weeks before he was able to sit up and feed himself. Soon after, he was able to walk stiffly to the kitchen table, leaning on Rosie for support.

Anarece said that Caleb was out of danger now and should be okay. She gave Rosie instructions on taking care of him.

When Anarece arrived home and told William that it would take more time for Caleb to heal completely, but he'd be okay. A heavy burden was lifted from William's heart.

After a month, Caleb was stronger and not as pale. He was able to walk to the barn with the aid of a walking stick. He'd lost feeling in part of his thigh and had a noticeable limp as he walked.

Rosie refused to let him ride a horse until more time had passed, so he worked around the barn and tended the garden.

Rosie watched him limp around the garden and thought, *'I'm okay with that limp, for I was afraid he wouldn't survive the attack of the panther.'*

Ira had taken over Caleb's work with the herd and spent more time taking the men supplies and helping brand and drive the herd. Sarah stayed home. Ira missed her company, making the time he could spend with her more precious.

One morning, as Ira and Sarah were having breakfast, Sarah said, "Ira, would you mind if we named our first son Caleb? We could call him Cal."

Ira said, "Okay. I'll talk to Rosie and get her thoughts."

Sarah smiled and said, "I already did and she said it would be fine to name our baby Caleb if it's a boy."

"Why would you ask her that? We don't have a baby boy or girl, for that matter."

Ira started to go to the barn to saddle Blaze, when suddenly it hit him. Incredulously, he stopped, turned, and asked, "Are we having a baby? Why didn't you tell me?"

Sarah laughed, "I just did silly. I wasn't sure until now. I hope you're happy about that."

Ira hadn't wanted to tell her how badly he'd hoped for children and was now elated at the prospect. In his happiness, a thought popped into his head. He looked at Sarah, and more to himself than her, said, "I suppose I won't be going to Texas after all, with a baby on the way."

She laughed and said, "I never planned on going anyway. Our family and lives are here."

When the time came, Anarece tended to Sarah and delivered a pink-faced miniature duplicate of Sarah. Ira held his newborn in his arm and said, "Little girl, your coming means I'll never get to Texas. So, I'll name you Texas Belle Sanders. That's as close to Texas as I'll ever be."

25

Changes

Many changes had come to Florida by 1882. A year prior, the State of Florida, hard-pressed for money, sold four million acres of land to Hamilton Disston, heir to the Disston Chainsaw Company. He also had an agreement with the State to drain an additional eight million acres for which he would be granted additional land.

His vision was to drain all the land in the central portion of the State of Florida stretching from north of Orlando all way south to the southern end of the state, including the Everglades.

To accomplish this, he ordered the construction of huge dredges to enlarge waterways including the Caloosahatchee River from Lake Okeechobee to the Gulf of Mexico.

Draglines deepened existing canals and dug new ones to drain water into the Kissimmee River. This would open vast acreage for farmland that was now underwater or subject to flooding. He formed a land company to resell the land.

Faster methods of shipping were needed now since steamboats and wagons were slow and restricted in the amount of cargo they could carry. Florida had no money to construct the railroads that were needed. So, to accomplish this the State made an agreement with Henry Flagler on the East coast and Henry Plant on the West coast. The State gave land to each of the men in exchange for every mile of railway constructed.

The men created a railroad line that stretched from Sanford to the town of Allandale and supplies were received regularly. Supplies were shipped further south by steamships traveling along the Kissimmee River. The years passed and many changes came to the State of Florida.

Meanwhile, Ira and Sarah had two more children. The first boy, as arranged, was named Caleb, and the second Andrew. Texas Belle, their daughter, was now a headstrong little girl of eight. She took her importance to the family as a natural thing. She looked down at her brothers as babies and expected to be treated with the respect of an eight-year-old, almost grownup in her opinion.

Caleb and Rosie remained unchanged. He had a permanently injured limb from the panther attack but otherwise could go about normal life. Callie, now sixteen, had grown into a young woman and was starting to get attention from boys her age and a little older. When Rosie commented to Callie that some boy was going to take her away someday, Callie, with downcast eyes, said, "Not much chance of that. There are no young men around here that I'm interested in. The only man I ever wanted is married to someone else. I'm afraid you're stuck with me."

Rosie felt a tightness in her chest at Callie's words. She knew that she and Caleb must come up with a plan for Callie's future.

William's family was also growing up fast. Jesse, now sixteen, spent more and more time in the woods. Unless William gave him specific jobs, he'd disappear in the morning and not show up until the late afternoon. He usually brought home skins of animals he trapped or shot with his rifle. The sides of the barn were covered with drying skins.

Selene complained when the wind blew the smell towards the house. William had hoped that Jesse would show more interest in the orange trees, but they held little appeal to him.

Adaza still accompanied William to attend to the trees as often as she could get away from housework.

Jairus was now fifteen years old. He had recovered as much as he ever would from his disease. His left arm had little movement or feeling. He was smaller in stature than his brother or William and spent most of his time painting and helping Selene around the house.

Hiba spent hours and hours with Anarece, walking in the woods or by the edge of the ponds collecting plants, roots, berries, and tree bark to make into medicines. She learned which plants were suitable for what ailment.

Often, when neighbors came to Anarece for treatment or medication, Hiba was the one who treated them and dispersed the homemade medicine concocted by both ladies.

Hiba did what housework was demanded of her, but showed little interest, for she was engrossed in the healing arts she was being taught by Anarece.

William had an additional person to help with the trees. One of the neighboring ranchers sent a black boy, named Isaiah, over to learn about the orange business. William agreed to teach him in exchange for his work.

It didn't take very long for Isaiah, to take an interest in Adaza. William noticed this and called Isaiah from the orange tree he was pruning.

"Isaiah, I notice you're showing an interest in Adaza. I understand she'll be of marrying age before long, however, it'll take a special person to win her hand. Let me ask you a question. Can you read and write? Can you do your numbers?"

Isaiah, looking embarrassed, said. "No, Sir. I've never been to school or learned any of those things. However, I'm a hard worker and will work hard to support a family someday."

William said, "That's all well and good, but see that mule? That mule works hard all day long, but he depends on me to reward him with food and a place to stay. Without me, he'd be just another stupid animal and would soon find himself as panther food. While it's a good thing, working hard isn't all there is. Do you want to be like that mule and be a hardworking, ignorant animal? If you're going to look after Adaza, you must learn to read, write, and do your numbers."

Isaiah was troubled by William's words, but ashamed of his lack of education. "How and where can I learn to read, write, and do numbers?"

"If you're serious, I'll teach you. We can work on the orange trees and devote part of the day to your education."

Isaiah replied, "As I said, that would be fine with me if you think I can learn."

"We'll find out if you can learn or not and, if you can't, you can give up hopes for Adaza."

Isaiah looked a little crestfallen but agreed that he would try to learn. William told him they would start lessons immediately.

William directed Isaiah to pick up the small green oranges that had fallen from the trees. William kneeled when Isaiah returned with them and told Isaiah to do the same. William took one orange and held it between his fingers.

William asked Isaiah. "How many is this?"

The reply came quickly with confidence, "That's one."

William then said, "Using your finger in the sand, make the mark for number one."

Isaiah felt good, for he knew that a single mark in the sand means one.

"That's very good. Do you know how to spell one?"

Isaiah didn't.

William, with his finger, wrote out 'one.'

"Pronounce after me, o,n,e. Those letters spell out 'one.' The alphabet contains twenty-six letters, each with a sound of its own. You'll learn those letters, one at a time, and you must know them to learn to read. So, one is the first number. Do you know how to write the word two?"

Isaiah said, "Well, it'd be two marks."

"No. That's not right."

William used his finger to write the numeral two in the sand. Beside the number, he placed two green oranges and spelled out two in the sand. He decided to only concentrate on the numerals today and wrote the numerals three through ten in the sand. Beside each, he placed a corresponding number of oranges.

Isaiah looked at the numerals and the green oranges beside each one. It was too much for him to comprehend. He was afraid he could never learn.

After going over the numbers several times with Isaiah, William erased them from the sand and carved them on a small branch.

"Take this," William said. "Carry it home. Practice it over and over and, when you come to work tomorrow, I expect you to be able to write the numbers in the sand like I did today,"

One morning, Caleb rode over for a talk with William. He arrived and, after learning that William was working on the orange grove, he rode off to find him.

Two men were working instead of William alone, and the other man was introduced as Isaiah. William added, "Isaiah is learning about the orange trees and making plans to steal my daughter away from me."

Isaiah shuffled his feet nervously, with eyes downcast, partially from Williams's words but also from the presence of a white man.

Caleb said, "We need to go to town and check out a rumor that I heard. Two men came by my house yesterday driving a wagon with a boat in the back. They claimed that all the land around here has been sold as underwater land and they're making plans to drain it all."

William replied, "If they think we're just going to take their word and move along, they better rethink. I'll saddle up a horse and we'll go to town and get this settled."

The two rode off together and, sometime later, came to the outskirts of the town. Both were surprised at the activity going on and the number of new buildings and houses built. Caleb inquired at the trading post about the rumor.

The attendant on duty answered his question. "You need to see the land agent. He's been selling a lot of land lately. You can find him in the new office building down the street."

"Where do we find this agent?" inquired William. The man led them outside and pointed out the building.

Caleb and William rode to the designated building, obviously new from the uncured lumber siding. After tying their horses to the hitching rail, they stepped upon a wooden porch and walked into the office.

A man sitting behind a desk was busy looking over papers scattered on his desk. The wall behind him displayed a large map of the immediate area around Allandale.

He stood as they entered and said, "Hello, my name is Tom Atkinson."

He held out his hand to shake Caleb's hand. Then, reluctantly took William's outstretched hand and limply shook it, then wiped his hand on his trouser leg.

Caleb explained to Atkinson the reason for their visit.

Atkinson moved to the map on the wall and said, "Show me where your ranch is located."

They looked at the map and, after getting their bearings, pointed out where they lived.

Atkinson said, "I'm afraid all the land in that area is listed as low land and belongs to the new owner. It'll be sold by the land office I work for, including the land you live on."

William walked up to Atkinson and, with a scowl,

said, "You mean a man can just come in and claim our land and get a deed to it from the State?"

"The land you live on was never deeded to anyone. I understand farmers and ranchers settled on land years ago and claimed ownership, but that doesn't give legal ownership." Atkinson continued, "I understand. I do. But, the fact is that the land is legally deeded to the new owner. On the good side, we'll give you the first option to buy the land and more if you'd like."

Caleb looked at William and then back at Atkinson. "We'll have to talk about this. How much will this land cost if we choose to buy the land we already own?"

The agent said, "Anything over one hundred acres would cost you one dollar per acre. You can buy up to one thousand acres each if we did it separately for you."

Caleb and William walked out of the land office and over to the horses. Neither mounted, they just stood looking at each other in disbelief. It had never occurred to them they weren't the legal owners of the property since Ira's father and mother had built there years ago.

Caleb said, "We can't take that man's word for it. Let's find the sheriff. He surely would know if that story's true or not."

They searched around town and found the sheriff's office. Once inside, Caleb asked a man sitting behind a desk, "Where's Sheriff Copeland?"

The man looked surprised and said, "There's no Sheriff Copeland. I'm the sheriff here and my name is certainly not Copeland. Why are you looking for him?"

Caleb told him the story of the rustlers they'd caught and turned over to a sheriff named Copeland. "He had a badge and introduced himself as Sheriff Copeland."

The reply came quickly, "What did this *so-called sheriff* look like?"

Caleb said, "He was a big man with red hair."

Caleb's description brought a rueful laugh from the man. "Red Copeland sells stolen cattle to a Cuban Captain that takes the cattle to Cuba. The Cuban doesn't care whose cattle they are or what brand they carry. He puts them on a boat somewhere south of Punta Rassa. Red has two or three gangs of rustlers working for him. The word is that he killed a sheriff over in Hillsborough County. That's probably where he got the badge. I'm afraid you turned over his own men back to him."

Caleb and William looked at each other, feeling foolish and embarrassed. William said, "We'll deal with that later. We're here to check on a story we heard from Tom Atkinson that he's selling land that folks think they already own."

The sheriff nodded his head and said, "That's the truth. The government gave title to four million acres to a man named Disston. Disston sold two million acres to a group from England. Disston and the English are selling land." The sheriff added, "Many people are starting to take notice of this area. Mr. Disston is doing a lot of advertising up North and the English plan on starting a settlement made up of English immigrants. If you want the land, you'd better act fast."

The two men left the sheriff's office and went back to the land office. They went inside and asked Mr. Atkinson if he could give them a few days to think this over and work things out. The agent readily agreed to provide them with three days to make up their mind before he offered the land to someone else.

A somber pair left Allandale that day and headed back to the ranch. There was little discussion, just a feeling of helplessness. Finally, William said. "If we have to buy it, I think we should buy as much as possible. We have enough gold coins that we've saved over the years?"

Caleb and William had placed the gold coins they earned by selling oranges and cattle in a heavy oak chest. The chest was buried in Caleb's barn for safety.

They arrived at the ranch and went to the barn. They raked away the hay covering the ground to the back corner stall. Grabbing a shovel, William dug into the earth and soon the lid of the cash box came into view.

The two men lifted the chest out of the ground. It was so heavy it took both men to lift it. They unlocked the lock and looked at the gold coins.

Caleb said, "There's enough here to buy two thousand acres.   With that much land, we can plant more oranges and have land for our cattle to graze if the open range ever ends."

They counted the required amount in gold coins and placed them in a heavy deer hide pouch. They replaced the chest in its place and covered it up with soil and then straw.

The next morning, the two men rode back to Allandale. Atkinson met and greeted them at the door. "I'm glad you came back so soon. What did you decide?"

William replied, "I want to buy one thousand acres and Caleb will buy one thousand acres."

"That'll be fine. So, you know that the two purchases will come to two thousand dollars. I assume you are in a position to pay."

William, in a brisk tone, said. "You make up the papers and this time we want to make sure we own it legally."

Atkinson nodded his head in agreement and began filling out the land purchase orders. He drew out the boundaries of where the land would be on the large map behind his head.

An hour later, the two men, now owners of two thousand acres of land, walked out of the agent's office carrying their two bills of sales. The agent told them that the proper deeds would be filed by the end of the week.

On the ride home, Caleb began talking, "We made a partnership based on the basis that neither of us owned one half but that we both owned one hundred percent. That meant no division of land, oranges, or cattle." He continued, "We now have acreage in each of our names. That's a legal separation of ownership and I think that's a good thing. We both have families now and someday will need to pass on the land to our children, who may not be in agreement about everything."

William thought about that for several minutes and then replied, "I can understand that. It makes sense. What about the cattle and orange groves? I don't want to separate those and I think we should keep our partnership on them."

Caleb agreed, "I don't want to divide anything we own together. I thought we should clear up the land ownership, that's all."

The two men hurried home to share the news with family.

William arrived home and, after unsaddling his horse, went to talk to Selene. They sat at the kitchen table, and he showed her the sales agreement.

"This is a legal deed to one thousand acres in my and your names, which means nobody can take it away or make us move."

Selene took the paper and silently sat as she studied the form. After reading it through, she said, "I can't believe it's real. I never thought we would own this much land. Our children's future is safe. Owning our own land is a dream come true."

William held her hands and said, "Our life is good. We have friends in Caleb and his family. The Yates family respects and tolerates us more than being friends. We still can't get too relaxed. We'll always have enemies in those who hate all black people just for being black. Our children have been protected so far, but the time will come when they must make their way outside the walls of our home. There's only so much we can do except prepare them as best we can. It won't be easy to teach them to maintain their pride and dignity while subservient to whites."

Selene replied, "That's all true, but we'll prepare them as best we can. After that, it'll be up to them, even though it breaks my heart to think of what could be if all whites were like Caleb and Rosie. It'll be true someday, but our people will suffer and even die before that day comes."

The two sat and held hands as each was lost in private thoughts.

Caleb was working in the garden the next morning and looked up to see William approaching.

William said, "We forgot something yesterday. What about Ira and Sarah? They're entitled to buy land just like we did. Ira is of legal age."

Caleb agreed and the two rode off to see Ira. He was tending his Holstein cows? when they arrived. They explained the land situation to him.

Ira asked, "You mean my folks never owned the land?"

Caleb answered, "According to the law, they didn't. But now, we have legal ownership of that land plus a lot more. We have enough gold to buy more land in your name."

Ira stood for a moment and pondered the news. His face suddenly brightened and he said, "I've been thinking about buying more Holsteins and starting a dairy. The problem I have is that Allendale would be the logical place to sell the milk, but the distance is too great to get the milk there fresh. If we can buy land closer to town, it'd solve that problem. That would mean I'd have to build a new house and move away from the ranch."

Caleb and William looked at each with this announcement.   Caleb replied, "We hadn't planned on your moving away, but I understand what you're saying. If that's what you want, we'll help. After all, your dad gave us our start."

The three went to Caleb's barn and retrieved gold coins with a value of one thousand dollars. They rode into Allendale and went directly to see Atkinson about another purchase.

He greeted them and said, "If you came for the recorded deeds, I told you it'd take a couple of days."

William replied, "We aren't here about the recordings. This is Ira Sanders. He wants to buy some land."

Atkinson walked over and shook Ira's hand. "Just come over to the chart and pick out where you want your land. How many acres?"

Ira said, "I want some land close to town for raising dairy cattle."

Atkinson pointed at an area marked in green and said, "Here's a nice tract of two hundred acres. It's close to town so the price is higher per acre. It'll cost you four dollars per acre or eight hundred in total."

Caleb spoke, "We brought one thousand dollars. What else do you have?"

Atkinson looked at his map and traced routes with his finger. "That two hundred is the nicest tract I have available. What I'd suggest as a good investment would be to buy that acreage and a few town lots. Many people are moving here and will want to build homes and businesses. The lots sell for one hundred each so you can buy twenty lots. I'd expect them to double in value in a few years."

Caleb, William, and Ira walked outside to talk in private.

Caleb said, "It's hard for me to believe that a small lot is worth as much as a hundred acres. Why, I can't imagine anyone wanting to live that close to someone else. But, before we pay for the land and lots, we should go look at the land to see if it's suitable for a dairy."

They went back into the land office and explained that to Atkinson. He readily agreed and said he'd close the office and take them to see the land and the vacant lots.

"Just wait out front for me and I'll get my horse and be right with you."

Atkinson joined them and led them out of town to see the acreage first. After about an hour of riding, he stopped by a big oak tree marked with white paint.

"This is the southwest corner of the land. You can see this land is level with a lot of open spaces with plenty of grass for cattle. You can see that a drainage canal has been dug to prevent flooding."

They looked and agreed that it looked like good cattle land and there was a canal running along one edge of the acreage and the water level well below the level of the land.

Atkinson began speaking again, "This canal is just the beginning of the changes Mr. Disston will make. There'll be a series of canals draining into the lake. He plans on lowering the water level in the big lake and surrounding land by four or five feet. This will prevent future floods and make more good acreage for farming. When this is completed, you can expect a lot more people to move here. There are already ads in the northern newspapers and even in London, England, extolling our warm temperatures and available land."

This was too much for the three to take in. They had enough to think about raising cattle and oranges.

Ira said, "I like the two hundred acres well enough and Mr. Atkinson seems like a truthful man and I'm tempted to go along with the idea of the lots."

They rode back to town and Caleb gave the gold to Atkinson. They walked out with a bill of sale for the acreage and lots in Ira Sander's name."

Caleb didn't like parting with that much gold, but felt good that the promise to Ira's father had been kept and Ira owned far more than his family had ever owned.

26

Jesse

Jesse arose early and, taking his rifle, quietly slipped out the door before anyone else was up. Sunrise was still an hour away, but he was at ease walking through the woods by moonlight.

Being inside the house made Jesse feel restrained and he spent many nights outside, under the stars. He felt guilty about it but he had no interest in the orange grove. His interest was roaming the woods and living off the land by hunting and trapping.

This morning, Jesse was heading to a meadow where he was sure a large buck deer would be feeding. He crept through the woods wearing moccasins that Oconee made for him when Pony was injured. The moccasins were light on his feet and made a quiet passage easier to accomplish than regular shoes.

As he neared the meadow where he expected to see the large buck, he was surprised to see the glow of a campfire. He knew of no one that would typically be in this area. Walking cautiously, he moved closer and saw an Indian man taking a coffee pot from the fire. The Indian man turned at the sound of Jesse's approach. "Good morning," the man said, eyeing Jesse closely to detect any threat, and then added, "Welcome to my camp. I have an extra cup if you would like to share my drink. It is not coffee but is made from pine cone seeds."

Jesse walked forward and said, "Yes. I'd like that. I left home this morning without eating, but I brought along some corn pone and will share it with you."

He removed pieces of corn pone and passed some to the Indian.

"My name is Jesse. Who are you?"

Handing Jesse a tin cup of hot liquid, he replied, "My name is Billy. I am going to the trading post to trade my furs for supplies my people need."

Since spending time with Pony, he wanted to know more about the Seminoles and the life they led. While sharing the drink, which had a slightly nutty taste, he asked Billy questions about his life.

Billy talked with ease to Jesse, relieved that his visitor hadn't been a threat. "I live south of here with my family and a few others. We hunt and fish for our meat and grow vegetables as well as wild plants that we use. My people have gotten used to white man's food; like coffee, sugar, salt, and flour. So, now we trade for those things."

Jesse agreed to go with Billy to trade his furs. As they neared the settlement, Billy stopped at a house on the outskirts instead of going to the trading post. He knocked on the door and a man opened it and stepped outside.

He looked from Billy to Jesse and said, "Good to see you again, Billy. Who's your friend?"

"His name is Jesse, and he is a new friend. Jesse, this is Cy. He takes the furs of mine and the ones of my friends and trades them for things we need. Too many times, white men will not give Indians a fair trade, so Cy does it for us."

Jesse said 'hello' to Cy and was greeted by a nod and grunt in return.

Billy told Cy what supplies he needed and handed over the bundle of furs. Cy took the furs and walked away toward the trading post.

Billy explained to Jesse, "Cy was at the trading post

one day when I came to trade. When the storekeeper told me what he would give me for them, Cy offered more. This made the man mad, but he agreed to give me what Cy offered. Since then, I get Cy to do our trading and give him furs for helping us."

Jesse understood what Billy was saying since he'd felt in the past that his furs didn't bring as much as those gathered by white men.

Cy came back, carrying the supplies Billy requested. Jesse and Billy took them and walked back the same way they had come.

Jesse said, "I never thought about it before, but Indians probably get the same treatment that we do at the hands of white people. My dad says someday it'll be different, but I see no signs of it yet."

The two walked along, talking as they walked. Jesse invited Billy to come by his house and meet his family. He assured him that Selene would feed them both. They arrived there late in the afternoon and William met them at the door. After introducing Billy, other family members came outside to meet their visitor.

When Anarece came out the door, Billy stepped back and said, "You are the Root Woman. I have heard of you."

Anarece nodded, "Yes. The Seminoles taught me much about medicines that your people use."

Billy was in awe of Anarece and had to be convinced to come inside to share a meal with them.

Jesse told William that he'd like to accompany Billy back to his village. William was reluctant to agree but, after discussion, agreed and added, "Take the mules and ride them. It'll be faster than walking, and you'll be back sooner to help with the work."

Billy slept on the front porch and, after breakfast, he and Jesse saddled the mules, loaded the supplies, and rode off. They rode all day, only stopping to rest the mules. They made camp late in the afternoon.

The ride was a joy to Jesse, for they saw no people on the trail. He found this pleasing. Jesse was happiest alone in the woods with just the animals for company. Oddly enough, he felt the same kinship with Billy and asked many questions about Seminole life.

As Billy answered the questions, Jesse became fascinated by all he learned about the Seminole way of life. It sounded more like the life he'd prefer to live.

On the third day, Billy turned the mule he was riding into a swampy area. He explained to Jesse that it was necessary to make their home in a secluded place where no one was likely to stumble on them. Too many enemies of the Seminoles traveled the main paths and were a constant threat.

After two hours of riding, they came to dry land. The camp was on a hammock that rose above the wetlands. The Seminole encampment was composed of seven palm-thatched chikees.

Children ran laughing to greet Billy but became shy when they saw Jesse. Adults emerged from chikees and formed a semi-circle in front of the riders.

One man stepped forward and said, "I am glad to see you safely home, Billy, but who rides with you?"

Billy replied, "This is my friend, Jesse. He helped me sell the furs, and these are his mules. Jesse, this is my father, Sam Eagle."

As he made the introductions, he dismounted, motioning Jesse to do the same. As they did, two men stepped forward and took the reins of the mules and led them away.

Sam stepped forward and, taking Jesse's hand, said, "Welcome to our home and thank you for helping my son. Come. It is time for our evening meal and we would be proud if you would eat with us."

He led Jesse to a chikee in the middle of the camp. A fire burned in a fire pit in the middle. Over the fire hung a black kettle filled with a bubbling yellowish mixture and a metal grate held cooking fish.

The three men sat on the ground around the fire. A woman walked over with three bowls made from dried gourds and each held a carved spoon. She filled the bowls with the mixture and added pieces of fish.

She took the first bowl to Jesse since he was a guest. The next bowl went to Sam as the elder, and the final one to Billy.

Jesse looked into the bowl.

Billy answered the unasked question. "That's sofkee, made from ground corn and water. We have that for most of our meals and add any meat we have."

Jesse tried a spoonful and the taste, while different, wasn't bad. He took another spoonful and replied, "I like the food, but why does your mother not eat with us?"

Billy looked surprised at the question and said, "It is not right for the women to eat until the men have finished. My mother and sister will eat soon."

Jesse looked to where the woman who served them stood, watching them eat. Standing behind her was a girl who stared intently at Jesse.

Billy followed Jesse's eyes and said, "That is my mother and my sister, Rona."

The men finished eating and stood up. Billy took Jesse on a tour around the camp and introduced the other adults. The names were hard to understand or pronounce, and most were forgotten.

Jesse spent a week in the Seminole camp and enjoyed each day as he learned more about the Indian way of life. He learned that everyone used one chikee for cooking and eating. Each family had a chikee to sleep in and keep their possessions. These encircled the cooking chikee.

Billy led Jesse to the chikee that belonged to his family. It had a thatched top but no sides. Sleeping platforms were along each wall, three feet above the ground. This is where Jesse slept for his entire visit.

Billy taught him to use a bow and arrow and, by the end of the week, Jesse could hit his target more than miss. When Jesse tried to use a dugout canoe, it overturned and he ended up in the water, to the delight of the onlooking Seminoles.

Billy stood with ease in the shallow boat and speared gar fish for the tribal meals. The craft had a rounded bottom and took a skill to use that Jesse wasn't sure he'd ever master.

After her initial shyness, Rona began accompanying the two as Billy continued showing Jesse around and taught him how the Seminoles lived.

One morning, Jesse arose and walked over to the central chikee, expecting to see Billy eating the morning meal. Instead of Billy, Rona was there and handed Jesse a bowl of sofkee and motioned for him to sit. She stood silently as he ate.

When he finished, Rona said, "Walk with me. Billy had to go away for a few days and asked me to keep you company."

Jesse stood and the two began walking away from the camp. No one seemed to notice. She led him to a stream that ran at the edge of the hammock. A dugout canoe was pulled up on the bank. Rona began pushing it into the water.

Jesse quickly helped move it into the water. Rona stepped into the canoe, motioned for Jesse to join her, and laughed at his clumsy entrance. He sat in the front with his legs straight out in front of him and held onto both sides of the canoe.

Rona lightly rose to her feet and began poling the craft upstream. Looking over his shoulder, Jesse marveled at her balance and the effortless way she handled the canoe. The water was stained a golden brown by cypress tree leaves and flowed by smoothly.

Jesse watched the banks of the stream as it glided along. A raccoon searched for crayfish along the shoreline and there were numerous swamp rabbits. He watched snow-white egrets and great blue herons wade the shallows, eyes intent on the water, looking for small fish.

Rona told him the large birds didn't only eat fish, but they also eat water snakes and even small alligators. At one point, the stream widened and Jesse saw what must have been over a hundred white ibis with their curved beaks.

Rona explained that the ibis was considered good to eat, but not the egrets or herons.

At a curve in the stream, a brown limpkin had impaled a large water snail and expertly extracted the snail from the shell. Rona said, "The limpkin is also good food and the snail he eats has been eaten by my people for many years. There are large mounds of shells left by those who lived here before the Seminole."

The water began to lose its color and, as it did, the bottom was visible. Soon, they traveled over a white sandy bottom instead of the dark muddy bottom further downstream.

The canoe suddenly exited the stream and Jesse saw the bank sweep away to both sides and form a circular enclosure of crystal water. He looked over the side of the canoe and watched as the boat passed over a spring with large amounts of clear water pouring out and down the spring run.

Rona pointed the canoe to the bank and held it steady with the push pole while Jesse got out and pulled the canoe higher onto the land.

The bank around the spring was all white and was, to Jesse, one of the prettiest sights he had seen. He held out his hand and helped her out of the boat.

Jesse said to Rona, "This is the prettiest spot I've ever seen."

Rona replied, "It is my favorite. I wanted you to see it.

I come here often to spend a day and swim in the clear water. We can swim today if you'd like."

It suddenly occurred to Jesse, *'We don't have swimsuits and sure can't swim in these clothes, which leaves only one possibility. I'm not ready to deal with an angry brother or father.'*

"No," he said. "We'll do that another time, but I'm happy that you brought me here."

Rona laughed at his discomfort and said, "Sit down. I brought our lunch."

She sat beside him and, reaching into a cloth bag, pulled out guavas and a gourd full of berries and pieces of cooked fish. They took their time eating the fruit and fish as Rona told him stories of her family.

Jesse thought, *'I would never get tired of hearing her soft melodious voice, no matter what she was saying.'*

The afternoon passed, and they returned the canoe to the water all too soon.

Jesse said, "Would you like to sit up front and let me pole us home?"

Rona laughed and said, "I do not think you want to go swimming, so sit in front this time. You can take me for a ride after you practice more."

They arrived back at the camp, and Jesse had never enjoyed a day more. The combination of the peaceful surroundings of nature and the pleasure of Rona's company made a day he'd not forget.

Jesse was unsure how everyone would react to his spending the day with Rona, but after a casual look at the couple, everyone went back to their normal activities.

Sam stood by the family chikee and motioned for Jesse to join him. Rona left his side and went to help her mother prepare the evening meal.

Jesse and Rona spent the next two days together and he became increasingly enthralled with this lovely copper-skinned girl. He was impressed with her knowledge as well as her quick laughter.

Jesse was surprised and a little disappointed when Billy returned the next day, riding a small brown horse. Everyone gathered to welcome him home. After everyone's greetings were complete, Billy explained that he'd visited another village and traded for the horse.

"Now," he explained, "I can carry more trade goods to Cy to trade for things the villagers need."

Jesse was reminded that he had been away from home for over a week and his family would be concerned. He spent part of the day talking to Billy but, after the evening meal, sought out Rona and asked her to walk with him.

They walked and neither spoke for a while. He didn't want to tell her that he must leave and she feared that he was going.

Finally, he said, "I must go home. I have been gone for a long time and my family will think something happened to me. I've enjoyed the last few days more than any in my life, and I want to thank you for spending them with me."

Rona took his hand into hers. Jesse stepped around and faced her, taking her other hand into his. She looked into his eyes and said, "It has been a wonderful time for me also. Will you ever come back?"

Jesse felt such emotion when he saw teardrops in her eyes that he almost said he wouldn't leave.

Instead, he said, "Rona, I promise to be back soon. I want to see you and be with you again."

They walked slowly back to join the rest of her family.

Before the morning meal, Jesse rode away to go home. He wasn't sure he would leave if he stayed to say goodbye to Rona. She watched him ride away, but believed in her heart that he would be back. She smiled at the thought and went to prepare the morning meal.

Jesse rode one mule and held a lead rope attached to the other mule. He urged the mule to go as fast as possible, often stopping to change mules, making much better time than on the last trip. He made camp late in the afternoon, wiped the mules down with moss, was up at daybreak, and continued his ride home, arriving there in the afternoon.

Jesse took the mules to the barn, unsaddled them, and turned both mules loose in the corral. Having done that, he turned to go to the house and saw Selene outside waiting for him.

"I'm glad you're home," she said. "You were gone longer than we expected."

Jesse replied, "I'm sorry for causing you concern, but I have much to tell you about my visit."

Selene listened attentively and didn't interrupt as Jesse told her about his visit to the Seminole village.

After he finished talking, Selene said, "The girl sounds wonderful, Jesse, but what are your intentions? She's an Indian and, although you were impressed by her, the fact remains that she and you have different lifestyles."

Jesse replied quickly, "I love the way the Seminole Indians live, free and in harmony with nature. I'd enjoy living that way, especially with Rona."

Selene nodded and said, "I'm sure it looks good to you right now, but I'd be careful how you tell your father. I'm not sure he'll share your enthusiasm."

When William came home that evening, Selene met him at the barn and watched as he unharnessed the team pulling the wagon.

Once he finished, she said, "I wanted to talk to you before you talk to Jesse."

William replied, "It's okay. I know he's home since the mules are back in the corral. Don't worry. I promise not to fault him for being gone so long."

Selene shrugged her shoulders, "I wish it was that simple, but I still want you to keep your promise. He's met a girl and seems to have fallen for her."

William laughed, "Well, why does that surprise you?

We met when we were his age. It's only natural that he meets a girl someday."

Selene smiled a wry smile and said, "Okay, just keep that attitude when Jesse tells you about her."

William wrapped his arm around Selene and they walked to the house. "You worry too much." He added, "You must let the children live their lives."

Adaza had the evening meal on the table when they went inside and the family sat down to eat. Everyone had questions about Jesse's trip. He answered them all without mentioning Rona

After dinner, when William went outside to smoke his pipe, Jesse followed. William lit his pipe, leaned back against the wall, and waited for Jesse to start the conversation.

Nervously, Jesse spoke, "I met a girl that I really like and would like you to meet her. She's not like anyone that I've ever met."

William blew out a puff of tobacco smoke and replied, "I'm glad you met someone. I'm sure she's special. Bring her around to meet the family."

Jesse hesitated and replied, "That'll be hard to do. You see, she lives in the Seminole village that I visited with Billy."

William turned to look at Jesse, "Why is she living in an Indian camp?"

Jesse said, "She's a Seminole girl and I want to live with her and live the Seminole life. You know I don't have an interest in growing oranges, and I already spend most of my time in the woods, just like the Indians."

William stood up from his seat and faced Jesse. "That's a crazy thought. We didn't raise and educate you so that you could live a life as an Indian. Get that idea out of your head. I don't want to hear anything about Indians or that girl again."

William went back inside the house, slamming the door behind him. Selene stood just inside, waiting for him, for she expected this reaction.

William said, "Do you know what Jesse wants for himself? To be an Indian and live with an Indian girl and waste all his education? We're trying to improve the life of blacks and he wants to throw it all away and revert to being a savage."

Selene took his hand and led him over to the table, sat, and motioned him to do the same. The two sat and talked for over an hour before going to bed for a troubled night's sleep.

Her final remark to William was, "We must let him go. Maybe we can get him back but, if we refuse and he goes anyway, he's lost to us. He must be allowed to live his life."

At breakfast, the family took their seats and began eating. William put down his fork and said, "Jesse, tell everyone about your trip and the special girl you met."

Unsure of his father's intent, Jesse began speaking, telling them of his visit with the Seminoles. He described how all village members worked together to grow crops, hunt, and fish for food. Everything was shared, no matter who the provider was. He told how they had respect for nature and the animals.

Two days later, Jesse rode away back to Rona and the Seminoles, unsure if they would accept him.

Jesse arrived at the Seminole village and was met by Rona, who had been looking for him to return. He dismounted and arm in arm they went in search of Sam. When they found him, he didn't look surprised to see Jesse again.

"Welcome," he said. "It is good to see you again."

Jesse stepped forward and said, "I came back for Rona. I would like to live here and do my share of the work."

Sam said, "I am not surprised, but for her to be your wife, it must be approved by the elders of the tribe. I will talk with them tomorrow."

Jesse spent a restless night, but Rona assured him that if no approval were given, she'd leave with him and live among his people.

The next day Jesse waited for the result of Sam's talk with the elders. He noticed that Billy rode away early in the morning without saying where he was going. Late that afternoon, Billy returned with another man following. All the men of the village gathered to greet the newcomer. Rona told Jesse that the man was a medicine man among the Seminoles.

Jesse watched as the medicine man and other men of the village sat in earnest conversation. After two hours, the medicine man rose and walked over to where Jesse stood.

The medicine man stood in front of Jesse and motioned for him to sit. Both men sat down cross-legged on the ground. The man began talking. "I am told that you want to take Rona for your wife and that you want to live among the Seminoles." He continued, "We are members of the Muscogee tribe and are planters and hunters. We came to this land to escape others who do not live as we do. We honor Ishtohollo, who is the peaceful God. We do not honor the vengeful God or mention his name. If you are accepted as one of our people, you must agree to our way of life. You will be forced to leave our village and never return if you harm another Seminole, if you steal, if you are not truthful, if you do not share in the work, if you do not honor our elders, if you neglect your wife or children, or if you bring alcohol into our midst."

Jesse said sincerely, "I'll live the life you describe and I'll share with others and obey your rules."

The medicine man arose and went to talk to Sam and the elders.

Jesse waited nervously for their decision. They didn't make him wait long.

Sam walked over to Jesse and said, "We are glad to welcome you to our village, to live as one of us. It is our custom for you to live in our chikee until you build one of your own."

Jesse looked for Rona to tell her the good news, but

couldn't find her.

Sam informed him, "Rona cannot see you until the wedding ceremony that will be held in the morning."

Jesse was wide awake before dawn. He sat down for the morning meal with Billy and Sam but had little appetite. After all the villagers finished their meal, Billy told Jesse to walk with him. Billy led him to one of the chikees and stopped in front of it.

"Stand here," he said.

The medicine man emerged from the chikee and stood in front of Jesse. Sam Eagle followed and stood to the right. Rona stepped out of the chikee with her mother, who took her hand, walked over to Jesse, and placed Rona's hand in Jesse's. She then took her place to the left of the medicine man.

Suddenly, all the villagers emerged from their homes, formed a circle, and began dancing around Jesse and Rona. The medicine man began singing a song in the Seminole language. Jesse would learn later that the song asks for a blessing for the wedding. When the song ended, the dancers stopped and were still in a circle, looking at the couple.

Rona turned to Jesse and said the Seminole wedding vow, "I will provide the bread if you will provide the meat."

Jesse, as prompted earlier, replied, "I will provide the meat if you will provide the bread."

The medicine man said, "You are now man and wife. You must go from the village for one week and then return to Rona's mother's chikee until you build your own."

With those words, he turned and walked away. The villagers went back to their homes.

Rona led Jesse to the stream where the dugout canoe still lay on the bank. The canoe was loaded with all the food the couple would need for a week, along with any fruit or berries they picked.

Rona said, "We will go to the spring where I took you before. We can be alone and live there for one week." With laughter in her eyes, she added, "Maybe this time we can go swimming."

They got into the canoe and began their journey to the spring and the rest of their lives.

27

Callie

One morning, Caleb, Rosie, and Callie were eating breakfast. Caleb said, "I need to make a trip to town to get a wagon load of supplies for the men tending our cattle. I plan to go today so, if we need anything, make a list for me."

Rosie spoke, "I'd like to ride along with you. I haven't been away from the ranch for some time and would like to see the changes I've heard about. Plus, I'd like to shop for a new dress for Callie."

Callie chimed in, "Me, too. I want to go. I never get away from home and I'd like to help pick out a new dress."

Caleb thought a moment before replying. "I guess that would be okay, but the wagon will be crowded."

Callie quickly replied, "I'll ride my horse and the two of you can ride in the wagon."

This was agreeable to everyone. So, Caleb went to the barn to harness a team while Rosie and Callie got ready for the overnight trip. He drove the wagon up to the house and led a saddled horse for Callie, who was soon mounted. Rosie climbed up into the wagon and Caleb slapped the reins, urging the team into motion.

They made camp late that afternoon and drove into town the next morning. Caleb drove straight to the trading post, which had a sign proclaiming it as 'Mason's Mercantile.' They went inside.

Caleb gave the clerk a list of all the supplies he needed. While the clerk went about filling the order, Callie and Rosie looked over the stock of cloth and ready-made dresses.

An older man walked up to Rosie and said, "Hello, my name is George Mason. I'm the owner and would be glad to help you since my helper is tied up."

Rosie explained what she was looking for and Mason excused himself and went to bring out more dresses from a shipment that he just received.

A young man walked into the trading post, saw the clerk was busy, and started looking around.

When he saw Callie, he walked over and said, "You must be new here. I thought I knew everyone around here, but I don't know you. Are you in town for the dance tonight?"

Callie looked to her mom for reinforcement, but Rosie didn't offer any aid.

Callie looked back at the man and replied, "My name is Callie. We just came in to buy some supplies and I don't know anything about a dance. In fact, I don't know how to dance, so no reason for me to go to one."

The young man laughed, "Well you're in luck. I'm not only the best dancer around, but I'm also the best teacher. My name is Anthony, but my friends call me Tony. Since you're new in town, I'd like to show you around town, if it's okay with your mom."

Mason returned with several dresses draped over his arm. He overheard the exchange between Callie and Tony and said to Rosie, "I know Tony. He's a good boy. If your daughter would like to walk around and see our town, it would be fine."

Rosie was doubtful, but looking at Callie's flushed face and realizing that Callie had never seen anything other than the ranch, she said, "Callie, it's okay to walk around town for a while, just be back in a couple of hours. We have to get an early start."

Callie hesitated, but her curiosity won out and she agreed to let Tony show her the town. Tony was pleased and took Callie's hand and led her outside after promising Rosie to have Callie back in two hours.

As soon as they were outside, Callie removed her hand from Tony's. He was surprised, but made no comment on her move.

Tony said, "Let's walk down to the lake and I'll show you where the dance is held, in case you ever want to go."

As they walked along, Tony talked about the town. "We're growing and have changed the name of our town to 'Kissimmee,' after the river. We have a new mayor as well as schools and churches. Trains stop here regularly coming and going from one coast to the other, carrying all kinds of goods."

Callie looked around in amazement. She'd never seen so many houses and people in one place. When they arrived at the lake, the size of the steamboat tied up to the dock was enormous to her. Men went up and down the gangway, loading and unloading cargo. She stared at everything, much of which she had never seen before. Tony laughed as her widened eyes showed her wonder.

"What would you like to see next?" Tony asked.

Callie looked at him and said, "The train. I've never seen a train."

He took her hand again and she was so interested in looking around that she took no notice. He led her along the shore of the lake until they came to an open-air building. It was painted white with latticework around the sides.

"This is where we hold our dances," Tony said.

"It's beautiful. I'd like to come back even if I can't dance. I'd be happy to watch."

They continued walking and soon came to the railroad tracks. As luck would have it, a train was arriving. A shrill whistle announced its arrival and Callie covered her ears with her hands to block out the noise. In a cloud of smoke, the train came to a stop at a building that Tony explained was the train depot.

Men and women began stepping down from the steps of the train cars and Callie marveled at the fancy dresses some of the women wore. After all the passengers departed the train, men began unloading cargo and carried it off to waiting wagons.

Callie could have stayed there for hours watching all the activity, but was reminded she had to be back at the store to join Rosie and Caleb for the trip home. Reluctantly, she told Tony that she must get back, so Tony took her hand again and headed back.

After Tony and Callie left for their walk, back at the store, the clerk finished writing down the order and looked to Mr. Mason for help checking it over.

Mason excused himself and walked over to the counter and, taking the order pad, began adding it up. Rosie picked out a dress and carried it over to add to the list.

Mason completed adding the amount of the bill and told Caleb the amount. Caleb counted out enough gold coins to pay the bill. He walked over, took Rosie's arm, and said, "We might as well take a little walk ourselves and see the changes going on."

Caleb led Rosie outside and they followed the wooden walkway in front of the store, looking at the stores and newly constructed homes. They came to a tall white building with a cross on top.

Just then, the front door opened and a familiar figure emerged. It was Reverend Sommers who, with a big smile, walked up to them. He shook Caleb's hand and then took both of Rosie's hands into his, all the time with a big smile.

"It's so good to see you folks again. What brings you to God's house today?"

Caleb replied, "We came in for supplies and are taking

a walk to see the town. We had no idea that you or the church was here, but it's good to see you also."

Sommers laughed, "Yes. Well, God never ceases to astound and amaze us with His callings. As you know, I was an itinerant pastor, going to any place that needed me for counsel, weddings, or funerals. I gave a sermon just outside town and one of the elders of this fine church liked what I was saying and convinced me to come here. I have a nice, friendly congregation. You must join us for services."

Caleb said, "While we'd love to, we're on our way back to the ranch shortly."

Sommers, never one to give up, said, "Okay. I understand. But. the next time you come to town, plan on staying over for Sunday services. You'll meet some fine folks and the Sunday dinners will prove we have some good cooks attending our church."

Caleb and Rosie promised to try to do that and, after bidding the Reverend 'goodbye,' walked back to their wagon. Once there, Caleb helped Rosie climb up and take her seat in the wagon.

Tony and Callie arrived and saw the wagon was loaded. Caleb decided to ride the horse, so Tony helped Callie climb up to join Rosie on the wagon seat for the ride home.

Tony said, "Can I come to visit your ranch?"

Rosie smiled and said, "We'd be glad for you to visit," knowing that he had no interest in the ranch but wanted to see Callie again.

Rosie gave Tony directions to the ranch and the wagon moved away with Caleb riding alongside.

Callie looked back and saw Tony watching them drive away. Tony saw Callie looking back and waved to her, she waved back.

Rosie had never seen Callie so excited as she described all the things she had seen in Kissimmee.

Callie said, "The town is wonderful and the people at

the train were so grand. Why, I've never seen or imagined clothing so fancy. Everyone in town must be rich."

Rosie smiled at Callie's enthusiasm. "I'm glad you enjoyed our visit and maybe we can come again. In the meantime, I'll teach you to dance, if I remember myself. Looks like you might have a boy very interested in you. Did you like him?"

"To tell you the truth, I was so interested in seeing the town, especially the train, that I didn't think much about Tony. He did say he'd come visit us at the ranch. Is that okay?"

Rosie smiled. "Yes. That will be fine. I told him he'd be welcome. But I must ask you, Callie, if some day you meet a boy, be it Tony or someone else who wants to live in town rather than on the ranch, what would be your thoughts?"

Callie's response was immediate. "I love the town and all the activity and look forward to going again. Maybe I'd even enjoy dancing, but I'll never leave the ranch. It's all I've ever known and I don't plan on leaving."

Caleb rode up to the side of the wagon where Rosie was sitting and asked, "Do you want to stop and rest?"

Rosie answered, "No. I'd rather keep on moving and get home as soon as we can."

They arrived home and began unpacking the wagon. When everything was unpacked that was intended for use in the house, Caleb drove the wagon to the barn and unloaded the supplies that would go to the men watching the herd.

When that was completed, he unhitched the team and unsaddled the horse. He brushed them all down and fed them some grain.

Rosie called out that she had dinner on the stove. When Caleb went inside the house, Rosie and Callie were sitting at the table and a plate of food was ready at Caleb's seat. They ate quietly since they were tired from the trip and went to bed and were soon asleep.

Three weeks later, Rosie and Callie were sitting on the front porch shelling cowpeas for the evening meal. They saw a rider approaching. Soon, Tony arrived riding a prancing black horse. The saddle on the horse was polished leather with silver trim. He had a matching bridle.

Tony removed his hat and said, "Hello. Do you remember me? I told you I would visit and here I am."

They both stood and Rosie said, "Get down, Tony. I'll get you a drink of water. I know you must be thirsty after your long ride."

"Yes, ma'am. I'd appreciate a drink. My canteen ran dry hours ago."

Tony stepped down as Rosie went inside for the water. She noticed he wore a black cowboy hat and boots. His denim trousers looked new and his grey shirt was store-bought.

"Hello, Callie," Tony said. "It's good to see you again."

Callie smiled, "You came a long way. I appreciate that you came so far to visit. Come sit by me while I finish with these peas."

Rosie came back with a glass of water and handed it to Tony. Then, she stepped over to Callie and took the bowl of unfinished cowpeas and said, "I'll finish these. You, take Tony for a walk and show him around after he finishes his drink."

Tony reached for her hand, but she avoided contact and began walking. He joined her and walked by her side with his hands in his pockets. She showed him the barn and the garden.

"Not much to see around here," Callie said. "Not at all like your town. No trains, no lakes, no place to dance."

"Nonsense," he said. "There's always a place to dance. Here, I'll show you. He stepped in front of her and, removing his hands from his pockets, he took both of hers into his. "Now, just watch my feet. When I move one of them, you follow with your feet."

Tony stepped back with his left foot. Callie stepped forward with her left foot and it landed on his right foot's shiny black boot.

She blushed and said, "I'm sorry. Guess I'm not meant to be a dancer."

Tony laughed, "Everyone is meant to be a dancer. It just takes a little practice. This time when I move my left foot back, you follow with your right foot."

Tony again stepped back with his left and Callie timidly moved her right foot forward. Tony then repeated the move with his right foot. Callie followed.

"Good!" Tony exclaimed. "Now this time, I'll move forward and you move back."

Tony slowly stepped forward and Callie stepped back and repeated with the other foot.

"See!" Tony exclaimed. "You're dancing! All we need is a little music."

Tony practiced the moves a few more times until Callie said, "That's enough for now. I'll practice later."

Tony laughed again. "That'll be great and the next time you come to town, we can go dancing. Make sure your folks show up on a Saturday for the dance is every Saturday night. There'll be lots of music and lights."

Callie took back her hands and they began walking again. "Your horse is very beautiful," she said. "He must have been expensive."

Tony replied, "He's a good horse. Sometimes I race him against other horses and have never lost. My father gave him to me for my eighteenth birthday."

"Your father must be rich."

"No, not rich. I guess he does okay. He's the captain of a riverboat and is gone a lot on trips upriver. Someday I'll take you on a riverboat ride. Would you like that?"

Callie said, "I don't know. I saw one when we walked by the lake. They're awfully big and smoke a lot. I thought it was on fire."

Tony laughed. "It wasn't on fire. It runs on steam and has boilers that are heated by fire to form the steam. That's what drives the paddle wheel."

Callie said, "It's time for dinner. Let's go back so I can help Rosie. You can stay for dinner."

When they got to the house, Caleb had come in from a ride, so Callie introduced him to Tony.

Caleb shook hands and said, "We can sit out front and talk while the womenfolk set the table."

The four sat around the dinner table. Caleb and Rosie had lots of questions about living in town. Tony answered their questions and asked questions about the ranch.

Tony asked if he could spend the night in the barn since it was too late to attempt the ride back to town.

Rosie said, "You don't have to sleep in the barn. We have an empty room that our son, Ira, used to sleep in. He's married and has his own home now. Maybe you and Callie can go for a horseback ride tomorrow and meet Ira and his family as well as our friends, William and Selene."

The next morning, Callie and Tony saddled two horses and she showed him around the rest of the ranch. They stopped at Ira and Sarah's house and were met by the children who were excited to see Callie, but were shy around Tony.

Only Belle stepped forward and asked, "Who are you and why are you with Callie?"

Tony laughed. "My name is Tony. I'm Callie's friend. She's showing me around the ranch."

Belle thought that over and said, "That's a pretty horse. Can I ride him?"

Sarah came out of the house in time to hear Belle's request and answered for Tony, saying, "No. You can't. I've told you not to be rude to visitors."

Sarah invited Callie and Tony to dismount and come inside and stay for lunch.

Callie introduced everyone, including Ira, who came in from tending the Holsteins. Lunch was a noisy affair with the children all vying for Callie's attention. Tony was at ease with Ira and the family and answered questions about living in town.

After lunch, Ira and Tony went outside while Callie and Sarah cleared the table and washed dishes. Belle walked outside and joined the two men.

Belle said, "Tony, I want you to see our Holstein cows. We have the only ones around."

She took Tony's hand and, accompanied by Ira, walked over to the pen holding the cows. After seeing the cows and hearing Ira's plans for a dairy farm, they rejoined Callie and Sarah.

Tony said, "Thanks for lunch and the tour. I enjoyed it, but we must go now. I plan on riding home and had better get started."

They said their 'goodbyes' and, as they rode away, Belle called out, "Come see us again, Tony."

He turned back and waved.

Callie said, "We didn't have time to meet William and Selene. Maybe, if you visit again, you can meet them."

They rode back and Tony said 'goodbye' to Caleb and Rosie and started his ride back to town after telling Callie to be sure and come to town to attend a dance soon.

Caleb said, "We'll be coming to town again in a few weeks. Maybe we'll see you again."

After Tony rode away, Caleb and Rosie waited for Callie to mention the day or her visitor. She didn't offer any comments, so Rosie asked, "How was your visit with Tony?"

Callie replied, "It was fine. I wasn't sure, but we had a good day and I'd like to attend a dance at least once."

Three weeks later, William knocked on Caleb's door and was invited to come in. Rosie poured him and Caleb cups of coffee and the two talked over their mutual interests.

William said, "We need some supplies, so I'm going to town tomorrow with Selene and wondered if you and Rosie want to go?"

Rosie heard the question and interrupted the two by saying, "Caleb, that would be a good idea. We need a few things and we could let Callie go to the dance in town. I've been giving her lessons and we can stay overnight and go to Reverend Sommers' church Sunday morning. I haven't been to church in years and would like to go."

Caleb looked at William and said, "Looks like I made up my mind to go to town with you."

Both men smiled.

The next morning the little procession began their journey into town. William and Selene rode in one wagon and Caleb and Rosie were in a second wagon. Callie rode alongside. They made camp that evening in the shade of a large oak tree outside Kissimmee. They rode into town the next morning.

They all gave Mr. Mason a list of the supplies they needed and told him they'd be staying over and going to church the next morning. They told him they'd be back later, but were going to look around the town

All five of them began walking and soon reached the church. Reverend Sommers was outside and welcomed them. Rosie told him they were coming to services the next morning.

He smiled and said, "You're certainly welcome. I'm glad you're here."

Rosie said, "This is William and Selene."

Sommers shook hands with both and said, "Sure, I remember both of you from Ira and Sarah's wedding. And will you two be coming to the service?"

William asked, "Are you sure we'd be welcome at your church?"

Sommers replied, "God welcomes all who come to Him and even though He is the ultimate power, I also welcome you."

William looked at Selene, who nodded

They all continued walking around town. The townspeople looked questionably at them as they walked, unaccustomed to seeing blacks and whites together. They ignored the looks and enjoyed the sights of Kissimmee.

Callie showed them where the dance was held and a passerby told them the time the dance began. They hadn't seen Tony. Callie realized that she had no way to contact him, but assumed he'd be at the dance. They spent most of the day walking around town and went back to Mason's Mercantile to pick up their supplies.

The two wagons, along with Callie, headed back to the campsite and Rosie and Callie fixed the evening meal. Once everyone finished eating, Callie went behind some thick brush and changed into her new dress that they bought on the previous trip.

Caleb drove the wagon. Rosie and Callie crowded together on the narrow seat beside him. When they arrived at the dance, the band was playing a lively tune to get everyone in the mood for dancing.

They sat in the wagon, unsure how to proceed. Their dilemma was solved when Tony, with a big smile, stepped down from the dance floor and walked over to greet them.

"Hello," he said. "What a pleasure to see all of you again. Why didn't you tell me you were coming to town? I would've met you. Anyway, you're here and I'm glad."

Tony offered his hand to help Callie down. Once she stood by his side, he looked at Caleb and Rosie and said, "How about you two, are you joining us?"

Caleb laughed, "No, I'm afraid not. These old bones are too old. Dancing is for young people."

Rosie didn't comment but thought, *'We're not that old and I might enjoy a dance or two, but Caleb still has a noticeable limp from the panther attack and he'd be embarrassed to try dancing.'* So, she said, "Caleb is right. We'll sit here and watch."

Tony took Callie's hand and led her to the dance floor. By this time, other couples were dancing, so they joined the crowd. They began dancing and he was surprised when she was able to follow his lead.

It was a magical night for Callie but she was nervous for a couple of reasons. She had never been to a dance before and felt like everyone in the room was watching her, waiting for a mistake. The second thing was Tony holding her left hand with his right hand lightly around her waist. Callie had never been touched this way before. But, after a couple of lively dances, she got in the mood of the dance and her nervousness disappeared.

Caleb and Rosie sat in the wagon and watched the dancers as they whirled around the floor. Rosie was particularly pleased to see the smile on Callie's face and hear her laughter as she danced.

After a few dances, Tony got two glasses of punch and he and Callie walked down to the wagon where Caleb and Rosie were sitting. Tony asked them if they'd like a glass of punch and both declined.

Tony then said, "Did you see Callie dancing? She did really well."

Rosie laughed and said, "Well she dances a lot better with you, Tony, than she did with me when I was teaching her the steps. You're a good dancer and I'm glad Callie has you to dance with for her first dance."

Tony said, "When are you folks going home?"

Caleb replied, "We made camp just outside town and we'll spend the night there. In the morning, we're going to church to hear Reverend Sommers give his sermon."

Tony replied, "That's great. My family and I go to that church regularly. May I join you and sit with you at church?"

Callie said, "Okay. I'll be sitting with my mom and dad

and also our friends William and Selene, but you're certainly welcome to join us."

Tony answered, "I look forward to that. I'll introduce you to my parents in the morning."

Tony and Callie went back to dancing and the night passed in a whirlwind of laughter and dancing. Callie danced with different young men who were anxious to meet a new girl in town.

Callie danced with one young man who introduced himself as Van Evans. Van was a terrible dancer and stepped on her toes more than once.

Van apologized and said, "I don't dance much, as you can tell. But, when I saw you, I just had to try. Hope I didn't do any permanent damage to your toes."

Before Callie could answer him, Tony came to reclaim her and danced with her the rest of the night. When the dance was over, Tony walked her to the wagon, helped her into it, and stood watching as Caleb turned the wagon and drove away.

The next morning, when they arrived at the church, Reverend Sommers met them at the front door. "Welcome," he said. "Come right in. Services will start shortly."

Callie told her parents and William and Selene she'd wait for Tony to arrive and join them later. The four went inside and hesitated, deciding where to sit. The room was partially filled.

A black couple sat just inside the door on the last row of pews. There was one pew farther up the aisle that had enough room for the four of them plus Tony and Callie.

William took Selene's hand and walked toward those seats, followed by Caleb and Rosie. William was aware that everyone was looking at them. He heard whispers as they neared the seats. Whispers of, "Where do they think they're going," and, "They should know their place."

William reached the pew and was ready to take a seat

when the black man in the back row stood and walked up to William and said, "I'd be proud for you and your Mrs. to sit with me and my wife."

William looked at the man, then the people around him who were all looking at him. Selene squeezed his arm and whispered, "It's not that important where we sit."

William hesitated. He wanted to sit where they were whether anyone liked it or not. He looked at Selene, then Caleb and Rosie, and turned and followed the black man back to the back pew. The black man and his wife slid down the pew, making room for them. Caleb went in first. Then came Rosie and Selene followed by William.

Callie waited only a short time when she saw Tony approaching with a prosperous-looking man and woman. Tony's face brightened when he saw Callie.

He walked over to join her and said, 'Good morning.'

Tony took Callie's hand and led her over to meet his parents. "Callie, this is my mom and dad."

They both smiled and Tony's dad said, "Glad to meet you, Callie. We feel like we already know you for Tony has told us about you in glowing terms."

Tony's mom gave Callie a hug. His parents went inside to take their seats while Tony and Callie talked. The church bell rang, signaling everyone to come in.

Tony and Callie went inside. She saw her parents and William and Selene sitting in the back row and took a seat by William, sliding over enough to give Tony a seat. He hesitated and then sat down.

Callie turned to him and said, "These are our friends, William and Selene Thornton." She said this, nodding to William and Selene. Then, she nodded to Tony and told William and Selene, "This is my friend, Tony."

Tony stiffly nodded at the two.

Reverend Sommers came in, closed the door behind him, and went to the front of the church. He took his place behind the pulpit. He nodded to the piano player who began playing a song.

Everyone in the church stood and Reverend Sommers led the congregation in singing three hymns. At the conclusion of the last song, he motioned for the congregation to be seated.

Reverend Sommers stood behind the pulpit and began talking. "Our town, our state, and our nation survived the horrible war between the States and, although the war is over, we face a time of rebuilding; not only our physical world but our spiritual beings. I'll start this morning at the very beginning. *'On the sixth day of creation,'* as all of you have read, *'God created man in His own image. In the image of God created He him; male and female created He them.'*"

Reverend Summers continued, "Now, I know none of you doubt that scripture or you wouldn't be here this morning. Where some differ in opinion is that some feel the man God created was white alone. I've even heard talk that God is the Father of white mankind and others - yellow, red, and black races - maybe prove the theory of evolution and came not from God directly, but from some sort of mutation from monkeys."

This remark brought laughs from some of the congregation who were starting to get uneasy at the direction of the preacher's words.

Sommers continued, "I'm sure none of you believe that but, just to clear it up, let's look at Acts seventeen, verse twenty-six."

He opened his Bible to that verse and read, *"'And He made from one man every nation of mankind to live on all the face of the earth, having determined allotted periods and the boundaries of their dwelling place.'"*

Reverend Sommers closed the Bible and continued, "Now, does that clear up the matter of where all races come from? The scripture says clearly, *'from one man.'* Who can that one man be? That man had to be Adam. He is the father of all men of all colors. This sort of clears up that issue. However, some men have told me this verse clearly states that men of different nations need to stay within their own boundaries. While that argument might have some validity, we must consider why men from different nations didn't stay within their given boundaries. In our case, greedy, ungodly men in violation of God's law captured and enslaved people of color and brought them unwillingly to this land and away from their boundaries. Now, we can say we'll send them all back, but how do you send back a child that was born here. The only back we can send them to is into slavery, which we now know is against the law. Slavery is against our law now, but was always against God's law, as we can see in Exodus twenty-one verse sixteen *'Whoever steals a man and sells him, and anyone found in possession of him shall be put to death.'"*

Reverend Sommers stood silent a moment, then continued, "Others say that God is the God of white people and other races have their own gods. So, we'll look at Revelation seven verse nine. *'After this I looked, and behold, a great multitude that no one could number, from every nation, from all tribes and peoples and languages, standing before the throne and before the Lamb, clothed in white robes, with palm branches in their hands.'"*

As the sermon progressed, some people listened with rapt attention but others began to fidget in their seats. Soon, a couple near the front got up, exited their seats, and walked down the aisle and out the door. Soon, another couple followed.

The Reverend ignored those departing and continued, "There is a lot of resentment and blame in our state and nation. We blame others for our problems and have hostility in our hearts for blacks, northerners, and yes, even our neighbors. I, no not I, God asks you to remove the bad feelings from your heart and mind. Only when the cleansing that forgiveness brings to your life can you be truly free and begin a new life. A life without bitterness and prejudice will bring a new beginning to us all and make you feel like a new person in a new world. God has given you that capability but you will have to accept and practice that kind of life. Begin a new life and encourage others to do the same. God will reward you and harmony can come to our town, state, and nation."

Tony's father and mother stood, walked down the aisle, and stopped by the pew where Tony was sitting. Tony's father looked down at him and then at Callie sitting by William. His mother turned her face away.

Tony's father said, "Well, Tony."

Tony looked up at his father and turned and looked at Callie and over to William and Selene and back up to his father. He turned to Callie and said, "I'm sorry." He stood and followed his parents out of the church.

The rest of the sermon continued without anyone else leaving. The collection plate was passed around. Caleb and William dropped gold coins into it. Reverend Sommers instructed everyone present to take part in the communion service. He led them in one more song, 'Blessed Be the Ties That Bind,' and, when the service was over, everyone went outside.

Reverend Sommers came over to them and thanked them for coming and hoped they'd come again. Rosie assured him they would, but not often as it meant an overnight trip.

William added, "Are you sure you want me and Selene to come back. You might lose your whole congregation."

With a wry smile on his face, Sommers said, "That might be, but right is right and if you can't encourage what is right in the church, then where?"

Callie was standing alone by the wagon when a young man walked up to her and said, "It's good to see you again. I'm glad you can walk after my attempts at dancing. In case you forgot, my name is Van Evans."

She remembered him from the dance and laughed at the memory. "You were pretty bad but it was my first dance, so I wasn't a good partner."

Caleb and Rosie walked up as Van turned to them and said, "My name is Van Evans. I work for the Roberts' ranch which is close to yours. I never met you folks, but someone at the dance told me last night who Callie was and it made me sorry we hadn't met. I saw you and the black man along with a younger man on the last cattle drive."

Callie spoke up, "That black man is William Thornton and his wife is Selene. They're my father's partner on the ranch and good friends. Does that bother you?"

Van looked at Callie, surprised by the anger in her voice. "No. It doesn't bother me. I never thought of it before, but a lot of what the preacher said made sense. If they're your friends, I'd like them to be mine, for I want to get to know you."

Rosie piped up and said, "We're glad to meet you, young man, but we must be leaving. We have a long drive ahead of us. If you'd like to visit, you'll be welcome."

Without hesitation, Van said, "How about next Sunday? That's my day off work."

Rosie replied, "That'll be fine. Come for dinner."

Caleb and his party went back to their wagons to start the journey home.

William laughed and said, "That preacher is going to lose a lot of his flock if he thinks they have to accept a black sheep into their fold."

Caleb drove their wagon with Rosie at his side. Callie chose to ride her horse. Rosie was concerned about Callie after Tony's abrupt departure. She thought, *'I guess getting hurt by someone else was part of growing up but I don't like to see my daughter mistreated.'*

When they reached home, Rosie tried to talk to Callie about what happened but Callie said everything was fine. A sure statement that everything was not fine. The next Sunday they had two visitors. The first was Van Evans who came to call on Callie. The second was a surprise when Reverend Sommers rode up on a white mule.

28

Thanksgiving

Van was the first to arrive on Sunday. Caleb was home, sitting on the front porch smoking his pipe. Rosie ran him out of the house when he tried to smoke inside.

Caleb stood when Van rode up and walked out to greet him, "Good morning. It's good to see you again. The girls are busy inside fixing Sunday dinner so you and I can visit a bit. Get down and I'll walk with you to the barn so you can unsaddle your horse and turn him loose in the corral. You can give him a little grain if you'd like."

They walked to the barn together with Van leading his horse. Once the horse was loosed into the corral, Caleb and Van walked back to the house and took seats on the front porch.

Caleb began talking. "If I remember correctly, you work for the Roberts' ranch. Is that right?"

"Yes. I've been with him for four years. I like ranching and the cattle business. I hope someday to have a place for my own."

Caleb said, "That's a good ambition. Ranching is a good way to make a living but it's going to be tough for a young man to get his start. Land is getting expensive and the range is getting pretty crowded."

Van replied, "I understand. Mr. Roberts told me much the same thing but, still, I'll find a way. I don't drink, smoke, or gamble. The only expense I have is clothing now and then, so I save most of what I earn."

Caleb thought, '*I like this young man. When I was his age, my mind was on staying alive. I hope he never has to face the things I did on my way to here.*'

Van continued, "I only spent a few minutes with your daughter but, in that time, I knew she was a girl that I wanted to spend more time with. I saw her dancing with others and the one dance we shared wasn't fun for her. I'd like to visit Callie and get to know her. I hope that's okay with you."

Caleb laughed. "It's okay with me, but I'm afraid Callie's the one you really need to ask that question."

Callie walked out the front door and, if she was surprised, she didn't show it. Van stood up quickly and took his hat off.   "Good morning, Callie. Do you remember me? My name is Van. We met at the dance."

Callie smiled and said, "Of course, I remember. Do you think there's something wrong with my memory?"

Van looked to Caleb for a hint as to how to answer her. Caleb looked away.

Van, twisting his hat in his hand, answered, "No. I don't think anything is wrong with you, but you danced with several guys. I wanted to make sure that you knew my name. We didn't have much time to get to know each other."

Callie reassured him, "Don't worry. I know who you are and you did say you were coming today. You two guys keep talking. Dinner will be ready soon. And, by the way, you're going to ruin your nice hat if you keep twisting it all up."

Callie turned and went back inside the house. Van sat back down.

"It's hard for me to talk to girls. I haven't been around them very much."

Caleb told him, "The first thing you have to do is relax or at least make her think you're relaxed. Girls like to keep you guessing. It keeps them in control. Women are born with that knowledge. About the time we think we know what to say or how to say it, the words always come out wrong. Don't worry. These things work themselves out."

They heard the sound of approaching hoofbeats and looked in the direction the sound came from. Reverend Sommers rode up. Before dismounting, he looked down at Caleb and Van and said, "I didn't expect to see you so soon but, after the sermon last Sunday, the elders of the church decided that I wasn't really the man for the job. They dismissed me and I'm back on the road again. One member of the congregation who wasn't in favor of me leaving the church gave me this mule and a saddle."

Caleb stood and said, "Get down. Dinner is about ready and we'll be glad for you to join us. I'll go in and tell Rosie to set another place." He went inside.

Reverend Sommers dismounted and walked up to Van and shook hands with him.

Sommers said, "I remember you from the church service on Sunday, but never got to meet you."

Van told him his name and that he worked at a ranch nearby and was a visitor himself. He offered to take the mule and put him in the corral. While he did that, Reverend Sommers took a seat on the porch.

Van came back at the same time Caleb came back outside followed by Rosie and Callie, who were pleased to see the preacher. He retold the story of losing his church and then they all went inside to eat.

After the meal was finished, the three men went back outside and sat on the porch.

Sommers started talking, "I'll miss the church for it had some nice folks that I'd gotten to know but the leaders didn't agree with my liberal ideas. While I'll miss the church, I'm looking forward to my itinerant pastoral duties. A lot of people live in isolated places and can't go to a regular church.

They need to hear the words of salvation, but mostly they need me for weddings, baptisms, and funerals.

Callie came outside and said, "Van, would you like to take a walk and look over our home?"

Van stood and quickly said, "Sure, I would."

He nodded at Caleb and the preacher and followed Callie as she stepped off the porch.

Callie and Van walked for a while, both lost in their own thoughts.

Van broke the silence by saying, "Callie, I haven't spent much time with you and have to say that I don't know you, your likes, or plans. What I do know is that I've been drawn to you since the first time I saw you at the dance. I rarely go into town and it was luck that I was there the same night you were. It could be that fate wanted us to meet."

Callie replied, "There's not a lot to get to know about me. I'm just a country girl that hasn't seen a lot of the world. As for my likes, I like pretty things just like any other girl. I haven't spent a lot of time on what my plans are. I've been content with my life and just expect that things will work out. What do you like and what are your plans?"

Van laughed, "My plans are simple. I want to be a rancher and I want a wife for a partner to share my life with. As far as what I like, I'm happy when I roll out of my bedroll in the morning with the morning dew still covering the ground. I like the sun coming up and seeing it glisten on the dew. I like the smell of coffee brewing over a campfire. I'm excited every time a new calf comes into the world. I guess you could say that I like life but most of all I'd like someone to share everything with."

Callie looked at him, "For someone who doesn't talk much, you say a lot."

Van added, "I saw you dancing with that fellow at the dance. You were laughing and seemed so happy. I was afraid that it was too late for me to know you. I'm such a terrible dancer and that didn't give me a lot of confidence."

Callie stepped in front of him and took his hands in hers. She looked into his eyes and said, "Van, I think I was waiting for someone like you to come along. I had fun with Tony but he's a town boy and I'm a ranch girl. It was exciting to be in town and I'd like to go again but I could never live there."

Van smiled in relief. They turned and walked back towards the ranch house. Meanwhile, Caleb and Reverend Sommers were deep in conversation.

Sommers said, "Caleb, I look around me and see a nice home and ranch that you've built. Plus, you have a good wife and a lovely daughter. You've raised Ira into a fine young man who's started his family. You should be very proud and grateful for what you've done."

Caleb thought for a few moments before answering. "While I'm satisfied with the progress we've made, I can't take all the credit. Good fortune made me meet William. Without him, I couldn't have accomplished near as much." He continued, "It was luck that brought Rosie into my life. If not for William looking for a length of cloth for Selene, I might have never met Rosie. Doing a favor for a soldier friend of mine brought me to this ranch and Ira. We worked hard, but a lot of things went our way that could have ended differently."

Reverend Sommers smiled. "I'm sure you earned all you have. But, I'm also glad that you recognize that not everything is in our control. Some call it luck, some call it fate, and I personally believe the hand of God is involved. It could be one of these or all of them."

Sommers paused a moment and then added, "In my case, I had a church and a congregation. I slept on a good bed every night and never worried about having food to eat. Then, last Sunday, you, William, and your wives came to my church. I'd heard of your friendship and now saw it for myself. That day gave me the motivation to deliver a sermon that I had long wanted to deliver but not the courage to do so."

Sommers sat silent for a few moments and then continued, "Now, I might have delivered that sermon someday, but probably not, for I had entered into a life of comfort and little risk. I say God didn't like that and sent you and William to church last Sunday."

Sommers laughed and said, "Enough of what might have been in both our lives. The thing is, we're here and both should be grateful for our lives. Thanksgiving is coming up in two weeks. What would you think of getting everyone together to celebrate?"

Caleb said, "That's a wonderful idea. Let me get Rosie and see how she feels about it."

Caleb went inside and came back out with Rosie. Reverend Sommers told her his thoughts about Thanksgiving.

Rosie said, "I like that idea. We have great, good friends, so showing our thanks is the right thing to do. Of course, we'll invite William and his family. Ira and his family are right here and we should invite the Yates family to celebrate with us." She turned to Caleb and said, "What about Tex, Joe, and Freman? They should be here."

Caleb replied, "We can work that out. I'll have them drive the herd close. The cattle will be okay for one day without the men."

Sommers clapped his hands and said, "Good. It's settled then. I'll be making my rounds and telling folks that I'll be visiting on a regular schedule to handle their spiritual needs. I'll tell the Yates and be back with them on Thanksgiving Day."

Rosie said, "No. Come the evening before. We can find a place for you to sleep and also tell the Yates' to spend the night with us. It's too far to come on Thanksgiving."

Callie and Van returned from their walk. Rosie smiled when she saw they were holding hands. She touched Caleb's shoulder and pointed at the couple. "Looks like we better invite Van to our little get-together."

The next morning, Reverend Sommers rode off on his white mule, singing happily as he rode. Caleb went to find William to tell him about the plans for Thanksgiving. He found him working in the orange grove. Isaiah was with him. Both stopped working when Caleb arrived.

William was enthusiastic about having a big Thanksgiving with both families attending. He told Caleb that Selene would probably go over to see Rosie the next morning to plan the meal together.

William said, "I guess you better plan on Isaiah coming also. He and Adaza have been spending so much time together that I have to include him or shoot him. I haven't decided which yet."

Isaiah, who never spoke around Caleb, surprised them all when he replied, "It wouldn't be smart to shoot me now after all the time you spent teaching me my numbers. Not to mention the time Mrs. Thornton has spent on my book learning."

Caleb and William both laughed. Caleb said, "I guess we better count on Isaiah for the dinner. As he said, it'd be a shame to waste all that time spent on education by shooting him now."

The next morning, William went in search of Pony. Luckily, he was home eating breakfast at his chikee. Pony welcomed him and invited him to dismount and join in the meal.

William declined the offer of food and said, "Caleb and his family and me and mine are having a big dinner to celebrate Thanksgiving. We want both of you to come, but I'd also like for you to go and invite Jesse and his wife to be there. Do you know where his wife's village is?"

Pony replied, "Yes. I have been there before. I will be glad to take him word of the dinner."

William said, "That'd be good. Come by my house and pick up a horse for the trip. I know you have a horse but it's unbranded. You might run into someone who would try and take it from you. Mine is branded and I'll give you a note that you're riding it with my permission."

The next morning, Pony and Oconee, on two of Williams's horses, began the trip to see Jesse.

The day before Thanksgiving, Reverend Sommers arrived with the Yates family. It had been a while since the two families had been together, so all were glad to be together.

Ira, Sarah, and their children came over to share the evening meal. As soon as the meal was finished, the women ran the men out of the house so they could prepare for the next day's celebration.

That same day, William and Selene arose early and went about their normal activities, anxious as to whether Jesse and his wife would arrive.

Their fears were relieved when Jesse and Rona rode up. Everyone rushed outside to welcome them. Jesse jumped off his horse and embraced Selene and then shook William's hand. He then turned to help Rona dismount.

Taking her hand, he led her over and introduced her to the family. Selene hugged her, not sure if that was the right greeting for an Indian, but Rona returned the hug. Rona was dressed in Seminole fashion with a bright-colored skirt and blouse.

Selene took Rona's hand and said, "Come inside and we'll get to know one another."

Rona looked questioningly at Jesse but, when he nodded his head, she followed Selene inside.

Thanksgiving morning was organized bedlam. William drove up in his wagon. Inside the wagon, were bowls of food that Selene and Adaza had cooked.

Caleb welcomed them and told William he was just in time to help set up a table for all the food.

William introduced Rona to Caleb. Selene took her inside to meet Rosie and Callie.

Ira and his family arrived with their laughing, chattering children. Sarah went inside to join the ladies and told the kids to stay outside and play.

Caleb and William came out of the barn carrying long wooden planks that they placed on wooden kegs set on end. Callie came out with an armload of table cloths and covered the planks.

Next, came a procession of women carrying bowls of food. The Yates' brought along fresh smoked hams. Mrs. Yates had pies made with fruit she canned last year since no fresh fruit was available this late in the year. Ira brought pitchers of fresh milk for everyone to drink.

While the women were setting the table, Caleb and Ira took a shovel from the barn and walked over to a mound of dirt that had smoke rising from it. They removed the dirt and uncovered a layer of bay leaves.

When they removed the bay leaves, a white sheet was left that covered two rear shoulders of venison, shielding them from sand that might sift through the bay leaves.

Together they removed the venison that had been roasting in the pit since the day before. The meat was golden brown and gave off a pleasing aroma.

Just as the meal preparation was about completed, the sound of hoofbeats announced the arrival of Tex, Joe, and Freman. They dismounted and drew taunts from the others that the smell of food drew the riders in.

Tex laughed and said, "You're mighty right. But, I don't expect anything for free so, to pay for my meal, I'm going to let Freman sing songs for you once dinner's over."

Everyone laughed at the steep price Tex was paying.

Next, Van and Isaiah rode in. Callie went to greet Van while Adaza welcomed Isaiah. Pony and Oconee had come over that morning bringing turkeys Pony had trapped.

Caleb looked at all the food and said, "There's enough food for a week."

Tex laughed and replied, "Don't believe that. We've not eaten home-cooked food for a while so you'd better not sit too close to me when I get started eating. You might get bitten."

Finally, everything was ready for the meal. As expected, Reverend Sommers would hone everyone's appetite with a long, detailed blessing of the food. He asked for a blessing on the food and each person in attendance, singularly and in combinations. Then, he went into thanking the Lord for providing the food, weather, and everyone's health. When it became apparent to him that attention spans were weakening, he closed his prayer.

Yates said, "It's amazing, Reverend, how you time your prayer to be about a minute short of a sermon."

Everyone laughed and turned their attention to the food. After eating, William and Caleb took a seat on the front porch and filled their pipes with tobacco they had grown and cured.

Selene, Rosie, and Mrs. Yates were covering up the food and left it on the makeshift table so the food would be uncovered again for the evening meal.

Van, Callie, Isaiah, and Adaza spent the afternoon together. Van and Isaiah offered different opinions on the value of raising oranges against that of raising cattle. Neither changed their minds.   The two girls mostly listened but occasionally joined the conversation.

After the talk slowed, the four played horseshoes, coached by Mr. Yates. Jairus brought along his paints and was busy painting a picture of the group. Anarece and Hiba watched, giving advice. Which, of course, Jairus ignored.

Tex walked up to Belle and said, "I understand your name is Texas Belle."

Belle replied, "Yes, it is. Everyone calls me 'Belle.' Who are you?

"Folks call me 'Tex' because I'm from Texas. Come over here and take a seat and I'll tell you all about the great State that you're named after."

Ira looked over and saw Tex talking to Belle. As Tex talked, he waved his arms in the air to make a point. Ira laughed and thought, *'Well here comes another Texas fan.'*

Everyone joined together again for the evening meal and, once it was over, the ladies began cleaning and packing up leftovers.

Freman took out his guitar and began playing and singing. Everyone gathered around and listened to his music. He played some of his favorites and then led everyone in the gospel songs they all knew.

During a lull in the singing, Jesse said, "Freman, I have a treat for you." He motioned for Rona and Oconee to step forward. "These girls will sing a song for us in the Seminole language."

Rona and Oconee started singing and Freman picked up the melody and played along with them. When it was over, everyone clapped their hands.

William and Caleb didn't join in the singing and took a seat on the front porch. William took a long puff on his pipe, blew out a big cloud of smoke, and said, "Well, General, it looks like you finally got an army of your own. It's sort of an odd army but we do have a good number of them."

Caleb replied, "I don't know about an army, but they are our future."

William looked around again and then back at Caleb and said, "Jairus is only interested in his paint and Hiba only in treating ailments. Jesse has joined the Indians. That leaves Adaza and Isaiah with any interest in taking over our work.

Ira is wrapped up in his Holsteins. There's only Callie and her new beau, Van, in your family to take over one day."

They sat lost in their thoughts of the past and future.

Reverend Sommers walked up and interrupted the silence, "Look at all God's children. I wish the rest of the world could see Indians, blacks, and whites enjoying life and themselves without bias or judgment. I'm pleased with this. I know God is too."

Selene and Rosie joined Caleb and William and stood by their sides. The sun was setting and cast an orange glow on the two couples who had overcome much, but still had challenges to face. Challenges they would face together.

Caleb took Rosie's hand and said. "From now on we'll do this every year.

Acknowledgments

A great thanks for the wonderfully informative references used to create this book:

Kissimmee : 125 Years of its Peoples and Progress by Jim Robison

Healing Plants : Medicine of the Seminole by Alice Micco Snow and Susan Enns Stans

The Seminole Indians in Florida by The Florida State Department of Agriculture

www.ingramcontent.com/pod-product-compliance
Lightning Source LLC
Chambersburg PA
CBHW030710190726
48286CB00001B/251